**His lips touched hers and
everything else ceased to exist.**

Noah plundered her with his tongue, an electric mating of
their mouths that made her wonder if he might just take her
here, in the middle of this glorious garden—

Elise gasped and yanked herself from his arms, horrified
and shaking and breathing hard. What the hell was she doing? What the hell was she *thinking*?

"I can't do this." Her voice was a ragged whisper.

"I'm sorry." He was breathing as hard as she was. "I
didn't mean...I shouldn't..."

Her heart twisted painfully. "Please don't be sorry," she
said miserably. "It's me who needs to apologize."

Confusion clouded his eyes. "Apologize for what?"

"For not telling you why I'm here."

ACCLAIM FOR KELLY BOWEN

DUKE OF MY HEART

"Wonderful! A charming, clever, and engaging storyteller not to be missed."
    —Sarah MacLean, *New York Times* bestselling author

"Top Pick! 4½ Stars! Bowen begins her Season for Scandal series with a nonstop murder mystery that sizzles with tension. This suspenseful tale unfolds quickly, and readers will be captivated by the well-drawn characters who move Bowen's inventive plot forward. Readers will savor this unconventional romance."
    —RT Book Reviews

YOU'RE THE EARL THAT I WANT

"This story has it all: romance, suspense, wit, and Bowen's trademark smart and slightly quirky characters. Bowen's thrilling plot, spot-on pacing, and savvy characterization will delight her current fans and seduce new ones."
    —*Publishers Weekly* (starred review)

"*You're the Earl That I Want* delivers with intrigue, chemistry, and humor."
    —HeroesandHeartbreakers.com

"4 stars! Humor shines throughout Bowen's final Lords of Worth novel. Her atypical characters' adventures quickly

move the story forward, enchanting readers with their esca-
pades and captivating them with their sexual tension. Bowen
is at the top of her game, and all readers could desire is
more."

—*RT Book Reviews*

A GOOD ROGUE IS HARD TO FIND

"Where have you been all my life, Kelly Bowen? If Julia
Quinn, Sarah MacLean, and Lisa Kleypas were to extract
their writing DNA, mix it in a blender, and have a love child,
Kelly Bowen would be it."

—HeroesandHeartbreakers.com

"Bowen's impish sense of humor is expressed by lively, entertaining characters in this wickedly witty Regency. This is
pure romantic fun."

—Publishers Weekly

"4½ stars! This is a shining example of Bowen's ability to
make readers both laugh (at the wry and witty dialogue) and
cry (at the poignancy within the romance). With wonderful
characters, a quick pace, and heated sensuality, Bowen has a
winner."

—*RT Book Reviews*

I'VE GOT MY DUKE TO KEEP ME WARM

"Kelly Bowen is a fresh new voice with a shining future!"
—Teresa Medeiros, *New York Times* **bestselling author**

"With this unforgettable debut, Bowen proves she is a
writer to watch as she spins a multilayered plot skillfully

seasoned with danger and deception and involving wonderfully complex protagonists and a memorable cast of supporting characters...a truly remarkable romance well worth savoring."

—*Booklist* (starred review)

"4 stars! In this delightful, poignant debut that sets Bowen on the path to become a beloved author, the innovative plotline and ending are only superseded by the likable, multidimensional characters: a strong-willed heroine and a heart-stealing hero. Get set to relish Bowen's foray into the genre."

—*RT Book Reviews*

"Fans of romance with a touch of suspense will enjoy the work of this new author."

—*Publishers Weekly*

a *Duke*
to
Remember

a *Duke*
to
Remember

KELLY BOWEN

FOREVER

NEW YORK   BOSTON

Copyright © 2016 by Kelly Bowen
Excerpt from *Duke of My Heart* © 2016 by Kelly Bowen

Cover design by Elizabeth Turner
Cover illustration by Judy York
Hand lettering by Ron Zinn
Cover copyright © 2016 by Hachette Book Group, Inc.

Forever
Hachette Book Group
1290 Avenue of the Americas
New York, NY 10104
forever-romance.com
twitter.com/foreverromance

First Edition: July 2016

Forever is an imprint of Grand Central Publishing.
The Forever name and logo are trademarks of Hachette Book Group, Inc.

The publisher is not responsible for websites (or their content) that are not owned by the publisher.

The Hachette Speakers Bureau provides a wide range of authors for speaking events. To find out more, go to www.hachettespeakersbureau.com or call (866) 376-6591.

ISBN 978-1-4555-6337-1 (mass market); 978-1-4555-3681-8 (ebook)

Printed in the United States of America

OPM

10 9 8 7 6 5 4 3 2 1

For my husband, Dave, who has always believed I could do anything.

Acknowledgments

I consider myself one of the luckiest of all authors; to have such an incredible and talented team behind each and every book is a truly wonderful and humbling experience. Thank you to my agent, Stefanie Lieberman, who has always steered me the right way, and my editor, Alex Logan, who knows how to make each story just that much better.

Thank you also to Elizabeth Turner for gifting my stories with such incredible covers. And to the entire team at Forever—my books would not be what they are without you.

And as always, a heartfelt thanks to my family for their unflagging support and encouragement.

Chapter 1

London, August 1819

Miriam Ellery, Dowager Duchess of Ashland, had her ankles chained to her bed.

It was for her own protection, the steward at Bedlam said. The chains prevented her from wandering too far, and possibly killing herself or another patient. Aye, she might not look dangerous, he warned, but you could never really tell when a madwoman might succumb to unnatural and violent impulses.

Elise DeVries looked on without comment from the narrow doorway. Her brown wig itched her head terribly, as did the stiff mustache and beard pasted to her upper lip and jaw. The arms of the spectacles she wore pinched at her scalp, digging into the tender skin just above her ears. But as she contemplated the pathetic figure of the chained duchess in front of her, Elise could not give credit to her own discomforts.

"What do you think, Doctor?" the steward asked, wiping his nose with the back of his sleeve.

I think you are every sort of fool, Elise wanted to say.

The very notion that the frail, elderly woman sitting slumped on the bed might injure another patient was absurd. It would be a miracle if the duchess could actually lift one of her legs under the weight of the heavy shackles, much less run amok through the hospital, endangering its inhabitants.

"These sorts of cases can indeed be tricky," Elise said instead, pitching her voice low in the same manner she sometimes used when performing on the stage. "How long has Her Grace been a patient here?" She ordered herself to concentrate.

"I was forced to bring my aunt to this place about a month ago," said Francis Ellery, nephew to the Duchess of Ashland. He put his hands on his hips, looming over Elise and the slight steward.

"Forced?" Elise prompted, trying to draw out Ellery's motives for committing his aunt to Bedlam's care.

"Her condition had deteriorated to the point where she could no longer look after herself, even with the assistance of servants. Someone had to do something," he said, just a little too smoothly.

Something, indeed, Elise thought to herself.

"Has she no husband?" she asked, feigning ignorance. She, like most everyone who read the papers, knew very well that the eleventh Duke of Ashland had recently died. Two years ago a seizure of some sort had left the old duke's muscles flaccid and had stripped him of his ability to speak and walk. Afterward he and his wife had both withdrawn from society. As far as Elise knew, Ashland had never recovered his faculties.

"The duke has passed on," Ellery informed her gravely. "I am quite devastated by the loss, as are all his closest companions."

Elise very much doubted that Francis Ellery, who, at the moment, stood to inherit the dukedom of Ashland, was at all devastated by his uncle's death.

"What a shame," *tsk*ed Elise. "And there are no children to look after the duchess?" she asked, turning her head in Ellery's direction.

"Only a daughter who has been estranged from her parents for over a decade." He shook his head sadly. "I am afraid it has been left to me to care for them in these difficult times."

"Mmm." Elise pretended to observe the duchess, tilting her chin this way and that. But it was Ellery whom she studied covertly. And the more she saw, the more her instincts recoiled. At first she couldn't say precisely why he repulsed her. Ellery was a perfectly groomed specimen of the ton with nary a blond hair nor a silk thread out of place. Nothing in his appearance branded him as someone overtly callous or cruel, or suggested he was the villain Elise rather suspected him to be. In truth, his expression was one of martyred benevolence, as if he truly believed himself to be an angel of mercy when it came to the welfare of his aunt.

Still, Ellery's eyes gave her pause. No matter how much duty and compassion he was trying to convey, the hard, raw ambition that seethed there was hard to miss. Elise had met many men with these very same eyes. And where they were concerned, she always trusted her gut.

"Have you tried to locate the daughter?" Elise asked. "Surely she would—"

"No. There is no point," Ellery interrupted. "Her Grace's daughter has been cut from the fabric of her life. From all of our lives. I have not seen her, nor do I expect to."

You are lying, Mr. Ellery. Elise gazed at him impassively. *But why?*

For it had been the duchess's daughter, Lady Abigail, who had arrived at Elise's office earlier in the week, frantic, desperate, and seeking help. It seemed Abigail had received a letter from the family's longtime and loyal housekeeper, informing her that the duke had died and that the duchess had been committed to Bedlam. Lady Abigail had hastened to the city, only to find the world she had left behind in London was now inaccessible to her. She'd been barred from her childhood home by Mr. Ellery and denied access to her mother by the doctors here at Bedlam. After several desperate days of making no progress whatsoever, and unable to find a sympathetic ear among her former friends, she'd been beside herself. Not knowing what else to do and with no one else to turn to, she'd hired Elise.

Which was why Elise now found herself in the bowels of Bedlam, wondering why an aging woman, who was of sound mind and relatively good health according to her daughter, had found herself chained to a bed in a hospital for lunatics. And wondering just how difficult it was going to be to get her out.

It had been necessary for Elise to call in a favor from a prominent London doctor, who had provided her with false credentials and a glowing letter of introduction, which together had secured her entry into Bedlam. Presenting herself as Dr. Emmett Rowley, a member of the Royal College of Physicians, she'd been granted access to examine Miriam Ellery. To deflect suspicion she'd selected three other random blue-blooded patients to examine, provided that the nearest relatives of these women did not object.

Elise had already seen the patients she was pretending to observe today, and none of the families of those other women had interfered or objected. None of them had even cared enough to respond to the notices the directors of Bedlam had sent to their homes. The fact that Her Grace's nephew had refused to allow Dr. Rowley to see his aunt unless he was also present during the exam with a steward of his choosing did not bode well. Elise was quite sure that there was a specific and self-serving reason that Francis Ellery had imprisoned his aunt in this place. She just didn't know what it was yet.

Elise glanced about at the private cell. "Her care must cost a fortune, sir," she remarked casually.

"I wish only to provide the best for my beloved aunt," Ellery said, clasping his hands behind his back.

"Mr. Ellery is a generous benefactor to the hospital," the steward added.

Elise pivoted back to the steward. *To the hospital or to you?* She wondered just how much of Ellery's generosity slipped into the pockets of the duchess's gaolers.

"Does Her Grace receive many visitors?" Elise asked next. "Friends?"

The steward shook his head. "No, she is too far gone for any visitors, Dr. Rowley. With this sort of condition, you can't have distraction, can you, sir? And it would interfere with Her Grace's treatment, of course."

"Of course." Elise nodded in feigned agreement. It wasn't just her daughter, then, who was forbidden to see her. It seemed the duchess had effectively been cut off from civilization as a whole. *Why?*

Elise pretended to make a note in the book she was carrying. Addressing the steward again, she asked, "And what are the signs and effects of the duchess's condition?"

"She is unable to remember recent events, even those that happened mere minutes ago. She often confuses individuals with people from her past. Babbles a great deal about things that happened twenty years ago as though they happened yesterday. The poor soul even insists her son is alive."

Out of the corner of her eye, she saw Mr. Ellery tense. That was interesting.

Lady Abigail had mentioned she was the lone survivor of two siblings, and it had been easy enough to check parish records to confirm the live birth of one Noah Ellery, the only son of the late Duke of Ashland. Yet the details surrounding Noah's death were vague. At some point someone had written the words *presumed deceased* next to his name in the church register. But there was no date, no reference to a riding accident, a hunting mishap, an illness, or any other cause. The implication was that he had simply...vanished.

"But she's wrong, I take it? That is to say, her son is, in fact, dead?" Elise asked, feigning ignorance once again.

"Yes," said the steward. He continued in a hushed tone, "But 'twere probably for the best anyhow. That young gentleman was never right in the head either."

"I beg your pardon?" This time Elise didn't have to pretend confusion.

The steward suddenly realized he might have said too much and glanced anxiously at Ellery. But the man looked pleased.

"It's true," Francis sighed heavily, and dropped his

voice. "My cousin was touched from birth. I suppose it isn't surprising that his poor mother now suffers the same mental defect."

Elise did her best to conceal her shock and keep an expression of mild interest fixed on her face. "Another hysteric in the family? Interesting." Elise pretended to make another notation in her book, if only to hide her annoyance that Lady Abigail hadn't mentioned this. Nor had it come up in her investigation. Which was vexing, if it was indeed true. "What were your cousin's symptoms, may I ask?"

"He was unable to speak. Can you imagine? A duke's son reduced to using hand gestures just like the monkeys in a menagerie. Just as well he died, I suppose." Ellery shook his head with more regret. "Certainly there was no cure for what ailed Noah."

Elise weighed this new information. Assuming it was true that Noah Ellery had been mad, it might explain the lack of precision in the church register. If the heir to a dukedom suffered an obvious mental deficiency, the family might indeed take measures to ensure such a child faded conveniently into the ether. And what was more, the family might then find a way to blot the child's name from the records. Money could rewrite history. Elise knew that better than anyone.

"Madness is something that quite obviously runs along this branch of the family," the steward piped up. "Through the maternal side in this case. I always say the apple doesn't fall far from the tree."

"Terribly distressing," Mr. Ellery said. "I must confess I am relieved that my relation is a paternal one."

"As you should be, sir," said Elise. "But what of the

daughter? Did she show signs of such madness when you were acquainted with her?"

"Well, she did abandon everything to elope with a blacksmith and run away to Derby. And that was after she took the patronesses of Almack's to task for their comments surrounding her fraternization with the lower classes. In a single public rant, Lady Abigail committed social suicide. Doesn't have a friend left in London. Unless, of course, you count the blacksmiths of the city." Mr. Ellery chuckled darkly. He seemed to find his little joke exceedingly funny.

"Ah. Perhaps a temporary spell of lunacy?" Elise suggested, her lips quirking.

Ellery looked delighted at this notion, just as Elise had known he would. "Most likely."

The steward was rubbing his hands. "Well, I can tell you this," he said. "The duchess will become more and more removed from reality unless she receives vigorous and sustained treatment. Purges, cold water treatments, and restrictions in diet—all of these must be applied in rotation if there's to be any hope of recovery."

Elise suppressed a shudder. "Indeed."

The steward shook his head. "The madness must be driven out, and sometimes it takes extremes to do so. She is a danger to others until it is, and as such, she must remain here."

Elise nodded. "I'd like to interview her."

Ellery frowned. "As you can see, Dr. Rowley, she's in no condition to talk."

"I'd like to ascertain that for myself." Elise allowed a tiny note of suspicion to bleed into her question. "No other family had a problem with this. Is there something you are hiding?"

"Of course not." Ellery looked on unhappily.

"Excellent. I shan't be more than a few minutes." Elise pushed by him before he had a chance to protest further.

"Do not get too close," Ellery warned. "I cannot be responsible for your safety from this point. The woman is quite unpredictable, you know."

"Thank you for your concern," Elise murmured, resisting the urge to turn and unpredictably kick the man in the shins.

Elise left the men at the doorway and approached the duchess, crouching in front of her so that they were almost eye to eye. While they were in this position, neither the steward nor Ellery would hear anything that was said between them. "Your Grace?" Elise asked softly, trying not to look at the chains that bound the duchess. Elise had once known what it was like to be held captive. She knew the feeling of utter helplessness that came with such restraint. And it made her even more determined to see this woman freed. "Your Grace?" she asked again, with renewed determination.

The duchess continued to stare at the wall, her lips moving slightly as though she was reciting a silent prayer, her grey hair falling in untidy clumps around her ears. Elise realized the woman had been drugged. She'd seen too many opium addicts not to recognize the signs.

Elise set her book aside and reached out, gathering the woman's cold, thin hands in hers. "Abigail sent me," Elise whispered. "Will you speak with me?"

The duchess turned from the wall then. Her eyes were red, but they met Elise's with no hesitation. "Abigail sent you?" she asked in a voice that sounded as though it hadn't been used in some time. "Where is she? Why isn't she here?"

"She wanted to be," Elise said, searching for signs of mental defect but finding none. All she saw was exhaustion and dulled confusion. "She isn't allowed to visit you. But she sent me to make sure you were all right."

"Are you a doctor?"

Elise smiled under her mustache. "I am today."

The duchess's eyes became a little sharper. "Francis wants to see me die in here," she said, straightening her spine. "But Abigail won't let that happen. There's nothing wrong with me, and they all know it. Abigail will fetch Noah."

Elise stilled. "Your son?"

The duchess tipped her head, her eyes losing their focus, her brief lucidity slipping away.

Elise cursed inwardly. "But your son is dead."

"Dead, dead, dead," the duchess mumbled in a singsong voice. "He's not dead. Just...gone." Her words slurred slightly.

Elise wanted to shake her but was careful to keep her expression neutral. "Gone where, Your Grace?"

"I never got him back," she replied, and there were tears tracking down her haggard cheeks now.

Elise stared at her. What did that mean?

The duchess was quiet for a few moments, and Elise wasn't sure if the woman was even aware of her presence now.

"He gave me roses for my birthday when he was seven," the duchess said suddenly, a wistful expression on her face. The slur had vanished, but she sounded distant now. "Not a bouquet, but an entire garden of damask roses. Fickle things, damask roses. But Noah grew them. That child could make anything grow. Such a sweet boy."

"Where is he now, Your Grace?" Elise prodded. Was it possible that the duchess was telling the truth? That the rightful heir to the dukedom of Ashland was still alive? Or was this a desperate, drugged wish, wrought by the grief and sorrow of a mother who had lost a son? "Where is Noah now?" Elise repeated.

The duchess was silent for nearly a full minute before her shoulders slumped forward once again. "Who are you?" she asked Elise. "Are you another doctor?"

Elise closed her eyes briefly. "Yes," she replied.

"I don't want to go in the cold water again," the duchess pleaded, and her voice shook. "Where is Abigail?"

"She's coming," Elise told her. "She's coming as soon as she can so you can go home."

"I don't want to stay here anymore." Withered, bent fingers clawed at Elise's own hands.

"You won't have to. I promise." She said it knowing promises were dangerous things. Especially when Elise was sure another month in this place would kill the duchess.

"I'm very tired," the duchess whispered.

"I know." Elise stood, and the woman's hands fell away from hers to rest lifelessly on her faded skirts.

Elise took stock of her surroundings—the heavy stone walls and the thick bars of the gates. This room was a heavily fortified dungeon, and it would be exceedingly difficult to break its prisoner out. Not impossible, of course, for Elise felt certain that there were many inside this place who could be bribed and leveraged if it came to that. But such things took time, especially when Elise did not have any established contacts. And the duchess did not have the luxury of time.

Ellery cleared his throat loudly behind Elise. "I think that is enough," he said. "It is clear that my aunt has been fatigued."

"Indeed." Elise retrieved her notebook from the floor, careful to school her expression.

"What did you discover about this patient?" the steward demanded as Elise approached him. Behind him Ellery was watching her keenly.

That she has been dosed with narcotics, probably by you. That she might harbor knowledge that would prevent Mr. Francis Ellery from getting what he wants.

"Her ladyship is clearly delusional," Elise said, choosing her words with care and telling the men everything they wanted to hear. "Confuses the present with the past, has only scant moments of lucidity, and is unable to recall even the most recent conversations."

As expected, both men relaxed. "So you see why the duchess must remain here, don't you?" Ellery prompted.

Elise didn't trust herself to answer. Instead she flipped open her notebook and scribbled *Where is Noah Ellery?* If only to keep herself from saying something she might regret later.

"Did you wish to see any of the other patients while you are here today, Dr. Rowley?" the steward asked. "We have one who thinks he's a dog. Barks till the wee hours of the morning and will only eat off the floor." He chuckled. "Most entertaining. A pity the public can no longer pay to witness it."

Elise took a steadying breath. "No, that will be all for me today. My area of interest is confined to ladies of pedigree."

"Too bad."

"My thanks for your time, gentlemen." She forced the words through her lips. "I'll take my leave now."

"Suit yourself." He frowned. "What hospital are you with again, Doctor? The directors didn't say."

Elise took a last look at the defeated, confused woman still sitting on the edge of her bed. "Neither did I," she said, and then hurried back toward the maze of corridors that would take her out of Bedlam.

Francis Ellery watched the detestable doctor go with a curl to his lip.

He was both pleased and relieved that the doctor had seen exactly what Francis had wanted him to see, but the insufferable arrogance and disrespect that he'd used to address Francis was enough to make him see red. But that would soon change.

His father had always been fond of telling Francis he'd been relieved that the burden of the duchy of Ashland had fallen on his older brother's shoulders. Being a younger son was a blessing. It had freed him from a landslide of responsibility and allowed him the liberty to choose how he lived his life and even whom he married. Being a duke wasn't as glamorous as one might think.

His father had been an idiot.

Not only did the Ashland title come with mind-boggling wealth, it came with power trumped only by the bloody monarchy. What sort of man would not want those things?

And now all of that could be his. Francis wanted—no, needed—it all. He was so close, he could almost taste it. The old duke had died. Francis's father was dead. There was only one thing stopping the courts from handing over everything Francis had ever wanted.

And that was his lunatic of a cousin. Who was very inconveniently missing.

Missing wasn't good enough for the courts to transfer the peerage from Noah Ellery to Francis Ellery. *Missing* wasn't even good enough to transfer any of the duchy's properties and wealth. Especially with the duchess running her mouth, trumpeting to anyone who would listen that her precious son was still alive.

Francis had certainly taken care of that problem. He'd then turned his attention to the one remaining and sought the sort of help that a situation like this required. That sort of help was expensive, but would be worth every penny in the end. If Noah Ellery was alive, he would be found.

And if the courts wanted a body, he would give them one.

Chapter 2

The offices of Chegarre & Associates were tucked into the clutter of Covent Square, hidden in plain sight in the shadow of St Paul's Church. The long piazzas that lined the raucous marketplace were crowded today, as they were every day. And being that the Covent Square neighborhood was populated largely by those who made their living as entertainers, of both the artistic and the intimate persuasion, the tenements saw traffic that ebbed and flowed at all hours of the day and night. No one had the interest or the time to notice the comings and goings of Elise DeVries. Which was exactly how she wanted it.

There was no sign outside the shabby-fronted building that housed Chegarre & Associates, nor did the consultancy advertise its services in the *Times*. Even so, every person in the ton—and many outside it—knew about Chegarre and the secret miracles it worked for its clients.

Chegarre & Associates was a firm dedicated to fixing

the private and personal problems of the very public people who were wealthy enough to afford Chegarre's astronomical fees. When faced with the threat of humiliation, scandal, or dishonor, one could do no better than to avail oneself of Chegarre's expert team for a solution. Elise had been a partner in the firm for just over five years, and there was little that surprised her any longer. She'd covertly tidied up inconvenient deaths, separated scandalous lovers, quashed illicit affairs, shut down illegal businesses, foiled kidnappings and extortion plots, and helped to zero out debts and addictions. The firm was masterful at making scandal simply disappear.

Which was not to say that resolving the Ashland matter would be easy.

Elise climbed the worn stone steps and let herself into the building, shutting the heavy wooden door firmly behind her. Immediately the din of the square vanished, replaced with a blessed silence. While the exterior of the once-luxurious town house still presented the same shabby facade as its neighbors, the interior had been restored to its former glory. The grandeur of the past was evident in the details of the polished wood on the walls and floor, the sparkle of crystal from the chandeliers and sconces overhead, and the subtle sheen of marble where it framed welcoming hearths. Elise leaned against the door and closed her eyes, suddenly exhausted in the absence of an audience.

She pulled off her spectacles and pressed her fingers to her eyes, making black spots dance behind her closed lids.

Seeing a woman restrained as the duchess had been had evoked unpleasant memories. And now, in the quiet and privacy of this space, it left her more than a little unsettled to be reminded of the lengths certain people would go to in the pursuit of their ambitions. Which was ridiculous, she knew. Greed and ambition were the very things that brought business to her doorstep, and the prevalence of both meant that all the members of the firm lived quite well. But for the first time since she had been hired by Chegarre, Elise wondered if perhaps she needed a break from the darker side of human nature. Perhaps she just needed to get out of London for a while.

Or perhaps she just needed a good, stiff drink.

"Miz Elise."

Elise's eyes snapped open. "Good afternoon, Roderick," she said to the boy standing before her. He was about eight, dressed formally as befitted a pint-size butler, though the entire effect was somewhat ruined by the untamable cowlick that stood straight up from the back of his head.

"Didn't recognize you from the window or I would've got the door for you," he said, scratching his head.

"That was kind of the idea," Elise replied, pushing herself wearily off the door and starting into the hall. Between this job and her work as a part-time actress at the Theatre Royal, she barely recognized herself anymore at any given moment. Every day brought a new role and a new deception to play out.

"I like that costume," Roddy offered. "That's a good one. You look like a real doctor."

But she wasn't a real doctor, Elise thought unhappily. She wasn't a real anything, in fact. She was a chameleon, paid to become whomever the situation required. And false credentials would get her only so far.

"Mr. Alex is in the drawing room waiting for you," Roddy continued.

"Good." Elise brightened at that. Alexander Lavoie was

not only her brother but a partner of Chegarre & Associates. As the owner of one of the most exclusive gaming hells in London, he was intimately familiar with the most influential and infamous members of the ton. And Alex had a particular talent for taking the secrets of these elite gamblers and depositing them into his coffers along with their money. This talent alone could turn a clever man into a very, very successful one.

And Alexander Lavoie was nothing if not clever.

"Lady Abigail is down in the kitchens," Roddy told her. "Baking again. Says she couldn't stand waiting and doing nothing. Do you want me to fetch her?"

"Not just yet." Lady Abigail had been staying in the upstairs guest rooms of the town house while Elise assessed her case, and Elise couldn't remember a time when their pantries had ever been as full of biscuits and breads.

"Are you sad, Miz Elise?" Roddy asked suddenly as they made their way toward the drawing room.

"What? Why do you ask?" Elise frowned.

"You looked kind of sad when you came in."

She paused in the hall just outside the drawing room door. "Maybe a little. People can be horrible to each other. And sometimes it makes me sad to think about it too much."

Roderick nodded sagely. "When I get sad or angry, I like to go down to the river and throw rocks into the water. It makes me feel better."

Elise smiled despite herself. "Are you suggesting that I go throw rocks into the Thames?"

Roddy made a face. "Of course not, Miz Elise. Unless you want to. But surely you have something you like to do that makes *you* feel better?"

"Cows," she said.

"Cows?"

"I used to milk the cows whenever I needed to think. Whenever I needed to let my mind rest and settle my thoughts."

Roderick wrinkled his nose dubiously. "Did you want me to fetch you a cow? There are some kept over on—"

Elise laughed. "No, thank you, Roderick. I think you've cured any sadness for now. I can skip the milking for today."

"Happy to help, Miz Elise." Roddy flashed her a smile before he disappeared back down the hall, presumably in the direction of the kitchens and the delicious smells that were wafting up.

"Things must have gone poorly if you're thinking of the old farm and wishing to milk cows again, little sister." The drawl came from inside the doorway and Elise turned to find her brother leaning against the frame, his booted feet crossed and a half glass of whiskey in his hand.

He had hazel eyes as Elise did, though his tended toward dark amber while her own languished closer to green. They also shared the same dark, coffee-colored hair, though his possessed none of the wave that made hers curl. He was tall and lean, and the scar that started at his ear and ran over his cheekbone to catch at his lip gave him an intimidating appearance.

He stepped forward and made to kiss Elise on the cheek, before eyeing her beard in distaste and thinking better of it. Elise plucked the glass from his hand and took a bracing swallow, allowing the liquor to blaze a trail of fire down her throat.

"That bad?" Alex asked with some sympathy.

"Worse." She drained what was left. "They have the

duchess chained to her bed and drugged, and I'm quite certain Francis Ellery is paying to have her kept that way." She pressed the cool glass to her forehead. "She's utterly helpless."

"Is she mad?"

"I don't believe she is. But even if she were, I wouldn't wish that on my worst enemy." She shuddered slightly. "I can't leave her like that, Alex. I'll do whatever it takes."

"I know," Alex said gently. "We'll get this sorted. But we'll do it one step at a time."

Elise nodded and took a deep breath. "Of course." She was letting too many of her own emotions muddy the waters here. And emotions had no place in this job. If she really wanted to help the duchess, she needed to focus on fact. "Tell me what you were able to find out about Francis Ellery," she said.

"Come," Alex urged, as he ushered her farther into the drawing room. "If we're going to talk about Francis Ellery, I'm going to need more whiskey."

Elise followed him into the room decorated in soothing shades of blue. A long Edward East clock kept time against the far wall, while beautifully carved furniture pieces upholstered in sumptuous brocades were arranged over the Aubusson rug at their feet. It was a room meant to impress and put even their most privileged clients at ease.

Alex plucked the glass from her hand and refilled it generously from a collection of crystal decanters along a rosewood sideboard. He handed the glass back to her before pouring another for himself and took a seat on the sofa, settling back into the plush cushions.

"Would you care to sit?" he inquired.

"I'll stand." It was all she could do not to pace.

"Suit yourself."

Elise took a more measured sip from her glass. "Tell me about Francis Ellery," she repeated.

"Francis Ellery"—Alex's top lip turned up, pulling at his scar—"does not gamble at my establishment."

"He doesn't gamble?"

Alex swirled the contents of his glass. "I didn't say that. He gambles heavily, but he no longer does so under my roof. He is a liar and a cheat. Two things I can never have on my gaming floor, if only because, together, they inevitably lead to violence. Which of course inevitably leads to the destruction of beautiful property, namely my own. You've no idea how difficult it is to get bloodstains out of baize. Ghastly expensive, those faro tables."

"So you've told me. On multiple occasions," Elise said dryly. "What else?"

"Mr. Ellery has a number of gambling debts. Very large debts. And word is that the collectors are becoming impatient."

"Ah. I can imagine Mr. Ellery is all the more eager to have the Ashland title in hand."

Alex peered at Elise. "Are you aware of how much wealth is associated with the dukedom? The real property alone is staggering. The last duke was one of the single richest landholders in all of Southern England."

"I am aware." She paused. "What about the late duke's son? Did you discover anything about him from your club clientele?"

"I did indeed. The Marquess of Heatherton, after a half-dozen glasses of my best French brandy, confided that there was, and still is, speculation about the boy. Especially now with the death of the old duke. Heatherton saw the boy only once when the child was near nine or ten—said he was the spitting image of his father—but after that he never saw him again. No evidence of him ever attending Eton or another school befitting a duke's son. No appearances at country shoots or hunts, even once he was old enough to take part. The old duke refused to speak his son's name, and the general consensus was that the boy had died, though no one ever confirmed it with any degree of confidence."

"Huh." Elise scratched at her beard.

"Heatherton did go on to say that he witnessed the duchess making a terrible scene when he called on Her Grace and Mr. Ellery to offer condolences after Ashland's death. The marquess said the duchess became quite agitated. In fact she begged Heatherton to help her find her son. When Mr. Ellery reminded his aunt that Noah Ellery was long dead, she began raving, insisting he was alive, and eventually Mr. Ellery had to bodily drag the duchess from the room to see her settled upstairs. He took great pains to later excuse his aunt's wild rant as a product of her mind-altering grief."

"Mind-altering?" Elise asked.

"Ellery's words, not mine. Though isn't it terribly convenient that the single person who believes that Noah Ellery is alive has now been committed to Bedlam?"

Abigail will fetch Noah. Elise heard Miriam's words echo in her head. "She isn't the only one who believes the heir to Ashland is alive. I think his sister does too."

Alex's brows rose. "And why, then, would Lady Abigail decline to mention this?"

"Perhaps I can answer that."

Elise froze, an unpleasant ripple of unease coursing

through her. Slowly she turned toward the voice that had spoken.

He was standing in the doorway of the study, one hand tucked into the front of his coat, the other resting on the top of a silver-tipped walking stick. He was a physically impressive man, with red-gold hair and pale-blue eyes set into an aquiline face reminiscent of early Tudor portraits, from before their monarchs had fallen victim to vice and the ravages of age. He was dressed expensively, the finest fabrics tailored to perfection on his sleek frame, a blindingly white cravat tied intricately at his neck. A gold ring glinted off a finger as he adjusted his grip on the head of his walking stick.

"King," she said by way of careful greeting. It was the only name the man had. Or at least the only one Elise had ever heard. But that was to be expected from a man with no past who had risen ruthlessly and violently through the ranks of London's underworld until he rested at the very pinnacle. He traded in rare antiquities, art, jewelry—anything, really, that could be obtained and that would fetch a price from discriminating buyers with very deep pockets and very few principles. Elise doubted that there existed anything in this world that King could not unearth. Assuming the money was right, of course.

"I let myself in," the man said. "There was a decided lack of opposition. You might want to think about addressing that."

"Come to steal the silverware, King?" Alex asked casually from the sofa, crossing his legs. He looked relaxed, but Elise could sense the hostility rolling off him in waves.

King's eyes flickered in the direction of her brother briefly. "Perhaps not today, Mr. Lavoie." He stepped into the room and walked slowly toward Elise. "By God, I can see why the duchess adores you." He came to a stop in front of Elise, examining her appearance. "I would wager your own mother would never recognize you."

"Miss Moore isn't here at the moment," Elise told him. Ivory Moore was both the founder of Chegarre & Associates and the former Duchess of Knightley. It was usually she who negotiated with King when necessity required it.

"I know. The duchess is in Chelmsford."

Elise narrowed her eyes at him. Ivory was indeed in Chelmsford, managing a situation there. But that was not common knowledge.

King shrugged in response. "One hears things."

And that was the problem, Elise thought to herself. The man was as dangerous and as unpredictable as a pit viper, but he had connections that ran as deeply into the upper echelons of London society as they did into the gutters of the underworld. And there were times when Chegarre & Associates needed his assistance.

King reached out a hand and touched the lapel of Elise's coat, rubbing the coarse wool between his fingers, as if testing its quality. It was everything she could do to remain still.

"I would trouble you to step away from my sister," Alex said, taking a slow sip of whiskey, his posture not altering, but the threat in his voice unmistakable.

The corner of King's mouth lifted, and he withdrew his hand. "No need to get so prickly, Lavoie. I am rather an admirer of Miss DeVries, if you must know. I have great respect for those who are good at what they do."

Alex made a rude noise. "Respect? A strange word coming from the mouth of a man who thought auctioning a wom—"

"Whatever business was between the duchess and myself was just that, Lavoie. Business." King looked at Alex coldly.

"Enough." Elise put her hands on her hips, drawing on those acting skills that King had so recently praised and cloaking her face in a mask of boredom. "We're wasting time, and I have clients waiting. Why are you here, King?"

King examined the ring on his finger. "I was made to understand that you were asking questions about Francis Ellery and the son of the late Duke of Ashland on behalf of a client."

Jesus, was there nothing that this man didn't hear? She glanced at Alex and saw him put his glass to the side. "Perhaps," she replied.

"In the spirit of the respect I have for this fine firm, I thought I might bring to your attention the fact that Francis Ellery has recently hired two assassins."

Elise felt her jaw slacken. "I beg your pardon?"

"Not good ones, mind you, because Ellery simply can't afford them. The vainglorious sot has galloped his way through whatever money was left to him and whatever he borrowed after that. And good assassins, the kind that can make murder seem like the most innocent of accidents, are heinously expensive. At least my favorites are. Highway robbery if you ask me, but then again, one gets what one pays for."

Elise was trying to make sense of this. "Why are you sharing this with us?"

"Because their target is Noah Ellery."

A deafening silence descended in the room.

"He's alive then," Elise said carefully.

"Yes. Or at least he was the last time I saw him. And I'd

very much like to locate him before these middling assassins do."

Elise's mind was racing. "When did you see him last?"

"Twelve years ago."

"Where?"

"Here. In London."

"Ellery was in *London*?"

"He was. Until Lady Abigail left the glitter of high society behind and married a blacksmith from Derby. Very dedicated to and protective of his sister, you know." His eyes slid to Alex.

Elise frowned. "Lady Abigail didn't mention any of this."

"That is because Lady Abigail never knew he was in London. It's possible she assumes him dead. I can tell you with certainty that she's never done or said anything in the past twelve years to indicate that she believes he's still alive."

"You've been watching her."

King smoothed a finger over the top of his walking stick. "Checking in occasionally, perhaps."

"And how did *you* know the duke's son was in London?"

"That is none of your business."

Elise regarded King impassively, knowing there was something much deeper here than King's professed respect for Chegarre & Associates. "Just what, exactly, is your interest in Noah Ellery?"

Something in King's face shifted. "That would also be none of your business."

"No, that is very much my business. For I am not in the habit of locating individuals if I know that exposing them will endanger their lives."

King's nostrils flared slightly. "You think I wish to harm him?"

Elise shrugged. "Do you?"

The man's pale eyes slitted. "If I had known before to-day that Francis Ellery had hired such men, I would have located these assassins and paid them double to forget the name Noah Ellery ever existed. I might have paid them double again to make Francis Ellery disappear instead. Still might." A muscle flexed along his clean-shaven jaw. "But they are in the wind at the moment. And I can't have Francis killed. Not yet. He may still be useful in locating the heir to Ashland."

"And just why do you wish to find him?" Elise prodded, deliberately ignoring King's casual threat to have Francis Ellery executed.

"Because I owe Noah a great debt." For a split second, there was emotion on King's face, a vulnerable pain, though it vanished as quickly as it had appeared. "And I do not wish to see him harmed."

Elise blinked. Bloody hell. Did a real human being dwell somewhere beneath King's icy, twisted exterior?

"If you know so much about this man, why do you need me to find him?"

"Because I have been unable to. And believe me, I've tried. But Noah Ellery has covered his tracks too well."

"I see."

"I am told you used to be a tracker for the British army. Somewhere in the Empire's colonies."

Elise stilled. That wasn't something she often shared. But it was a waste of time wondering how King had come to know it. "Yes."

"Further, I am told that you are the best."

"At what?"

"At finding people who don't wish to be found."

"Yes. I am," said Elise. She knew King had little tolerance for false modesty.

"I know Lady Abigail is here at present," King said. "And I am hopeful that she can offer a clue as to her brother's whereabouts that I have yet to uncover. But I know she does not have the funds to pay all of the charges that will be incurred in this matter. I do, and I wish Chegarre to look to me for compensation. But do not, under any circumstances, divulge my involvement in this matter to anyone. This conversation never happened, do you understand?"

"Yes." Elise paused, frowning. There were more important issues at hand than invoicing details. "How does Francis Ellery even know his cousin is alive?"

"There are some very thin rumors surfacing now," King said, tracing the tip of his walking stick over the pattern in the rug. "Among those who knew the late Duke of Ashland had a son. Among those who remember that child. Among those who have discovered that there is no credible record of death for that child, who, as far as anyone can determine, has not been seen in over twenty years. Rumors enough to stay Francis's hand on the duchy of Ashland. At least for now. At least until Noah Ellery can be confirmed dead." King looked up at her, and his eyes were as flat and as frigid as Elise had ever seen them.

She felt her skin crawl.

King's cane stilled on the carpet, his knuckles tightening on the handle. "I take exception to a man who thinks to claim something he has no right to from someone who…" He trailed off, and Elise wondered silently just what the hell Noah Ellery had done to earn such devotion from a man as terrifying as this one. "You'll advise me of your progress?" King's hand relaxed, and he straightened.

"Of course," Elise murmured.

"Very good. Mr. Lavoie, Miss DeVries, always a pleasure." He offered them a smile with no warmth. "I'll see myself out."

A silence fell as both Elise and Alex considered the empty doorway through which King had just vanished.

"Is he telling the truth, do you think?" Alex asked presently, pushing himself to his feet.

"I think King was as honest as he's ever been," Elise said slowly.

"More than we can say about Lady Abigail."

"Yes." Elise put her glass down on the sideboard and pulled off her beard, wincing as the glue tugged at her skin. "It won't be the last time a client tries to conceal something of importance from us. Though for the life of me, I can't begin to guess why Lady Abigail hasn't contacted her brother if she knows he's alive. He could free his mother from Bedlam in less than a moment." She rubbed at the reddened skin on her jaw, thinking of the duchess imprisoned in chains.

The same sense of weary sadness she had felt earlier pressed in on her again.

"Are you all right?" Alex had stepped closer to her.

"I'm fine."

"You're not. You were talking to Roddy about milking cows."

"Do you ever miss it? Home, that is?" Elise asked suddenly, thinking of the orchards and the pastures and the forests that they had grown up in. Where things had been simple and straightforward.

Alex was quiet. "I don't miss the war," he said.

"I'm not talking about the war, or what it cost us. I'm talking about the farm. When we were still a family."

"You're still my family, little sister," Alex reminded her. "And it doesn't matter if we're in York or London."

"I know."

"I try not to look backwards, Elise. Makes it hard to see where you're going."

Elise looked down. Alex was right. But it was also hard to see where you were going when you couldn't even be sure who you were anymore.

"Do you want me to handle this, Elise?" Alex asked. "I can close the club for a week—"

"Don't be ridiculous," Elise said, raising her head. "I've got nothing holding me here. The theater is closed. The ink isn't even dry on Elliston's lease, and he's talking about repainting the entire interior. It will be months before he'll reopen." She had no idea where this melancholy was coming from, but she needed to focus on the task ahead of her. If she was to help the Duchess of Ashland, she would need to be at her best. "I'll handle this, Alex. If Noah Ellery is alive, I'll find him. It's what I do, after all."

"Right." Alex was still watching her. "Well, do you want me to help you talk to Lady Abigail at least?"

"No, I think this will go better if I interview Lady Abigail alone. I don't want her to feel ambushed."

"Understood." Alex glanced in the direction of the hall. "But I insist you send me word about the outcome. Especially," he added, "if you come across a living, dead heir."

⁓

Roddy fetched Lady Abigail from the kitchens at Elise's request, and she arrived in the drawing room slightly out of breath, a look of hopeful expectation stamped on her face.

"Were you able to see my mother, Miss DeVries?" Abigail asked, hurrying forward.

"I did," Elise answered, removing her wig and running her fingers through her hair, massaging her scalp.

"Was she all right? Surely you could see that there was nothing wrong with her?"

Elise let her hands drop as she regarded the woman standing in front of her. Abigail had her hands on her sturdy hips, her blond hair escaping the tight crown of braids at the back of her head. The seconds ticked by, and still Elise said nothing. The hope in Lady Abigail's eyes faded and was replaced by deep apprehension.

"Where is Noah living at the moment?" Elise finally inquired. She had no interest in wasting any more time.

The woman paled, before bright spots of pink burned into her cheeks and she looked away. "My brother is dead."

Lady Abigail was lying. She, like King, knew Noah Ellery was alive.

"You are right about one thing, my lady," said Elise. "I don't think that there is anything wrong with your mother or her mind. Yet your cousin pays handsomely to keep her locked up, subjected to torturous treatments that have no curative benefit, but will likely kill her within a month. Maybe two."

"Oh God." Lady Abigail sat down heavily on the settee.

"Let me tell you what I think, my lady, and you can simply agree or disagree. I think one cannot inherit a dukedom if the current, *sane* duchess insists that her son, the rightful heir, yet lives." Elise came to sit next to Abigail. "With such a claim, the estate could be tied up indefinitely."

Lady Abigail had her face buried in her hands. "This is such a bloody mess," she mumbled through her fingers.

She sounded on the brink of tears. "Damn Francis and his damn greed."

"Did you never consider what would happen when your father died?"

"Of course! But I didn't think Francis would do...this." Abigail's voice was barely audible.

"Is there no one you can appeal to for help?" Elise asked. "Old friends? Surely someone with enough political and social leverage could look into this on your behalf? You are, after all, the daughter of a duke."

Abigail shook her head. "I have no friends in London anymore. I'm afraid I burned all of those bridges, though I can't say I've ever regretted it until now. The members of the ton are more eager to align themselves with the next Duke of Ashland than the daughter of a madwoman." She made a rude noise. "And people wonder why I left London and never looked back."

Elise sighed. None of what Abigail had said was surprising, but they were still back where they had started. "Is your brother truly mad, as Francis implies?" Elise tried a different tack, though she winced slightly at the cruel manner in which her words came out. "Is that why he doesn't wish to be found?"

Abigail was worrying a loose thread on her sleeve. Her lips were pressed in a thin line. "He might not have spoken as a child, but Noah is not mad."

"Nor is he dead," prompted Elise.

The woman shook her head miserably.

Elise felt a small rush of satisfaction. Now they were getting somewhere. "Where is he then? For I fear that he is the only person who has the power to save your mother in time. He must be fetched back to London."

"I don't know where my parents sent him. One day I came home and he was simply gone. I was only fourteen at the time, and they refused to tell me anything. His name was never mentioned in our household again until five years later when my father sat my mother and me down and told us that Noah was dead. He offered not a single detail about how he died, but demanded we accept my brother's death as fact and move forward."

Well, that didn't help. Abigail clearly had no idea where Noah had gone. It could have been Scotland. Or France. Or it could have been the moon. But if she had no idea where he had gone... "Then how do you know he is alive?"

From the front of her dress, Abigail carefully removed a brooch and handed it to Elise. It was heavy, crafted not by a jeweler but more likely by a smith. It was a piece of crude simplistic beauty, tiny strands of steel woven into the shape of a rose.

"He sent this to me, six months after my wedding day, along with a letter."

"A letter? Your brother announced his resurrection with a *letter*?" Good Lord.

"Yes." Abigail sniffed, sounding a little defensive. "Once I got over the shock, it was the best wedding gift I could ever have dreamed of."

"And did this letter tell you where he was?"

"No. It only said that he loved me and that he was proud of me for finding the courage to choose my own happiness. He asked me not to look for him, but to trust that he had found his own measure of happiness."

"Did it say where he had been sent as a child?"

"No." She twisted her hands in her lap. "But..."

"But what?"

"Even if you could find Noah, I don't know if he'll come back to London."

"I beg your pardon?" Elise wasn't sure she'd heard correctly. "Your mother—*his* mother—might die imprisoned, your cousin stands to steal the entire dukedom out from under him, and he won't return to London?" Abigail had said Noah Ellery wasn't insane, but Elise was beginning to wonder.

Abigail looked at Elise unhappily. "The only other thing he said in his letter was that our parents were dead to him. And that he would never return to the world that we had both been born into."

Elise stifled a groan. This was getting more complicated by the second.

"But there was a Nottingham postmark on the letter," Abigail rushed on. "And my husband recognized the workmanship of the brooch. He apprenticed together with a blacksmith who enjoyed making pieces like this out of leftover bits of metal. And sure enough, we found the man's initials on the bottom of the piece."

Elise turned the brooch over and squinted at the tiny letters worked discreetly along the lower edge of the steel stem. "J. B."

"He's a smith by the name of John Barr. He lives and works in Nottingham."

And right now he was the only link to a missing duke. A long shot, to be sure. But a starting place. It was doubtful that Noah Ellery was still in Nottingham. But no matter how carefully a person tried to cover his tracks, small clues were inevitably left behind. And Elise was very good at finding such clues.

Unfortunately, others were already looking as well.

"Does anyone else know about the brooch or that your brother is still alive?" Elise asked urgently.

"Just my husband. And my mother."

That much had become obvious. "Was it you who told her?"

Abigail nodded. "When I married, my father disowned me. But she defied my father and came to visit me secretly when my first son was born. She was still so heartbroken over Noah. And holding my son in my arms, it broke *my* heart to think about what it would be like to lose a child. Maybe it was a mistake. But I told her. Showed her Noah's letter."

"I see. But you're certain you never showed the letter to anyone else?"

"Oh God." Abigail's face had suddenly gone ashen. "The letter. I kept it in a box that held a pair of sapphire earrings I'd saved from my youth. And it was stolen."

"When?" Elise demanded. King hadn't mentioned a letter, or the burglary of Abigail's home. As implausible as it seemed, the all-knowing King had missed two critical pieces of information.

"The day before I left to come here to London. I thought it was the jewelry the thieves were after. But it wasn't, was it?"

Elise ran her hands over her face in frustration before shaking her head. "No."

If Abigail was right that she and her mother were the only people who had known about Noah's letter, it was clear that Ellery, or the men he'd hired, had gotten very, very lucky. They'd targeted Lady Abigail's house without much hope of finding anything useful and had stumbled upon a gold mine.

"Francis has people looking for Noah, doesn't he?" Abigail whispered.

Elise debated the wisdom of telling Abigail the rest of it. In the end she said, "Yes. And it is absolutely necessary that I find him first."

Lady Abigail pressed a hand to her mouth. "They'll kill Noah if they find him."

Elise nodded reluctantly, though she was relieved that Abigail understood. "Yes." She paused. "*If* they can find him. It would seem he's hidden himself quite well."

Abigail's eyes had filled with tears. "What am I going to do?"

"You are going to do nothing," Elise told her. "You will stay here as our guest and avoid Francis Ellery. And whatever you do, do not mention your brother, or the fact that he is alive, to anyone outside of these walls. The last thing I need is to return to find out your cousin has somehow managed to have you locked up in Bedlam as well."

"But—"

"I can find your brother," Elise told her, trying to infuse her tone with a calm reassurance she wasn't feeling at the moment. If Noah Ellery had managed to stay invisible for so many years, it wouldn't be easy. "I am very good at finding people who don't wish to be found." That part, at least, was true.

"I can't lose him again," Lady Abigail whispered. "Please, Miss DeVries. Find my brother and bring him back."

Chapter 3

Elise had forgotten the freedom that came with living rough.

Freed of the congestion of London, freed of the constraints of skirts, freed of the expectations demanded of a young Englishwoman, Elise felt almost giddy despite the circumstances. Everything she needed to live was on her person, or strapped to her saddle. The boy's clothes she wore were comfortable, the horse she rode agreeable and fast, the sun on her face divine, and the forested country she passed through picturesque. Aye, it wasn't the rugged, rough beauty of the Canadian wilderness where she had grown up, but then again, there was something to be said for the comfort of a wide, maintained road.

And the lack of American snipers.

Elise pulled her cap down lower over her brow as she guided her gelding toward the bridge crossing the River Leen that would lead her into the center of Nottingham.

In another life, before she had come to England, she had been recruited by the British in their war against the Americans and had become one of their best trackers and scouts. Years of practice looking for people who didn't want their presence known had honed her skills and now served her equally well in the employ of Chegarre.

Up ahead on the left, Elise took in the grand edifice of the castle that loomed on a rise and stood watch over the town. Straight ahead, on another rise, the sturdy square tower of St Nicholas Church rose, buildings clustered at its base. Pastureland fell away from the road, divided by stone fences and dotted with homes. Clumps of trees hid the town proper, but wisps of smoke rose beyond, betraying a busy settlement.

She'd start at a tavern, Elise figured, to determine if a smith named John Barr was still in residence. Taverns were always fonts of information, especially if the ale was flowing liberally. And a well-placed question about the availability of a good smith to shoe her gelding wouldn't be out of place. If there were others on Noah Ellery's trail, Elise did not want to draw unwanted attention to herself. Or to John Barr, for that matter. Not until she could determine if there was any evidence that John Barr knew the whereabouts of Noah. Or even knew him at all.

As it was, she harbored hope, but her expectations were low. It was entirely possible the smith had moved on. Or died. It was entirely possible that the only connection Noah Ellery had ever had with him was the coincidental purchase of a rose brooch.

She scowled at herself, unwilling to consider defeat before she had even started, and urged her gelding into a jog.

Up ahead on the bridge, a group of boys were playing,

long sticks waving wildly in the air as each brandished his wooden sword. Two daredevils had climbed up on the narrow stone wall that ran along the edge of the bridge, parrying and lunging at each other in what sounded like an epic battle between pirates along the rail of a galleon's deck.

Elise couldn't help but smile. The scene before her brought back happy memories. She too had played with mock weapons as a child, until she'd been old enough to acquire real ones. Cheered on by their friends, the two boys were becoming bolder. Elise glanced down at the swirling river beneath them and grinned, thinking it was only a matter of time before one of the pint-size sea captains would find himself overboard and sputtering.

Her horse slowed to a walk as she began making her way across the bridge, the gelding pricking its ears as the battle on the bridge wall reached a fever pitch. And then suddenly there was a shriek, and the boy closest to Elise lost his footing on the wall and disappeared over the side, a resounding splash audible a second later.

Every boy on the bridge froze, the color draining from each one of their faces as they rushed to peer over the wall of the bridge. Elise frowned. Where she had expected squeals of laughter and triumph, there was only an awful silence. One of the boys took off, running in the direction of town. From the back of her horse, Elise caught a glimpse of a dark head above the water before it disappeared again. With a sickening lurch of her gut, she realized the boy couldn't swim.

"*Merde*," she swore, swinging down from the gelding, yanking her boots off, and shucking her coat as she stumbled to the edge of the bridge. She stepped up onto the stone wall, searching the water below her. The boy's head surfaced again, and without any hesitation, Elise jumped.

She hit the water cleanly, the cold water that closed over her head a jolt to her heated body. She stroked to the surface, searching for the boy. A flash of color, pale against the dark water, caught her eye before it disappeared again. She dove, extending her hands in front of her. It was eerily silent under the water, the sound of her blood pounding in her ears the only thing she could hear. Her lungs started to burn, and she kicked forward once more, her hand suddenly coming into contact with a small body.

Grabbing a fistful of the boy's shirt, she kicked desperately upward and reached the surface. Drawing in deep breaths, she adjusted her hold on the boy so that her arm was around his neck, keeping his small face above the water. He was struggling wildly, which relieved Elise to no end, but it also threatened to drag them both back under the water.

"Stop moving," Elise snapped at him, her mouth against his ear.

He tried to turn, his hands flailing.

"I said stop moving," she growled again. "Or so help me, I'll let you go."

The boy stilled.

"Very good. Stay like that." Elise kicked slowly through the water, allowing the current to drag them downriver. She angled toward the closest bank, trying to pace herself, though it took a long time for her feet to find the bottom. With an effort she tried to push herself forward, only to find her legs were far more fatigued than she'd thought.

"Dammit," she gasped as the water nearly went over her head.

Suddenly there were strong arms beneath hers, and the weight of the boy vanished from against her body.

"Let go," someone instructed. "We've got him."

Thankful, Elise released her grip on the boy. The arms beneath her didn't vanish, however, and she leaned into their steely support, grateful for the help. Now that the melee was over, she found herself suddenly shaky. With the assistance of her rescuer, she half stumbled, half crawled up the bank. The strong arms deposited her carefully, and she sprawled amid a thick blanket of marsh grasses. She was aware she was breathing like a winded racehorse, but couldn't bring herself to care.

"Is the boy all right?" she managed.

"He's fine." The words were slow but clear, and they came from somewhere up above her. "His father has him."

"Good." She looked up, but all she could see against the glare of the sun was the blurred outline of a man. She gave up and lay back against the grass, trying to slow her breathing. "I do hope his father is taking him to swimming lessons now."

There was a bark of what sounded like surprised laughter.

Somewhere farther up the bank, Elise could hear the babble of voices raised in agitation. She closed her eyes. It sounded as if half the town was standing on the road beyond her. So much for avoiding unwanted attention. What a debacle.

"You're not going to die on me, are you?" The voice came from lower down, almost directly in front of her this time, and Elise opened her eyes, staring up at a collection of clouds scudding across the blue sky.

"Not yet, I think." She struggled to sit, her tired muscles still refusing to obey.

A warm hand caught hers and pulled her forward, and Elise was suddenly presented with the most beautiful eyes she had ever seen.

They were smoky green, the color of pine wreathed in mist, the color of still waters that hid great depths. They were ringed with blond lashes, set in a strong, rugged face that spoke of hours spent outdoors. Pale-blond hair fell around his ears in careless waves, the ends damp where they brushed his bare shoulders. Incredible shoulders, wide and powerful, droplets of water sliding over the ridges of muscle to disappear down the front of his chest.

Her mouth went dry, and whatever breath she'd thought she had caught deserted her once again.

He was crouched before her, a look of concern tempered with a half smile stamped across his striking features. "Hmmm. Well, if you die, can I have your horse?" he asked. "As fine an animal as I've seen in a long time."

"My horse?" she repeated. Good Lord. Her wits had completely scattered under that smoky gaze.

He glanced over her head up in the direction of the road. "One of the boys brought it off the bridge for you."

Elise struggled to draw a normal breath and formulate a thought. The man was trying to put her at ease. It wasn't his fault that he looked as he did. It wasn't his fault her body was threatening to make an utter fool of her because of it.

But clearly it had been too long since she had invited a man to share her bed, because she was shamelessly staring at the way his body moved as he shifted. Subtle shadows carved their way across his torso, created by lean muscle rippling under golden skin. A scattering of dark-blond hair covered his chest and trailed down past his navel. Her eyes dropped farther south, and she let her gaze wander over the sharp ridges of muscle that formed a V over his hips before disappearing into the front of his breeches. His free hand rested on a powerful thigh, long, capable-looking fingers spread out over the top of his knee. She imagined what those fingers would feel like against her bare skin. Because she already knew what his arms had felt like beneath her, the hard strength of his body against hers.

When he was pulling you from the water like a drowned river rat, you fool, not drawing you into a lover's embrace.

A terrible realization struck her with the completion of that thought. Without needing to check, she knew her cap was gone. Her braid had come unpinned, and she could feel the heavy weight of her sodden hair on her back. A glance at her waterlogged clothes plastered to her body confirmed her worst suspicions. When she'd bound her breasts tightly beneath her loose, baggy shirt, they were unnoticeable, but there was nothing unnoticeable about them now. The bindings had come loose and slid down to bunch at her waist. Worse, the threadbare fabric of her worn shirt was almost transparent, and stuck to her skin as it was, she might as well have been wearing nothing. The curves of her breasts were clearly visible, as were the dark areolas of her peaked nipples.

The man's eyes were still on her face and not on her chest, which Elise was choosing to interpret as a testament to his chivalry, but no one in his right mind would mistake her for anything other than what she truly was. A woman dressed as a boy.

"No, you can't have my horse," she muttered, attempting to peel her shirt away from her breasts with her free hand. "I need it to flee a lot of awkward questions."

The man was watching her again. "They are going to want to know who you are," he said quietly, jerking his chin in the direction of the voices beyond them. The understanding she saw in those incredible eyes made her blink.

She managed a weak smile. "Do you suppose anyone will notice if I just swim back to where I came from?" She was trying to make her mind work, but like her muscles, it seemed lethargic, her usual ingenuity depleted. "You can tell them that I was a mermaid."

"A mermaid." His mouth twitched and he glanced over her head again. "You have to give me something better than that. I'll tell them whatever you want, but a mermaid might be reaching."

Elise frowned at his question. *I'll tell them whatever you want*? Not *Who are you?* Or *Why are you dressed like a boy?* Those were the questions most people would have started with. "Why are you being so…kind?" she asked, not sure if *kind* was the right word. *Perceptive* might be better. Or *accepting*.

"Someone was kind to me once in a situation not so different from this one." His eyes flickered to her unorthodox trousers and her bare feet before returning to her face. "And you saved the son of a dear friend minutes ago."

"Right." Elise sighed, knowing that there was going to be no avoiding what was coming next. She gazed down, startled to realize that this man still held her hand, as though it were the most natural thing in the world. Unnerved, she withdrew it and wrapped her arms around herself, not sure if it was her exhaustion or the physical beauty of this man that was still addling her wits. Why could she not come up with something clever to say? Why could she not come up with the myriad of plausible excuses and explanations that were always ready? Why did she not want to?

"It is safer to travel alone as a boy than as a woman," she said. There, that was a truth. Simplified truths were always better—safer—than elaborate lies, anyway.

"Ah. Well, then, I can work with that. I'll keep the worst of the questions at a distance for you."

Elise could feel a smile tugging at the corners of her mouth. "You drag me out of a river, threaten to claim my horse, and now you appoint yourself my knight-errant?"

"Well, if you're not going to die, I think you're owed at least a little errancy for saving a lad."

"*Errancy*? Is that even a word?"

"It is for a heroine." He smiled at her then, and Elise felt the bottom of her stomach pitch wildly. Oh, dear God. The man had dimples. She was not going to survive this. Not without giving in to the insane urge to kiss him silly if only to discover if he tasted as good as he looked.

She uttered a strangled laugh that sounded a little unstable in her own ears, and his smile disappeared back into a look of concern.

That was better. "I'm not a heroine." At present she was a part-time actress and a woman people hired to make their problems go away. There was nothing heroic about that.

"I'm afraid you are at the moment. You should prepare yourself to be treated as such. What you did was—"

"Reckless? Foolish?" She didn't want to hear any more compliments from this man. If he didn't stop with all this gentle kindness, she couldn't be held responsible for her actions. Which would undoubtedly be both reckless and foolish.

"Brave." He smiled at her again, and she had to look away as her insides went molten. "Here."

Elise reluctantly turned back to find him holding out a ball of damp linen. "What is that?"

"My shirt. It's mostly dry. You can...on. Put it on. If you wish. Yours is, ah..." He made an inelegant motion at her torso before looking away.

Elise watched in fascination. Was he blushing? Holy hell, he was, and the urge to reach out and run her fingers along those warm, chiseled cheekbones was a tangible thing. To follow her fingers with her lips and her tongue...

Elise cleared her throat forcefully. This was absurd. *She* was being absurd. A man who looked like this and who treated a woman with the dignity and respect and *kindness* he had just shown her would not be single. He would be married. With strapping sons who looked just like him and lovely daughters who looked just like his beautiful wife.

Right?

"Thank you." She reached out and accepted his shirt. He stood abruptly, and Elise's gaze followed him up. He held out a hand to her, and with only a slight hesitation, she took it, allowing him to pull her to her feet. They stood there in the muck and the tall marsh grass for a long minute, facing each other, Elise's hand still caught in his.

She could feel the heat of him rolling off his bare skin, and still more warmth bleeding through his palm into hers. Saints help her, she wanted to feel more of him. Wanted to run her fingers over the planes and ridges of muscle, wanted to feel the sun-warmed skin beneath her fingers. She had never, in all her life, been so instantly, desperately attracted to a man. And one who blushed. And used words like *errancy* and *heroine* without apologizing. And who gave her the shirt off his back in an effort to provide her with modesty and protection.

It would be easy to become completely besotted with a man like this. He had the power to make her forget everything around her with a simple smile. It was just as well she would be gone within a day or two, as soon as she completed her search for John Barr here in Nottingham. She couldn't afford the distraction.

She forced her eyes from his and stepped back slightly, pulling her hand from his. She shook out the rough linen shirt and yanked it over her head, struggling to pull the loose garment over her wet clothes. As soon as she could get this damn shirt on and deal with whatever waited for her up on that road, she would be on her way.

Elise cursed silently, the dry shirt stuck halfway over her head. The muscles in her arms threatened to give out on her as she fought the restrictive wet fabric of her own clothing.

"Do you need help?" There was amusement lacing his words.

"No." Elise struggled for a few seconds longer. "Yes." Her arms were trapped at strange angles, and she couldn't see a thing.

"Hmmm."

"Are you laughing at me?"

"No." He laughed.

She felt his hands slide up her arms, the linen untwisting and sliding over her limbs. He gently tugged the collar of his shirt over her head, his fingers traveling over her shoulders to straighten the seams before deftly tying the laces at her throat. "There you are, milady." His mouth was curved into a half smile again. "Your knight-errant has slain the beastly shirt with his bare hands."

And become the first man ever to dress me.

Elise had never experienced anything so strangely intimate in all her life, and it had left her gasping. Gooseflesh rippled over her skin, and heat gathered in her belly. "Thank you," she whispered.

He gave her a brief bow. "Might I have the pleasure of your name, milady?" he asked.

Elise started with the realization that she didn't yet know his name either. An entire conversation, an entire tangle of debauched fantasies—she was wearing his shirt, for pity's sake—and she hadn't even stopped to ask his name.

"Elise," she said. "DeVries," she added as an afterthought. There was something liberating about simply telling this man her name. Because for once she was no longer in disguise. She didn't need to pretend to be someone else. The river had made sure of it. "May I have the pleasure of yours?"

"Noah," he said.

Elise froze, using every ounce of experience honed on the stage to keep herself from reacting. "Noah." She forced a soft smile.

He was about the right age. He was blond, like Lady Abigail. Which might mean nothing. The odds of finding a man who didn't want to be found before she'd really begun to search in earnest were slim. The odds of finding that man in the mud and vegetation of a riverbank were astronomical. Impossible, she might even venture. "So am I to call you Sir Noah?" She said it lightly.

"Lawson. My last name," he clarified unnecessarily. "Though Sir Noah has a definite ring to it." He was teasing her again.

Noah Lawson. Elise felt an irrational stab of disappointment. Of course he wasn't the man she was looking for, and the fact that she had harbored such a thought for even a second made her feel not a little foolish. There were many men in England named Noah. Had she truly believed it would be that easy? That she would ride into Nottingham and be met by a man who would simply introduce himself as Noah Ellery, lost heir to the title of Ashland? That he would smile and inquire when they would be leaving for London?

Had she not been so distracted, Elise would have remembered that Noah Ellery would not have introduced himself at all—he lacked the powers of speech to make that possible. But there was nothing wrong with Noah Lawson's powers of speech. Most of what came out of his mouth was leaving her weak at the knees.

"Lawson!" The shout came from above their heads through the tall grasses. "Are you all right? What are you doing down there?"

Noah glanced at her. "We're fine," he shouted back. "Just giving the lass a chance to catch her breath."

His statement was met with utter silence, followed by a low murmur of male voices. Next there came the sound of snapping twigs as booted feet started down the bank in their direction.

"'Lass'?" Elise asked.

Noah gave Elise an apologetic shrug. "Better that they have a little warning that you're probably not what they're expecting." He jerked his head in the direction of the road. "Come." He reached for Elise's hand again, and she gave it willingly, her legs still feeling leaden and not at all up to the task of climbing a steep riverbank on their own.

He went slowly, allowing her to lean on his arm, and

they were halfway up when they met a bear of a man on his way down, his face pinched in concern.

"God's teeth, man, but we thought you'd fallen back in." There was relief in the man's words. His bright-blue eyes went from Noah to Elise. "And I thought you were jesting when you said 'lass.'" He pushed by Noah to stand in front of Elise.

Elise gazed up at him warily and then, without warning, found herself enveloped in a smothering embrace.

"Thank you," the man muttered gruffly. "That was my fool son you saved just now." He drew back just as abruptly, running a hand through his dark hair, liberally sprinkled with grey.

Elise could only nod.

"Well, come on with you two," the barrel-chested man ordered roughly. "Before people start talking." He turned back in the direction of the road. "There's a lot of folk wanting to meet this...lass. You can't have her all to yourself."

"I wasn't ravishing her in the reeds," Noah said sardonically to the man's back.

Elise swallowed hard and looked back at the concealing vegetation with some regret. Lust swirled through her veins, and she stamped on it before her thoughts could be detected.

"You're mostly naked, and she's wearing your clothes," the man replied over his shoulder.

"Better mine than yours," Noah replied.

The bear up ahead laughed, a deep, rolling sound, and Elise wondered at the relationship between the two men. Friends? Family? Either way, their conversation spoke of an easy familiarity, not so different from what she shared with Alex.

Elise started forward again, staggering at the incline, and in a heartbeat she found herself swept up and trapped within a pair of strong arms.

"Put me down," she demanded, not knowing where to put her hands or where to look. A familiar panic gripped her. "I can walk."

"No you can't. You're stumbling like a drunken sailor," Noah retorted, tightening his arms around her.

Alarm skittered through her. "I don't need to be carried."

"I'll miss dinner if we go at your pace to the top of this hill. Probably breakfast too." He continued up the bank, ignoring her resistance.

Elise struggled harder, trying to quell her rising panic but failing. "Please. Put me down. Please." She knew she sounded desperate and unhinged.

Noah stopped.

Elise shoved herself from his arms and landed gracelessly on her feet, staggering to one knee painfully before righting herself. She couldn't look at him.

"I'm sorry," he said. "I thought..."

"It was a nice gesture, Sir Noah," she said weakly, aiming for humor and failing. "But I can't..." How could she explain herself? What woman panicked the second she was restrained? What woman did not have dreams of being swept up into the strong arms of a handsome man and carried away? "It's just that I don't like to feel..." God, she was making a mess of this.

"Helpless," Noah suddenly supplied. "You don't like to feel helpless."

Startled, she looked up at him. "Yes."

His face was stark. "I'm truly sorry."

"Don't be." She shoved her tangled hair off her forehead in agitation. "It's ridiculous, I know. But I can't—"

"I understand." He said it so quietly that Elise barely heard him. Yet she believed him.

She took a deep breath. "Thank you."

"Come, milady." The haunted expression that had touched his features was gone, replaced once again with a teasing smile. "I would be delighted to have the honor of escorting you up to the road. I will be hungry, probably, but delighted all the same."

"I promise you won't miss dinner." She couldn't help the smile she felt creeping across her own lips in response.

She tucked her hand under his arm again, wondering why it was so easy to be with this stranger. Why he seemed to understand her and accept her in ways that no stranger ever should. He had, in the ridiculously short time she had known him, set her off course and peeled back layers that Elise had thought she'd made impenetrable.

Just as well she would be on her way within the hour.

Chapter 4

Noah Lawson leaned on the back of a cart and studied the woman who called herself Elise DeVries, trying not to appear as if he was doing so.

He'd been driving with John and Sarah, almost at the foot of the bridge, when he had heard the shriek and the splash. With stunned disbelief he'd watched as an unfamiliar lad on a rangy bay gelding had vaulted from his horse, jumped up on the low wall, and without a second's hesitation, thrown himself off the bridge.

Except it hadn't been a lad. It had been a woman—something he had discovered the instant he had waded into the river to help her as she struggled with the current and the weight of the boy. She'd tensed at first and then relaxed and allowed him to help her up on the bank. And after that—Noah wasn't sure what had happened after that.

She had made a joke, he remembered, as she lay back against the thick grass, her wet clothes clinging to her body, leaving nothing to his imagination. She had curves that positively begged to be touched. Glorious breasts that her threadbare shirt couldn't conceal. Hips that flared and framed a beautifully rounded backside that would feel decadent beneath his hands. Long legs that he instantly imagined wrapped around him. It had been almost embarrassing, his immediate carnal response to the sight of her, and he had been relieved to crouch as long as he had with her in the grass. It had taken him long minutes to get his body under control, and his wet breeches would have done absolutely nothing to hide his desire.

He'd concentrated on keeping his eyes on her face and his mind out of the gutter.

And then she'd sat up and smiled at him, and whatever physical response he'd had seemed to pale in comparison to the instant connection he'd felt deep into the very marrow of his bones. It defied reasonable explanation, but he'd forgotten to be cautious and careful. He'd forgotten to focus on his words, the way he did with people he didn't know. He'd simply been…captivated. Completely disarmed.

She was beautiful in an unexpected way, her complexion darker than was common, with hazel eyes that danced unapologetically with humor, and thick hair the color of dark coffee that he wanted to touch, even as disheveled as it was. Within seconds he'd found himself teasing her, unable to help himself, caught in the warm rays of her smile. Feeling as if he had known her for a lifetime, instead of scant minutes. Feeling dangerously at ease.

Perhaps it was this that now, upon reflection, unsettled him. He didn't really know who she was or where she was from. That lack of knowledge should have put him on edge. Should have sent him running as quickly as he could in the opposite direction. Except he wasn't running. Instead he was trying desperately to figure out how he might keep this extraordinary woman close to him for just a little longer.

Perhaps because he saw in her himself as he had been years ago. One did not disguise oneself without cause. Without cause one did not react like a panicked wildcat when one's free will was taken away, however innocently. He of all people understood that, and for some irrational reason, he wanted to assure her of it. Wanted to help her. Wanted to know her.

And then, of course, there was the fact that she had saved a boy he considered family.

John would undoubtedly thrash his son to within an inch of his life, once he stopped shaking and convinced himself that Andrew was truly fine. His wife, Sarah, hadn't let go of Andrew, and their son's expression ranged through excitement at the attention, embarrassment at the cause, and apprehension for the repercussions he knew were coming.

Miss DeVries, on the other hand, had fixed a pleasant smile on her face as she was interrogated by a crowd of townspeople who, alerted to the commotion, had come running. The group was dwindling now, its curiosity sated. The strange novelty that was Miss DeVries would be put away for later discussion and retellings.

Noah had hovered at first, deflecting the most brazen of the town gossips, but Elise had waved him off, advising him that she could hold her own. And she had, but now her smile was starting to fray at the edges, and Noah could recognize the signs of strain. He had felt her muscles trembling with fatigue as they climbed that damn hill, and he couldn't imagine she had many reserves left.

As if she could read his mind, Elise turned, making her way toward him. Or, more accurately, making her way to her gelding, which was currently tied to the back of his cart.

She gave him a tired smile and went to her horse's head. "Can you recommend an inn?" she asked wearily. "Something with a good stable and a reasonable ale? And maybe the possibility of a warm bath?"

Noah frowned at the request. After everything, it seemed unconscionable to simply send her on her way. He couldn't send her away. Not only did that strike him as terrifically callous, he suddenly, more than anything, needed more time with this woman. The strength of that impulsive desire startled him. "You'll sleep with me tonight," he blurted.

Elise jerked her head up so fast that it startled the gelding. "I beg your pardon?"

Dammit, that had come out wrong. "You'll *stay* with me tonight. I have a bath."

Elise's mouth had slackened slightly, and Noah could feel a faint heat climbing into his cheeks. Hell, that wasn't at all what he was trying to say. He hated when this happened.

He took a deep breath and concentrated. "What I am trying to say is that I can offer you a place to stay for the night. I have a good stable for your horse and a bathtub. And dinner. I can feed you dinner."

"Ummm." Elise blinked at him.

"I have a housekeeper," he hurried on before she could say no. "Cooks. She does. Very well." He was inexplicably anxious now, afraid she would slip away from him, and his words were coming in the wrong order. "Please. Least I can do."

Elise was shaking her head. "Thank you, but I'm afraid I must keep moving—"

"There you are." John was hurrying toward them, Sarah on his heels.

The petite woman was paler than usual, and she went directly to Elise, clasping her hands briefly in her own. "You are our guardian angel," she said, a slight wobble to her words. "We owe you a debt that can never be repaid."

Elise nodded, looking a little uncomfortable under the weight of so much gratitude. "Thank you, but I am only happy that it ended well."

"Thanks to you," Sarah said, her grey eyes warm. "And if there is ever anything you need, anything at all, please, all you need to do is ask."

"Thank you," Elise said again. "But all I need is directions to an inn—"

"Never! You'll not be staying at some flea-ridden, hole-in-the-wall inn by yourself." Sarah sounded horrified. "You can stay with us—"

"She can stay with me," Noah said hurriedly. "And Mrs. Pritchard. I've already offered."

John and Sarah both stared at him, and Noah willed himself not to look in their direction. He knew very well why they were looking at him the way they were. This was a complete departure from his usual aversion to strangers.

"There are six children who live in your home, one of whom I think will benefit from having his family close to him tonight. Your beds are full. But I have the space. And Mrs. Pritchard will be pleased to have someone to cook for besides me." He knew John and Sarah couldn't argue with that logic.

Elise was shaking her head again. "While those are both generous offers, Mr. Lawson and..." She trailed off, and a faint crease appeared in her brow as she gazed at John and Sarah. "I'm sorry, I do not know how to address you."

"Have you not introduced yourself to her?" Noah asked John with incredulity.

The bear of a man blinked at Noah and then at Elise.

"I believe you introduced yourself earlier as the father of the fool son I saved," Elise said with a faint twitch to her lips.

"I beg your pardon." John sounded as horrified as his wife had earlier. "John Barr at your service. And this is my wife, Sarah." He glanced at Noah. "And I beg you to reconsider Mr. Lawson's offer of hospitality."

Elise had gone quite still, a peculiar expression on her face. She clasped her hands in front of her then and smiled. "Very well. I would be pleased to accept your offer, Mr. Lawson. Thank you."

A thrill of something he couldn't quite identify shot through Noah's gut. He wondered briefly at her sudden change of heart but realized he didn't really care. The idea of having this woman in his house was making it hard to breathe. Hard to think.

"Splendid." Sarah clasped her hands and turned her gaze to Miss DeVries, though every few seconds she'd glance at Noah out of the corner of her eye. "Then you simply must come to the summer ball tomorrow night. Well, we call it a ball, but it's not so much a ball as a picnic with dancing under a large tent later," she clarified. "You must come as our guest."

Miss DeVries shifted. "That is a lovely offer, I'm sure, but—"

Sarah took her hand again. "Say you'll come. Please. It would be an honor to have you there."

Miss DeVries hesitated a second before replying. "It would be my pleasure."

Another thrill danced along Noah's spine.

"Thank you," Sarah said, squeezing her hand one more time. She smiled and drifted back to where her son waited, gathering him in her arms again and pressing a kiss to his damp hair.

"Come," Noah said to Elise, trying to sound casual. "Leave your horse tied to the back." It was easier to concentrate on his words now. "Ride up front with me."

Elise nodded slowly. "Yes," was all she said, and Noah suspected she had simply run out of energy to argue. "A pleasure to meet you, Mr. Barr."

"And you, Miss DeVries. I look forward to seeing you again soon under more ordinary circumstances."

She smiled tiredly at John before she headed to the front of the wagon.

"A word, Noah." John caught him by the arm before he could follow her.

"What?" Noah turned to face him.

"What are you doing?"

"What are you talking about?" Noah frowned in confusion.

John pulled Noah back, farther away from the cart, his voice low. "Miss DeVries. Who is she?"

"What?" That made no sense. "What are you asking?"

"Why did you offer to take her back to your home?"

"Because she needs a place to stay for the night. Because she saved your son from drowning." He knew he sounded defensive and strove to lighten his tone. "You should be kissing her feet right now."

John raised his hands in a conciliatory gesture. "I know. I might yet." He smiled faintly. "I will never be able to repay that debt. It's just…"

"Just what?"

John shuffled his feet, looking almost embarrassed. "In all the time I've known you, I've never seen you like this. Comfortable with anyone so quickly."

Noah knew what John was implying. He knew that Noah avoided busy coaching inns and kept away from taverns that served the travelers who came from London and the surrounding areas. John had never asked for details, but he knew very well that whatever was in Noah's past was meant to stay there.

And it had been fifteen years. Fifteen years since Noah Ellery had ceased to exist. Fifteen years since he had rebuilt his life as Noah Lawson.

At the very beginning, when he'd first landed on London's streets, he'd feared men in woven smock coats armed with chains and rope would appear to drag him back to the cage he'd fled. At the beginning he'd been convinced every unfamiliar man might be a Runner, hired privately to hunt him down and arrest him. But no one had ever come. And then, when he had left London, distance accompanied by more time had dulled any lingering fear. No one had come looking for the man once known as Noah Ellery. And the notion that Elise DeVries was here in Nottingham for that reason was so patently far-fetched that it didn't merit further consideration.

"I like her." It sounded odd, even in his own ears. "She's different. I just… I don't know how to explain it."

John gave him a long look and scratched his head as if the conundrum of a pretty woman in the front of Noah's cart was in equal parts amusing and baffling. "I like her too, but you know nothing about her. I think you're bewitched."

I know she is kind. And funny. And fierce. And maybe I am bewitched.

⁓

She was watching him.

Noah could feel Elise's eyes on him as he turned his mare in the direction of home and set it to a steady trot. He said nothing, comfortable with the silence. It was always others who struggled with the quiet, who felt compelled to fill the void with chatter, or expected him to do the same. But Elise said nothing. A mile slipped by. And still she simply watched him as he drove.

Another mile passed.

"Is there a piece of river weed in my hair?" He found the fact that it was he who spoke first vastly ironic.

"No." If she was embarrassed to be caught studying him, she didn't show it.

"My teeth?"

Her lips twitched. "No."

"Are you cold?"

She made a strange sound, and he took his eyes off the rump of his mare long enough to see her bite her lower lip. "No," she said. "No, I'm quite warm, thank you." She gestured at his shirt still draped over her own wet clothes.

Noah nodded, returning his attention to the road. The sight of her in his shirt was stirring things in him he hadn't experienced before. He hadn't noticed it earlier, perhaps because they were surrounded by people, but now, on this road, alone, it made him feel…possessive. Protective. Made him remember how she had felt beneath his hands when he had drawn the linen over her head and down her body.

Made him want to know what it would feel like to take it back off. What it would be like to peel those damp layers from her skin and run his hands over every curve and—

"You should take your boots off now," Elise said beside him.

"I beg your pardon?" He was horrified to think that the licentious direction his thoughts were headed in was so clearly apparent on his face.

"Your boots. They're soaked. If you leave them to dry on your feet, it'll take a team of oxen to pry them off later."

He almost sagged in relief. But he was not taking his boots off. Or any other article of clothing. He'd borrowed the only shirt available, one that was uncomfortably small, specifically so she wouldn't have to endure a three-mile-long cart ride next to a half-naked man. He might not be a knight, but nor was he a cretin. "I'll take them off when we get back."

"Suit yourself." She shrugged before turning slightly to look at him again. "Thank you," she said suddenly.

"For not taking my clothes off?" *Boots.* He'd meant to say for not taking his *boots* off. The wrong word had slipped out. He felt heat rise in his face and braced himself for a well-deserved set-down.

Elise laughed.

He turned to stare at her.

"I think, Mr. Lawson, that there were not so many

women standing up on that road this afternoon who weren't secretly delighted that you'd taken your clothes off."

The heat that had been creeping into his face flamed. He looked away, unsure what to say.

"You are a very handsome man, Mr. Lawson," Elise continued beside him, sounding vastly amused. "And while a proper lady would pretend otherwise, and certainly never be so uncouth as to mention it in conversation, I find ignoring the truth a rather pointless endeavor."

Noah didn't know what to do with this woman who had taken his blunder and turned it into an unexpected compliment. "Thank you?" he tried.

"You're very welcome," she said with satisfaction.

"But you are very much a lady," he protested, shifting uncomfortably.

"Kind of you to say so to a woman wearing wet trousers." She grinned at him, the corners of her eyes crinkling in unrestrained humor.

In a heartbeat Noah found the air squeezed from his lungs. God, she was beautiful. Even with her hair drying into a matted cloud of rich brown waves and a streak of mud at her temple, she was the most beautiful thing he had ever seen.

"Have I embarrassed you?" she asked.

"No."

Her eyes danced.

"Maybe a little," he admitted.

"Again, I fear I cannot apologize for the truth." She smiled wickedly at him, and he found himself smiling back, caught in her contagious happiness. He heard her draw a sharp breath, and she looked away.

"What I had wanted to thank you for was your help at the river." She was looking into the distance somewhere over the rump of his mare now. "I'm glad you waded in when you did."

Noah felt the edges of the leather ribbons cut into his palms as he tightened his hands around them. In hindsight, that he had waded in at all shocked him. He hated the river and its dark, cold water. Though he hadn't been thinking about the water when he had seen her struggling with the boy. Old memories surfaced, bringing with them the ugliness that accompanied them every time. "Yes." It was a poor reply but it was all he trusted himself to say.

She nodded slightly and tucked a rebellious curl behind her ear, seemingly finding nothing odd about his response.

"London from?" he blurted, meaning to redeem himself, but not finding the right words. *Are you from London?* he had wanted to ask, before the dark memories had needled their way into his consciousness and made it hard to concentrate.

"I am," Elise replied. "And I must confess it was good to get out of the city. Some days the stench in the summer is enough to fell a horse."

Noah stared straight ahead, unwilling to believe that she could or would simply ignore or accept his bizarre speech. Again. She must think him a half-wit.

She twisted in her seat, pulling the wet fabric from her legs with an absent look of annoyance. "Have you been there?" she asked. "To London in the summer?"

Yes. He shuddered. He remembered very clearly what London in the summer was like. And what London in the winter was like. And the seasons in between. "No."

"Well," she said, flapping her arms in an apparent effort to dry herself faster, "you're not missing much."

Noah watched her out of the corner of his eye. The

thought struck him that, in his billowing shirt, she looked like an oversize stork trying to take flight, and he suddenly found himself smiling, the ugly memories receding as quickly as they had surged.

"You're laughing at me again," she commented wryly.

"Yes."

"At least you're honest, Mr. Lawson."

His smile slipped. He wasn't honest about anything. He hadn't been honest about anything in well over a decade. And he found himself wishing he could be. Just for one moment, he wanted to tell this woman something about himself that was true. "I mix up my words," he said suddenly. There. He was honest about that.

Her flapping stopped, and she peered at him, a faint crease in her forehead. "So?"

"So?" he repeated.

She turned her palms up. "So?"

Noah wasn't sure what to say. Absent were the pity and the suspicion and the distaste he usually encountered when others became aware of his difficulty. "Does that not bother you?"

"I can't sing," she mused.

"You can't sing?" He was confused. What did that have to do with—

"Does that not bother you?"

He blinked at her. "What?"

"I can't tolerate being restrained, but you know that already. I cannot abide rats, and when I'm angry, I tend to curse. Very offensively, I might add. In French."

Noah was aware his jaw had slackened.

"Anything else?" Elise was wrestling with her thick hair now, trying valiantly to twist it back into a braid.

"What?" Well, if she hadn't thought him a half-wit before, she would now.

She gave up on her hair with a sigh. "I thought we were comparing our shortcomings. Or at least our shortcomings as others may view them."

"Um."

"Do you want me to think of some more?" She cocked her head and started counting on her fingers. "I'm not a proper lady, but that is probably obvious since I'm wearing trousers. I don't let anyone handle my rifle—"

"Your *rifle*?" Noah wasn't sure where and when this conversation had gone so completely sideways. "You have a rifle?"

She gave him a strange look. "It's strapped to my horse. It's not exactly small. I would have thought you'd have noticed it."

"Why do you have a rifle?"

"I would expect for the reason most people have a rifle," she answered, not answering him at all.

Noah remembered the long bundle wrapped in oiled cloth. "I thought that was tent poles. Or something." In truth he hadn't thought much about the contents at all.

"Tent poles." She chuckled. "You're very funny, Mr. Lawson." She shook her head and considered the next finger on the hand that she was counting on. "Now let's see. I've been told I sometimes snore when I sleep—"

"Stop," Noah managed. "This is not what I intended at all." He'd not intended this comparison of supposed failings, this absurd discussion of things that were irrelevant. These...shortcomings she seemed to think she had were not shortcomings. They were things that made her one of the most intriguing people he had ever met.

Elise met his eyes. "I don't really care that you can't find the right words all the time, Mr. Lawson. But I will care if you touch my rifle without asking."

A bubble of something unfamiliar was rising in his chest, compressing and squeezing his heart. Something that was flooding through his veins, something reckless and wild that made him want to abandon all caution. It was all he could do not to touch her. Not to bury his hands in her mud-streaked curls and kiss her senseless. He had never met anyone like her. He was terrified that he never would again. "Fair enough," he managed.

"Glad we got that out of the way." She leaned back, wincing as the cart hit a hole in the road. "Who is John Barr?"

Noah took a deep breath, trying to find his equilibrium again. "John? He's a smith. And one of the best. Nothing he can't fix. Ploughs, weapons. He'll shoe your gelding for you too, if you need. He's a fair hand with even the most fractious of horses."

Elise was shaking her head. "No, I mean, who is John to you? You said his son was like family. Are you related?"

It was a completely reasonable question. He answered carefully. "He is my family. Not by blood, but family all the same." Out of the corner of his eye, he saw her smile.

"Ah." There was understanding in that single syllable.

"Do you have family?"

Her hazel eyes were on him again. "I do. A brother by blood. And a sister. Not by blood, but family all the same."

He found himself smiling along with her.

"Do you have brothers or sisters?" she inquired.

His smile evaporated. "No." It was the immediate, safe response, but memories of Abigail's gentle eyes and her fearless heart flooded his mind.

"I'm sorry," Elise said from beside him.

"I beg your pardon?"

"I didn't mean to bring up painful memories."

Jesus, had he been that transparent? "I had a sister once," he found himself admitting. And then he couldn't bring himself to say anything else.

"What was her name?" she asked.

"Abby," he said, realizing that he hadn't spoken his sister's name out loud in over a decade. "Her name was Abby." He felt Elise's hand on his arm, a light, fleeting touch. She looked as though she wanted to ask him another question, but then reconsidered.

Bloody hell, it was just as well that they were almost home. Another mile in this cart and he'd be confessing every deep, dark secret about his past to a woman he barely knew. It was terrifying, how easily small truths slipped out of him in her presence.

"We're almost there." He turned his mare down the familiar lane that wound through a copse of trees.

Elise wriggled again, presumably against the discomfort of her wet clothes. "Thank goodness."

A sentiment he shared wholeheartedly.

Chapter 5

Elise had found Noah Ellery.

The dawning of that fact had left her reeling. It defied the odds. Approached the realm of the bloody miraculous. Elise still struggled to believe that the gods of fate could have chosen to amuse themselves in such a fashion.

She hadn't prepared any sort of a plan, which in hindsight was appalling. And embarrassing. And unprofessional. But in her defense, what Elise had prepared herself for when she rode into Nottingham was an arduous search for John Barr in the hopes that he might offer a clue to the whereabouts of Noah Ellery. Well, John Barr had certainly done that.

He had hugged her, introduced himself, and then insisted she have dinner with the next Duke of Ashland.

On the ride back, Elise had interrogated the man who called himself Noah Lawson. Subtly, using every ounce of cunning and care that she had ever learned; and the coincidences had started stacking themselves up like so many pieces of driftwood until they formed a wall that was impossible to ignore. And Elise had long ago learned that there were no such things as coincidences in the business of Chegarre & Associates.

Noah had lied when he said he'd never been to London in the summer. That had been easy to read. He had a sister named Abby. That revelation had been luckier. Elise had wanted to press further, but the shuttered look on his face had made it clear he would not say more on the subject. At least at that time.

I mix up my words.

That remark had wiped away her lingering disbelief. His confession had both touched her and relieved her beyond measure. Aye, he did that when he was flustered, that much had become obvious, though he seemed to think it an insurmountable flaw. Elise had dealt with many men and their *flaws* in the time she'd been with Chegarre & Associates, and compared to the dangerous and destructive vices and predilections of those individuals, the occasional twisted phrase didn't even signify.

And it wouldn't prevent him from speaking up for himself and telling Francis Ellery to go to the devil, she thought with fierce satisfaction.

Elise had made the unforgivable error of assuming that Noah Ellery couldn't speak. Which made her squirm. Assumptions were dangerous things. In hindsight, Noah's sister had never said that he couldn't speak. She had only said that he *hadn't*. Elise could only guess that Noah's tendency to use the wrong word on occasion had kept him from speaking as a child, though that was hardly a question she could simply pose while bouncing along a country road.

In fact she was at an utter loss as to how to best broach the subject of the true nature of her presence in Nottingham. A man who had fled his past, allowed everyone to believe him dead, and built a new life complete with a fictitious name would not be in a hurry to go anywhere with her. Elise simply couldn't blunder in and blurt out the truth. She'd need to approach this situation carefully, and in a nonconfrontational manner, to secure Noah Ellery's cooperation. Her job would be so much easier if he wasn't fighting her and she didn't have to worry that he might simply disappear again. But for all of that rationale, Elise felt a little as if she had stepped onto a stage with no script memorized and no idea what part she would need to play to see this act to an end.

"My house is just over the ridge," Noah said beside her, interrupting her thoughts.

He'd barely finished the sentence when they crested that same ridge and Elise looked down into a gently sloping vista. The late-afternoon sun had touched everything with gold, creating a backdrop that seemed magical. Thick clumps of oak, birch, and hawthorn surrounded the yard, casting deep shadows that fell on the roof of a large barn, and obscuring what Elise guessed must be the house. A handful of cows grazed placidly in a fenced pasture carved into a blanket of trees, and a small herd of hogs milled about under a partially covered enclosure. Sunlight sparkled off the river, just visible beyond cropland and the trees that edged the shore.

The air was still thick with the heat of the day, and the breeze had submitted to stillness. Birdsong resonated around her, and occasionally she caught a glance of plumage winging through the leafy boughs.

"This is all yours?" she asked as they started down the gentle incline.

"Yes."

She closed her eyes and breathed deeply. It had been a long time since she had felt... as if she were home. A fragile blanket of peace descended. These were the sounds and the smells that put her in mind of her childhood. Of a time when things had been simple. Until they hadn't.

Until the war had cost them their home. Until they had fled across an ocean to escape an uncertain future.

Elise opened her eyes to realize too late that Noah was watching her. She bit her lip, wondering what he had seen on her face in that unguarded moment. But he said nothing, only guided his mare around the last bend of the lane and brought it to a stop in front of the barn.

Noah hopped from his perch, and Elise did likewise, going directly to her gelding and untying him.

"Your home is beautiful," she said, waiting, her horse's lead rope grasped tightly in her hand.

"You haven't seen the house." Noah had unhitched his mare from the cart and was leading it toward Elise.

"Doesn't matter," she murmured. And it didn't. The natural beauty and peace that surrounded her here were worth a hundred gilded palaces.

"Well, I built it, so have a care with my pride when you do see it." He was grinning at her as he gestured for her to follow him into the cool, dim interior of the barn.

Every fiber in her body ignited. Bloody hell, but she couldn't think when he smiled at her like that. The urge to taste those gentle, curving lips overwhelmed her again. She let Noah walk on ahead of her, her eyes lingering on the way his ill-fitting shirt pulled across the width of his shoulders, the way his breeches clung to his hips and powerful legs.

"You can put your gelding in the first stall on the left if it suits," he said over his shoulder.

Elise jerked, startling her horse for the second time in as many hours. "Thank you." She berated herself under her breath. Whatever happened, she could not allow herself to be smitten by a man whom a client was paying her to retrieve. Well, she amended, if she was being honest, she was probably already smitten. But she could be smitten from a distance. What she couldn't do was become involved with Noah Ellery. Intimately, emotionally, physically. Not only was it unprofessional, the distraction could be dangerous.

She sighed. This all would have been a great deal easier if the heir to Ashland had been an arrogant pig.

"You can put your tack in here," he added, his voice muffled and floating from an unseen alcove. "There's space for a few saddles and hooks for bridles beside the harnesses."

Elise realized that Noah had already unharnessed his mare while she was still standing motionless, lost in her musings. Quickly she led her gelding into the barn, and was greeted with a neatly swept dirt floor and the clean scent of good hay. She untacked her horse, setting her pack and rifle to the side, and secured the horse in the stall Noah had indicated. By the time she'd put away her saddle and bridle, Noah had already tossed hay into the stall and hung a bucket of water on the inside.

"Ready?" he asked.

No, she wasn't ready. She wasn't ready at all. She hadn't yet prepared a single argument, nor organized a well-rehearsed explanation that would build her case to convince a dead man to return to London.

Noah bent, swinging her pack effortlessly over his shoulder.

"I can carry that," Elise protested.

"I know you can." He made no move to give it to her.

He had to stop doing things like this. "Thank you."

"You're welcome. Now come. I'm starving." He headed out of the barn.

Not knowing what else to do, Elise grabbed her rifle, still wrapped carefully in its cloth, and followed him as he headed up the lane toward the trees.

~

The house was beautiful.

Elise didn't have to pretend admiration as they drew nearer. She supposed it would be called a cottage, but it wasn't like the many small, poorly erected abodes she'd passed on her way through the countryside. This was a solid building, and the attention to detail and careful crafts-manship in its construction were obvious. The walls were built of stone, almost a honey color in the late light. It was a single story, sprawling away from the lane, the small panes in the many windows glittering in welcome. The roof wasn't thatch, as she'd been expecting, but covered in slate, much like a London home. But for all its beauty, it faded into the background, for surrounding the cottage, as far as Elise could see, were gardens.

Roses in shades of brilliant pink exploded from a sea of green, competing with the vibrant crimsons and purples of hollyhocks and cornflowers. It lacked the precise severity that so many of the London gardens boasted and instead had been allowed to flourish, empty spaces filled with color. It was a little as Elise imagined a fairy garden would look if such a thing existed.

"Damask roses," Elise whispered.

"You know your roses," Noah said beside her, sounding pleased.

No, I don't. I don't know anything about roses, except that a seven-year-old boy once planted them as a gift for his mother.

Elise stopped next to a profusion of blooms and reached out to touch a pink rose, the petals impossibly soft beneath her touch. "Is the garden yours?" she asked, though she already knew the answer.

"Yes." He had come to stand beside her.

The intoxicating scent of roses swirled around her, accompanied by a subtle concert provided by a host of bees and birds. "It's..." She paused, thinking *beautiful* seemed inadequate. "Exquisite."

He was silent, though Elise could feel his eyes on her.

"I think perhaps I should like to sleep out here tonight," she said softly. "Amid all this perfection."

He chuckled, a deep, rich sound. "Mrs. Pritchard would have a fit if I let you sleep out here," he told her. He paused, his laughter fading. "But thank you. Perhaps after dinner I could show you the rest."

Elise took a deep breath. She should not be complimenting him. She could not be standing in his rose garden, discussing things that would never come to pass. She would not be touring his gardens after dinner. She should be having a very frank conversation with him that she very much doubted he would want to participate in. This was pointless, this subtle but deliberate probing. She could beat around the bush forever, poking and jabbing randomly at the periphery, hoping that something useful would emerge. And in the meantime the Duchess of Ashland would be dead, and Francis Ellery would have inherited a fortune.

The better course of action was to simply tell him the truth. Did she really think that if she confronted Noah he would run? And if he did, then he was not the man she needed him to be anyway. Not the man his sister needed him to be. And there was nothing that Elise could do to fix that, no matter how much she might wish otherwise.

If the worst happened, Elise would be better off cutting her losses and returning to London to start exploring other options.

And really, the rose garden was as good a place as any. "Mr. Lawson," she started, unsure how to phrase what she had to say, but knowing she needed to say it.

Noah reached past her and selected one of the blooms, neatly snapping the stem. He held it out to her with a soft smile. "For you, my lady."

Elise thought she might never remember how to draw a full breath again. "For what?"

"For being you."

No man had ever given her a rose for simply being herself. And certainly not while standing in a magical garden bathed in golden sunlight. All thoughts of London slipped away, and she was overcome by such longing that it robbed her of whatever wits she had left.

Very slowly she reached out to accept the rose, her fingers brushing his. Neither made a move to pull away. She ventured a glance up at his face, and the possessive look she saw reflected in his eyes made everything around her fade to nothing. In that moment she couldn't remember where she was, or what she was doing there. Couldn't remember why it was impossible for her to reach out and touch him, or simply step forward and kiss him.

"Heavens, Mr. Lawson, but I was starting to think you'd been kidnapped by faerie folk— Oh my." The sound of a door banging and the abrupt end of a sentence had Elise whirling in alarm.

A woman was standing frozen just at the front of the house, a cloth dangling from her fingers unheeded. Her brown eyes were opened in shocked surprise, wisps of silver hair falling around her flushed face.

Noah retreated hastily, his hand dropping from Elise's. "My apologies for the lateness of the hour, Mrs. Pritchard," he said, adjusting the pack on his shoulder and heading toward his housekeeper.

Mrs. Pritchard's gaze flew to Noah, then to Elise, and back.

"May I introduce Miss DeVries," Noah said as he gave the older woman a quick kiss on the cheek. "Miss DeVries, this is Mrs. Pritchard."

The expression on Mrs. Pritchard's face was one of stunned astonishment.

"A pleasure to meet you." Elise spoke up, trying her best to inject warmth and normalcy into her words. As if she hadn't just been caught in a rose garden, dressed in wet trousers, a breath away from kissing a man she should never kiss.

Mrs. Pritchard blinked at her, as if believing her to be real for the first time. "And you," she replied faintly. "Welcome."

"Miss DeVries will be staying with us tonight," Noah continued conversationally, as if this sort of thing happened regularly.

Which, Elise suspected, based on the comically bewildered look on Mrs. Pritchard's face, was far from the case.

"What happened to your shirt?" She was staring at Noah's bedraggled, ill-fitting garment.

"I loaned mine to Miss DeVries," Noah told her.

Mrs. Pritchard's eyes snapped back to Elise. "You what?" She wheezed slightly.

"Hers was wet."

The cloth dropped from Mrs. Pritchard's hands to flutter unnoticed to the ground.

"It's a bit of a long story," Noah hastened to add, no doubt catching sight of his housekeeper's face.

"I was in a position to help Mr. Barr and his son this afternoon," Elise said, wondering why she felt the need to explain.

"She didn't help Andrew; she saved him from drowning," Noah said, giving Elise an exasperated look.

"Um. Yes, well, since I was traveling through Nottingham, Mr. Lawson was kind enough to offer me a place to stay for the night. And the chance to dry my clothes," Elise clarified.

"I see," Mrs. Pritchard said, clearly not seeing anything.

"Why don't we go inside?" Noah suggested. "Then I can tell you the whole story. I am being a poor host by leaving Miss DeVries standing dripping in my garden. Perhaps, Mrs. Pritchard, you might see Miss DeVries settled while I change?" He bent and retrieved the fallen cloth and handed it back to his housekeeper.

"Of course." The housekeeper seemed to give herself a mental shake, and her face creased into a beaming smile. "Please do come inside."

Noah held the door for her, and the housekeeper bustled

back in, Elise following a little more slowly. She had gone but four steps when the sound of joyous barking split the silence and a blur of white fur streaked by her, gravel scattering beneath scrabbling paws.

Three paws, at least, Elise realized, watching the creature that was bouncing around Noah, its entire back end wagging with the force of its tail. It was of an indeterminate breed, its head and body not quite matching, its ears sticking out from its head at illogical angles, and it was missing the lower part of a front leg.

"My dog," Noah said almost apologetically. "I call him Square."

"Square?" Elise repeated.

The mutt turned at his name, and within a second it was Elise who found herself the object of much happy attention.

"He doesn't realize he's a triangle," Noah said in a stage whisper. "Don't tell him."

A bubble of laughter escaped before she could stop it. She bent to rub the belly of the dog, who had rolled over at her feet and was looking at her hopefully.

"What happened to his leg?"

"Got caught in a poacher's trap, I suspect. I found him out by the river eating what was left of a rotting fish. Leg was already half-healed."

"A survivor," Elise said quietly, stroking the soft fur.

"Yes." She could feel the weight of Noah's gaze on her. "That's why I couldn't just..."

"Destroy him."

"Yes."

She wanted to look up at him, wanted to discover what she would find in his eyes. Wanted to know what Noah

Ellery had survived to become the man he was today. Except she couldn't. Because she was too afraid of what he might see in hers.

"You can trust me," he said into the quiet, and his odd words betrayed that her silence had already told him too much. Told him that she understood the meaning of the word *survivor*.

Elise straightened, and the dog gave a disappointed woof. The word *trust* suddenly stuck in her throat like a sharp bone, making it difficult to swallow, difficult to think about anything else. She had no business speaking of trust. She was not at all who he thought her to be. She was a wolf in sheep's clothing, come to yank the proverbial rug out from under his feet.

"Come inside," he said in that same gentle voice.

She glanced down at the pink rose she still held in her hand. She couldn't go into this man's house. She couldn't eat his food, sleep under his roof, accept his generosity—his flowers, for God's sake—while pretending to be something she was not. While harboring ulterior motives. Guilt soured in her stomach.

Bloody hell, what had happened to her? She was never this...scattered. She was always professional and composed, even when a situation went sideways. Her brother had accused her on occasion of being mercenary, though she'd always considered that a compliment and not a criticism. She never allowed her emotions to swing wildly back and forth, but in the past few hours she had been battered by too many. And this growing feeling of guilt was the last straw.

She should leave, find some space, regroup, and come up with a plan for how to handle Noah Ellery.

"I think it would be best if I found an inn—"

"No. I won't hear of it. Besides, Mrs. Pritchard is quite pleased to have a guest to dote on. If I send you away now, she'll likely serve my head on a platter tonight." Noah was smiling at her again, trying to make her feel at ease, she knew. "Surely you don't want to be responsible for that."

Elise found herself smiling back despite all her best intentions. "Pleased? She looked at me like I was a unicorn that had just sprouted out of the rosebushes."

"You can't blame her. I'm not in the habit of bringing home strange women. Especially ones dressed in trousers who have asked me to pretend they're mermaids." He reached out to touch a long ribbon of her hair that was curling damply over her shoulder.

A new riot of butterflies swarmed and banged against her ribs.

"Very well." She tried to think rationally. She was not going to win this argument. She was miles from town, darkness was not far off, and all her worldly possessions were either slung over this man's back or eating hay in his stable. Perhaps this was best. She would use this small window of time to study this man and determine exactly what might best convince the next Duke of Ashland to return to London.

She stepped away, and her hair fell from his fingers. If she was to keep her head, she couldn't do it while this man was touching her.

"Lead the way, Mr. Lawson."

Chapter 6

Noah had been right.

Mrs. Pritchard, once over her initial shock and given an explanation of the afternoon's events, had proven to be a warm, cheerful woman who had bustled about, fussing over Elise as though she were a lauded royal guest and not a bizarre interloper. She'd shown Elise to the back of the house and let her into a room filled with late-afternoon sunlight streaming through large windows that faced the river. The inside of the house, like the exterior, was a testament to careful design, simplistic, but all the more pleasing because of it.

"I think this room will be suitable," Mrs. Pritchard said as she moved about, pushing open the windows to let in the breeze.

"It's lovely," Elise assured her. She glanced around, taking in the pale walls, the carved headboard of the bed, the washstand, and the large wardrobe against the far wall.

"The tub is just beside the kitchen," Mrs. Pritchard said, sticking her head into the wardrobe and extracting a folded towel, which she placed on the edge of the bed. "I've got some water heating."

"Please don't go to too much trouble." That damn guilt was pricking again. She didn't deserve this kindness.

"Nonsense. It's no trouble at all. I can offer you better than the River Leen can."

"Thank you." She wasn't sure it mattered that she would be clean when she brought Noah's secrets tumbling down around him.

"Do you have dry clothes?"

"In my pack." Elise gestured to where Noah had left it, just inside the door.

Mrs. Pritchard opened her mouth and then closed it again.

"I have a dress," Elise told her. "Don't worry. The trousers were just for travel. And, as it turned out, for swimming," she added with a rueful twist to her mouth.

The woman gave Elise another warm smile, even as she considered her intently. "You are very courageous."

Elise shrugged, uncomfortable under the scrutiny. "Anyone else would have done the same."

Mrs. Pritchard looked dubious. "Not many people would have thrown themselves off a bridge after a boy they didn't know."

"It was more of a controlled leap," Elise hedged, thinking the woman's description made her sound a little like a deranged bat.

Mrs. Pritchard laughed before she once again considered Elise, delight now evident in her expression. "I can see why he's so taken with you."

Taken with her? Dear God, but she couldn't encourage that vein of thought, even if it did make her pulse accelerate. "Mr. Lawson is very kind." It was all she could think of.

"He certainly is that," Mrs. Pritchard agreed. Her eyes lingered on the single pink rose Elise still held in her hand. "Though he doesn't..." She trailed off with a slight shake to her head, and whatever she had been about to say remained a mystery.

Doesn't what? Elise wanted to demand. What did the man who called himself Noah Lawson not do? A thousand questions swirled through Elise's mind, questions that she could ask—needed to ask—about Noah. "He doesn't often bring strange women home," she said, forcing a light tone to her voice.

"He doesn't bring anyone home," Mrs. Pritchard murmured, barely loud enough for Elise to hear. "Aside from the Barrs, of course."

Elise looked down at the rose in her hand, tucking that bit of information away and trying to pretend that the admission didn't make her irrationally happy. "You've worked for Mr. Lawson for a long time then?"

"Ten years. Don't know what I would have done if not for Mr. Lawson. My husband, rest his soul, was the coachman at Corley House for Baron Corley. But after my William died, I was turned out. Had nowhere else to go."

"I'm sorry."

"Don't be. Mr. Lawson is one of the good ones. He's become like the son I never had. I've been happy here." Mrs. Pritchard was still for a moment before suddenly dusting her hands on her apron. "Well, let's see you clean," she said, reaching for the towel. "I'll put that rose in some water for you, if you like, while you bathe."

"I'd like that very much." Elise brought the bloom to her nose and inhaled deeply, longing and desire rising sharp and fast before she could remember why that was unacceptable. Impossible.

～

Elise DeVries was running from something. Or, more likely, someone.

Noah had considered all the possibilities while he had washed and changed, and that had seemed like the most obvious. She was traveling in disguise. With a rifle, for God's sake, though that didn't necessarily mean she knew how to use it. He wondered if Elise was her real name even. Not that it mattered. Bloody hell, he would be the last person to cast stones on that account.

He'd considered the possibility that she might be a criminal—but in his experience criminals were not in the habit of risking their lives to save people they didn't know. And she lacked the wild, hunted look of someone relentlessly pursued by the law. But it was obvious she was hiding something. She had agreed to his hospitality out on the river road, but once they had arrived here, she'd become quieter. A faintly troubled look had shadowed her features, and her easy smile had dimmed.

Well, for one night at least, Noah could make sure she felt protected. Protected and cared for, no questions asked.

John Barr had done the same for Noah a dozen years ago. He hadn't known Noah's secrets the winter day he had found a wary eighteen-year-old hiding in his shop close to the forge in an effort to stay warm. In fact John didn't know his secrets even now, but it had never mattered. He had helped Noah then, and he had helped him throughout the years. Helped him reinvent himself. Helped him find happiness in a new life.

Noah could never repay that debt, but perhaps he could help someone else who might have found herself in a similar situation.

He was powerfully attracted to her; there was no point in pretending otherwise. But there was more to it than just physical magnetism. The moment Elise had jumped off the bridge, the moment she'd smiled up at him with those beautiful eyes, she'd become more than a simple stranger.

And the moment she had sat beside him on a farm wagon and listened to him and not the order of his words, she'd become more than someone he didn't know. She'd become someone he wanted to know very much.

There were delicious smells coming from the kitchen, and he could hear Mrs. Pritchard humming happily to herself. He paused for a moment, unseen, watching his housekeeper chop vegetables, a satisfied smile on her face. It seemed Mrs. Pritchard was no more immune to Elise's vivacity than he was. His housekeeper was probably already considering what sort of cake she might bake to celebrate their engagement.

Noah shifted, his pulse leaping. He would have kissed Elise in the garden. Never, in all his life, had he wanted to kiss a woman the way he wanted to kiss Elise DeVries. But he'd hesitated, unwilling to scare her. Hell, it scared him, the way his emotions and desires were piling up in a jumbled order that he couldn't seem to sort out. Honestly, what sort of man kissed a woman the same day he met her?

A bewitched one, a voice in his head suggested.

"Mr. Lawson." Elise was standing at the end of the short hall, the door to the small bathroom ajar. Her cheeks were faintly flushed, her long, dark hair pulled back neatly from her face, though a few tendrils had already escaped their confines and curled damply along her cheek. "I hope I haven't kept you waiting long." She smoothed a hand almost self-consciously over the creases in her dress that betrayed her travels, and Noah found himself mourning the loss of her shirt and trousers.

Which was silly, he knew. If anything, he should claim to have been scandalized at the sight of her in trousers and relieved that she was now garbed in something more... appropriate. Yet this plain, nondescript brown dress she was wearing did not do this extraordinary woman justice. Did not do her spirit justice. If Elise had to wear a dress, it should be vibrant. A crimson or sapphire silk that would shimmer when she moved. No, on second thought, it should be emerald satin, embroidered with crystals that would glow and sparkle when they caught the light. Just as she did.

"Mr. Lawson?"

He started. What had she asked? Something about keeping him waiting long? "Not at all." He might wait until the end of eternity for this woman if that was what she required. "Though I had thought it was possible you had turned into a mermaid," he said, and was pleased with how easily that had come out.

She smiled at him then, and the entire hallway lit up. His heart stuttered.

"I'm not sure if you are disappointed or pleased that I didn't," she replied.

"Pleased, I think. I would imagine a tail a devilishly

hard thing to manage at the dinner table. Though you must admit, you were in that tub a long time."

"I had to give you time to get your boots off." She cocked her head and raised a single brow wickedly. "Tell me, Mr. Lawson, how long did that take?"

Noah looked at the ceiling briefly. He'd been ready to cut his boots off with his hunting knife by the time he'd finally managed to struggle out of them. "It doesn't matter."

"Ah." Elise was smirking at him. "If you recall, I did suggest you take them off earlier to avoid such difficulties. Yet you chose not to listen to the voice of reason."

"Yes, well, that particular voice of reason had just thrown herself off a bridge," Noah pointed out. "The presence of reason was debatable."

"I didn't throw myself off anything. It was a controlled leap. Why must I keep saying that?" she muttered, but there was laughter dancing in her beautiful eyes, and Noah had quite forgotten that anyone else in the world existed until he heard Mrs. Pritchard clear her throat behind him.

"Dinner will be ready shortly, Mr. Lawson," she said. "I'll serve in the dining room."

He started and turned. "Thank you." Mrs. Pritchard looked between Elise and Noah with a delighted, slightly misty expression before disappearing back into the kitchen. Bloody hell, forget the cake, his housekeeper had already selected the clergyman to perform the wedding ceremony.

He turned back to Elise and offered his arm. The laughter had faded from her eyes, and that troubled look was back. After a second's hesitation, Elise moved forward and slipped her hand under his arm, allowing him to guide her toward the dining room.

"The dining room?" she asked. "Your house has a dining room?"

"It's not a grand room," he said, seizing on a distraction that would smooth the troubled crease between her brows. Nothing like the opulent St James's Square dining room he remembered from his childhood. "But the Barrs all fit at the table when they come."

He stopped just inside the door. The gardens were visible through multiple windows, affording its occupants a beautiful view. There was a long, serviceable table in the center of the room, a table he had built with timber from his own land. Though the chairs didn't all match, and two of them had tall blocks of wood placed on the seats. "For the smaller children," he told Elise, catching her studying them. "They are always included."

She nodded silently, and he couldn't tell if she approved or thought it absurd.

"I was never allowed to share meals with my parents as a child," he said, having no idea why he felt the need to explain himself to her. "I ate in the nursery. Alone."

"Your family was wealthy then." It was more a statement than a question.

"Yes." His explanation had betrayed another bit of his past, and it seemed pointless to deny it now. If she was surprised, she hid it well.

"Your parents are—"

"Gone." An old pain, one that time had managed only to dull, twisted.

"I'm sorry."

"Me too." It was easier if she believed them dead. It was what he did.

"Mmmm." Her hand slipped from his arm, and she

walked farther into the room, putting the bulk of the table between them.

At the near end of the table, Mrs. Pritchard had put out place settings for two. The single pink rose he had given Elise had been put in a jar of water between the settings. He always ate with his housekeeper, usually at the small table in the kitchen, but it was clear tonight that Mrs. Pritchard had no intention of joining them, visions of a romantic evening no doubt dancing in her head.

Noah watched Elise walk past the crockery and glass, her fingers trailing over the surface of the table. She stopped at the far end, where a chessboard had been pushed to the side, a small box of brightly painted lead soldiers beside it.

"Do you play?" Noah asked.

"Chess or soldiers?" A ghost of a smile touched her lips.

"Either one." He said it in jest.

She picked up a small rifleman, its deep-green coat vivid in the last rays of sunlight streaming in the windows. "Yes," she whispered, and Noah had no idea which part of his question she had answered.

"The soldiers are Andrew's," he said slowly, filling the strange silence. "And he maintains my dining room table makes the best battlefield. It's his older sisters who wage war on the chessboard, and if you find yourself sitting across from either of them and let your attention slip, they will show you no mercy."

Elise turned the little soldier over. "Do you have children?" she asked suddenly.

"No." The question startled him with its abrupt directness.

"A wife?"

"No."

"Are you engaged? Or otherwise promised?"

"No."

"Mmm."

Noah blinked, the rapid questions having left him slightly off balance. "Are you?"

"Am I what?" Elise asked.

"Married. Or otherwise promised?" He realized he was holding his breath waiting for her answer, and forced himself to exhale.

"Oh." She looked nonplussed. "No."

They stood, gazing at each other. Noah wasn't entirely sure what was going on. There were strange undercurrents swirling in the room that he didn't understand. Her expression was intense, her eyes troubled once again.

"Will you accompany me outside?" Noah asked impulsively. "There is still time before dinner. And I'd like to show you the rest of the garden." And he hated this... distance that he could feel her putting between them in this room.

Very gently she put the toy rifleman back in the box. "Yes."

⁓

Noah led her out into the warmth of the early evening, the shadows long and the breeze calm. Elise walked beside him, not touching him, though she was aware of his every move. She kept her eyes fixed somewhere beyond the garden and on the dark smudges of trees near the river as they approached the edge of the rose beds, afraid that, if she looked at him, her wits would scatter and her train of thought would be lost. Again.

Noah had caught her in the hallway after her bath, unprepared and unready for the sight of him. He'd changed into clothes that were more formal, and his coat and breeches, though simple in style and suited for the country, were exceptionally tailored and perfectly fitted. Elise caught her breath. Dressed as he was, with his graceful, powerful carriage, it was easy to imagine him in evening wear, commanding a ballroom. He looked every inch a duke.

And then he'd smiled at her and the world around her had dimmed and she'd struggled once again to remember why she was here. Struggled to remember that Noah Ellery was a job.

This had to end. There was no point in prolonging the inevitable confrontation. The confrontation that, in all likelihood, would turn this man against her with every fiber of his being. And if that was the case...then so be it. Lady Abigail hadn't hired her to behave like a love-struck fool. She'd hired Elise to find her brother and bring him safely back to London.

Elise stopped near the edge of the rose garden, unwilling to walk any farther. It wasn't as if she could outrun what was coming. Noah came to a stop beside her.

"I'm not who you think I am," she said quietly. Which was a ridiculous thing to say. She had no idea who Noah thought she was, though she couldn't think of another way to start.

"Are you in trouble with the law?"

Elise looked at him with surprise. That wasn't a question she had been expecting. "No."

"So you're not a thief?"

"No."

"Is someone trying to hurt you?"

"What? No." She could feel her brows draw together. "Why do you—" She stopped, understanding. He thought she was running from something. Or someone. A reasonable assumption. One that, in his place, she might have been tempted to make. Yet still he had offered her his home.

She thought of Mrs. Pritchard. *I had nowhere else to go*, the housekeeper had said. Somewhere down near the river, Square barked. Another lost soul that Noah had extended his care and protection to. And now he was trying to do the same for her.

Mr. Lawson is one of the good ones. Noah certainly was that.

"No, I am not a thief." Elise sighed heavily, wishing for an irrational moment that it were just that easy. "But that doesn't mean you know me or—"

"What you did today on the bridge told me everything I need to know about you." He moved in front of her so that she was forced to look up.

"No." She closed her eyes briefly. She couldn't go down this rabbit hole again. "Not everything."

"I know you don't like rats, you swear in French, and you sometimes snore."

"That's not—"

"I know I don't mix up my words with you."

"I beg your pardon?"

Noah was searching her eyes. "Today, when I misspoke, you didn't care."

"Of course not." She wasn't sure where he was going with this. "Does it happen often?"

"When I'm anxious."

She'd already guessed that. "I made you anxious?"

"Not you. It was me. At the time I was worried that you'd think me too forward. Or foolish. Or both." He paused. "I didn't want you to go. I wanted you here. I wanted..."

Elise looked up at him, her gaze caught in his smoky green one. "You wanted what?" She wished that question back the second it left her lips because the answer was clear in his smoldering eyes.

In the fading light, his hand found hers where it rested against her skirts. His fingers twined through hers, warm and strong. "I wanted to know what it would feel like to touch you," he whispered. "I wanted to know what it would feel like to kiss you."

Desire ripped through her, an intense, primitive thing that left her trembling, a throb building low in her belly. He lifted his other hand and drew his finger along the side of her face, his thumb brushing the sensitive skin of her lower lip. She was aware that her breath was coming in shallow gasps, but then so was his. This...thing that was arcing between them was beyond anything she had ever experienced—beyond anything she had ever needed to control.

She put her free hand up to catch his, intending to pull it away, but his fingers simply curled around hers, imprisoning them in his warmth and sending more heat licking through her limbs. He shifted, stepping closer, his body a breath from hers. She should pull away. She should say something. She tried desperately to think, but it was as if she were drugged, unable to form even the most rudimentary of—

His lips touched hers and everything else ceased to exist.

He kissed her gently, reverently, as though afraid she might shatter. He let go of one of her hands, his fingers sliding around the nape of her neck, caressing the soft skin beneath her heavy braid, and she melted into his touch, unable to resist. He deepened the kiss, his tongue teasing the corners of her mouth, and the throb that had started in her belly became an unbearable ache. She opened beneath his advances, drawing him closer, needing more of him. She heard him groan softly, and her fingers convulsively tightened on his, her other hand coming up to curl into his coat.

His mouth left hers to skim her jaw and the side of her throat, each touch of his lips precise and deliberate and leaving her gasping. She pressed herself against him, feeling the hard evidence of his desire through the fall of his breeches, and he brought his mouth back to hers, more demanding now. She slipped her other hand from his, letting both hands move around his neck, tangling her fingers in his hair as his own hands slid down the curve of her back. He plundered her with his tongue, an electric mating of their mouths that made her wonder if he might just take her here, in the middle of this glorious garden—

She gasped and yanked herself from his arms, horrified and shaking and breathing hard. What the hell was she doing? What the hell was she *thinking*?

"I can't do this." Her voice was a ragged whisper.

"I'm sorry." He was breathing as hard as she was. "I didn't mean...I shouldn't..."

Her heart twisted painfully. "Please don't be sorry," she said miserably. "It's me who needs to apologize."

Confusion clouded his eyes. "Apologize for what?"

"For not telling you why I'm here."

"I don't understand."

Elise took a deep breath. If there was even the smallest doubt that this incredible man who had just kissed her witless in a rose garden was Noah Ellery, she would know within a moment.

She looked him squarely in the eye. "Your sister, Abigail, sent me to find you."

Chapter 7

He couldn't breathe.

The air was sucked from his chest in a whoosh, and blackness crowded the edges of his vision. It was only through sheer force of will that Noah managed to stay on his feet, for his knees were threatening to buckle and his stomach was threatening to rebel. An icy sweat covered his skin, and nausea was rolling through him in waves. Nothing could have prepared him for the beautiful ambush that was this woman.

She was watching him silently, those hazel eyes of hers almost gold in the setting sun. She knew. She knew, she knew, she knew. It pounded through his head, echoing deep in his bones.

She knew who he was, or who he had been, though how she had discovered his identity was horrifyingly unclear. He tried to put his thoughts in order, but his mind refused to cooperate.

She reached out a hand, as if to steady him, but he jerked away from her.

"I'm sorry," she said again, her voice seemingly coming from a great distance. "This was..." She blew out a breath. "This was not how I intended this at all."

"No," he managed to say, the words jumbled in his head and not making sense. He wanted to deny everything, but he couldn't seem to form the necessary sentences.

"Just hear me out—"

"No."

Elise looked down at her hands. "I know very well that you are Noah Ellery, heir to the duchy of Ashland. Pretending otherwise is a waste of our time."

His breath was coming back, small sips of air that were pushing the darkness from the edges of his vision. "Not me."

Elise sighed in obvious frustration, and with what looked like regret on her face. "You're a terrible liar."

He wasn't a terrible liar. He was a brilliant liar. He had lived a lie for fifteen years, and no one had ever discovered his secret until now.

"Abigail needs you."

He focused on those words, focused on the implications of that sentence.

Abigail needs you.

She had not made mention of his father. Or his mother. Only his sister.

The one person in his childhood who had not looked at him with pity. Or anger. The one person who had defended a small boy when no one else would. The one person who had never tried to fix him.

The urge to retch diminished slightly, though a new

dread curled through him. What had happened to Abigail? Was she hurt, was she—

"She's fine." Elise was watching him carefully, and he hated that her blindsiding him had made him give so much away. "But she needs your help. She needs you to come home. To London."

He stared at her before he spun, charging out of the garden into the darkening pastures. He didn't know where he was going, but he needed to move. He could no longer simply stand still under the assault of the secrets that Elise DeVries wielded.

He wasn't sure how far he had gone before he stumbled to a stop, the greyness of twilight making a valiant effort to stay the shadows. Somewhere closer to the river, an owl hooted, an eerie sound that echoed across the pasture. With a start he realized that Elise stood beside him. He'd not heard her, nor had he expected her to be able to keep up over the uneven ground.

"Who are you?" he asked abruptly, a welcome anger replacing the shock. Replacing the feeling of betrayal and the humiliation. He had trusted her. Let down his guard and allowed himself to believe that he felt a connection with this woman. Jesus Christ, but he had *kissed* her.

"I work for the firm of Chegarre and Associates in London. I was hired to find you."

"What is Chegarre and Associates?" he snapped. "Lawyers? Investigators?" Though if they were investigators somehow tied to the Runners, he would already have been arrested.

"Not exactly. We help people find solutions to situations that are…difficult. People turn to us when regular channels of the law or society have failed them."

That meant nothing to him. "And I'm...believe—" He stopped and concentrated on his words, letting the anger run freely, letting it crystallize his thoughts. "And I'm supposed to believe anything you say?"

He heard Elise sigh unhappily. There was a faint rustle of fabric, and she held something out to him in the palm of her hand. Something that gleamed dully in the fading light. "Abigail gave me this to give to you. So that you would know I spoke the truth when I found you."

He recognized it instantly, though he'd never expected to see it again. He reached out and took the brooch from Elise, careful not to touch her. The steel rose was warm against his skin, the edges smooth where it lay in his hand. He remembered the day he'd had John make it for her. He wrapped his hand around it tightly and closed his eyes.

"Abigail's husband is a smith. He recognized Mr. Barr's work, so I came to Nottingham to find him, and hopefully, a clue to your whereabouts." Her voice was quiet and without inflection. "I didn't expect this. I didn't expect you."

Noah opened his eyes and stared out at the river, a silver ribbon now just beyond the trees. He knew exactly what Abigail's husband did for a living. It had been one of the reasons why he'd chosen such a gift. But he'd never considered the possibility that the workmanship of the brooch would ever be recognized.

When news of Abigail's defection from the ton had first broken, Noah had read the details of it in the scandal sheets in London. Each report had been vindictively exhaustive, a spiteful and malicious account of how the daughter of a duke had thrown her entire future away and soiled the Ashland name with disgrace and humiliation.

When Abigail had fled London for Derby, Noah had followed, choosing Nottingham to settle in. Close enough that he might check up on Abigail from time to time, but far enough away that an accidental encounter was improbable. Noah had never been prouder of his sister in his entire life. And he'd asked John to make her that brooch so that she might know it. It had been a risk. But he had trusted her to keep the secret of his existence to herself. And it would seem she'd kept that trust. Until now.

"Is Abigail all right? She has her health?"

"Yes, but—"

"Her husband, her children—they are well?"

"As far as I know. That's not why—"

"Do they need money?" Noah didn't have much compared to the Ashland fortune, but he would sell whatever he had to if she needed help.

"No. But—"

"Who else knows that you're here?" he demanded.

"No one, of course." Elise was looking faintly annoyed. "Chegarre and Associates deal in secret and confidential matters, and we take that very seriously. I've been doing this a long time, and I doubt there is anything you can tell me that I haven't already heard. But I am uninterested in the contents of your past, aside from the few facts that relate directly to our current predicament. It is not my job to judge people, or form opinions. My job is to assist those who need it. Like Lady Abigail. Like you."

Noah wondered exactly how much this woman really knew about his past. If she knew what he had done, what he had become.

"Your father is dead," Elise said before he could finish that thought. "And your mother—"

"Stop." Hatred, resentment, and the old echoes of

terror—they all rose up with a strength that almost choked him. It was stupid, he knew. He should be beyond this sort of reaction, and further, he should be feeling regret or sorrow or grief. A normal person would feel such things when informed of the passing of a parent. But he couldn't muster any of those emotions. They'd been snuffed out long ago in the hell into which he'd been cast by the two people he'd trusted most. "You came all the way from London to tell me that my father was dead?"

"Yes, but that's not all—"

"You should have saved yourself the trouble," he snapped. "There is nothing you can tell me about the Duke or Duchess of Ashland that I want to hear. As far as I am concerned, they both died long ago."

Elise's lips thinned. "Abigail said you might say that—"

"Further," Noah gritted through clenched teeth, "know that there is nothing that will ever entice me back. Tell me, am I still assumed dead in the hallowed halls of London?"

She narrowed her eyes. "Yes."

"I plan to stay that way, Miss DeVries. Nothing you do or say will change my mind."

"You have a responsibility to—"

"I do not have a responsibility to anything," he growled. "Not to my father, not to my mother. Not to Ashland's piles of properties and strings of titles and coffers of money."

"If you ever let me finish a sentence, I was going to say you have a responsibility to your sister."

He resented the faint wash of guilt even as he pinched the bridge of his nose. "You have told me that Abigail is not in any danger. Or distress."

"Perhaps, but the same cannot be said for your mother—"

Noah held up his hand. "You will return to London, or wherever it is that you came from—"

"London. Your sister is in London at the moment."

He hadn't known that. But it didn't matter. "Then tell Abigail that you were unable to locate me. Or tell her whatever you need to make her understand that I can't go back. Ever." *To London. To who I once was.*

"You want me to lie to your sister?"

"You seem quite good at it. Lying, that is." Noah saw her flinch, but he hardened his heart.

"I never lied to you."

"You knew who I was and let me believe—" He couldn't even say it out loud.

You let me believe that there was something between us.

He had believed that there existed a connection that he had never felt with another woman, something extraordinary. The disappointment was as humiliating as it was excruciating.

Elise looked away. "I didn't know who you were right away. And if you are referring to what happened in the garden...that was real." She sounded subdued. "It should never have happened, and for my lack of professionalism, I apologize. But only for that."

A tiny fragment of hope twisted in his gut, and he hated himself for it. He knew better. "You need to go." She couldn't stay here.

"No." She turned back to him, gazing at him steadily. "I will not leave here without you."

"You will." It was a command.

"Your cousin, Francis Ellery, knows you are alive." She said it with no warning.

"What?" For the second time, it was as if she had gut-punched him.

"The letter you sent to your sister with that brooch was stolen from her home very recently. I believe it was taken by Mr. Ellery, or individuals working at his behest. Further...er, investigation on my part has also indicated that Francis Ellery has hired two assassins to find you and make sure that your death is not just an erroneous rumor."

"Assassins." He had never heard anything so utterly ludicrous in his entire life. Especially in light of the fact that she said *assassins* the same way others said *tax collectors*. "You can't honestly expect me to believe that."

Elise cocked her head. "You should. You sent that letter to Abigail via the regular post. And while it certainly arrived anonymously, that letter bore a Nottingham postmark that will inevitably lead these men here, if it hasn't already."

Noah threw up his hands in a show of exasperation, ignoring the uncertainty that was gnawing at him.

Elise frowned. "I don't think you truly understand what is at stake here. How much wealth. How much power. And the lengths your cousin will go to to ensure he becomes the next Duke of Ashland. I cannot—will not—leave here when your safety may be at risk."

"First, Miss DeVries, I am perfectly capable of looking after myself. I do not need you to tend me like a nursemaid. Second, my cousin, like everyone else, believes me dead. There is no reason for him to be looting my sister's house looking for evidence of my existence or hiring *assassins*." He sounded like an idiot saying that out loud. It was preposterous.

Elise shook her head. "Unfortunately not. The reason

Abigail returned to London—the reason she hired me is because, upon the death of your father, your mother made the mistake of publicly insisting that you were alive."

Noah felt his stomach drop again. "How...mother..." He couldn't find the words.

Elise winced. "Abigail told her. She regrets it now. But perhaps you can understand the dilemma I'm faced with. I will not leave you unprotected."

Noah laughed, a sound that was dry and humorless, thinking of the rifle that now leaned against the wall in Elise's room. He no longer doubted for a second that she knew how to use it. "How do I know you're not an assassin?"

She was quiet for the space of two heartbeats. "I'm not an assassin." She sounded strange. "If I were, you'd already be dead."

"Jesus." He rubbed his hands over his face. He felt as if he'd stepped into the pages of a story where reality had been discarded in favor of fancy and farce. He didn't know what to believe. "I don't want the title," he said, pretending, just for a moment, that everything Elise had told him was true. "Go back to London and tell Francis he can have it with my compliments."

"He's in the process of murdering your mother."

"What?"

"Since her public claim of your existence, Mr. Ellery has had your mother committed to Bedlam to discredit those claims. And the duchess will be dead within a month unless you can prove her right."

He thought he'd heard her wrong. "Bedlam," he repeated slowly.

"That is correct. Last I saw her, she was shackled and in an opiated haze." Elise was watching him intently again.

"Abigail wants me to return to London to rescue my mother from Bedlam." The irony was too much, and Noah found himself laughing, great heaving breaths that bordered on hysterical. There was no humor in his laughter, and after a few seconds, it faded as fast as it had risen, leaving nothing but a great yawning pit of . . . nothingness. After everything—the years of terror and despair and pain— he should have taken an unnatural satisfaction in such a predicament. But it was all he could do to keep his own memories of that hell from becoming completely unleashed and crippling his ability to think.

It had been his father who had woken him in the dead of night, cajoling his sleepy son from the warmth of his bed with murmurs of new puppies in the stables to see, leading him out of the house to where Noah had found not pups but grim-faced men with unforgiving strength. His father had given his captors a brisk nod, ordered Noah to behave, and left him struggling as the men locked Noah into a barred carriage as though he were a dangerous beast. He'd pressed his face up against those bars, terror coursing through his small body, and seen his mother watching from an upstairs window. And as the carriage had bumped and jarred its way to the top of the drive, she'd simply let the curtain drop.

Noah wondered, not for the first time, if Abigail had ever known where he'd been sent. If she'd known the torture he'd been subjected to at the hands of mad-doctors who had told him that they would fix him. Promised that they would have him speaking like an Eton grad within a few months, their treatments guaranteed to work. He wondered if Abigail had known of the cruelty and callousness of the stewards and keepers, who had viewed the patients as less than vermin.

Noah had spent those first months praying that his mother would intervene and save him from Bedlam. But the summer had turned into fall, and then winter, and the cold winds had howled through the cracks in the walls. The keepers continued their torture, and other patients around him fell ill and died from dysentery and cholera and things Noah couldn't name. And he'd stopped praying. Stopped hoping. He'd accepted that no one would ever come to save him.

And no one ever had.

"You're the only one who can have her released," Elise was saying. "Well, there are other avenues I can explore, but I fear they will take too much time and will not save your mother."

"No." He turned away from her and started back in the direction of the garden. Miss DeVries had no idea what she was asking him to do. "Like I said, both my mother and father died a long time ago."

She was suddenly in front of him, as silent and quick as she had been earlier, and her ability to navigate in the darkness was unnerving. Her expression was hard to read in the failing light. "How many times has Lady Abigail asked you for help?" Her voice was deceptively neutral, but the barb jabbed deep, and the wound bled guilt.

Never. Not once.

"I thought so." She must have read the answer in his silence, and her voice now had a brittle edge. "If you maintain your refusal to help, then at least have the decency to face your sister and tell her that yourself."

"I can't. You don't understand."

"You might be surprised," she said, and it wasn't unkind.

"No."

"Then I fear, Your Grace, we are at an impasse."

Noah froze before reflexively glancing around. "Don't…me…" He stopped. "Don't address me as such. Ever."

Elise was silent for a long moment. "No one else here knows who you really are, do they?" she asked abruptly.

A bead of cold sweat ran down his back as it dawned on him the power this woman now held over him. Yet he could answer her with nothing less than the truth. "No."

She was watching him again, her eyes glittering in the last of the light. "What about John Barr?"

Noah shook his head. There was little point in lying, and the last thing he needed was for her to pose the same question to John. "He knows I am not Noah Lawson. That is all," he said hoarsely.

"And he's never asked?"

"No."

"Mmm." He thought he detected a note of approval in her mumbled response. "Tell me why you won't return to London. The real reason."

He took a steadying breath. He felt a tiny measure of relief that she didn't know all of it. She didn't know the truth. "It doesn't matter."

"I rather think it does." There was a gentleness to her words that he couldn't bear.

Noah stepped around her and kept walking. There was nothing in this world that would ever entice him to speak more about his past to a woman who already knew too many of his secrets. "Get your things. I will drive you into town."

"And tell your housekeeper what?"

He stumbled before stopping. "Are you threatening me?"

Elise heaved a sigh. "No, I'm not threatening you. But the thing with secrets and lies, Mr. Lawson, is that they have a habit of becoming complicated very quickly. They pile up, they become twisted and convoluted, until you can't remember what is real anymore."

Noah could feel the threads of the life he had carefully woven starting to unravel, row by row, stitch by stitch, and there was nothing he could do to stop it. His emotions were churning wildly, a mess of things he couldn't begin to sort out. He couldn't concentrate, couldn't put his words into the right order to verbalize any of what he was thinking.

In the semidarkness Elise put her hand on his arm. "Don't say anything right now," she told him, and he wondered, again, how he was so transparent in front of this woman. He pulled away from her, hating how logical she sounded. He heard the compassion, yet the steely strength that lay beneath it was unmistakable.

"Know that whatever secrets of yours I hold will remain just that. You have my word. I will never use them against you. But no matter your decision, you owe your sister an explanation. And it will come from you, not from me. Whether you elect to return to London as Mr. Lawson or the Duke of Ashland is your choice." She paused. "But I will not leave you unprotected. And I will not leave this farm without you."

Chapter 8

Dinner had been a silent affair, save for the expected murmurings of thanks as Mrs. Pritchard presented them with a simple yet delicious meal of stew and fresh bread. She had thrown both of them quizzical looks, but hadn't commented on the strained silence, and instead announced quite loudly that she was retiring early. Elise might have found it amusing had she not felt so utterly wretched.

Never had she handled anything as badly as she had the situation with Noah Ellery. She should have done some more digging before she left London, but she had been in a rush, and now she regretted her haste.

That young gentleman was never right in the head, either.

I don't know where my parents sent him.

Those two statements, made a world apart, suddenly came together to make the hairs on the back of Elise's neck stand up. Suspicion warred with doubt.

She didn't want to believe it. She didn't even want to think it. But if Noah's reaction when she had informed him of his mother's current imprisonment in Bedlam was any indication, Elise rather thought she already had her answer. Never, in all her life, had she seen such a visceral, bleak response to a simple reference.

And if what she suspected was indeed true, and Noah Ellery had spent time as a patient—prisoner—in Bedlam as a child, Elise wasn't entirely sure she wanted to know what memories haunted this man. Nor, she thought to herself, were they any of her business. But she genuinely regretted not having been adequately prepared. And as a result, the man who had sat across the table from her during that excruciating meal had looked at her only once.

"Have your bags packed at dawn," was all he'd said before vanishing back out into the night.

Elise had given him a minute and then silently followed him, old instincts taking over. He hadn't gone very far—only to the edge of the trees at the far end of his pasture, where he had stood staring out at the river for the better part of an hour. Elise had circled and scouted the surrounding forests and bush, but had found no sign of another human. No sign that anyone else had found or followed Noah Ellery. That knowledge made her breathe a little easier, though the similar knowledge that she should have done that the second she had arrived at this farm left her uncomfortable. She'd allowed herself to become distracted and, as a result, exposed them both to a potential danger.

She'd waited with him, unseen, until he had returned to the house. She'd slipped into her bedroom and tried to find sleep, though she had done nothing but toss and turn all night, the bed ropes creaking beneath her and her thoughts in a turmoil. But the only thing that had been clear, when she had finally abandoned her efforts at sleep and stolen from the house, was that she wasn't packing any bags unless the Duke of Ashland was riding with her.

The cow she was milking shifted, and Elise started, realizing she had lapsed into inactivity. She sighed and readjusted her stool, resting her forehead against the animal's warm side, and resumed her rhythmic motions. In the east the sky had been washed a pale platinum that heralded the beginning of sunrise. She closed her eyes briefly, the familiar routine going a long way to soothe her troubled mind, even if it hadn't inspired any answers.

Maybe she should have told Roddy to fetch her a cow—

"What the hell do you think you're doing?" Noah's demand came from the barn door, and Elise started, yanking harder on the teat than she had intended. The cow stomped its hind leg in annoyance.

"I would think that would be obvious," she said mildly, unable to see him. "And I'd trouble you to keep from yelling at any female in the immediate vicinity until I'm done."

"Why are you milking my cow?"

"Because it helps me think. And it needed to be done."

Noah muttered something vile, and there was a thump from the other side of the animal. A faint cloud of dust rose, the first rays of dawn illuminating the motes dancing in the beams. From beneath the animal, Elise could see the edge of her pack on the ground.

"You forgot your things in the house," Noah said. "And your rifle. I took the liberty of fetching both for you. Please step away from my cow."

Elise continued to milk, the steady gurgle of the streams hitting the bucket the only sound in the silence.

"Did you not hear me, Miss DeVries?"

She didn't respond.

"Do you require me to saddle your horse for you?" he asked.

Elise remained mute.

She heard a string of muttered curses. "Are you ignoring me on purpose?" Noah demanded from somewhere on the other side of the bovine barrier that still stood between them.

"Yes."

"You have to go." She could hear the frustration in his words.

"And I will. So long as you're with me." There was no way she was surrendering ground on this. Her hands kept a steady pace, the streams of milk starting to subside as the bucket filled.

"I'm not going anywhere with you, Miss DeVries. Nor can you stay in my house."

"That's fine. I'll sleep here." Probably made more sense anyway. Staying in that house would render it much more difficult to come and go undetected if there was indeed someone watching. It would be smarter for her to stay in the barn.

"What do you mean, here? In Nottingham?"

"No. In your barn." The last of the milk dripped into the bucket.

"I—you—*no*." The chain of syllables was strangled. "You'll sleep in my barn over my dead body."

"And that would be exactly what I'm trying to prevent."

Noah made an inarticulate noise. Elise ignored him and

reached for the bucket, setting it carefully aside next to the others, before standing from where she'd been crouched on the stool. She gave the cow a pat on the rump, shooed the animal out of the barn, and turned to face Noah.

Whatever she had been going to say next died on her tongue. He was still standing near the doorway, beams of new sunlight illuminating the lines of his body and gilding him. He was dressed in rough clothes, and the worn fabric of his breeches and coat hugged his frame and did nothing to conceal the power that lay beneath them.

Just like that she was back in the rose garden, remembering how he had felt beneath her hands. How his warmth had bled through fabric and into her skin, joining the heat that had been building from within her. Her eyes came to rest on his lips as she remembered just how masterfully he had kissed her, how breathless he had left her. How utterly unable she had been to resist him and the powerful attraction that had caught her and held her fast. And based on the shiver that rippled across her skin now, it would seem that after everything, nothing had changed.

The desire to kiss him again, to touch his face and erase the worry and frustration and anger that creased it now, was overwhelming. Until she remembered that it was she who had put all those things there.

She swallowed, that unhappy guilt sitting like a weight in her chest along with an equal measure of regret. The sense that something irreplaceable was irrevocably slipping away from her was acute.

Collect your damn wits, she ordered her consciousness. Noah Ellery was a job, not a suitor, and she needed to remember that. Otherwise emotions would start to get in the way of good judgment and common sense, and that was a dangerous place to be. She raised her eyes, hoping her expression hadn't given any of her thoughts away, but he wasn't looking at her.

Instead he was staring at the buckets of milk. "You milked *all* my cows," he said, and she had no idea if he was angry or pleased. At least they were no longer discussing sleeping arrangements.

"You have excellent milkers," she said. "Lovely dispositions. Makes everything so much easier when you're not fighting for cooperation." She put emphasis on the last sentence.

He glanced at her, his brows drawn together. "I thought you were from London."

"I am."

He frowned at the buckets.

"Believe it or not, people from London know how to milk cows," she told him. "They do have cows in London. Lots of them."

He was shaking his head. "You didn't grow up in the city."

Elise bent to lift two of the heavy buckets. "No," she agreed, looking down at the milk in her hands and thinking that was likely obvious and not worth arguing.

Noah moved to block her way, his hands over his chest. "Where are you from? Originally."

Elise readjusted her grip on the handles. "The country." She smiled blandly at him. "Now, if you'll excuse me, I'll take these up to Mrs. Pritchard. There are two more buckets that need to be brought up." She jerked her head toward them.

"That's not how this works," Noah said, not budging. "You owe me a truth about yourself since you seem to know so much about me."

Elise hesitated. She didn't owe him anything. And she did not often share much about her past with anyone. But on the other hand, Noah was no longer ordering her to leave, or threatening to saddle her horse, or otherwise dragging her off his property. Perhaps this was an opportunity. She'd offer him an abbreviated, carefully censored version of her past, if only in an attempt to make inroads with a man whom she needed to trust her again. "Near York."

"You're from Yorkshire."

"No. Canada."

Noah stared at her. "In the colonies."

"That is correct. Now get out of my way. These are heavy." She pushed by him, but he was faster.

"You grew up on a farm there."

"Yes."

"Is that where you were born?"

"It's where my brothers and I were all born."

"Your brothers? You said you only had one." His words were laden with suspicion.

Elise closed her eyes, cursing herself for the slip. "My oldest brother died. Only Alex is left." A swell of sorrow caught her off guard, and she bit the inside of her cheek. Perhaps it was the surroundings that raised old, happy childhood memories, bittersweet now with the reminder of so much loss. Her brothers had been the world to her—they'd raised her from the time of their parents' death, when she was six. "Alex and Jonathon were both soldiers. Third York Regiment under Major William Allen. Jonathon was killed in the defense of York." She had no idea why she'd felt compelled to explain that, other than to remind herself that he had died fighting for something that they had all believed in.

Alex had been fighting beside him when he'd died. Though to this day, he had yet to speak about what had happened out on the battlefield. Elise had been there that day as well, though she had never been issued a regimental jacket or trousers. As always, she'd been a ghost, her commanding officers sending her deep into enemy territory to find their troops and observe them and collect information on their movements, positions, and capabilities. Information that had not, in the end, been able to save her brother.

"I'm sorry," Noah said, and his words sounded stiff, as if even the smallest acknowledgment of sympathy or compassion would derail his determination to keep her at a distance.

Elise just nodded and ducked by him, continuing up toward the house.

"Is that why you left your farm?"

Elise had a momentary flash of blackened timbers and smoking ruins. "There was no farm left. After the British retreated, the Americans razed the buildings, slaughtered the animals, and burned the orchards." She saw Noah glance around him as though he was imagining what it might be like to return home after a long absence to find everything you had built destroyed.

"I'm sorry," he said again.

"So am I." But that was the nature of war.

"Why did you come to London?" Noah was in front of her again, and she was forced to stop.

Because the militia had been left behind when the British regulars had retreated and there had been nothing left in York except danger. Angry American officers looking for excuses to punish those who had remained loyal to the Crown. She wasn't sure she was at all comfortable with the direction his questions had taken. "For the theater." That was suitably flippant and misleading. Yet partially true.

"The theater?"

"Yes. I am a part-time actress at the Theatre Royal in Drury Lane. When I'm not busy locating missing dukes, that is." She edged by him and resumed walking toward the house.

"You're an actress?" He was beside her now, and he sounded incredulous. He could make of that what he would. But better incredulous than angry.

"Sometimes." She adjusted her grip on the heavy handles, making sure not to slosh the milk.

"Well, that would explain a lot," he muttered under his breath.

Elise stopped abruptly. "What is that supposed to mean?" she demanded.

"You're quite accomplished at deceiving everyone. You had me fooled from the very beginning. You had us all fooled."

Elise put the buckets down and put her hands on her hips, anger rising at the suggestion that everything that had happened since she had ridden out onto that Nottingham bridge yesterday had been some sort of diabolical plot. "You think I arranged to ride into Nottingham and save a drowning boy so that I could worm my way into your presence? You think that I take pleasure from being the one who has brought the past crashing into your very peaceful existence here?"

Noah was silent, and for the life of her, she couldn't read his expression.

"There is something that one learns when one is an actress," Elise said. "Every night you go out on that stage.

Every night you pretend to be someone you're not. But eventually the curtain is drawn, and your audience goes home, and the costumes and the face paints get put away." She looked up at him. "No one can pretend forever to be someone they're not."

"I'm not pretending, if that is what you are implying." His face was set in angry lines. "The man you came here to find no longer exists."

Elise shook her head. "You are not ten years old anymore, Your Grace," she said, deliberately using his title. "You are a duke, whether you like it or not. You are a man with wealth and power at his fingertips should you choose to use them. But most importantly, you are a man with a sister and a mother who need you very much."

She saw a flash of fury in his eyes. "Are you questioning my honor now?"

Elise took a step closer to him, refusing to be cowed by his ire. Just as well they got this sorted out now, standing in a deserted lane between the barn and the house where there were no witnesses save for a handful of sparrows. "I am not questioning your honor. I am merely presenting you with the facts."

"The facts," he repeated, his lip curling. "You have no idea what facts you speak of."

"Then tell me."

He looked away and then looked back at her, an angry flush climbing into his cheeks. "Tell you? Just like that?"

"It would be a start. I will be of far more help if I fully understand what it is we might face when we return to London."

"Jesus. There is no *we*. You...nerve..." He trailed off, searching for words, and judging by his expression, Elise had no doubt they weren't going to be pleasant when he found them.

"Your sister begged me to find you," she said, cutting off whatever he was going to say. "And I did. I will not apologize for doing my job. You're not the only one who has things in their past they'd rather forget. You're not the only one who has had to do whatever it takes to survive." There was a part of her brain that was cautioning her to stop, to simply leave well enough alone, and let Noah Ellery think of her what he would. So long as the job got done, it didn't matter.

Except, she realized with no little dismay, it did matter. She cared very much about what he thought of her. She cared about him. Dammit.

She softened her tone. "I am not your enemy, though I understand it might seem like it now. I am with you, not against you."

"Really?" There was an edge to his words. "Is that what you were trying to prove last night in the rose garden? That you are *with me*?"

She could feel the heat rise in her face. "No. That wasn't—"

"Wasn't what? Something else you don't feel the need to apologize for?"

"What happened last night between you and me was...perfect. If only for a moment." She was looking up at him, standing so close that she could see the dark-green flecks in his irises. "So no, I won't apologize for that."

He blinked at her, and his expression shifted, as if he too had suddenly become aware of how close they were.

Yet neither of them moved away.

Elise could feel her pulse pounding in her veins, feel

a longing ache igniting and thrumming through her body. She tried to suppress it, but it was far too late, common sense and intelligence evaporating in the face of so much heat. She curled her hands into the fabric of her skirts to keep from reaching out to touch him.

His hair was loose and falling over his ears and forehead and was begging to have her fingers run through it. His strong jaw was covered with a day's worth of stubble, entreating her to feel its texture. There was a ragged edge along the collar of his shirt at the base of his throat, and it was imploring her to run the pad of her thumb over the tear and then along the darkened skin beneath it and across his—

"Anything else?" Noah asked hoarsely.

"I beg your pardon?" Dear God, but it was hopeless. She couldn't even remember what they had been talking about. After everything, after her lectures and rigid reminders to herself, after carefully cultivating and bolstering her resolve, a second near this man reduced reason to a smoldering pile of ash. She had never wanted a man the way she wanted this one.

"Is there anything else you'd like to not apologize for?"

Elise gazed up at him, realizing with a jolt that the anger had faded from his face altogether and been replaced with something far more dangerous. His smoky gaze caught and held hers, and there was that intense longing she had seen in the rose garden, the want and need that had turned her knees to liquid and her insides to fire. He was still no more immune to whatever arced between them than she was. A reckless hunger pounded through her now with every beat of her heart.

"Yes," she said. "I will not apologize for this."

And she kissed him.

It was a rash indulgence, a desperate need to prove that what had happened in the rose garden had been perfect. And right. And inevitable. And she'd meant this kiss to be quick, a brief slaking of a thirst that would likely never be truly satisfied.

Except his hand came up and caught the back of her head, and then he was kissing her back, and whatever shreds of control and restraint she'd been hanging on to disintegrated. She wrapped her hands around his neck, her fingers curling into the tousled blond curls she had so longed to touch. She nipped at his lower lip before letting her mouth travel over the roughness of his jaw, finding that spot at the base of his throat where she could feel his heart hammering. He tasted of salt and heat and man, and she let her hands drop, sliding them under his coat and over the linen of his shirt. Her hands wandered over his chest and around to his back, each ridge of steely muscle defined beneath her touch.

He hissed against her ear, before the hand at the back of her head urged her lips back to his, his mouth coming down hard on hers once again. His free hand slid down her spine and over her rear, pulling her against him. She was straddling one of his thighs, her skirts bunched around her legs, and powerless to move. Not that she had any interest in doing so. The feel of his body pressed against the length of hers was devastating. It robbed her of breath, of thought, of focus, leaving only a mind-numbing need roaring through her body. She made a muffled sound of frustration and yanked the tails of his shirt from his breeches, slipping her hands under the linen and allowing them to roam over his skin.

She felt him shudder beneath her touch, the muscles beneath her palms flexing as he moved. She shifted, the rigid bulge of his erection trapped against her hip. Another sound of frustration rose in the back of her throat. There was nothing in this world that she wouldn't give at this moment to be able to feel all of him against all of her. All of him within her.

Noah's hands had caught her head now, keeping her at the mercy of his wickedly talented tongue. He dipped his head, his lips moving from hers to the underside of her jaw, and his hands trailed over her collarbones to her shoulders, then down to her breasts. Involuntarily she arched against his touch, every nerve ending in her body demanding more. He stroked the slopes of her breasts, first with his hands and then with his mouth, before his palms cupped their heavy fullness through the fabric of her dress and his thumbs circled and teased the sensitive peaks of her nipples. Her head fell back slightly, her thighs clenching the hardness of his thigh as her body sought release. She was wet and aching and somewhere she had lost control of what she had started, but she was long past the point of caring.

He moved slightly, and his hands dropped to her waist, pushing her harder against the steely length of his thigh. She was unable to do anything except revel in the feel of this man around her and beneath her. His breath was ragged and uneven. It gave her an unseemly amount of satisfaction to know that her touch undid him as completely as his did her.

"Noah," she managed to whisper, not sure if it was a plea or a warning.

Her voice seemed to penetrate his skull, for he jerked back and swore softly.

Saints help her, she was in trouble. Her world had tilted from the pleasure she had found in this man's arms while they groped and fumbled at each other's clothing like a couple of frenzied adolescents. She couldn't begin to imagine what it might be like to take this man to her bed and allow him to do what he would.

But they were still standing in a middle of a lane, forgotten buckets of milk at their feet and a sea of discord between them. She straightened, her fingers smoothing the fabric of her skirts.

Noah was jamming the tails of his shirt back into his breeches, his movements erratic. He stopped. His eyes searched hers, desire shadowed by confusion. "I don't understand what you do to me."

"That makes two of us then," she replied softly. A world of regret and self-reproach would descend on her the moment she walked away. Never had she allowed so much control to slip so far. "But whatever this is, it changes nothing."

Chapter 9

He'd lost his mind.

For real this time. Noah might have found that funny had his life not been crumbling under him.

He swung the ax down harder than was necessary, and another log split beneath the blade, the pieces sent flying from the force. He left them where they lay, among a hundred similar pieces, and seized another log, setting it up on the wide stump. He swung the ax again, and his muscles screamed in protest, but he ignored the pain. Embraced it, even. He needed something mindless, something to drive out whatever madness had gripped him since he had pulled a beautiful woman from the River Leen.

He'd gone down to the barn this morning, certain he had a firm grip on what he needed to do, determined that he would see Elise DeVries safely away from his farm. Away from him. Except...except somehow he'd found himself kissing her again. And not just kissing her. Wanting her with an intensity that defied reason. Ignoring everything that had brought her into his life in the first place.

I don't understand what you do to me.

He'd blurted out that truth while his mind was still sluggish and drugged with lust. She was like an addiction, something that he was powerless to resist, even though he understood just how dangerous she was. He'd never experienced anything like it before, and it disturbed him beyond words.

Thwack. Another log fell victim to his blade.

Even now he could feel his blood heat and his groin tighten just thinking of her. Thinking of her lush curves, her clever mouth, the way she seemed to know how to touch him exactly as he wished to be touched. She was not shy, nor was there a trace of coyness or guile. She was a woman who knew exactly what she wanted, and it aroused him to no end.

And then there were her words that he had tried not dwell on.

I am with you, not against you.

Well, she wasn't, really, was she? Her very presence threatened everything he had built.

Yet deep down, had Noah truly believed that his past would stay buried forever? Had he really expected that no one would ever recognize him? He'd been told from an early age that he was the spitting image of his father. It was likely that time had only amplified the likeness, and there was probably a good amount of luck involved in the fact that no one had ever recognized him. Or, at the very least, questioned his origins. Yes, he might avoid busy coaching inns where travelers from London were likely to congregate, but unless he was to become a total recluse, it would be impossible to avoid strangers completely.

When Noah had left London for good, he'd not given much thought to the distant future, other than his wish to stay invisible and remain reasonably close to Abigail so that he might watch over her undetected. Once he'd settled here, days had turned into weeks and then months and then years, and Noah had allowed time to create an illusion of safety.

But it had been just that, really. An illusion. And perhaps he should be thankful it was Elise DeVries who had shown up on his doorstep and not a Runner or a magistrate. Which didn't mean he was going anywhere near London. No matter what sort of tale she spun.

"You expecting winter early?" Mrs. Pritchard was standing near the corner of the house, her hands on her ample hips, surveying the carnage around him that had once been a neat stack of logs waiting to be split.

Noah yanked another log from the dwindling pile and set it on the stump. Sweat was running into his eyes, and his shirt was plastered to his body.

Thwack.

"Needs to be done sooner or later," he mumbled. "Wood'll dry faster this way."

"Mmm-hmm." Her skepticism was loud and clear.

Noah avoided looking at his housekeeper. Instead he reached for yet another log and heaved it onto the stump. He gazed down at the rings just visible in the stump where a long saw had severed the trunk. They circled around and around, getting smaller and smaller the closer they got to the center. Just like his thoughts, piling into indecipherable circles, leading nowhere logical.

"I have a sister," he said abruptly, leaning on the handle of the ax and staring down at the gouges and slashes that covered the top of the stump. He had no idea why he'd said that. Except that Abigail had been his only regret. It was strange, how much he still missed someone who had been gone for so long. And speaking about her out loud suddenly made her seem closer.

"You do?" He could hear the surprise in his housekeeper's voice.

"She lives in Derby. With her husband and her children."

"You're an uncle." Now Mrs. Pritchard sounded delighted.

"Yes." It struck Noah that he had never really thought about it like that. That he had never really considered what Abigail's children would be like. If they would be gentle and generous in the same way she had been as a child. Another layer of guilt settled over him like dark coal dust. Noah had spent so much time focusing on his own life, on maintaining and protecting his new, perfect reality, that he had given very little thought to the reality of hers, save the thought that she was content. "She needs my help. My sister, that is."

"So when are you leaving?"

Noah glanced up. "What makes you think I'm leaving?"

Mrs. Pritchard frowned. "She's your sister."

"I haven't seen her in a very long time."

"So?" His housekeeper was starting to sound like Elise.

"She wants me to come to London."

Mrs. Pritchard's frown deepened. "If you're worried about the farm, you don't need to be. I'm here, and the Carters' youngest two boys are always looking for work. They were an excellent help last year at harvest."

"I wasn't worried about the farm." The farm was the last thing he was concerned about.

"Then what are you worried about?"

Everything else. But nothing he could tell Mrs. Pritchard. Nothing that would take away the damned guilt that had been building since the moment Elise had uttered the words *Abigail needs you*.

"She's your sister," his housekeeper repeated firmly, piling more guilt onto the already substantial pile. "You do what you need to do. Nothing else really matters."

"It's not quite that simple."

"Only if you choose to make it complicated."

Noah sneered to himself silently. He hadn't chosen anything. *Complicated* had been chosen for him. *Complicated* had been set in motion the day his parents had arranged to have him smuggled from their house in a carriage with bars. "Maybe," he said, if only so he didn't have to argue. He pulled the ax off the stump and raised it over his head.

"Has your sister ever helped you when you've needed it?"

Thunk. The ax glanced off the log awkwardly, and the wood thudded to the ground. Memories of a defiant girl in pigtails and pinafores leaped to his mind. Abigail had been his biggest champion and his most valiant defender. At least until he had grown big enough to fight his own battles. And then she'd taught him how to fight smart and fight dirty.

Noah kicked the fallen log to the side and jammed the blade of the ax into the stump again in frustration.

"Does this—whatever involves your sister—have something to do with Miss DeVries?" his housekeeper asked.

"Yes. No. Sort of." He mopped his face with his sleeve,

not even knowing where to begin if he had to offer a further explanation.

"I think you need to tell me exactly what is going on."

"What do you mean?" It was a pathetic attempt to stall.

"Do you think me a complete bottle-head, Mr. Lawson?" Mrs. Pritchard asked, though there was no venom in her words.

"No." He cleared his throat. "Of course not."

"I have been with you now for ten years, Mr. Lawson. Ten years, and in those ten years, I have never heard you mention a sister. Or a mother, or a father. Or a childhood home, for that matter. Did you think that I never noticed? Never wondered?"

"But you never asked."

"Because it never mattered. Until now, it would seem."

"It's complicated."

"Yes, so you keep saying. And now you're out here chopping wood like a man possessed, avoiding Miss DeVries and more likely to give yourself an apoplexy than resolve whatever it is that needs resolving."

Noah ran his hands through his sweat-soaked hair. "I've tried talking to El— Miss DeVries. She refuses to listen to reason." That, and he seemed unable to keep his hands off her. Which was a whole different kettle of unreasonable. And unacceptable. "She'll be returning to London shortly." Alone.

Mrs. Pritchard crossed her arms over her ample chest. "Is she in danger? Your sister?"

Noah shook his head. If he believed that, he'd be halfway to London already and damn the consequences. "No. She's fine."

"Are you in some sort of danger?"

"What? Why would you think that?" Noah stared at Mrs. Pritchard.

"Miss DeVries asked me if I had noticed anything odd lately." There was a worried frown on her face now. "She wanted to know if there had been any strangers stopping by, anyone asking questions about you or another man named Noah. Anyone I might have noticed in town who wasn't known, or that another local may have remarked upon."

"When did she ask you this?"

"This morning. When she was making jam."

"*What?*" He wasn't sure what bothered him more—that Elise had alarmed his housekeeper with her ridiculous stories or that she seemed to have absolutely no intention of leaving. "Where is she now?" he demanded.

Mrs. Pritchard shrugged. "I don't know. But she changed back into that awful shirt and trousers that had been drying in her room and left."

"Left for where?"

Mrs. Pritchard's frown had turned into a scowl. "I don't know, Mr. Lawson. I wasn't the one giving her roses in the garden last night and ignoring her the next day."

⁓

Noah shoved his way into the darkened interior of the barn, letting his eyes adjust to the light. In the corner Elise's pack still rested on the floor where he had deposited it earlier. A bizarre mixture of relief and annoyance washed through him. His eyes scanned the wall, and he noticed that her gelding's bridle was still hanging from its hook, along with its saddle.

Wherever she had gone, she hadn't gone far. His eyes turned back to where her pack lay. The heavy buckles gleamed dully in the light, peeking out from under an oiled cloth. He froze. Her rifle was missing.

Where the hell could the woman have gone?

He stalked out to the rear of the barn, allowing his eyes to roam over the pastures where they rolled down toward the trees. In the distance a movement caught his eye—a familiar waving tail and a lopsided gait. The dog lifted his head and sniffed the air and then, with a bark, disappeared into the trees. What the hell was Square doing down by the river?

Was that where Elise had gone? Had she gotten it in her head to go hunting after she had made jam and milked his cows? It wouldn't surprise him, but bloody hell, this had to stop. Before he could reconsider, he was striding toward the thick ridge of trees. Whatever the woman was doing, it wasn't anything good. He needed her on her horse and down the road back to London, not roaming about his property and threatening his sanity.

He reached the edge of the trees and paused. The wind was up today, and the leaves danced above his head, the branches of the hawthorns and birches rattling and swaying. He entered the forest, and as he went deeper, the sound became muted, the larger, thicker oaks spreading their limbs to provide a thick canopy above. He followed one of the many deer trails that wound its way through the trees in the direction of the river, but there was no sign of Elise. No sign of Square either. He pressed on.

The sunlight here was shut out, the forest darkened and cool, though none of this bothered Noah. He came here often just to stand in the peace and the silence. The branches were thick, the ancient trunks twisted and gnarled, and the very air itself whispered of the magic and legends that abounded in these forests. But today the forest was silent.

Too silent.

Something was out of place.

Very slowly Noah drew his hunting knife from its sheath at his waist.

"You shouldn't be out here alone."

Noah spun, every muscle in his body tensing, his knife coming up in an instinctive arc.

Elise was standing not three feet from him, her eyes flitting over his knife briefly before coming back to his face. "That knife will be useless if they have pistols."

She was indeed dressed again in her shirt and trousers, a faded and worn blue coat of some military origin buttoned up over her torso. Her hair was pulled back tightly from her face and covered entirely by a battered cap. There was a collection of pouches strapped to her waist and across her chest, and her rifle was cradled in the crook of her arm. Had he not heard her speak, he would have dismissed her as a young soldier. He barely recognized her. And she looked nothing like the woman who had been bent over a milk bucket this morning. A woman who had looked at him with desire and then kissed him senseless in the middle of a lane. This Elise looked hard and remote and...dangerous.

"Where the hell did you come from?" he demanded, if only to cover the sound of his heart pounding in his ears.

Elise glanced pointedly up at the limbs of a massive oak above them.

Noah forced himself to take a deep breath and impaled her with a stare. "And just what the hell did you think you were doing?" he growled through clenched teeth. "Swinging through the trees trying to find your inner Robin Hood?"

Elise gestured to the forest around them. "Reconnaissance."

"You can't be serious." He forced his eyes to remain on her and not dart away to examine his surroundings. He would not acknowledge the absurdity of such a notion. He could not—*would* not buy whatever blarney she was still trying to sell.

Elise only gazed at him, her hazel eyes like darkened caramel in the shadows of the forest. "I could have slit your throat. Or shot you. You need to be more careful."

Noah let his irritation show. "First, I'm not sure why I need to say this again, but I am perfectly capable of looking after myself. Second, you need to stop suggesting otherwise. Not only is it alarming my housekeeper, your continued suggestions that I am helpless are damn insulting. Any other man might demand pistols at dawn."

"And any other man would lose." The rifle remained steady in her hands. "And I never said you were helpless."

"Are you always this arrogant?"

"I prefer *proficient*. And for the record, duels are asinine. There are always witnesses, the terrain and conditions are not always optimal, and most dueling pistols are unreliable. Both in accuracy and performance. There are much better ways to deal with such situations. I can offer a selection of other options if you find yourself in such circumstances in the future." The last was delivered with such cool detachment that a small shiver chased itself down Noah's spine.

"What, like knives and chains?" he asked carelessly, trying to mask his sudden disquiet. He didn't want to imagine what "other options" might entail, nor did he want to acknowledge that a future with both of them in it existed.

"Not quite what I had in mind." She assessed him for a long moment. "You're familiar with street fighting." It was a statement more than a question. Her eyes flickered over the knife in his hand again. "You are most comfortable with a blade in close quarters. And I suspect you are very…proficient." Again a statement, and this one seemed to please her.

Noah opened his mouth to answer but discovered he couldn't find anything to say. There was nothing pleasing about the memory of the acid taste of fear in his mouth, the burn of blood on his hands and arms, the metallic scent of death. There was nothing pleasing about his proficiency with a knife. There was nothing pleasing about killing. Even if it meant that you got to live.

Noah felt his jaw clench. "We're not having this discussion." He sheathed his knife deliberately and turned on his heel, heading back along the path toward the house and weaving his way through the thick foliage. "And another thing," he tossed back over his shoulder, trying to affect a sangfroid he didn't feel, "I want you to stay out of my kitchen." He shoved a branch out of his way and waited for the rebuttal that was sure to come.

Except it never came. Instead all he heard behind him was the chattering of a squirrel and the trilling call of an unseen bird. He stopped and turned but saw…nothing. It was as if Elise had vanished into thin air. He glanced up at the branches over his head, but nothing moved save the occasional leaf.

"Elise?" he said into the space around him, feeling foolish and not a little unnerved.

"I'll stay out of your kitchen if you stay out of this forest. It's unsafe. At least for now."

Noah nearly came out of his skin. He whirled and found Elise standing on the path, only somehow she'd gotten ahead of him. "Bloody hell," he swore, "stop sneaking up on me like that." She was like a damn phantom in this damn forest.

"Better me than someone else. I'm trying to ensure that, when you return to London, it is not in a pine box. You are of no use to me or your sister in a pine box."

Noah threw up his hands.

"Your cousin has hired—"

"My cousin wouldn't know how to hire a footman, much less an *assassin*," Noah snapped at her.

"And how do you know that? When was the last time you spoke with your cousin?" Elise gazed at him impassively. "Was that before or after he grew up and gambled away whatever money he had? Was that before or after he found himself in debt to a number of men who are long on memory and short on patience?"

That Francis would have lost money gambling wasn't surprising. He had never been overly clever as a boy. Though he'd made up for that with sheer meanness. He'd been the type that had taken pleasure in pulling the wings off butterflies and poking the eyes from frogs. But to go to the lengths that she was suggesting...Noah scowled. "That is not the point. Francis was always cruel but—"

"But now he is no longer a child. Now he is desperate. And desperate men are dangerous men."

"Tell me exactly how you came to be in possession of such information. That Francis Ellery hired men to assassinate me."

Elise's face shuttered. "That doesn't matter—"

Noah barked a rude laugh. "I thought so."

"Are you insinuating I'm making this up?" Elise asked, color staining her cheeks.

"Have you met these men?" he asked.

"Who?"

"These so-called assassins who are hot on my trail?"

Elise's mouth tightened. "No."

"Know their names? How much they were paid?"

"No, but—"

"But nothing. You have nothing."

Her beautiful eyes narrowed into slits. "I have far from nothing. I have the Duke of Ashland standing in front of me—"

"I. Don't. Want. The. Title." He bit off each word.

"I don't really care if you aspire to be a pauper or the bloody king of England when it comes down to it, *Your Grace*." There was a razor edge to her voice that was not lost on him. "But I do care if you get your fool self killed because of it. And I care that you have a sister and a mother who need your help. My job is to make sure they get it one way or another."

The guilt that had been simmering for too long, stirred by dark memories of fear and death, bubbled over, turning into anger. "If I thought Abigail was in any sort of danger, there is no force on this earth that could stop me from getting to her. But she's not."

"The same cannot be said for your mother."

Noah turned away, every muscle in his body tense, an icy cold settling through his bones. It was wrong, he knew, to feel so much hatred and resentment toward someone after so long. A better man would have forgiven his mother for her betrayal and abandonment. A better man would have forgiven or, at the very least, tried to forget the consequences of that abandonment. But he had been unable to do either. He was not a better man. "That is not my affair," he hissed.

"You are not a man who allows others to suffer." Elise's voice had risen.

Noah's head jerked around. "You don't know me, Miss DeVries. You have no idea what I would or would not do."

"I know—"

"You...nothing...you know nothing." His blood was surging through him, emotion making it difficult to think, difficult to breathe.

"I know enough to know you would not leave your mother in Bedlam."

"That's where she left me when I was ten!"

A silence fell hard on the end of those words. A silence that breathed with the forest around him, echoed in the canopy of silvered leaves overhead.

At his sides Noah's hands were clenched into fists, yet the regret he had expected to follow that confession did not come. In fact there was an immeasurable, if inexplicable, sense of relief. His admission, his release of that secret to this woman had been reckless and rash and utterly unfathomable. He could not begin to explain why he had told Elise DeVries something that not even John Barr knew. Perhaps because she already held so many of his secrets. Perhaps the admission was like a crack in a dam where a steady trickle of truth had eroded the edges until veracity burst through all the lies and secrets, leaving him exposed. Perhaps it was an unacknowledged need to have another soul on this earth to whom he might reveal his true self.

But whatever the reason, standing here, with only the trees to witness his folly, Noah wasn't sorry.

Presently he became aware that Elise hadn't spoken. He met her eyes, only to find them watching him, betraying no emotion. No horror, no disgust, and, most telling, no surprise.

"You already knew that." His words were barely a whisper.

She tipped her head as if considering her answer. "Yes. I think I did."

"I...you..." Noah had no idea what to say to that. "You think? Did Abigail tell you that?" he managed.

"Abigail doesn't know."

"Thank God," he mumbled.

"No one knows where you disappeared to. Only that you vanished as a child and, until very recently, were presumed dead."

"I almost died in that place," he said, feeling a little numb. "A number of times." And there had been even more times he'd wished for death. Prayed for it. Begged for it.

Elise set her rifle down and leaned it against a tree. She stepped closer, so that she was directly in front of him. She put a hand on his chest, directly over his heart, where it beat steadily. "But you're not."

Noah dropped his head. "I'm not dead? Or I'm not a lunatic?"

"Well, the former is rather obvious. As for the latter... are you?"

"Am I what?"

"A lunatic?"

"No," he spluttered.

"Good. I'm so very glad we got that sorted out." Elise

sounded as if she was smiling, but he was a little afraid to look at her.

It was exactly what she'd done on the road when he'd blurted out his first confession. His admission that he got his words mixed up. Somehow she'd reduced it from something looming and horrific to something...less. Something that simply was. A part of his past, a part of him that deserved no more or less attention than any other part.

She raised her other hand and placed it against his chest. He could feel the heat from her touch permeate the cold that had settled into his bones earlier. It was everything he could do not to simply draw her into his arms and bury his head in the softness of her neck and let her strength chase away all his ghosts.

And on the heels of that came a wash of embarrassment. When had he become so maudlin? So weak? Since when did he need a woman to find courage and to stand firm? And a woman who had her own agenda at that? "I don't want your pity," he mumbled, trying to reassert whatever dignity he still had left. There could not be a repeat performance of the debacle in the lane this morning, when he had allowed the base demands of his body to obliterate all his resolutions and intentions and good sense.

"No, I never expected you would," she replied. Her hands suddenly slid up and caught his face when he would have pulled away.

He froze before raising his eyes to hers. She was gazing at him in that level, intense way she had, as if she were peering past his exterior and reading his soul.

"You have the corner on my aggravation and frustration at the moment, if I'm being honest," she said, though she said it with a small smile. "Though that is simply because you're making my job somewhat arduous and we are not yet on the road to London." She paused. "But you will never have my pity. A survivor is not a man to be pitied. He is a man to be respected."

Something in Noah's chest lurched. With sudden clarity he realized he wanted this woman's respect with a force that he wasn't prepared for. It was one thing to know that she desired him on a physical level. It was something deeper, something so much more significant, to know he held her regard.

"I can't go back to London," he said, needing her to understand more than he had ever needed anything.

She didn't argue or remind him about Abigail or his title or any of the things she'd presented to him already. "Why?" Her hands still rested against the sides of his face.

"I...killed."

"Ah." She didn't flinch or recoil. There was no gasp of dismay, no shadow of trepidation. Though by now Noah should have known better. "Tell me," was all she said.

He stepped away from her then, afraid that, if he remained where he was, he would give in to the urge to simply kiss her and use that as an excuse to stay this conversation.

"I was in Bedlam for five years," he said, trying to keep the facts separate from the emotion that was twisted through them. "From the time I was ten until I was fifteen." He pulled a leaf off a bush and traced the tiny lines on its emerald surface with his fingers. "My father told the men who came for me that I was the gardener's son, and I was committed under a false name. Presumably to spare the dignity of our family until such time that my faculties of speech could be fully restored."

"What happened when you were fifteen?" Elise asked, and he was reminded of just how perceptive she was.

"We escaped."

"We?"

Noah forced himself to speak evenly. "A boy, Joshua, the same age as me, who was committed before I arrived. Often, throughout the years, they would keep us chained together. Part of our individual recoveries, we were assured by the mad-doctors and the keepers, though Joshua had no trouble with speech. The night we escaped, we were such—chained together. One of the keepers on our ward had taken a fancy to Joshua. Abused him often in a manner I will not detail further. Fully intended to do the same on this particular night, regardless of the fact that we were shackled together. *Because* we were shackled together. The man told me to watch. He told me I might learn something before it was my turn. He never got the chance." Noah realized he had shredded the leaf in his hands and he let the pieces fall, watching them flutter over the toes of his boots. "Along with the keys, the bastard carried a knife at his belt. I waited until he was…distracted. And then I was quicker than he." He dropped his head. "And I can't be sorry for it. I'd do it again."

Elise was watching him silently, her eyes shadowed by her cap and completely unreadable.

"There were others. After I escaped. I lived on the streets of London for three years, and there were those who would have seen me gutted if only for the clothes on my back." He dropped his head. "I was quicker than they as well."

A quiet settled and stretched on, the wind whistling through the braches overhead before subsiding again. A raven cawed loudly before it too fell silent.

"I am no use to Abigail if I am arrested for murder upon my return," Noah said, if only to break the stillness.

Elise tipped her head but still remained mute.

"Say something," Noah demanded.

"Why are you glad that Abigail is ignorant of what happened to you as a child?"

"What?" That wasn't what he had been expecting. He'd been expecting platitudes, reassurances that he'd done what was necessary, appeals to ignore any lingering guilt. All things that Joshua had continually intoned in the months after their escape.

"Do you not think Abigail is strong enough to handle the truth?"

Noah blinked. "My sister is one of the strongest people I know."

"Then why keep her in ignorance?"

"Because I do not wish her to know what I did. What I became." That sort of darkness was his burden, not hers.

"What you became," Elise said, "is the man you were always meant to be. Every tragedy, every joy, every achievement and every failure has made you the man who stands before me now. You can't hide from him forever."

"I..." Noah trailed off helplessly.

"This is why you haven't seen or spoken to your sister? Why you've hidden on a farm in Nottingham?"

"Yes."

Elise shook her head before looking up at him intently. "Your parents abandoned the Duke of Ashland when he was ten years old, because they incorrectly believed him to be incapable. Incapable of one day embracing the power and wealth and responsibilities and all the good that might come of those things when that child grew into a man. Do not allow Noah Lawson to do the same. Come with me to London. Your sister deserves to know the man you've become."

"Did you not hear me?" Noah finally found his voice. "I'll be arrested." He hated how defensive he sounded.

"You will not be arrested. Thanks to your parents' vanity, or desperation, or both, Noah Ellery did not exist in Bedlam. Further, the old building and most of its records no longer exist. If you desire to return to London as the Duke of Ashland, I can provide you with a fully plausible explanation for your lengthy absence, complete with any required paperwork and evidence."

Noah stared at her.

"Chegarre and Associates is a firm with far-reaching resources, Your Grace," Elise told him. "I would suggest that you use them."

Noah's fingers curled into fists, a faint sense of unreality encroaching on this entire conversation. "Has nothing I've told you disturbed you?" he asked roughly. "Does the fact that I am a killer not give you pause?"

For the first time, Elise looked away, her composure slipping ever so slightly, a shadow of what looked like grief passing over her features. "No."

"How can you say that?"

"Because I understand that what you had to do is not who you are."

She was standing stiffly, and with a dawning comprehension, Noah realized that the soldier's clothing was not a disguise. The rifle she carried was not a theater prop. No more than the haunted look that had crossed her face was fabricated. This soldier standing before him was part of who she was. "You know what it's like. To kill."

"Yes." It was barely audible.

"You were a rifleman." It wasn't unheard of. Noah had heard tales from Waterloo of women who had followed their men into battle and fought at their side. He couldn't imagine that the colonial armies were any different.

"No. I was a tracker, meant to locate American troops and guns and report their movements and numbers." She was studying the forest, and Noah recalled exactly how easily she had vanished through such terrain. "I too did whatever was necessary so that I might live to see the next sunrise."

She was paler than he had ever seen her, her eyes fixed inwardly on something that only she could see. But in her voice he could hear the same note of despair and desolation that was so familiar to him. She understood what it was like to be forced into situations where there were only two outcomes. Kill or be killed.

Noah moved then, coming to stand before her, his fingers cupping her jaw, and without thinking about what he was doing, he kissed her.

It was a brief, gentle kiss, one that simply offered the things that she had already offered him. Understanding. Strength. Compassion. He felt some of the stiffness drain from her body, and he dropped his hands, gathering her close to him. She let herself be drawn into his embrace.

"Why did you do that?" she asked.

"Because you were looking back," he whispered, resting his forehead against hers.

"You sound like my brother."

"Smart man."

"He has his moments." They were silent for a long minute.

"Why did you fight?" Noah asked into the silence.

"Why are you in Nottingham?" She answered his question with her own.

"Because I couldn't leave Abigail. I needed to know she was safe."

Elise pulled away from him then. "And I couldn't—wouldn't leave my brothers. They were my entire world." Elise ran her fingers down the barrel of the rifle that still rested against a tree trunk. "This Baker rifle belonged to Jonathon. My oldest brother. But I was always better with it than he." She smiled sadly. "Our venison stores for winter made it hard for him to argue the fact, though it didn't stop him from trying."

"You miss him."

"Every day." She raised her eyes to his. "Like you miss your sister. But unlike my brother, Abigail is still here to see. To touch, to talk to—" Elise stopped abruptly, her entire body stilling.

Noah frowned, before he became aware of the sound of Square barking in the distance.

"Does your dog usually bark like that?" Elise asked, picking up her rifle.

"When we've visitors." Noah didn't like the unease that rooted within him. Bloody hell, but Elise had him jumping at shadows.

Elise was already moving, slipping through the trees and the thick foliage. Noah followed, nearly crashing into Elise's back as she stopped abruptly near the edge of the wood. He peered over her shoulder, feeling ridiculous, and even more so when a wagon pulled up in front of his house and Sarah was helped down by her husband. At their feet Square bounced happily and was rewarded with a rub from John.

"It's John and Sarah, for God's sake," Noah grumbled. He watched as Sarah carefully lifted a bundle of green fabric out of the back of the wagon and headed toward the house, raising a hand in greeting as Mrs. Pritchard opened the front door.

"Sarah looks pretty," Elise commented by his side.

For the first time, Noah noticed that Sarah was indeed dressed up, in a gown of pale blue. Beside her John had on neat breeches and a coat Noah had never seen before. They looked as if they were going to—

"Bloody hell." Noah ran a hand through his hair.

"What's wrong?" Elise turned to look at him in concern.

"They're here to pick us up. For the picnic."

Elise blinked at him.

"The one they invited you to after you plucked Andrew out of the river. The one you agreed to attend as their guest of honor."

"Ah." She closed her eyes briefly. "I had forgotten."

"Will you come?"

She hesitated. "Is it necessary for you to attend this picnic?"

"Why wouldn't I?"

"Attending will leave you exposed. There will be crowds."

Noah marshaled his patience. "The crowds that you mention are made up of neighbors. Friends. People who know me. Though I can make excuses on your behalf."

"Absolutely not. If you are going, then I must as well."

"You *must*?" Noah raised his brows.

"Yes."

"As what? My bodyguard?"

"If you insist on calling it that."

"For the love of—" Noah ran his hands through his hair. "We've been over this. Even if I believed that there were assassins on my trail, I do not need you hovering over me."

"I won't hover. In fact, you won't even know I'm there. I'll channel my inner Robin Hood."

"That's absurd. I know these people. There will be no *assassins* at the picnic." He let sarcasm creep into the last.

Elise shrugged. "I'm not leaving you alone."

He tried to be irritated, but something in the way she said it made him feel warm inside. It made him want to kiss her all over again. He cleared his throat. "Fine. Then you will attend the picnic with me like a regular human being. You will not hover. You will be a gracious guest of Sarah Barr's. And you will not bring your rifle."

"Yes to the first three. But I'm bringing my rifle." Her jaw was set.

"Tell me you're jesting."

"Does it look like I am? I need to be sure I can keep you safe."

"So what? You're going to walk around with a loaded rifle and point it at everyone until I give you some sort of secret signal that they are a friend?"

Elise flushed. "If I have to."

"You do not need a damn rifle at a damn picnic."

"Fine. I'll leave it hidden in the wagon if that sounds better."

"No, it doesn't sound better. It still sounds crazy." He laughed without humor. "And I would know, wouldn't I?"

Elise's lips thinned, and she looked away. "I don't like fighting you," she said suddenly. "I wish you would trust me."

"Trust you?" Noah felt his forehead wrinkle. "You are the warden to my darkest secrets. You know more about my past than any other person. I have no choice but to trust you."

Elise shook her head and met his eyes again. "You've confided in me, and for that I am grateful. Honored. And there will never come a time when I betray that confidence. But trust is very much a choice. And if you truly trusted me, we would not be having this argument."

It was Noah's turn to look away.

"You're wanted, Noah. Needed. Loved. Not just for what you have the potential to do, but simply because of who you are." The steel was back in Elise's voice. "Your sister believes in you. She always has, and I think you know that."

Noah didn't give a damn about Francis Ellery or his debts or whatever designs he had on the Ashland fortune, though it angered him that he had drawn Abigail into his greed-driven machinations. But Elise was partly right. For the first time, Abigail needed her brother more than he had ever needed her. At the very least, she needed to know she wasn't alone. And as for his mother...Noah closed his eyes. Every time he tried to find the forgiveness he knew he should possess, all he could see in his mind's eye was the curtain at the window dropping as she turned away from a terrified child.

He suddenly felt the brush of Elise's lips over his and his eyes snapped open. "Don't look back, Noah Ellery. Because I believe in you too. And when you understand that, then you'll trust me."

Noah stared at her, a tiny ember of impossible hope igniting and struggling to cast light into the dark pit that was his past.

Chapter 10

Elise gazed at herself in the long cheval glass, not knowing whether to be dismayed or pleased.

"The color suits you." Behind her, Sarah beamed. "You look beautiful."

She did look lovely, Elise admitted without conceit, considering her reflection with the same objectivity she applied backstage at the theater when evaluating a costume. The dress Sarah had presented her with was not elaborate, suitable for a country picnic, but all the more striking for its simple lines. It fit her almost perfectly, save that the bodice was a little tight, but the skirts flowed softly over her hips and swirled around her ankles. It was lawn green, and against her skin and her brown hair, the hue was flattering. A band of white embroidery in a whimsical pattern edged the bodice and the hem, and the whole effect was, indeed, beautiful.

But beautiful was noticeable. Elise did not want to be

noticeable. She bit her lip. Her brown dress would be far better. No one remembered a woman in a mousy brown dress who, with enough skill, could simply fade into the background and remain invisible for as long as required.

"The dress is gorgeous," Elise said, framing a suitable excuse in her mind. "But I can't borrow such finery—"

"It's yours." Sarah smiled at her.

"I beg your pardon?"

"The dress. It's a gift. I know I can never repay the debt our family owes you, but please accept this as a token."

Well, hell. There was no way to duck out of this one without being grossly insulting or just plain rude, and Elise had no desire to be either. "Then thank you," she said, meeting Sarah's eyes. "It is my privilege to accept it." She ran her hands over her dress.

"Mr. Lawson will have a heart seizure when he sees you," Sarah said, sounding infinitely smug and satisfied at once.

Elise ignored the way her stomach flip-flopped and the sudden self-consciousness that assailed her. "I hardly think my appearance will affect anyone's health one way or the other," she muttered.

Sarah made a noise of disbelief. "Any red-blooded male will—"

"Will there be many people there?" Elise asked, not wishing to continue along a vein of conversation for which she had a dearth of clever answers. And, she reasoned, if she would not be able to remain wholly unnoticed, then at least she could educate herself on what to expect.

"It is always well attended," Sarah told her, slanting Elise a look to let her know she'd fooled no one. "Everyone from the area is invited. Landowners, tradesmen, merchants. The local gentry often stop by, though they tend to simply parade about in an effort to remind everyone why they should be admired. There are games before supper; a shooting contest for the men, croquet for the women. And after, there is music and dancing." Sarah grinned at her. "Even if Mr. Lawson tries to hoard you all to himself, I'll make sure to introduce you to some people I think you'd really like."

"Sounds delightful." It did sound like fun, Elise reflected. It sounded a great deal like the harvest dances that they'd had in York when friends and family would gather to let loose and enjoy an evening of revelry before the cold came and winter set in. Except she wasn't here to have fun. She wasn't here to dance. And she certainly wasn't here to make friends.

The last left her strangely sad.

"Here." Sarah was reaching into a small bag that rested on the bed. "Your outfit is not yet complete. John made this for you."

Elise shook her head. "No, please. I don't need anything else—" The words died as Sarah ignored her and bent slightly, fastening something to the front of her bodice.

The woman stepped away, and Elise gazed down at the brooch that now rested against her chest. It was done in fine steel, similar to the rose Noah had given to Abigail, except this one was the silhouette of a tree. Twisted strands of steel were bound together to form a trunk before they spread out, each delicate branch interlocking with another.

Sarah met Elise's eyes in the mirror. "It is an oak, meant to symbolize strength and family. The courage and strength you gave so selflessly to our family will never be forgotten."

Elise reached up to touch the brooch. "Thank you," was all she managed through a throat that had gotten suspiciously tight.

"You will be a part of our family forever," Sarah said. "Even if your travels take you far away."

Elise tightened her fingers over the brooch just as Sarah put her arms around her and gave her a gentle hug. How had this happened, this enfolding into the lives of people she had never intended to know? Since she had arrived in England, Elise had always been content to dwell around the edges of relationships, either intimate or otherwise. Mostly due to the fact that she was almost always in character, and each association, however enjoyable it might be, was fleeting. Because eventually she would need to become someone else.

Until now. Now there was a part of her that wished for something...less calculated. Less simulated. Something more real. Perhaps it was her rural surroundings that brought back this desire to belong. Perhaps it was the realization that there were, indeed, places left to her where people required nothing more from her than...herself.

Noah, freshly scrubbed and changed, was leaning against the wagon, deep in conversation with John, when the women emerged from the house. He looked up and caught sight of Elise, and his conversation ended abruptly mid-sentence. John too fell silent, his eyes widening slightly in his broad face.

For all the time she had spent on the stage, for all the provocative roles she had played in her tenure at Chegarre & Associates, she should be inured to the attentions of any man. But she felt the weight of Noah's gaze all the way through her body and down to the very tips of her toes. It made her feel flushed and restless and shy all at once.

"Doesn't Miss DeVries look lovely?" Sarah said from beside her, giving her husband a meaningful look.

John straightened and cleared his throat. "You do look exceptionally lovely tonight, Miss DeVries," he said, immediately going to his wife's side. "Almost as lovely as my Sarah."

Sarah swatted at John's arm but she was smiling as she did so.

"I'm biased." John grinned at her.

"Mr. Lawson?" Sarah prodded.

"Yes," Noah whispered hoarsely. "Lovely." His eyes were still on Elise, an intense stare that was doing nothing to put her at ease. He covered the distance between them, gathering Elise's hand in his and pressing his lips to the backs of her knuckles. His eyes never left hers as he released her hand, though she could still feel the dizzying sensation of his lips on her skin. His eyes dropped, and his hand went to the brooch pinned in the center of her bodice. Very gently he traced the edges of the steel, the backs of his fingers grazing the slopes of her breasts. Elise sucked in a breath, her nipples tightening instantly, and resisted the urge to arch against that tantalizing touch. John and Sarah still stood not four feet away.

"The brooch is stunning, Mr. Barr," Elise said, trying desperately to keep her words even. "I will treasure it always."

"You're very welcome," John told her, though it seemed

as if his words were coming from a distance, because all she could concentrate on was the feel of Noah's touch.

"Truly beautiful," Noah said then, though Elise had no idea if he was speaking of the brooch. She had a brief vision of him pushing the edges of her bodice aside and replacing his fingers with his lips, and heat streaked through her.

"It represents her courage and her strength," Sarah supplied.

"It's perfect," Noah said, his hand dropping from the brooch to skim her waist before it fell to his side. Elise released a breath she hadn't realized she'd been holding, and the world came back into focus.

John and Sarah moved away, John helping his wife up onto the front seat. Noah led Elise closer to the rear, where a second bench seat spanned the width of the wagon. She chanced a look at him and swallowed. His eyes were hot, his jaw tight, and he looked as if he wanted to devour her.

"Do I have a piece of river weed in my hair?" she whispered close to his ear, trying desperately for a light tone.

He started. "What?"

"Or in my teeth?"

Noah blinked.

"You're staring."

Noah laughed and ducked his head. "You're stealing my lines."

"Yes."

"You're magnificent," he said, the laughter fading as his eyes dropped to her mouth and Elise took a hasty step back. If she didn't put some distance between them, she would give him exactly what he wanted regardless of where they might be standing because, God help her, she wanted it too.

It had been easier earlier when he'd been immersed in his memories, the old remnants of fear and anger enough to suppress the heat that seemed to flare every time they drew near each other. In that forest his touch had been one of gentle understanding, offered in support, not desire. A shared acknowledgment of things that had come to pass and had made both who they were.

Elise had been horrified at Noah's confession, unable to imagine what it would be like for a child to endure what he had. She'd been furious on his behalf that it had been allowed to happen. Though she could admit to none of those things. Demonstrate none of those emotions. Noah had been right. He didn't need her pity. He didn't need her outrage, her horror, or her anger. Those were all emotions that amplified the destructive power of secrets like those that Noah had entrusted to her care. Secrets like those had to be handled carefully.

Elise straightened her skirts, which didn't need straightening, unable to meet Noah's eyes at the moment. She fumbled for something benign to say. "You look very handsome yourself." Dear God. She sounded like a stammering debutante. She, who had cleverly conversed with princes and generals and governors when circumstances required. And she had been good at it. But then again, she hadn't been violently attracted to any of them.

Noah extended his hand, and after a second's hesitation, she placed hers in it. He squeezed it, a slight pressure that nonetheless sent new sparks shooting across her skin.

"I put your rifle in the back," he said quietly. "It's under the bench."

Elise stilled. "Thank you," she whispered.

"It seemed easier than arguing with you about it in front of John and Sarah." His voice was gruff.

She slanted him a look. It wasn't exactly a victory, but she would take it. "Of course. How thoughtful."

"Yes, well." He cleared his throat. "Come. Your chariot awaits, milady."

Elise glanced at the back of the wagon and the wooden bench seat.

"I regret it's not a carriage," Noah said.

She looked down at her hand still clasped within his. At this moment there wasn't anywhere else she'd rather be. "I don't."

◦────◦

I regret it's not a carriage.

Noah had made the remark flippantly, his mind addled by the vision that was Elise DeVries. But now Noah wondered if it might be worth embracing his title if only to have a fleet of carriages at his disposal. Enclosed, private travel spaces where he might draw the curtains and then draw Elise onto his lap and have his way with her.

The tough soldier who had listened to him with a steady and unflinching heart that emotionally charged afternoon had been replaced with an ethereal princess. The transformation was as unnerving as it was breathtaking. Elise was every inch a woman, and it was an effort not to let his hands run over her beautiful curves, displayed to perfection in that green dress. Her hair had been pinned up in some fashion, though long tendrils had escaped to caress the gentle slope of her neck and frame her face. It required all his concentration not to bury his fingers in her hair so that he might taste her lips and her skin. He'd sat ramrod stiff beside her on that damned wagon bench, a bench not wide enough to afford them separate spaces. Every bump, every lurch of the wagon had nudged them together, thigh against thigh, hip against hip. At one point Noah had put a hand at her back to steady them over a deep rut in the road. He'd felt her shiver in the summer heat and he'd withdrawn his hand, afraid her reaction would make him forget that they weren't alone. Given the time and place, this temptation that was Elise wasn't fair.

And then, when they'd arrived, he'd regretted even more the lack of a private carriage where he might simply keep Elise hidden away and all to himself.

As the Barrs' wagon had joined other similar equipages, there'd been shouts of welcome over the sounds of a pipe and fiddle already pulsing through the air. They'd joined the jovial crowd, making their way through knots of people, Sarah's arm linked securely through Elise's as Sarah embarked on a series of exhausting introductions.

Elise was a picture of relaxed politesse, but she turned back often, as if to make sure Noah was still there. He trailed behind and watched as the women turned curious but friendly smiles on Elise. The older men doffed their hats with a flourish and a twinkle in their eye, and the younger men stammered like fools as they tripped over themselves in their introductions.

Noah had forced himself to relax his jaw, aware he was gritting his teeth.

"I see you're still bewitched." John appeared suddenly by his side and thrust a cup of ale into Noah's hand.

"I am not bewitched." Noah watched as a man in a dark

coat bent over Elise's hand and was rewarded with a pretty smile.

"You look ready to strangle Stuart Howards." John gestured to the dark-coated man, who was now waving his hands expansively and telling some sort of tale with great animation, much to Elise and Sarah's amusement.

"I have no interest in strangling anyone," Noah replied testily. "Miss DeVries is very . . . amiable."

"Amiable? You're full of it, Noah Lawson."

"I beg your pardon?"

"You're bewitched, and so is she." John laughed, a deep rumbling sound. "I may be older than you, but I'm not blind. Or stupid. The two of you nearly incinerated the back of my wagon with the looks you were giving each other."

Noah felt himself flush. "It's complicated." He took a deep swallow of ale.

Beside him John snorted. "As a man with six children, I can, with good authority, say that it's not."

Noah choked, and John cheerfully pounded him on the back. "I heard she made blackberry jam after she milked your cows this morning," his friend said. "She saved my son and my wife rather adores her. And she makes you smile. Forget whatever I said about being cautious. You might want to think about keeping her." John thumped Noah on the back one more time before heading off.

When Noah caught his breath, he looked again for Elise, but she was gone from where he'd last seen her. A flash of green coupled with blue caught his eye, and he saw that Elise and Sarah had wandered close to the edge of a field, to an area surrounded by a low stone fence and dotted with wooden targets. A handful of men stood casually in conversation under the shade of an open-sided tent, and a collection of firearms leaned against the fence. He could see Sarah gesturing to the field, no doubt explaining to Elise the rules of the shooting contest that would start shortly. Elise was listening with half an ear, her eyes scanning the edges of the pasture before perusing the knots of people standing nearest to them.

Her casual mien had slipped a little, and she looked wary and watchful now.

Noah shook his head and made his way over to the women.

"Mr. Lawson." Sarah greeted him happily as he approached. "I was wondering where you'd gotten to."

"Your husband led me astray," he said lightly, gesturing to the ale in his hand.

"That didn't take long," Sarah said wryly. She glanced past Noah's shoulder and suddenly waved at someone. "Excuse me for just a moment," she said before slipping past him.

"Would you like a drink?" Noah asked Elise, who was still watching their surroundings as though she expected a horde of Huns to pop out from the trees.

"No, thank you," Elise murmured.

"Let me rephrase." Noah held out his cup to her. "Please have a drink."

Her eyes came back to him. "No, thank you. I need to keep my wits sharp."

"You need to relax."

"I can't. There are a lot of people here."

"Yes, and they all belong here." He held her gaze. "My life is not in danger." He felt foolish saying that, surrounded as he was by people he had known for a decade.

Elise's posture eased slightly. "You will tell me if anything changes?"

"Tell you if what changes?" Sarah was back, slightly breathless.

"Tell her if I change my mind about participating in the shooting contest," Noah said smoothly.

"You're not going to compete?" Sarah asked.

Noah eyed the field. "I haven't decided."

"Well, you should." Sarah turned to Elise. "Mr. Lawson won the shooting contest last year, you know," she told her.

"You won last year?" Elise's eyes bored into him. "You never mentioned you were . . . proficient with firearms."

He met her eyes. "You never asked."

"Touché." He thought he saw Elise's lips twitch. "Just how proficient are you?"

"Oh, I do all right."

"He beat thirty other contestants," Sarah offered.

A dark brow went up. "Thirty?"

"Half of whom were in their cups, I'm sure," he told her.

"*Pfft.*" Sarah made a noise of disbelief. "No one was in their cups, and you well know it, Mr. Lawson." She poked him in the chest. "I can't think of anyone who would participate in anything that involved firearms and vast quantities of alcohol. It's why they have shooting first and croquet second. Because unlike shooting, croquet is much improved by vast quantities of alcohol."

Elise laughed at that, and Noah found himself laughing with her. "Agreed," he said.

Her posture had eased, Noah saw. In fact Elise was smiling wickedly now as she walked over to the guns that were leaning against the stone fence. She selected a long smoothbore military musket, running her hand over its iron barrel. "If you're not going to compete, would you care to give a demonstration of your proficiency, Mr. Lawson?" she asked.

Noah set his ale on the top of the fence and stepped forward, feeling lighter than he had in a long time, and not a little reckless. "What's in it for me?"

"The preservation of your pride, for one." Elise said, examining the gun with a critical eye.

"I'm not worried about my pride."

"Says the man who hasn't had the privilege yet of losing to a girl." She advanced toward him, stopping only a breath away.

"Is that a challenge, Miss DeVries?"

Elise smirked and tipped her head. "Yes."

Noah felt a thrill of anticipation, and something else entirely, race through his veins. "Then I accept."

"What are the stakes?" she asked. "Besides your pride, that is."

"You seem certain I will lose."

"You will."

Behind Elise, Sarah was listening to their exchange with wide eyes and a great deal of interest. "You think you could beat Mr. Lawson in a shooting contest?"

"She might." Noah grinned, loving the way Elise grinned back. "She's very fond of firearms. And I've been advised she's very, very good."

Sarah's brows shot to her hairline, even as she joined Elise with a delighted smile. "Then by all means, Miss DeVries, I think you should show Mr. Lawson a thing or two about—"

"Mr. Lawson!" The address rang over whatever Sarah had been about to say next. "Mr. Lawson!"

Noah turned to find a woman riding toward them on a fine grey horse, scattering people standing in her way like water in front of a ship's bow. He groaned silently.

"Oh saints preserve us," Sarah muttered under her breath, echoing his thoughts. "It's Her Majesty come to torment the serfs."

⸻

The woman on the grey mare was young, probably no more than twenty, dressed in an elaborate riding habit. Her blond hair was glossy and tucked stylishly beneath a brimmed hat that shaded her flawless, milky complexion. The groom who had been traveling with her dropped back at the careless wave of her hand, and she reined her mare to a stop just in front of them.

"Mr. Lawson," the woman said, a soft breathlessness to her voice, "I am so relieved to see you hale." Her eyes traveled over Noah from head to foot as though she were evaluating a prize bull brought to market.

"Miss Silver"—Noah straightened—"a pleasure to see you." The way he was holding himself told Elise it was anything but.

"Of course," the woman said, her eyes skipping to Elise.

"Miss Silver, may I introduce Miss DeVries." Noah's introduction sounded stiff.

"Indeed." Miss Silver's eyes were now busy evaluating Elise's gown, her hair. Her lip curled slightly as she eyed the long gun Elise still held in her hand. "I heard you saved a child from drowning, Mr. Lawson. And I just had to see for myself that you were fine. I was overset with worry."

I just had to see for myself. Elise bit back an amused snort, knowing the woman's interest had nothing to do with Noah's health and everything to do with rumors of a lass.

"It wasn't me."

"Hmmm?" Miss Silver was still examining Elise.

"Wasn't me," Noah repeated patiently.

"Do speak up, Mr. Lawson. I can barely hear you." The woman's crop tapped impatiently on the edge of her sidesaddle, and her mare shifted nervously, only to be brought up short.

Manners were preventing Noah from addressing this woman the way she deserved to be addressed. Luckily, Elise suffered no such problems. "Mr. Lawson was trying to find a polite way to tell you that you are in error while sparing your pride, Miss Silver," she said.

"I beg your pardon?"

"I regret to tell you that you've been misinformed."

"Do you know who I am?" Miss Silver demanded, each syllable icy.

"Should I?" While Elise didn't know *who*, she certainly recognized *what*. Dismissive. Spoiled. Entitled. Inconsiderate. She had dealt with too many to count in her service to Chegarre & Associates, and they were all the same. And it was generally expedient to simply tell them what they wanted to hear and send them on their way.

"The Honorable Miss Silver is Baron Corley's daughter," Noah said, sounding weary.

"Yes, and you would do well to remember that," she snapped.

"How impressive," Elise murmured, making sure to put a believable amount of reverence into her words. "I've never met a baron's daughter before," she continued with perfect honesty. Her clientele tended to trend toward women addressed as "Your Grace."

Miss Silver preened slightly.

Noah slanted Elise an incredulous look. Belatedly she became aware that a number of men had gathered, presumably for the start of the shooting contest, and were listening to the conversation.

"It was Miss DeVries who saved the child from drowning," Noah interrupted, his voice tight, his patience clearly coming to an end. "Andrew Barr was extremely fortunate to have had someone of such capability and courage near at hand when he fell from that bridge."

"*Pshht.* Anyone could have saved that boy," Miss Silver pouted under her breath, seemingly taking a great deal of exception to Noah's referring to Elise as capable and courageous.

"No, they could not." Now Noah sounded thoroughly annoyed. "It took an extremely strong swimmer to preserve his life."

Miss Silver's face set mutinously. She stared at the rifle in Elise's hands, letting her contempt show. "And I suppose you think you can shoot as well as you can swim, Miss DeVries?"

"Better." It was Sarah who snapped out that answer, furiously indignant on Elise's behalf. "She can shoot better."

An interested hum went up from the crowd behind them, which had overheard the conversation, and Elise groaned to herself. The last thing she needed was a spectacle.

For the first time, Miss Silver seemed to become aware that she had an audience. She allowed a smug smile to creep across her face. "Ah, Mrs. Barr. You sound very confident. I didn't expect such from you. But as it happens, I am an excellent shot. A little hobby of mine, if you will. Perhaps, if the gentlemen allow us, we might discover just who is the most...accomplished." She aimed a self-satisfied, triumphant look in the direction of Noah.

Elise resisted the urge to snort. She had seen such posturing in Mayfair ballrooms, but never had she had the privilege of witnessing it in the middle of a fenced sheep pasture. "I don't think that there is any need to prove—"

"Of course you feel the need to refuse. I didn't imagine that you were actually as courageous as Mr. Lawson seemed to think you were." Miss Silver sniffed.

"*Merde*," Elise said under her breath. Had this chit just called her a coward? In front of a crowd of people? This bird-witted woman had just backed her into a very awkward corner.

Noah stepped forward, his posture rigid, his fists clenched at his sides. "Have a care with your words, Miss Silver."

Elise stared at Noah, startled. It didn't matter that Miss Silver and all her juvenile opinions didn't signify, or that Elise was perfectly capable of taking care of herself. Noah had still leaped to her defense. A warmth such as she had never known spread through her, suffusing the smallest corners of her heart. She wanted to touch him, slide her arms around him, and never let go.

Miss Silver had recoiled, her eyes narrowing spitefully. "Have a care with *your* tone, Mr. Lawson," she sniped back. "Do not forget that you are addressing your better. I am the daughter of a baron, and you are...*nothing*."

"Miss Silver has caused me no offense," Elise interrupted hastily. Beside her the tension in Noah's body was a palpable thing. She leaned into him. "While I appreciate your knightly errancy, Sir Noah, please endeavor to remember what I said about duels," she whispered in his ear.

He frowned fiercely. "I wasn't about to challenge an idiot of a girl to a duel," he hissed back.

"Good to hear." She paused. "Perhaps you should mention to her that you're a duke and that you take exception to *her* tone."

Noah goggled at her.

"It would be fun to see her faint right off her pony. A shilling says she goes ass over teakettle right over the rump of that mare, as opposed to sliding off the side like a sack of turnips."

"*Elise*," he hissed in horror.

"Or perhaps I might come back here and pay her a visit as a French princess. On second thought, I've got a Bavarian empress who owes me a favor."

"*What?* What the hell are you talking about?"

"It might be fun to knock Miss Silver off her sanctimonious social perch, don't you think?" Elise mused.

"You're insane." Noah was gaping at her.

"My brother often uses the word *diabolical*." But Noah was now fighting a smile, so whatever diabolical insanity she wielded was well worth it.

"What are you whispering about?" Miss Silver demanded.

Elise raised her voice. "Oh, teakettles and turnips—"

"Perhaps you might like to challenge me to a contest instead, Miss Silver." Noah cut Elise off, giving her a warning look that lacked any real threat.

"Why on earth would I want to do that?" Miss Silver asked. "You won the shooting contest last year, Mr. Lawson.

What is the point in competing against someone you're unlikely to beat?"

Elise swallowed a smirk. "What indeed?" she murmured.

Noah elbowed her.

"I want to shoot against Miss DeVries." Miss Silver banged her crop on the edge of her saddle like a petulant child, and her mare pinned her ears. "And I can think of only one reason why she would refuse."

Elise could think of many, but it seemed pointless to argue any of them. "Very well, Miss Silver. If the gentlemen agree to postpone their own contest for a short while, I would be happy to accept your challenge." She glanced around her at the ever-increasing crowd and was met by vehement agreement. Dammit.

"Good." Miss Silver looked pleased with herself.

Noah muttered something foul under his breath before he suddenly slid from her side and disappeared into the crowd. Where the hell was he going—

"What is going on here?" The demand came from a man pushing his way through the onlookers.

"Papa," Miss Silver exclaimed from her horse. "You're just in time."

Lord Corley frowned, the lines on his thin face deepening. "Just in time for what?" He shot a suspicious look at the men who had gathered around his daughter's mare, and smoothed the front of his fine coat. His aura of self-importance was nearly as glaring as the top of his scalp through his thinning hair.

"I'm going to participate in a shooting contest."

"I think not." His small eyes narrowed even further.

Miss Silver waved her hand in the direction of Elise and

Sarah. "But Mrs. Barr said I'm no good. She said Miss DeVries is a better shot than I," she sulked, her lip trembling and her eyes filming on cue. "And I know that to be impossible since it was you who taught me how to shoot."

Elise watched in utter amazement. The girl had missed her calling on a London stage.

"Is that true, Mrs. Barr?" the baron demanded, turning his narrowed gaze to Sarah. "Because my daughter is a very accomplished marksman. Or -woman, as it may be. To insult her competence is to insult me as well. Not something that you would wish to do, I think."

Sarah made a small sound of unhappiness, and Elise resisted the urge to heave an exasperated sigh. Of all the pompous idiocy.

Miss Silver beckoned to her groom impatiently, and the man appeared at her side and assisted her with dismounting, Miss Silver apparently taking her father's statement as approval of her participation. She strode over to Elise and held out her hand. "Give me the gun."

Wordlessly Elise passed the musket to Miss Silver. It was a good one, a newer version of the standard infantry musket. Its gleaming walnut stock was not yet gouged and chipped, and the brass plates were yet unmarred by scratches. The girl returned to her father, the two of them now engaged in a conversation Elise couldn't hear. She made a show of examining the piece and sighting a target down the barrel.

After interminable minutes Miss Silver and her father nodded. "I have used such before. This will do nicely," she decreed, before the pair of them moved off to parade along the base of the field, squinting in the direction of the targets.

"Here." Noah's voice was in her ear suddenly, and Elise found her own rifle and pouches pressed into her hands. Beside him Sarah waited, looking terribly worried.

Elise looked up at him in surprise. "Thank you."

"I'm sorry about this," Noah said abruptly. "Miss Silver is—"

"A child," Elise supplied. "With a child's view of how important she is in the world."

He looked at her, his jaw still set. "Yes. But her father indulges her whims. In his eyes his daughter can do no wrong, and his belief of that borders on the irrational."

"You don't say," Elise replied, sarcasm dripping.

"The baron also owns the parcel of land next to John and Sarah's. The land they are currently in the process of purchasing to expand John's business."

"I should have kept my mouth shut," Sarah said unhappily.

"I see." Elise rested the rifle's familiar weight in her hands.

"Do you?" Noah asked.

"Of course. You need me to lose to this child."

"Yes." Regret filled his words. "It would be within the baron's nature to punish Mrs. Barr or her husband in some manner for, as he would see it, goading his daughter into a fixed contest in which she grievously loses, causing his daughter untold distress." His face twisted unpleasantly.

Elise sniffed. "What's in it for me?"

Noah blinked before his lips curved. "You're stealing my lines again."

"I'm an excellent actress. I have a knack for remembering good lines," she agreed. "But surely I should expect some favor from my knight-errant?"

He patted his pockets. "I'm all out of silk ribbons and posies."

"Pity. Think of something else."

"What do you want?"

Elise smiled up at him, a slow, wicked smile. She stepped forward and went up on her tiptoes. "You'll think me forward. Or foolish. Or both," she whispered against his ear.

She saw the way his breath caught in his chest, heard his faint exhalation even as his fingers curled and then uncurled. The look he gave her was scorching, and Elise wondered if perhaps she had gone too far. "Those are my lines again, Miss DeVries," he said in a low voice.

"Like I said, Mr. Lawson, I remember the good ones."

"Very well, milady." Noah bowed slightly, though his eyes never left hers. "You have yourself a deal."

Chapter 11

Elise took a deep breath, releasing it slowly, relaxing her body. She looked down the barrel, her eyes picking out the clear mark on the very outside edge of the target made by Miss Silver's shot. It was a wonder the woman had hit the thing at all, given that she had been using a musket and not a rifle, but Elise had to give her credit for being able to handle the heavier weapon with a minimum of fuss.

All the targets had been whitewashed, black circles in diminishing sizes painted on their faces, and the one Miss Silver had chosen was a middling distance away. But it was not moving. Nor was there wind, or rain, or smoke, or fog. No screams of wounded or dying men, no thunder of feet or hooves marking the hunters and the hunted. No shouts, no whistle of artillery. It was distracting, this absence of distraction, Elise thought. But regardless, she would put her shot where she needed to.

It galled Elise to fail intentionally. It was so tempting to simply put a clean shot through the center of that target, if only to see Miss Silver's face. But Miss Silver was not worth whatever repercussions the Barrs or anyone else might suffer because of her ability to manipulate her father's fragile ego.

With some regret Elise picked a spot on the edge of the target, debating just how close she should come to Miss Silver's shot. And then, beyond the target, a movement caught her eye. A blur of grey along the top of the stone fence at the end of the field. Elise smiled. And fired.

Noah watched as Elise fired her rifle, absorbing the kick of the gun with such ease that it was obvious to anyone watching that she had fired that weapon a thousand times. The rifle was an extension of her hand, her stance sure, every movement expert. Particularly the minute yet deliberate adjustment of the barrel in the second before she fired. While every other pair of eyes flew to the target, his stayed on the woman in the green dress, who had straightened. A small smile played about her lips, as though she was privy to an amusing secret.

"She missed," Miss Silver announced waspishly from where she had been watching, and clasped her hands together in delight. She turned a victorious smile on Elise. "Perhaps some more practice will improve your shot, Miss DeVries."

"I'm sure it will." Elise had arranged her face in an expression that looked suitably chastened and grave, and Noah wasn't sure if he should laugh at her acting ability or be furious on her behalf at the entire condescending farce.

But then Elise caught his eye and winked, and whatever anger he'd been harboring vanished, because suddenly they were partners.

I am with you, not against you.

There was a battle going on inside him, an epic tug-of-war, in which on one side caution and bitterness had dug in deeply. It was this that had kept him distant and safe from his past for years, things that had ensured his solitary survival. But now Noah was questioning whether he wanted distance and safety anymore. For on the other side, admiration and hope were hauling on his heart and his conscience. Because when Elise DeVries had ridden into his life, she had brought with her the realization that he wasn't really alone. And an insistence that, if he chose to, he could be everything Elise seemed to think he might be.

She believed in him. Even knowing everything that she did, she believed in him. More than he had ever believed in himself.

And that knowledge was making it hard for Noah to concentrate on anything other than the beautiful woman still holding a Baker rifle.

He couldn't take his eyes from her. He ignored the knots of men murmuring and gesturing at the targets. He ignored Miss Silver where she was accepting congratulations from her father near the edge of the field. He ignored the people still lingering and staring at Elise with curiosity. He went directly to her side and stopped, simply needing to be near her.

Elise smiled at him briefly before bending to examine the edge of the flint on the Baker. "Where's Sarah?"

"She's with John," Noah said, trying to affect a cavalier demeanor in an effort to distract himself from the overwhelming urge to kiss her and so maintain this exhilarating sense of alliance for just a few moments longer.

"Of course. Please advise me if that little troll of a baron causes trouble for her, or anyone she's related to, in the next while."

"Why? You'll arrange to have him transported?" Noah's brows bunched, her statement providing the distraction he needed to focus on something other than the desire pounding through his veins.

Elise lifted her head and gazed at him with approval. "Why, that's an excellent suggestion, Mr. Lawson."

"I was jesting."

"I wasn't."

"You could make that happen?"

"Yes. Though there are others at Chegarre and Associates who have far better connections in that department than I. I would refer Mrs. Barr to them."

Noah felt his jaw slacken.

"I trust my performance was adequate?" Elise asked, returning her attention to the Baker.

Noah cleared his throat. "You didn't have to miss entirely."

"I didn't."

"There wasn't a mark on that target."

"Ah. Yes, well, I wasn't shooting at that target," she told him, brushing out the priming pan.

"Then what the hell were you shooting at?"

"There was a rat."

"A rat?" Noah stared at her. "What? Where? I didn't see a rat."

"On the far fence. Running along the top. About a yard to the left of the gate." She finished her ministrations and raised her head. "I told you I hate rats. There are some who say they are a harbinger of the Black Death, you know."

"The far fence." Noah was aware he was repeating her words like a half-wit, but that far fence was at least twice as far away as the target.

"Yes." She swatted at a fly that buzzed near her waist. "Listen, I'm starved. All this losing has made me famished. Do you think we might get something to eat?"

Noah pinned her with a hard look. "Stay here."

"What—" she started, but Noah was already jogging across the field, heading to the far fence. He reached the wooden gate and turned to the left, taking measured steps along the rough stone wall. If there had truly been a rat then he should find—

He stopped abruptly, then vaulted over the fence. Lying in the fragrant grass, a good number of feet beyond the fence, was a rat. Or what was left of one. He nudged it with his toe, fleas jumping from its fur, its body still warm.

He turned and stared back in the direction of Elise, her green dress easy to pick out among the men who were still milling. He could see her put her hands on her hips and shake her head. Slowly Noah made his way back to the tent.

She cocked a brow at him, her jaw set. "What did you find on the other side of that fence, Mr. Lawson?"

"A rat."

"Good heavens. You don't say. Was it dead?"

"Yes," he muttered.

"Imagine that. You know you could have saved yourself a long walk if you had only believed me," Elise said with a sardonic edge to her voice. "A lesser woman might start taking exception to your complete lack of faith in her."

Noah winced. "That's not fair."

"Yes, well, not much in life is fair, Mr. Lawson. I just lost a shooting contest on purpose to a silly girl who would be dead within a week of a Canadian winter if she had to rely on her skill with a gun to feed herself. That is not fair."

"You picked a rat off a fence at the far end of the bloody field. That's..."

"Proficient?" she prompted, sounding testy.

"Far-fetched. Almost impossible."

"Impossible?" Elise made a rude noise. "Good thing you're not relying on your skill with a gun to eat either." She sniffed. "Are you always this complimentary to women you escort to summer picnics?"

Noah ran a hand through his hair, feeling like an utter cad. She was right. "I'm sorry."

Elise sighed. "Apology accepted." She put a hand on his arm. "One of these times, Mr. Lawson, you're going to surprise me. You're going to simply believe me when I tell you something." She patted his arm, and Noah caught her hand in his.

He drew her closer, unwilling to let go of her hand. "Thank you for losing."

"You're welcome." She gave a wry shake of her head. "Please don't ever ask me to do it again."

"I won't." He paused, letting his eyes roam over her beautiful face.

"Good." She was smiling at him again. "I'll happily lose at a lot of things if it's required, but shooting cannot be one of them. I have some pride, you know."

"You are..." He trailed off, unable to choose the right word. *Incredible. Incomparable.*

With me.

And she truly was. For the first time in his adult life, he was no longer alone. Aye, he had wonderful friends and people he cared for who surrounded him, but they'd always been kept at a careful distance. Even John, his closest friend, didn't know his real name. He'd pursued very few relationships with women, knowing that such unions would always be bereft of any real intimacy beyond physical pleasure. There could be no whispered sharing of hopes and dreams and histories because Noah had been unable—unwilling—to disclose anything real. Women, like everyone else, knew only the individual he had diligently presented, the carefully curated persona of Noah Lawson.

And all of that vigilance had been, indeed, a lonely endeavor.

Until Elise. Until he'd met the woman who knew his secrets. Until that woman had refused to leave him, refused to back down, refused to accept his rebuffs. Instead she'd taken a few more secrets from where they rested heavily on his shoulders into her own unflinching heart.

And, in doing so, made his burden lighter.

"I am what?" Elise prompted, giving him a slightly puzzled look.

He started, realizing she was still waiting for him to finish what he'd begun to say. Except he couldn't. There were words and feelings and longings piling up in his head and heart, and he couldn't sort any of it into a sentence that might express just what Elise DeVries was to him. He reached out and touched her face, using the only language he could articulate just now.

Her pupils dilated, and her breathing became shallow, and it was an effort to remember he was standing under a tent, surrounded by people milling about, conversations rising and falling around him. It was an effort to remember why he couldn't kiss her right here. The aching need for her was about to trump every ounce of his common sense.

"If you keep looking at me like that, Mr. Lawson, I'll do something stupid, then you'll do something even more stupid, and we'll find ourselves married by morning," she murmured.

"We're not in a London assembly room," he said, if only to cover the yearning that ripped through him at the prospect of taking this woman to his bed. And keeping her there indefinitely.

"No, we're in a damn sheep pasture. Surrounded by guns. And people. And sheep shit. I fail to see the advantage." She sounded breathless.

He ran his thumb along the edge of her jaw. "I really do need a carriage. One with a lock on the door."

She shivered and licked her lower lip.

Every drop of blood in his body pooled in his groin. "You have no idea how much I want you right now." He had nothing but the truth to offer her, standing here in this tent. "I would give you—"

The crack of a musket snapped through the air as the shooting contest got under way.

"Food," she said, stepping out of his reach.

His hand fell to his side. "What?" He could barely think through this haze of lust.

"You can get me food." Her voice was unsteady.

Noah took a few great gulps of air.

"I'm going now, Mr. Lawson." She turned and headed away from the field, away from him. Away from the recklessness that had gripped them in its thrall.

"Where?" He hurried after her. Enough blood had returned to his brain to penetrate his daze.

"To find something to eat."

"Then at least give me your rifle. I'll put it back in the wagon."

She opened her mouth as if to argue.

"There are no unfamiliar faces here, Miss DeVries. And anyone who might wish me harm would be an utter idiot to do anything in front of a small army of men whom I count as friends." Another crack of a musket punctuated his words. "Friends who are currently using firearms, at that."

She fingered the stock of the Baker uncertainly. "You're sure?"

"I'm sure." He held out his hand.

Still she hesitated.

"If you're worried about dinner, everything that's being served is already dead."

She made a face. "Very funny."

"I try."

Slowly she placed the rifle in his outstretched hand. "I'm trusting you to tell me if anything changes, Mr. Lawson."

"Understood. And thank you."

"For what?"

"For trusting me."

Elise shook her head. "I don't need your pretty words, Mr. Lawson. You can thank me by returning the favor one day."

⁓

"I'd bet every brass button I've ever sold in my store that Miss DeVries lost that shooting match to Lord Corley's daughter on purpose," Stuart Howards said, nearly shouting to be heard over the music that was pulsing around them. The ground beneath Noah's boots vibrated with the feet of dancers as they swirled by.

Noah was listening with half an ear. The slightly inebriated Howards was one of a dozen men who had brought up the afternoon's shooting contest with Noah, hoping that he might confirm or deny that statement, which seemed to be the general consensus of the crowd. There had been too many veterans looking on who had recognized not only the somewhat uncommon weapon but the expertise of the hands that had held it.

"Perhaps," Noah answered vaguely. It was the same answer he had given to everyone else. His eyes were searching the crowd, looking for the woman in question.

Howards took a deep swallow from his cup of ale. "Where is Miss DeVries from?" he inquired, his face flushed from the heat or the alcohol or both.

Noah's eyes fell on Elise then. She was standing near the edge of the dance floor, her foot tapping in time to the music and an expression of wistful longing on her face. For once she wasn't watching the crowd, looking for a threat that he knew didn't exist here. Instead she was gazing at the dancers, looking as if she very much wished to join them.

"York," Noah said, distracted.

"Ah, a Northern girl." Howards nodded to himself as if this explained everything.

Through the bodies spinning in a country dance, Elise's eyes met Noah's, as if she had felt him watching her. He tipped his head toward the dancers and raised a brow. Her face broke into a sudden, radiant smile. In an instant Noah's blood heated and his pulse accelerated.

He was lost. He wanted this woman beyond anything that was reasonable or rational. He'd settle for a dance here, now, but he knew it wasn't going to be enough.

Howards was wiping his mouth with the back of his sleeve. "Lots of visitors coming through town this time o' year," he said. "Good for business, you know, though you got to keep a careful eye. Couple coves in my store jus' yesterday askin' around about—"

"Excuse me, Howards," Noah interrupted. "But there is a lady who is looking for a dance partner." And Noah would be damned if she would dance with anyone else. Elise belonged to him and only him. He was already making his way toward her before Howards even had a chance to answer. Which was somewhat rude, but Noah couldn't seem to bring himself to care. He had no interest in talking about brass buttons and store sales with Howards. His only focus was on the woman in the green dress who had his insides twisting in anticipation and desire.

Within seconds he'd pulled Elise from the edge of the spectators into the mass of dancers, reveling in the joy and delight that shone from her eyes as she threw her head back and laughed.

Chapter 12

The ride home had been one of contented happiness, the Barrs keeping the conversation lively and finally leaving Noah and Elise in front of the cottage before they turned their wagon and headed for home.

Square greeted them from where he had been sleeping near the front door, with a stretch and a happy wag of his tail.

"Did we beat Mrs. Pritchard home?" Elise asked. "The house is dark."

"I suggested to Mrs. Pritchard that perhaps she might want to stay with a friend in town for a few nights," Noah told her.

Elise turned to him in surprise, moonlight chasing silver streaks through her hair. "What? When?"

Noah reached out and brushed a loose tendril behind her ear. "I asked her right before we left for the picnic. Because if, in fact, my cousin has completely lost his mind, and someone is indeed looking to murder a duke who no longer exists, I don't want to put her in harm's way."

"Thank you," Elise said. "Thank you for believing me."

"For the record, I still feel like a fool," Noah said, adjusting his grip on Elise's rifle, which he had taken from the back of the wagon.

"I don't care how you feel. Only that you still can. And I'd like to keep it that way. What did you tell Mrs. Pritchard?"

"Nothing."

"Nothing? Didn't she ask why—"

"No, she didn't ask. She simply jumped to all sorts of conclusions. And I let her."

"Indeed?" Elise's serious expression was replaced with a grin. "What sort of conclusions?"

"The kind that will break her heart if you don't marry me by next Thursday. Friday at the latest."

"I'll clear my calendar."

"I'd appreciate it." He laughed.

A strange silence fell between them, the scent of roses drifting around them on the warm summer air, the bright moonlight creating strange shapes and shadows around them.

"Did you enjoy yourself tonight?" Noah asked into the silence. He had no idea what had made him ask that.

"I did."

"You sound surprised."

"Maybe I am. Tonight reminded me of a time when things were . . . simpler. It brought back a lot of happy memories." She paused. "Thank you for that."

"I didn't do anything."

"You danced with me."

"Not well."

Elise smiled up at him. "I disagree. I thought you were rather dashing, Sir Noah."

Noah felt as if a giant fist had squeezed the inside of his chest. It was moments like this that nearly undid him. In another lifetime they could have been an ordinary couple, two lovers simply standing under a full moon in a rose-scented garden. And there had been other times this evening, other moments filled with dancing and music and laughter, when he had forgotten why Elise was here. Moments when he had forgotten that her very presence represented a world that was waiting to claim him, a world full of complexity and bitterness.

But those tiny snippets of time were fleeting. And in this lifetime, in this reality, they stood on the edge of desire, a strange cauldron of circumstance swirling beneath them, making each step they took perilous and uncertain.

He reached for her hand as if that gesture might provide him with balance. She let him take it, and he felt her fingers curl into his.

"What are we doing, Noah?" Elise asked suddenly into the stillness, and her voice was bleak, stripped of any laughter.

He didn't want this conversation. He wanted to hold on to the fantasy for just a few minutes more that he might take Elise inside and undress her. Lay her down on his bed and make love to her the way he had wanted to since the very first time she had smiled at him. He would make her his for this night and forever. So that she might always dance with him at picnics. So that she might milk his cows anytime she wished. So that he could finish falling completely and utterly in love with her.

"I don't know."

"We can't go on like this." In the wash of pale light, her eyes were desolate. "Pretending. Wishing that things were different. It will only make everything harder, and in the end it will solve nothing."

She was right, and he hated that.

"I need you to give me an answer, Noah," Elise whispered. "I need you to tell me you will come back to London."

Noah felt the familiar hollow open up inside him, that black void that was full of pain and resentment. The joy and the happiness of the evening slid into that pit in an instant, leaving him bereft. He wanted to tell her what she wanted to hear. That he would abandon everything he had built in Nottingham. That he would storm into London, seize a title he had never wanted, and in doing so rescue a mother who had never wanted him.

"I want to. But I can't. Just...not yet."

"You won't. Two very different things."

Noah looked away. The void became a pressure, a crushing weight that was constricting his ability to breathe.

"I made a promise to help your mother, Noah, and that is a promise I intend to keep. Even if the Fates are whispering that she doesn't deserve it." Her voice wavered slightly. "I said I wouldn't leave here without you, but I lied. Because, in truth, I can't force you to do anything. I can't force you to get on a horse and ride to London. I can't force you to assume a title that is rightfully yours."

Noah gazed unseeing into the night, as miserable as he'd ever felt. Elise had a way of flaying everything to its bare bones, stripping away the pretensions and the excuses that covered truths. And in her wake she left the carcasses of fears and doubts and secrets sticking up like bleached bones in a harsh light.

"I can't give you the answer I want to give you because I don't know if I can ever forgive her," Noah rasped. It was the truth. And it was awful. He hated himself for it. "I don't know if I can ever forgive my mother for what she did."

"Then don't."

Noah's head snapped around in shock.

Elise looked up at him. "You blame her for what you endured. What you had to do. And I can't tell you that you are wrong to do so."

Her understanding was like a knife twisting deep into his heart. It would have hurt less had she railed at him, accused him of being dishonorable, callous, or cruel. All accusations he had already leveled at himself more than once. "I lived like a feral animal in that cage for five years." The words escaped, like poison oozing from an infected wound. "I still have scars from the chains. They tied me down and spun me on swings or poured icy water over my head for hours until I passed out. I slept on rotting straw and vomit and shit, frozen in the winter, unable to escape the heat in the summer. I fought other children for scraps of food because otherwise I might starve. I killed a man who was raping a boy barely older than I." He was breathing hard. "I became—"

"You." She interrupted him, her eyes blazing. "You became you. What you survived did not break you, Noah Ellery. It made you strong. Stronger than any man I've known." She was breathing as hard as he. "I can't tell you that one day you'll find forgiveness. I don't know that. But I do know that your mother's actions once defined your life. Do not let her define it anymore. You have all the con-

trol now, Noah. Decide what you want to do with it." Elise
let her hand drop from his, and reached for her rifle, taking
it from his grasp.

Noah stood motionless.

She went up on her tiptoes and brushed her lips against
his, a gentle, heartbreaking kiss that was over before it
started. She withdrew and started up the steps of the house,
turning back only once.

"I'll leave at first light," was all she said.

Sleep came slowly, and when it did it was troubled, filled
with uneasy, restless shadows. Noah woke suddenly,
bathed in sweat, unsure of how long he had slept, but it
was still dark. A strange sense of disquiet had settled about
the room. He could hear the crickets outside, and the air
around him was still thick and humid. A shaft of moonlight
shone through the window, though it faltered briefly as fingers of clouds drifted by.

He rolled over as quietly as possible, slipping from his
bed and from his room. He did not bother lighting can-
dles, the moonlight illuminating everything in the rooms he
knew by heart. He paused by Elise's door, barely breathing, trying to listen for anything that might tell him she was
still awake. A snore, perhaps.

But not a sound came from within.

"Elise?" he whispered.

There was no answer. He stood outside her door, un-
sure. And feeling more foolish than he had in a long time.
Which, considering recent events, was saying something.
But what the hell did he think he was doing, creeping

around his house in his bare feet, considering spying on a woman who was no doubt asleep in her bed? They had names for men who did that. And none of them were complimentary.

A faint bark brought his head up. He frowned and left Elise's door, padding silently into the dining room. Through the tall windows, the gardens sat still and quiet, bathed in pale light. He could see the line of trees at the edge of the pasture, a dark smudge against the silver of the river beyond. A blur of white caught his eye, and another bark reached him as Square disappeared into the trees.

An unpleasant chill crawled down his spine. Square never left the house at night. Occasionally he slept in the barn when the weather turned wet or cold, but on nights like this, he slept at the front of the house. There was no reason for him to be down by the river. Unless...

Noah froze for a paralyzing moment before he hurried back to Elise's room and pushed open her door.

The sheets were rumpled, the pillows askew, but the bed, like the room, was empty.

"Bloody hell," Noah swore to himself. He could see her new green dress, hung with reverence on the pegs anchored to the wall. Her ugly brown dress was also there, along with what looked like the faded blue coat she had worn this afternoon. But her shirt and her trousers were missing.

She had to stop doing this. This disappearing. Not only was it objectionable, it was dangerous. Forget lurking assassins, there was always the possibility of poachers and thieves. Or holes into which one might stumble and break an ankle. Or trees from which one might fall and break a neck.

He hurried away from the window, not bothering to return to his room for his shirt, but lifting his hunting knife from its hook by the door. He stepped out into the night and whistled for Square. There was no answer. Unease slid through him, and he forced it aside.

She was fine, he told himself. Probably swinging through the trees or doing whatever it was that Elise DeVries did on moonlit nights. The woman was probably nocturnal. Hell, he wouldn't be surprised if, on nights like this, she turned into an owl. Or a bat. Or one of Mrs. Pritchard's faeries. Elise had proven more than once that she could morph into about anything.

He made his way toward the river, not acknowledging that he was jogging now. He gave another shrill whistle, fighting down a rising sense of panic. This time he was rewarded by a yip from the direction of the river, followed by an abrupt silence. The icy dread he'd pushed down curled its unforgiving fingers through him, raising the hair on his neck. Something was wrong. Something had happened.

Noah was sprinting now toward the thick foliage, hurdling the fence and racing across the fields. Another bark, and he pushed himself harder. The moon became obliterated by a drift of clouds, plunging his surroundings into darkness. He ran on and reached the trees, just as the moon reappeared to at least afford him the ability to maintain his bearings. He crashed through the brush like a panicked animal, bursting out onto the banks of the river, gasping for air. The light dimmed again, and he struggled to see in the darkness. He felt a cold wet nose against his palm at the same instant that something soft landed on his bare foot. He recoiled instantly, the knife drawn before him, feeling exposed and blind.

The curtain of clouds moved on. Instantly he could make out the shaggy white coat of Square, sitting expectantly in front of him, his mouth pulled back in a drooling grin, his white tail thumping against a carpet of dried leaves. The warmth that covered Noah's foot proved to be a limp rodent of indeterminate color.

What the hell was going on? Surely if Elise was in trouble, the dog would be agitated, not bestowing him with gifts of dead rats. He lowered the knife, feeling foolish. Again. But if Square was here, Elise couldn't be far.

Reconnaissance, he was sure she'd tell him whenever she chose to appear out of the forest like a wood elf. And then she'd ask him why he was breathing like a winded bull, sweat pouring down his face and his chest, his pulse hammering in his ears from his sprint from the house.

He would thrash her to within an inch of her life the moment he found her. That was, if the poachers and assassins and thieves and faeries were done with her. The dread that had almost choked him faded. He bent down and picked up Square's gift, tossing it back in the dog's direction with an unsteady word of thanks. The damn dog was at least considerate.

He watched as Square slid awkwardly down the bank and lay near the water's edge, dropping the rat. He saw the animal prick his ears at something out in the river, before resuming careful inspection of his latest prize.

Noah followed the dog's gaze, and his heart stopped.

She was floating face-up in the water, dressed only in her long shirt, her hair swirling around her in a cloud of dark against the silver surface of the water. Her eyes were closed, and her face was slack, the color of her skin blanched pale in the moonlight.

She wasn't moving.

With a tortured cry, Noah jerked into action.

Chapter 13

The water was cool against her hot skin, the feeling of weightlessness that came with the sensation of floating soothing and calming.

Unable to sleep, Elise had stolen out of the house and down to the trees, seeking space from the man who slept only a wall away from her. She'd emerged on the bank and had been unable to resist the silver water that beckoned in the heat of the night. She'd slipped into the water, rolling onto her back, and gazed up at the blanket of stars overhead. The sounds of the world were silenced under the water, and Elise embraced that quiet, using the hush to calm her racing mind and set her thoughts in order.

She would return to London without him.

The disappointment cut deep, deeper than she would ever admit. She had believed that Noah would do for his mother what the duchess had refused to do for her son. And Elise had believed that if she could only make Noah realize that he wasn't alone, he might be able to overcome the un-fathomable pain and hurt of abandonment. They had both failed.

But if Elise put herself in Noah's shoes and peered into the dark recesses of her own conscience, she couldn't say with any confidence that she would have reacted any differently from the way he had. Elise might know what he had endured, but she hadn't lived it. She hadn't been the child consigned to a fate worse than hell by the two people that same child had trusted to keep him safe and protected. It made her want to cry.

But crying solved nothing. So now it was time to move on from failure and seek out other options.

She would, of course, insist that Noah disappear for awhile—perhaps now would be the perfect time to travel the Continent. Bavaria was pretty this time of the year, she'd heard. She could certainly provide him with connections. Once he was on his way, she would tell King that she had located Noah Ellery and that he had declined her offer of help beyond what would get him safely away from England for the time being. Though King was a suspicious bastard and would likely demand some proof of Noah's safety. She'd have to put some thought into what she might provide that would convince him she spoke the truth.

And then there was the loose end that was the urchin named Joshua, who had suffered alongside and escaped with Noah from Bedlam, though it was likely that Joshua was dead. Boys on the streets of London rarely survived to adulthood, no matter how capable they might be. If they didn't succumb to starvation or disease, violence or vice, they might find themselves the victims of a press-gang, or thief takers. Boys like that tended to disappear.

Though she certainly wouldn't give any further thought to the inevitable disappearance of one Francis Ellery. She just hoped that King had the foresight to make sure his body was found. The last thing the dukedom needed was another missing heir tying up the succession. There would be others crawling out of the woodwork in line for the title, and she was confident any one of them would be better than the current conniving contender.

The removal of Francis Ellery would likely solve the problem of the duchess as well. A part of whatever money Ellery had managed to beg or borrow was still being used to keep his aunt in chains. Without that money or the promise of more, it would likely be a great deal easier to arrange the extraction of the Duchess of Ashland.

Perhaps this was best for everyone. Perhaps Elise should have suggested this a long time ago. It certainly had its advantages, the least being that it would work in the absence of the true heir to the dukedom of Ashland. Which was fine, if not wholly unsatisfying.

So unsatisfying, in fact, that it was everything Elise could do not to scream in frustration. Despite everything, she wanted Noah to polish his damn armor, get on his damn white horse, and skewer Francis Ellery with the point of his damn lance. She wanted him to lay claim to a title and a fortune that would flourish under his command and his valor and his principles. Because he was capable. And incredible. And—

A stream of water blasted up her nose as her head was jerked roughly below the surface. A steel vise closed around her wrists and dragged her down. Her eyes flew open even as she instinctively fought free, her mind registering the feel of fingers pressing painfully into her skin.

Elise twisted and jerked, but her assailant's grip didn't loosen. Fear surged, along with the immediate instinct to fight. She brought her legs up and kicked out, and her foot caught an exposed midriff with a satisfying force. The fingers around her wrist loosened, and she yanked herself free, stroking powerfully away from her attacker.

She surfaced, coughing, and tried desperately to identify where the next attack would come from. She wondered if there were two of them in the water. Or if one assassin had swum out and the other yet waited on shore. But all she could see was the shape of a dark head above the water, thrashing arms and legs causing the moon's reflection on the surface of the river to fragment. She trod water where she was, her eyes scanning the shore. Where was his partner?

In hindsight she'd been unforgivably stupid, leaving herself so exposed. But she'd been lulled by the absence of any sign of human activity and the added company of Square. She'd relied on the knowledge that the dog would detect another presence long before her senses would. Though the beast had failed on a grand scale in that regard. The damn thing hadn't even barked.

Her eyes came to rest on the dog, sitting on the bank, watching the spectacle, his head cocked, his tail wagging happily.

She stared in disbelief. She had been accosted by at least one intruder, and all the dog was doing was watching? And wagging his tail? Not that she expected defensive devotion, but a response of some sort would have been nice. How had her attacker gotten down the bank and into the water without the dog at least getting up to investigate?

Unless Square knew the attacker.

Her eyes snapped to the thrashing form in the water between her and the bank. She heard a vicious curse.

A gurgle of laughter escaped, relief making her giddy.

She could see Noah kicking frantically, trying to keep his head above water as he vainly fought his way back to shore. Her would-be attacker had apparently been her would-be rescuer. She could only imagine what she had looked like floating there in the moonlight, her eyes closed, her body relaxed.

He had thought she had drowned. And he had jumped in to save her, though it was becoming vastly apparent he couldn't swim. Whatever had he been thinking?

She quickly swam over to Noah, careful to keep a distance between herself and the struggling man. "Take a deep breath and stop your thrashing," she commanded.

He jerked in surprise but did as he was told.

"And don't touch me." She slipped an arm around his neck, much as she had done with Andrew Barr, and pulled him slowly toward the shallows. She could feel every muscle in his body tense, either in fear or in rage. She very much doubted it was the former.

Her feet touched the soft ground, but she did not let go, nor did she give any indication that she had found her footing. Noah was still facing out toward the center of the river.

"What were you thinking? You should never have jumped into the water when you don't know how to swim," Elise chided.

She felt him twitch. "What was *I* thinking?" His voice rose and bounced across the water. "I wasn't thinking anything. I was trying to save you," he gritted through clenched teeth.

"I'm sorry."

"You're sorry? I thought you were *dead*."

Remorse warred with annoyance. "If you had taken but a moment to think about it, you would have remembered that dead people sink. They don't float." She paused. "At least not for a few days."

"If that is an attempt to be funny, Miss DeVries, you may be assured I am not laughing."

Elise scowled. "You need to learn how to swim. The only one in danger of dying tonight was you. You would have ended up at the bottom if it hadn't been for me."

"It was because of you that I nearly went straight to the bottom!" he snarled.

"You can stand up now," Elise said abruptly, and released her hold on him.

Noah spluttered and lunged to his feet, turning to glare at her.

She swam out of his reach judiciously. "I didn't mean to scare you."

"I wasn't scared," he snapped.

"Of course."

He glared at her some more before he turned and waded closer to the bank, wiping water from his face.

"How the hell do you not know how to swim?" Elise asked, taking a chance and treading a little closer. "Surely you had ponds and such on whatever country piles your family owned? Surely some idiotic friend dared you to jump in at some point. That sort of stupidity is like a bloody rite of passage for every boy on earth."

Noah made a rude noise. "And how would you know that?"

"I had two brothers, in case you've forgotten. I was five when Jonathon dared me."

"I never went near the water as a child."

"Never?"

"Are you deaf, Miss DeVries?"

"Just surprised."

"As I got older, I was kept out of sight and away from anyone who might notice that the Duke of Ashland's son was defective. There were no friends to dare me to do anything." He said it with a harsh twist to his mouth.

Elise's heart hurt for the little boy who had been left alone to watch the world go by without him. Her heart broke for the child who had deserved none of the anguish and sorrow he'd suffered. She stroked closer to shore and stood, putting her hands on her hips.

"I dare you," she said.

"What?"

"I dare you to jump in."

"Don't be asinine."

She crossed her arms over her chest. "Do it. I dare you."

Noah threw his hands in the air. "I'm going back to the house."

"And then what?"

"And then nothing. I'm going back to bed like a normal person." He started up the bank.

"What happens the next time a child like Andrew Barr falls in the river? Or a lake? Or a pond? What happens when someone needs help and you can't give it to them, because on this night you refused to take a chance? Will you stand by and watch?"

She had done it on purpose, appealed to his protective nature. Appealed to his sense of gallantry and kindness, and she was not disappointed.

He stopped and turned. "I'll sink straight to the bottom."

Elise could see the planes of his face, stark in the moonlight. Drops of water still slid down his chest, tiny diamonds that fell and vanished with each breath. "No, you won't. I'll be with you."

He stood in silence, and Elise let that silence stretch, unwilling to break the fragile possibility that was slowly unfurling. "You can't teach me how to swim in five minutes," he said finally.

"No. That takes some time. And practice. After tonight you won't be able to cross the Channel, but I can at least teach you how to float."

"I can float," he scoffed.

"Mmmm."

"You don't believe me."

"Not at all."

"I can."

"Then prove it, Sir Noah. Unless..."

"Unless what?"

Elise tucked her hands into her armpits and wiggled her elbows, clucking as she did so.

"Did you just call me a chicken?" His mouth had fallen open.

She dropped her hands and smirked. "If the feather fits, Sir Noah..."

He made an incredulous face. "You're acting like you're twelve years old."

"I was aiming for about nine."

"You're impossible."

"You're stalling."

He raised his hands in a gesture of defeat. "Fine. I float for a minute and then we will get out of the water and return directly to the house. Am I clear?"

"Crystal." She gave him a winning smile. "Now let's see you float."

Noah frowned, but waded back into the water. He stopped when he had gotten chest deep. He took a deep breath and kicked his legs out in front of him. His entire body disappeared from view.

Elise was laughing as he pushed himself to the surface again, coughing and spluttering. "Well done, Sir Noah, well done." She moved toward him. "You float like a rock."

"I wasn't ready that time," he bit out defensively.

"Well, by all means, please do not let me stop you." She was standing next to him now.

He scowled fiercely at her, but took another deep breath. This time as he kicked his legs out, Elise stepped forward and placed one arm beneath his lower back. Noah immediately tried to jerk his head up, but she pushed his forehead back with her free hand.

"Look up at the moon," she told him. "And for pity's sake, relax."

He did as he was told, though she could still feel stiffness coiled through his body. She took her hand from his head and pried his arms away from his sides so that they were spread on the surface. She moved slowly down the length of his body, keeping one hand always at his back. She ran a hand down underneath his thigh and pulled his legs up so that they too were on the surface of the water.

"Close your eyes," she instructed. "And breathe deeply."

"What are you doing—" Noah started, but she shushed him.

"Trust me," she said.

His eyes searched her face. After a moment he closed them.

Elise smiled as she studied him in the pale wash of light. This was how she wanted always to remember him. Like this, the lines of worry erased from his face, his strong features a portrait of peace and what seemed a little like wonder. The water lapped gently at his sides and chest as she supported his back, and the tension and stiffness that had been so evident earlier were gone. She was supporting him, and he was letting her.

He had finally allowed himself to trust her.

For just a few stolen moments, she allowed herself the indulgence of feeling the rightness that engulfed her. For this moment he was hers, and she would give anything to keep him with her forever. But nothing was forever, and no matter what happened, a day from now, a week from now, years from now, she could not keep this duke for herself. With a bittersweet smile, she gently removed her hands from his back to let him float free on his own.

She saw his fingers curl, but he stayed buoyant on the water's surface. Elise slowly moved away from him, toward the shore. She climbed up on the grassy ledge, donned her abandoned trousers, and sat on the bank, water sluicing down her back from her hair. She was not sure how much time passed before Noah's feet found the riverbed once more, and he waded out of the water toward her. She was struck by the sheer beauty of him, made more intense by the absence of a frown. He lowered himself down on one side of her, both of them gazing out at the water in silence.

Elise shivered slightly, and Noah put a hand around her and pulled her closer to him. His fingers slid over the bare skin of her back where the loosened laces of her shirt had pulled the neck wide enough to expose her shoulder. His touch came to an abrupt halt just above her shoulder blade.

"Elise?" His fingers moved again, exploring the ruined skin at her back and the ridges of scar tissue that had never healed cleanly.

He would not have seen the old wound earlier, as it had always been covered by clothes. She forgot about the injury most days, though sometimes in the damp chill of the winter her shoulder ached.

He leaned back, pulling her shirt farther over her shoulder and down her back, and she heard his swift intake of breath.

"You can blame my brother Alex." She sighed, putting a hand on the warmth of Noah's thigh. "It's just as well he's good with money and numbers and such. He makes a ghastly surgeon."

His fingers were tracing the worst of the scar, and she could imagine him trying to determine exactly what sort of injury made such a mark. "You were shot." It was exhaled on a horrified breath.

"Yes."

"Jesus, Elise. When?"

"When I wasn't as invisible as I thought myself to be."

"What?"

Elise sighed. "American pickets have keen eyes and good aim. Or maybe just mediocre aim. They didn't kill me, after all, though the wound almost did."

"And your brother was there? He couldn't get you to a proper surgeon?" There was an edge to Noah's voice, as though he blamed Alex for what had been her failure.

Elise frowned. "It took Alex three days to find me. When the men who shot me discovered I wasn't dead, they bound my hands and feet and carried me back to the vicinity of their camp. They left me there, tied upright to a pine for the better part of the day." She stopped. "That feeling of helplessness was worse than any pain."

Noah's hand tightened on her shoulder. She didn't need him to say anything because he, of all people, understood that better than anyone.

"By the second day, infection had set in, though I have vague recollections of them pouring water down my throat and demanding answers to questions I could no longer comprehend. On the third day, they gave up and left me for dead. I am told Alex found me that night. Took the bullet out of my shoulder with his knife by the light of a single candle, too afraid to build a fire in case we were discovered. He laid me in a stream and sat with me for the next two days, trying to cool a fever that I can't remember." She stopped suddenly, realizing she had probably said more than was necessary, but unwilling to let Alex be cast in a poor light. "So no, my brother couldn't get me to a proper surgeon. He was two miles behind enemy lines and nine miles from a proper surgeon with nothing but a knife, a rifle, and a dying sister."

"I'm sorry."

"Why are you sorry? I survived because of Alex. He came for me when I had already been crossed off the lists as missing and presumed dead. He came for me when I needed him most. And then he did what he had to."

Noah was silent, his hands quiet on her skin. The moonlight blinked out and plunged them into darkness as clouds rolled and built.

"Then I am in his debt," Noah said finally.

Elise turned, wishing she could see his face. "You? He saved my life, not yours."

"No. I think he saved mine as well. Because he gifted me with you."

"Perhaps you might wish to thank him in person," Elise suggested softly.

"I believe I shall." Noah found her hand in the darkness and threaded his fingers through hers. "But first I will see Abigail. Because it's been too long since I did so. Because sometimes sisters need their brothers."

Elise froze and tightened her fingers around his. Moonlight flooded down around them again, flickering once before steadying. "They do," she agreed, almost afraid to breathe.

"It took too long for me to understand that." It was barely audible. "And for that, I am truly sorry."

"I think Abigail will forgive you," Elise whispered, her throat thickening.

"I hope so. Will you?"

"There is nothing to forgive."

"But—"

She pressed her free hand against his lips. "I do not wish to fight with you, Sir Noah."

Noah gazed at her for a long moment before releasing her fingers and pushing himself to his feet. He held out a hand to her. "Neither do I."

Elise put her hand in his and allowed him to help her up, and she was struck that it was this gesture, this extension of a strong hand on a grassy riverbank, that had first stolen her heart. They stood on the bank, neither speaking, as if terrified they might shatter the eerie spell that seemed to have been cast at the river's edge.

The air began to move suddenly, the sultry heat being touched by the first stirrings of a cool breeze that was gaining momentum and rattling the leaves. The moonlight vanished again before reappearing as more clouds drifted past. In the distance Elise could see brief flashes of light. A low rumble reached her ears.

"We should hurry," Noah whispered.

Elise nodded wordlessly and allowed herself to be guided through the trees and across the fields toward the house. The heat from Noah's broad palm was creeping up through her arm and warming her entire body, though the temperature outside was dropping rapidly.

The first raindrops fell just as they hurried into the yard, Square making a beeline up the narrow lane for the shelter of the barn, and Elise and Noah slamming the door of the house behind them as the wind suddenly gusted.

The house had descended into utter blackness, making it almost impossible to see him. She could only feel him, his heat, his touch. She concentrated on taking steady breaths, desire making her ache everywhere. Nothing that she hadn't felt the last time they had stood before each other, their clothes wet and dripping, her hand caught in his.

But this need was different. Something had changed. Something harder, hotter, more desperate than ever before had settled within her, demanding release.

A flash of lightning illuminated everything for a brief second before thunder rolled. It would seem the gods of the sky were as restless as she.

"You would have beaten me, you know," Noah said quietly.

"I beg your pardon?" She tried to see his face but it was impossible.

"If I had tried to best you on that shooting field, you would have beaten me."

"What are you talking about?" She was momentarily distracted. "Why is that important?"

"I've never met a woman with your confidence."

Elise smiled faintly. "I think you called it arrogance."

"I was wrong. It's confidence. And it's breathtaking." He pulled her closer, and she stumbled forward, her other hand coming up to rest on his chest. Beneath her palm she could feel the scattering of hair and the heat from his bare skin. Outside, the wind gusted again and rattled the glass panes.

"Thank you," she whispered, not sure what else she should say.

"I want to be able to do what you can."

Her head came up in surprise. "What? You mean with a rifle? Because I can assure you I can teach you how to handle the Baker far faster than I can teach you how to swim—"

"I'm not talking about swimming and shooting. I'm talking about..." He stopped. "Knowing who you are. I don't know if the man I have become here, now, can ever reconcile with the man who needs to exist in London."

"They are the same person, Noah. Lawson, Ellery, Ashland, the name matters not. Your journey is only relevant to the lessons it has taught along the way, not to its final destination."

In the dark his other hand found the side of her face, his fingers pulling her wet hair over her shoulder before tracing the edge of her jaw. "But you are so sure. So sure of who you are."

"I'm sure when I'm with you." That uncomfortable truth slipped out before she could stop it, before she could return it to the deep recesses of her mind where it had dwelt unobserved and unacknowledged.

The hand that still held hers tightened. "I don't understand."

"Never mind. It doesn't matter." Elise dropped her head, resting it against the broad expanse of his chest, listening to the steady beat of his heart.

His free hand settled gently against the back of her neck, keeping her close against him. "I rather think it does."

Elise felt her lips curl. "Now you're stealing my lines."

"You owe me a few."

A silence fell as Elise tried to find words that would explain, while Noah waited patiently.

"When I'm with you, like this, without an audience, I forget myself. I forget the role I am supposed to play, forget the lines I am supposed to deliver. With you I can step from the shadows," she said quietly. "But the rest of the time, I'm an actress, Noah. A woman who manipulates illusion to achieve whatever ends have been set out for me, whether it's on a theater stage or in a London ballroom. Today I was just a girl with a gun. Tomorrow I might need to be someone else. A week from now, you'll no longer recognize me. *I'll* no longer recognize me."

"You're so much more than just a girl with a gun." He said it fiercely and with such passion that she felt her stomach drop and her pulse race. "I see you, Elise DeVries. No matter what clothes you might wear or what mask you might assume, I see your courageous heart and I see your beautiful mind. I see your compassion and your hope, your resilience and your strength. If you do not know who you are, know that I do."

A blinding flash of light assaulted her eyes, followed by an instant rumble of thunder. His words made her want to weep with their quiet conviction. It was ironic, really. Each one so sure of the other. Both seeing more from without than they could from within.

"I'm so tired of pretending," she whispered. "Sometimes I'm not sure I can even remember who I once was. Or even who I want to be tomorrow."

"Who do you want to be tomorrow?" he asked, his voice hoarse.

Elise closed her eyes. "I don't want to talk about tomorrow."

He stilled. The hand at the back of her neck tightened, his fingers threading through the hair at the nape of her neck. His other hand released hers, and his fingers traveled over her upper arm, over her collarbone, coming to rest against the side of her face. "Then let's talk about now." His mouth was an inch away from hers.

She could hear his hunger and his need in the rasp of his words. She raised her other hand to his chest and ran both over the planes of his pectorals, down over his abdomen, and around his back, pressing her body against his. Her breasts were heavy, and the damp fabric of her shirt was chafing at her sensitive nipples.

He pulled her head back gently. "Who do you want to be right now?" he asked, his mouth against her ear. His voice was rough and full of promise. Her insides melted into a pulsing liquid heat. Dampness gathered between her legs. He would claim her now, unless she stopped him. Unless she pulled back out of his reach and retreated.

She swallowed, the words stuck in her throat.

"Right now, at this very moment, who do you want to be, Elise?"

"Yours," she whispered. "I want to be yours."

He found her lips in the darkness as a rumble of thunder ripped across the sky and the rain pounded on the roof and the windows. It mirrored the tumult that was coursing through his body, the need and hunger for this woman eclipsing everything that was reasonable and comprehensible. He had kissed her before he understood who she was and what she would ask of him, caught up in a vortex of intense desire he was powerless to fight. And he had kissed her after, still unable to resist her, but this, this was different. This was a melding of hearts and souls, a gut-wrenching acknowledgment that they were bound by more than just circumstance and fate. This was far more than a mere kiss, and there would be no going back from wherever this led them.

He pushed his hands farther into the mass of her wet hair, his lips slanting hard across hers. It was a confession, an assertion of the kaleidoscope of emotions that were warring for supremacy within him. And beneath this onslaught, she met him halfway. Exactly where he knew she would be.

He tried to pace himself because, God help him, he knew he should be gentle and patient and careful. He wanted to be all those things—she deserved all those things—but this need that filled him was wild and like nothing he had ever experienced before. He was unbearably hard, his erection throbbing at the wet restriction of his breeches. Against his chest he could feel the firm pressure of her breasts, and he ran his hands down the length of her spine, gathering her tightly within his embrace. The urge to claim her, to take her swiftly against the wall, on the table, on the floor, anywhere he might bury himself deep within her heat and find release from this torment, was making him light-headed.

Another roll of thunder crashed across the sky, shaking the very walls of his house. He dropped his hands to her ass, pulling her hard against him, desperately afraid he wouldn't have the control to make this perfect for her. His hands moved to stroke the sides of her breasts, her skin fiery beneath the sodden coolness of her shirt, but it wasn't enough. Nothing was enough. He wanted all of her against all of him. His hands moved to the hem of her shirt and pulled up at the fabric, trying to work it from her body and over her arms, but it was wet and twisted and uncooperative, and against his mouth, Elise made a sound of frustration.

Without his thinking, his fingers released the hem and moved to the ties at the neck of her shirt, curling into the seams, pulling at the worn linen. The threadbare fabric would rip, he knew, if he pulled hard enough, rending from her throat down the length of her torso. His fingers tightened, and he felt the first frayed edges give way. Somewhere beyond his haze of lust his conscience reminded him that this was not careful or patient. He felt completely out of control, and he barely recognized himself at this moment.

Without warning, Elise broke their kiss. "Do it," she gasped.

Noah went still. She couldn't possibly have divined what he'd been thinking.

She brought her hands up to his and covered them with her own. "I want nothing between us." Her breath was coming in shallow gasps. "Nothing."

Noah squeezed his eyes shut briefly, trying to find his control. Her words were pushing him further and further away from whatever shreds remained of his gentle intentions.

"Do it, Noah." Elise slid her hands up and twisted her fingers in his hair, her mouth against his ear, her tongue grazing the sensitive spot in the hollow of his neck beneath his earlobe.

"Elise—"

"I dare you."

Noah groaned and pulled hard, the fabric in his hands giving way easily. She stepped back as he shoved the wet linen back over her shoulders, her hands dropping so that he could push the sleeves down her arms. Her shirt fell to the floor behind her, forgotten, and her trousers followed. He could still hear her rapid breathing, could smell the rain on her skin, could feel the heat of her body so close to his.

Lightning flickered again through the windows, and for an ephemeral moment, he could see her. And then the blackness returned, but the sight of her bared to him sucked the air from his lungs and forced a sound from his throat he didn't recognize.

In the next instant, her hands were on him, the slide of her fingers and palms over his chest, along his ribs, down to the waistband of his breeches. With deft movements she went to work on the buttons, each brush of her fingers against his throbbing erection an exercise in torture. His breeches loosened and her hands delved beneath the waistband, pushing the wet fabric over his hips and down his thighs. She had gone down on a knee, he realized, as he felt her hands sliding along the rigid muscles of his thighs and then his calves as she worked his breeches from his legs down to his ankles. He stepped out of them, kicking them to the side, and then stood frozen as her hands skimmed his knees, then the insides of his thighs. He felt the brush of her hair against his cock as she bent, and then her mouth replaced her fingers as she left a fiery trail of kisses along the insides of his legs and ever higher.

She cupped his balls in her hand and then stroked the length of his erection, and he moaned at the indescribable pleasure of her touch. His fingers tangled in her hair as her hands slid around his thighs and over his buttocks. And then she took him in her mouth, and he nearly came right there as her tongue swirled around the tip of his cock. Lightning flashed, and Noah had a sudden glimpse of Elise kneeling before him, her dark head bent as she explored him with her mouth. He had never, in all his life, seen such an erotic, perfectly wicked sight, and the smoldering lust he'd fought to control ignited into a firestorm that ripped through his veins, lodging itself deep in the base of his spine and making his cock pulse in anticipation.

He staggered slightly and forced himself back, dropping to his knees in front of her.

"I won't last," he whispered raggedly, his hands still in her hair.

"I never intended you to," she murmured, finding his mouth again in the dark with her own and kissing him deeply.

He shuddered at the rawness of her words, a feeling of such possession coursing through him that it left him reeling. He took control of the kiss and dragged his teeth over her lower lip, his tongue sparring with hers. "I want you to feel what I feel when I'm with you," he rasped against her, his mouth moving down the edge of her jaw to the long column of her neck. "I want you to know what you do to me."

Elise's hands came up to grasp his wrists, her fingers quivering against his muscles. "Can you feel that?" she asked. "Can you feel me shaking?"

He might have nodded, but it was becoming a chore to breathe, much less speak.

"You do that to me." She guided one of his hands down over her breast to cover her hardened nipple. "You do this." She pulled his fingers down farther, over the gentle swell of her abdomen, and pressed them between her thighs. "And you do this."

It was Noah who trembled now, even as she released his hand. She was wet and hot, and he slid a finger through that glorious heat, the heel of his hand rocking hard against her pubic bone. She hissed and arched against him, her hips jerking as he pushed one finger into her, then two. She grasped his shoulders, her head falling back. Noah withdrew before pushing back into her, and she whimpered, her hips rolling down against the pressure. He bent his head, his mouth finding the swell of her breast and then her nipple, his teeth grazing the hard peak before he sucked gently.

Every muscle in Elise's body went taut, and she pushed herself back with the same desperation with which he had only a moment ago.

"I won't last," she panted.

"Never my intention," he managed.

"Oh God." She made a muffled sound that might have been laughter.

Chilled air intruded into the space between them as a fork of lightning sent a blinding flash through the room and thunder crashed overhead. Noah leaned forward, despising even that small distance between them. He ran a finger over her bottom lip, now swollen and soft. Another surge of possessiveness roared through him, a craving so acute that it was physical pain. "Tell me, Elise. Tell me what you want."

He heard her suck in her breath, heard the unevenness of her voice when she spoke. "I want you to make me yours. I want to feel you deep inside me. I want to feel your skin against mine. I want to hear you say my name when you come. I want your nights and your deepest fantasies that go with them. And when I come, I want your name on my lips."

Noah closed his eyes, knowing that he was forever lost. He would never recover from her. Never find another who would give what she had already given him. She owned his heart and his soul and all the dark and the light that might be found in both. He found her hand, shoving himself to his feet and pulling her with him.

Without a second's hesitation, he swept her into his arms.

⁓

Noah carried Elise into her room, and the panic that she always felt with such loss of control was wholly absent. Everything had tilted between them, altered beyond what she once recognized. He was a part of her now, woven into the tapestry of her being, and she would trust him with her very life. She kept her hands wrapped tightly about his neck, felt his strong hands supporting her even as he kissed her, tiny tastes that left her gasping and needing more.

She had nearly climaxed the first time he had slid his finger through the folds of her sex. She could have let him bring her to the edge and take her over simply with his hands. But she knew that wasn't going to be enough for her. Not this time. Maybe never. She wanted all of him, wanted to feel all his strength and his power when he took her.

There would come a time when she would watch. When there would be light enough to look into his eyes as he made love to her, see the splendor of his body, watch their bodies join. But on this night she would rely on her other senses. Taste the sweat of his skin, hear the sounds of his pleasure, feel his body reach for release.

He stopped abruptly in the darkness and bent, and Elise barely had time to register the cool sheets of her bed beneath her back before he came down, bracing himself above her, his kisses no longer a series of tastes but a hungry plunder that she was only too eager to comply with. He nudged her thighs apart with his knees, kneeling between her legs and straightening, his mouth leaving hers, but his hands now traveling over her collarbone to explore the generous swell of her breasts. He covered them with his palms, his thumbs scraping the sensitive peaks of her nipples. Elise made a sound of pleasure even as her back came off the bed, arching farther into his touch as her legs tightened on either side of his hips.

"So beautiful," Noah whispered into the blackness.

Elise couldn't answer, the feel of his hands, of his skin against hers, wiping her mind of everything except the sensation of his fingers as they traveled over her ribs, spanned her hips, and then slid along the insides of her legs, urging them wider. He bent, pressing his mouth to her navel, then to the soft skin of her inner thigh, tormenting touches that robbed her of breath. The want that had pooled low in her belly swelled to a throbbing that intensified with each touch that only teased.

And then his mouth was *there*, his tongue doing unholy things that had her fingers curling into the bedding in an attempt to anchor herself to something. Something that would keep her from flying into tiny pieces.

"Noah," she gasped. She needed him to stop. She needed him to never stop.

He raised his head, the immediate loss of his ministrations a horrible, cruel thing, but then his body covered hers, and his weight and his heat pressed her deep into the mattress. The rub of his chest hair against her breasts was an intoxicating friction, and his heart pounded beneath his ribs in time with hers. He braced himself on his elbows, and Elise wrapped her legs around his waist, her hips straining. Beneath her calves, the muscles in his buttocks flexed, and she could feel the tip of his cock nudge against the entrance to her folds.

She tightened her legs, her hands sliding over his back, urging him against her. She could hear his labored breathing, could feel the perspiration on his feverish skin as he fought for control.

"Not enough," she panted. "All of you."

He made a tortured noise and thrust into her, burying himself to the hilt.

Elise moaned, her hips tipping, reveling in the rightness of his filling her, stretching her, truly making her his. He stayed motionless for an exquisite moment, time suspended in sensation before he moved, withdrawing and then pushing back into her in a long, smooth stroke.

Behind her eyelids stars danced and exploded. She teetered on the precipice, wanting, needing, to take him with her when she went. She shifted her legs, her heels now braced against his ass, her inner muscles clenching around the length of him as she rocked her hips.

He groaned and slid out before impaling her again, harder this time.

"Don't stop," she breathed.

He gasped, a harsh, desperate sound, and he obeyed with hard, deliberate thrusts that sent perfect arrows of agonized pleasure spiraling through her. She met him stroke for stroke, feeling the tension within her build, the coiling of energy and anticipation winding tighter and tighter. Beneath her the bed pitched and rocked, while above the thunderstorm still raged, drowning out the sounds of flesh on flesh and the small noises of desire.

She felt the first ripples of release descend through her body, and her hands grasped at his back, her legs tightening around his hips before the wave of her orgasm slammed through her. The force of it sucked the air from her lungs and tore the voice from her throat as her body convulsed upon itself, leaving her insensible to anything except the excruciating pleasure that hammered mercilessly through her limbs.

Elise came back to herself enough to hear Noah moan, pushing hard into her, his hips jerking, before he yanked out of her and thrust himself against her belly, spending himself in the soft hollow of her hip. His head dropped into her shoulder, his breath coming in great heaving gasps, his hips still thrusting in small, slow movements.

She stroked the back of his head with her hand, trailing her fingers through his hair and over his shoulders, languidly, with no thought other than for the contentment it gave her to simply touch him, here, like this. This was where she belonged. No matter who she might have been or who she might yet become, she belonged to this man. In her search for Noah Ellery, she had found something she hadn't even known she'd been looking for. Here, in the security of his arms, she had found a sanctuary, uncluttered by secrets and artifice. Here she'd found only a feeling of rightness and a bittersweet ache in her chest that told her that her heart was no longer hers to give. He had claimed it as surely as he had claimed her body.

Noah stirred, pushing himself up on his elbows. The rain that had pounded on the windows and the roof had let up, but the thunder still echoed, though it had moved off into the distance. He bent his head and kissed her, a butterfly touch of his lips against hers, gentle and soft. "Don't move," he said.

Elise was reasonably sure that she wouldn't be able to move for a long time yet, her body sated to the point of immobility. "Mmmm," was all she could put together, hoping he would take it as a sign of her acquiescence.

He rolled off her and stood, disappearing somewhere into the house before returning less than a minute later. He lowered himself to the edge of the bed, letting something drop to the floor next to her with a muted thump.

"What was that?" she asked.

"My knife. My clothes. What's left of your shirt. And a replacement."

"You brought me a shirt?"

"One of mine. In case you were cold."

His hands found her in the darkness, and Elise started as he pressed something cool and damp to her stomach.

Belatedly she realized it was her ruined shirt that he was smoothing over her skin, wiping traces of his semen from her. His fingers followed the path of the cloth, tracing the curve of her hip and the swell of her breast.

"Thank you," she murmured.

Noah let the wet linen drop to the floor and ran a hand along her cheek, bending to press his mouth to her shoulder, another sweet hail of kisses against her damp skin. She felt worshipped and treasured and devastatingly happy.

Elise heard the bed ropes creak as he shifted, moving over her and stretching out on the far side of the bed, his body pressed against hers. Water dripped from an eave somewhere, the last lonely remnant of the deluge. Outside, shadows were shifting, glimpses of silver moonlight shining through as the last of the rain clouds parted and scudded across the sky.

"Go to sleep," he whispered against her ear. "Dawn will come soon enough. And the road to London is long."

Elise nodded, though she didn't ask who Noah would be when he rode into London. She didn't ask about the title or the fortune or the solicitors who waited with bated breath, wondering if the heir to Ashland would materialize. She didn't ask about Francis Ellery, because it was enough, for now, that Noah would be there for his sister.

Because it was enough, for now, that he would be with her.

Chapter 14

Something jarred Noah awake.

He opened his eyes, the room still dark, though through the windows the sky had lost the depth of black velvet and had been tinted with the faintest wash of grey. Dawn was not far off. Beside him he could feel Elise's warmth where she was curled against him.

He listened hard, and he heard it then, a faint creak. And he knew then why he had woken.

Very slowly, feigning a sleepy stretch, Noah turned, burying his face against Elise's shoulder, his mouth near her ear. "Elise," he whispered.

She came awake almost instantly.

"There is someone in the house," he whispered.

Her breathing remained slow and even, but against his body her muscles tensed. She nodded and rolled away from him, but was back in a second. She leaned forward, brushing a kiss to his lips, covering the movements of her hand

as she brought it to his under the sheets and pressed something hard into his palm. His fingers closed around it, and
with a start Noah realized it was his hunting knife. She
must have retrieved it from the floor next to the bed.

Through the open door, another creak reached his
ears, then an indistinct scrape. He would have known
that sound anywhere. It was the sound of a blade being
drawn. With slow movements Noah drew his own from
under the sheets and positioned his body so that he was
between Elise and the doorway, as if shifting in sleep.
They were cornered in this bedroom, and his only advantage would be surprise.

"I want you to get on the floor when I tell you to, understood?" Noah whispered, his head still against her neck.

Elise hesitated.

"You have no weapon."

"It's under the bed," she murmured.

"What?"

"My rifle. It's under the bed. It's loaded."

Noah closed his eyes. Of course it was.

There was another creak, followed by silence, and the
faint smell of an unwashed body and wet wool reached his
nose. In the corner of his eye, a shadow moved in the doorway, followed by a faint catch of breath. There was at least
one intruder. In the suffocating silence came a grunt, the
sound of fabric flapping damply as an arm was waved in
some sort of gesture.

Noah watched from beneath lowered lashes as another
figure separated from the one at the door, moving into the
room and now faintly outlined in front of the bedroom window. The second man made a motion at the still form of
Elise and then made a crude gesture at his crotch.

An icy calm settled through Noah's body then, one he had not felt in a very long time. It bled through his veins, slowed his heart, focused his thoughts, and heightened his senses. In the blink of an eye, he was fifteen years old again, on a dark London street, fighting for his life, facing those determined to take whatever meager coin or possessions Noah had on him or die trying.

Noah had lived that day, and many others just like it in the years that followed. Just as he would live now.

If these men were smart, they would try to kill him first. One always removed the biggest threat as quickly as possible. Not only did it improve one's chances at survival, it often broke the confidence of the others. He knew this from experience. Experience he had not wanted or asked for but had gotten all the same. Ironic that he had thought it something best forgotten. Because at this moment he was drawing on every ounce of it.

If they thought to rape Elise, they would need to kill him first. Because God help him, he would carve them apart piece by piece if they so much as laid a hand on her while he was still breathing.

The smell of the intruders became stronger. They were farther in the room, closer to the bed now, and he could hear a faint hiss of breath. Beneath him Elise pressed her fingers against his arm, just once.

And then the air around him moved and all hell broke loose.

Noah reared up and struck out as the man closest to the bed lunged down toward him, a short dagger clutched in both hands and raised over his head. Noah's left forearm blocked the assassin's stroke while his hunting knife caught the killer at his exposed throat. Blood spurted heavily and the man dropped the dagger, the blade clanging off the wooden floor. His hands clawed at his ruined neck, and Noah shoved him back, away from the bed.

Elise had vanished from sight, and Noah desperately hoped that she was safe where she was, somewhat protected. But he had no time to make sure because he was already on his feet, turning to face the second man, who still waited at the foot of the bed.

The stench of death now filled the room, the coppery tones of blood mixed with the darker musk of fear. The shock of the demise of his partner made the second man hesitate, enough to cost him any advantage. With a snarl Noah was on him, his mind evaluating the threat of the long dagger the man wielded. Good for stabbing, useless for slashing. They'd meant to kill them silently. They'd meant to use stealth while Elise and Noah slept, a brutal, quick attack that would have delivered a slow death, their life's blood leaking out onto the white sheets, pooling on the floor. These men had come to kill and then slip away. They had not come prepared for a fight.

The remaining assassin struck out with his dagger, and Noah dodged back easily, hearing the man grunt with the effort. He adjusted his grip on his knife, circling slowly, cold fury making every movement deliberate and sure.

They'd have killed Elise, after they had raped her, of that he had no doubt. She might be strong and tough and resilient but she would not have been able to overpower two men on her own. Because this wasn't a space where a rifle would be an advantage. This was an arena for the type of fighting he had learned to excel at. The type of fighting that had no rules and no conscience and where the winner got nothing except a reprieve from death.

"Drop your weapon," Noah said evenly, "and I might let you live."

"No." The killer was breathing hard and backing up.

"Pity. Though I promise to make your death quick," Noah told him, adjusting his grip on the hilt of his knife. "Which is more than you deserve." He cocked his head, crouching slightly, simply waiting for his opportunity.

The killer wheezed and groped behind him for the door frame, his dagger wavering in the grey dark. Noah could see the whites of the man's eyes, see the wild cast to his movements. He had suddenly realized that this was not a fight he would win and was retreating, though Noah had no intention of letting him go.

Noah lunged then, his knife slashing across the assassin's abdomen. The man grunted and staggered back, but Noah's hand shot out and he caught a fistful of the man's coat. The man flailed and twisted, and yanked his arms out of the coat in utter desperation. With a sudden jerk, the killer turned faster than Noah would have thought possible, throwing a nearby chair between them, and dove through the door, slamming it behind him. Cursing, Noah kicked the chair aside and wrenched open the door, but the assassin had already retreated down the hall and was gone from view. Noah followed, but was forced to measure his movements to avoid a potential ambush.

Halfway down the hall, he became aware of a presence by his side.

"Get back in the room," Noah hissed.

"He's running," Elise said, ignoring him. Her voice was cold and remote, and Noah wasn't even sure she was talking to him.

He tried to angle himself in front of her but she was low

to the ground, moving soundlessly and swiftly. She was dressed in a shirt and nothing else, her rifle in her hand, and she looked like a specter gliding through his house. It was enough to send a jolt of shock through his fury. They reached the kitchen and Noah paused, the door out to the gardens swinging, still moving on its hinges. With no hesitation Elise skirted the room and slipped through the door, Noah now hard on her heels.

On the other side of the roses, a white shirt billowed in the grey light as the assassin fled across the pastures. The man stumbled, his arms windmilling before he righted himself and kept running. Elise was still ahead of Noah, and as they cleared the rose garden, she pulled up. He heard her exhale, saw her bring the rifle to her shoulder.

"Don't kill him," Noah said coldly. "Dead men don't talk."

She didn't look at him, but nodded almost imperceptibly. Her hands readjusted, and her finger caressed the trigger.

She fired.

In the distance the man fell, his momentum carrying him forward so that he somersaulted in the grass. Birds rose from the trees in startled surprise, careening out of sight toward the river. The killer flopped on his side and then pushed himself to his knees, crawling unevenly toward the trees.

Elise lowered her gun, the smell of powder sharp in the air.

Noah released a breath he hadn't realized he'd been holding and crossed the remaining steps toward Elise. Elise turned to him, her face pale against the darkness of her hair.

"Are you hurt?" he asked, his eyes and his hands examining her body. He was afraid to touch her and afraid not to, all at once.

"No." She shook her head. "I'm not hurt."

He enfolded her in his arms, crushing her to him, his face buried against her hair where it tumbled across her shoulders. His hand rested on her back, and he could feel her heart pounding. The barrel of the Baker was caught between them, and it was pressing uncomfortably against his ribs. It didn't matter. He needed this contact, needed to know that she was whole. And still his.

After a minute Elise struggled to pull back, and he released his grip on her. Dark smears of blood now stained her shirt where she had been pressed against him. Her own fingers skipped over his chest, his ribs, his lower abdomen, searching for injury in the grey light.

"It's not my blood."

Her fingers stilled, and she looked up at him and simply nodded. It was nothing less than what he'd expected. Because, like him, she had been here before.

"Thank you," she said.

He bent to kiss her, a hard, possessive kiss that was born of the madness and danger of the last few minutes. He did not ask her what she was thanking him for, just as he did not try to minimize his actions in that bedroom. He had done what was necessary to protect her, and he would do it again—

His mind cleared, his thoughts snapping into focus.

The icy calm that had gripped him earlier still pulsed through his veins, though it was different now. In the cells of Bedlam and on the dangerous streets of London, that same cold composure had saved his life more times than he cared to remember, but it had always been accompanied by an underlying sense of desperation. The knowledge that each situation pitted him against death. A perpetual state of kill or be killed, and one never knew where or when the next threat would come.

This was different. He was different. Standing out here, in a Nottingham rose garden, he was not a desperate youth any longer, powerless to prevent the next threat of violence that would inevitably come, directed at himself or Elise, or even Abigail. Or anyone else who might be under his protection.

The power to control the future, should he accept it, was his for the taking.

～

Noah had dragged the assassin back and bound the man's feet and hands. He'd left the man lying on the packed earth in the middle of the rose garden before he'd disappeared into the house and collected the body of the first killer. Without a word Noah had slung the dead assassin over his shoulder and set off across the pasture, vanishing into the trees that lined the river. When he returned he'd been empty-handed, his face set into hard, unforgiving lines.

He'd left Elise to watch the killer who yet lived, though even had the man not been bound, he wouldn't have been going anywhere fast. She'd hit the assassin in the back of the thigh—not her best shot, but it had done the job. The bullet was buried deep within the muscle, and his woolen breeches were soaked with blood. He'd need to find a surgeon within the next few hours. Ugly things happened to deep wounds like that if they were not attended to promptly.

Now Noah prowled across the garden and back. He'd

donned his breeches but not his shirt, and his chest and arms were streaked with blood and sweat. Muscles and sinew flexed and rippled as he moved, slowly and with cold purpose. His hair hung over his forehead, damp curls plastered to his skin, and beneath his brow his eyes blazed with a chilling, feral fury. His hand was still wrapped around the hilt of his hunting knife, and the blade gleamed with a wash of crimson, a macabre color in the early rays of dawn.

Elise watched, silent. This was a Noah she'd never seen. It had startled her at first, this transformation. This was a street fighter, a man pushed to his limits who had pushed back and done so with a lethal efficiency. He fought hard, he fought smart, and in the end he had fought for her and beside her. There had been no hesitation. There had been no second-guessing. He'd been powerful and magnificent, dangerous and utterly ruthless. And it stole her breath and left her weak-kneed. And wholly aroused.

Noah stopped near the feet of the assassin. A man who made death his trade could recognize it when it stared him in the face, and he struggled before collapsing back into the dirt.

"How much did Francis Ellery pay you to kill me?" Noah asked in a bored, detached tone.

The man set his mouth into a hard line. "I'm not going to say nothing," he muttered.

"Yes, well, that is certainly true." Noah crouched down and gestured to the man's leg with the tip of his knife. "You'll be dead in two hours. Maybe three. And any chance you might have had to say something and save yourself will be long gone."

The thin-faced assassin glared at Noah through reddened eyes.

"Never mind. It doesn't matter. Whatever it was Ellery paid you, it wasn't enough to cover your life."

"Fifty pounds," the man blurted. "He paid us fifty pounds."

"Fifty pounds?" Noah repeated.

"Twenty-five up front, twenty-five when it was done."

Noah examined the tip of his blade. "Bloody hell, but have I been away from London so long that dukes are worth so little?" His face was set in hard lines, and his words were sharp. And deliberate. And sure.

Elise felt something soar within her.

"A duke?" The man's head fell back on the ground, and he groaned. "He never said you were a duke."

"Ah well, I'm sure that little detail slipped his mind in his clumsy rush to claim the ducal throne. I know I probably don't look the part at the moment, but then I hadn't expected your colleague to bleed quite so much in his attempt to kill me. A very unpleasant business, the assassination of a duke. Really, you ought to have demanded more money."

The man at his feet swore.

"And then there is, of course, the issue I have with your intentions toward the lady."

The assassin's eyes cut toward Elise where she was leaning on the Baker, still dressed only in her shirt. "That ain't no lady—" he managed to sneer, before the tip of Noah's knife twisted into the fabric of his trousers near his groin.

"Careful," Noah said.

"She shot me!"

"And I might ask her to do it again." Noah considered him, his knife twisting just an inch. "Or not. I should think you owe her an apology."

"What?" The killer looked at Noah as though he'd lost his mind.

"You were planning on raping her, then killing her, I believe. Or perhaps the other way around? Either way, I take exception to it. Apologize."

"You're crazy," the assassin wheezed.

"So I've been told." Noah smiled an empty smile. His knife slid along the fall of the man's breeches, the buttons sliding to the earth as the threads were neatly sliced.

"I'm sorry," the killer gasped in Elise's direction.

Noah pushed himself to his feet. "I thought so. Don't go anywhere," he said, his voice glacial. "If you behave, I might remember to take you out towards town when we leave and deposit you in the vicinity of a proper surgeon." He glanced at Elise before looking back. "Everyone knows the forests can be dangerous. Poachers and the like. Bad luck to be mistaken for a side of venison, though a sight more believable than explaining how you got shot while trying to kill a duke."

The assassin cursed again.

Noah turned to Elise. "Come with me." His eyes were hot and hard, and an electrified thrill went straight up her spine and her skin pebbled with gooseflesh.

He caught her hand in his and led her into the house through the open kitchen door, slamming it behind him with his foot. Noah turned, spinning her around and pressing her back against its solid surface. "You're shaking," he said. He took the rifle from her hand and set it aside, along with his knife.

"Yes." She hadn't known until he said it. She'd been aware only of the arousal that was clawing its way through her, a desperate need that had left her wet and wanting and unsteady.

"You're safe, Elise."

"I know that," she breathed, looking up at him, drowning in the heat and the power that blazed from his every pore. "That's not why I'm shaking."

⁓

He went still before his mouth was on hers, his fingers yanking at the bottom of her shirt, shoving it up over her hips, his hands on the smooth skin of her ribs and her lower back. He had known it was coming, this storm. It had been building in him, emotions dammed inside that demanded a physical release. A release that would validate the realization that they were still alive when death had come so very near. It heightened his senses, set fire to his blood, and made every touch almost unbearable in its sharp ecstasy.

Elise was wrenching the buttons of his breeches, pulling at the fall until it fell open. His cock sprang free from where it had been straining against the fabric, and she took his length in her hand, closing her fingers around him, and white-hot pleasure roared through him. He groaned, a guttural sound that was torn from somewhere deep within.

"I need you," he said hoarsely, and it was the only warning she had before he bent, his hands cupping her ass, and he hauled her up against him.

Elise wrapped her legs around his waist, her arms around his neck, inching herself up until he could feel the length of him slide through the slick heat of her sex. He pushed them harder against the door, pinning her back and shoulders and moving one hand between them, guiding the head of his cock to her entrance. Her head fell back against the door, her eyes glittering, a feverish color staining her cheekbones. Without a second's hesitation, he thrust himself deep.

She whimpered and tightened her legs, a vise of trembling muscle wrapped around his waist. Her entire body was straining now, and her hips jerked, hard, fast movements that lacked control as she sought release. He didn't want control. He wanted her, all of her as she was, uninhibited and unreserved. Alive.

He tightened his hands on her backside, and he moved then, deliberately driving into her wet heat, hearing the tiny, broken sounds of pleasure she made with each thrust. The friction of their bodies was relentless, the pleasure vicious and hot. It was too much and not enough at the same time. She bore down on him, and just like that, he felt her inner muscles convulse around him and she cried out, her fingers clamping into the muscles of his shoulders, her face buried in the hollow of his throat.

His vision dimmed, the roar of release streaking through his very bones, an inferno of fire and flame. Then the waves of pleasure came, one after the other, with such savage intensity that it left him gasping for air. He thrust hard, once, twice, before he pulled himself all the way out and spilled himself at the cleft of her buttocks. He was shaking and spent, and if Elise hadn't been wrapped so tightly around him and braced against the door, he might have simply slid to the ground.

He held them there, each of them breathing hard. Presently Elise unfolded her legs and slid along his body to find her own feet, her arms still wrapped around his neck.

"I was afraid," he said, realizing the truth as he spoke it.

"Not for me. For you. Afraid I might have lost you." His forehead was against hers, their sweat mingling.

"I'm right here," she whispered, her breathing not yet settled.

"I know."

Elise lifted her head, and her eyes searched his. "What happens now, Your Grace?"

She had called him by his title before and he had always rejected the address, resisted the truth. But then he hadn't been ready. Perhaps then he had lacked the understanding or the faith in himself to do what needed to be done. No longer.

"Collect the sheets in the bedroom and burn them. See what you can do about the floor. I'll leave her a note, but I don't want Mrs. Pritchard thinking I killed you when she gets back. Or alternatively, that you killed me."

There was a heady power in those words, a beginning of…something that had been missing for far too long.

"Very good, Your Grace," Elise replied, her mouth curving into a slow smile.

"I'll need to send word to the neighbors and arrange to have the Carter boys look after the farm for a while." Noah was thinking out loud. He glanced down at his blood-stained chest and then at Elise's wildly tumbled hair and her soiled shirt. "How long until you can be ready to depart?"

"Not long, Your Grace." There was approval shining from her eyes. Approval and something else that made him catch his breath.

"Good." The Duke of Ashland met her eyes. "We're going to London."

Chapter 15

In the end they took the mail coach back to London, sacrificing any personal comfort for the swift, punishing pace of multiple teams, something that their own horses could never have survived. There were no stops along the way save those where the horses were changed and mail and passengers loaded and unloaded. Conversation was limited, not only by the presence of the other passengers who rode with them, but also by the sense of urgency that had suddenly asserted itself. Every mile that passed saw Noah retreat deeper into a contemplative silence. Elise did not try to fill the quiet with inane conversation. Both she and Noah needed time to think, because weighty issues drew nearer with each town and hamlet that they passed through. The Duke of Ashland would need a very clever plan.

It was unlikely that anyone had followed them or had any reason to suspect they were anything other than a pair of weary travelers, but they had taken no chances.

Both wore caps to partially conceal their features and had dressed in simple, unmemorable clothing. A country man and his younger brother, traveling to London in search of work in one of the many factories, if anyone should ask.

No one did.

They disembarked in London under heavy skies and a steady drizzle, which suited Elise immensely. There were no showy open equipages on the road, filled with dandies and their ladies hoping to see and be seen. Pedestrians kept their heads down and their steps brisk, no one wishing to linger in the damp. Not that she expected to be recognized, but Elise was nowhere near ready to present the Duke of Ashland to London. She led them south through the streets on foot, wending past familiar landmarks as they drew closer to Covent Square.

Noah's face was set in hard lines, his eyes guarded, his expression grim and unreadable. She admitted that there was a small part of her that mourned for Noah Lawson. Mourned on his behalf the loss of a life so very different from the one he would step into. Mourned the loss of the simple pleasures like games of soldiers and chess with children at a dining room table where the chairs didn't match. Noah was doing the right thing, she knew. But it wasn't without cost.

They reached Covent Square, skirting the northwest corner of St Paul's Church and making their way along the piazza to the old townhome. As they climbed the worn steps, Noah glanced up once at the building's worn facade and then met her eyes, a faint shadow of uncertainty flitting across his face, the first she'd seen since they'd left for London.

"Is Abigail here?" he asked, gesturing at the heavy wooden door.

"Yes," she told him. "She should be. Your sister agreed to stay with us until such time as the matter with your mother could be resolved. Or until you might be located."

She saw a muscle in his jaw flex.

From her pocket Elise withdrew the steel rose she had collected from Noah's room before they'd left Nottingham. "I think she'd like this returned to her in person," Elise said quietly. She pressed the brooch into Noah's hand. His fingers closed over hers, the warm steel caught between them.

"Elise—"

The door suddenly swung open. "It's raining enough to drown the ducks," Roderick said unnecessarily. "Are ye coming in or not?"

Elise started, and her hand dropped from Noah's. "Hello, Roderick."

"Good afternoon to you too, Miz Elise." He peered past her to examine Noah. "And a good afternoon to ye, sir," he said.

"Er, good afternoon," Noah responded, sounding a little taken aback.

Roddy beamed and swung the door wider, and Elise and Noah stepped in. The boy closed the door smartly behind them, following them farther into the hall.

Elise turned to Noah. "Your Grace, may I introduce Roderick. Roddy, His Grace, the Duke of Ashland."

"Ah." Roddy's eyebrows rose just a fraction. "Then my greeting was lacking. A good afternoon to ye, Your Grace," he said with cheerful aplomb. "And a pleasure to make yer acquaintance."

Noah was studying the boy curiously. "A pleasure to meet you, Roderick."

"The duchess is in her study," Roddy volunteered. "Got back just this morning. Shall I fetch her for ye?"

Elise would speak with Ivory soon enough. "No, I'll find her a bit later. Is Lady Abigail available, Roderick?"

Roddy's face brightened. "Oh aye. She's in the kitchens with Cook again. Been baking all afternoon." A small hand disappeared into the pocket of his coat, and he withdrew what looked like a tart wrapped in a handkerchief. "She gave me *five*," he said, before he frowned, looking disgruntled. "Told me to eat them all. Said I needed some more meat on my bones."

Out of the corner of her eye, she saw Noah smile.

"Could you fetch her, please? And accompany her to the drawing room? We'll wait there."

Roddy stuffed his tart back in his pocket. "Aye. D'ye want tea brought up too? I can ask Cook while I'm there."

"No, thank you," Elise said. "We just need Lady Abigail."

Roddy shrugged. "As ye wish," he said, and disappeared into the bowels of the house.

Elise turned back to Noah. "Roderick is—"

"I know exactly what Roderick is," Noah said, his mouth curling slightly at the corners. "He had his clever hands in my pockets within three seconds of me stepping into this house."

Elise bit her lip. "He's slipping."

"No, he's quite good. Unfortunately, I have more experience than I care to remember with boys just like him."

"You didn't say anything."

"I didn't want to hurt his feelings."

Elise felt her heart squeeze. Of course he hadn't.

Noah held up the brooch still in his hand. "Would he have taken it?"

"No. Roddy generally looks for small concealed weapons or anything else of interest that might be problematic. Or helpful, depending on the situation."

Noah gave her a long look.

"Come," she said, pulling him farther into the hall. She led him deeper into the house, the scents of wax polish and baking mingling pleasantly. Wood paneling gleamed on the walls, reflecting the soft glow from the sconces that had been lit against the gloom of the day. She ducked into the drawing room.

A fire had been lit in the hearth, chasing away the damp, and Elise moved directly to the long windows overlooking the square and released the heavy drapes, allowing them to close over the glass. Elise doubted very much that Francis Ellery had any idea where Abigail was, or that he cared where she had gone, but she didn't wish to take any chances. Certainly not with Noah here.

She set about lighting the candelabra to provide supplementary light. Surreptitiously she watched Noah as he wandered the room, his fingers trailing over the back of the upholstered rosewood sofa. He stopped near the tall, narrow bookcase that towered to the high ceiling and pulled out an expensively bound book, opening it and closing it once before replacing it on its shelf. He continued to the hearth and past, pacing to the window, where he pulled back a heavy curtain before letting it drop.

"Noah."

He stopped and raised his head.

Elise crossed the room and stopped in front of him. She took his hand in hers, pulling his fingers open to reveal the steel rose. The edges had pressed deep grooves into his palms where he'd been gripping it hard.

"I was ten when she saw me last." He was staring down at the brooch.

"A long time," Elise agreed softly.

"I don't know what to tell her." His lifted his eyes. "I don't know what to say. I thought I did, but I don't. What if I'm not what—"

"She's never wanted perfect, Noah. She only wants you."

She heard him exhale heavily.

She closed his fingers back over the brooch. "Don't forget how strong your sister really is," she whispered. "Let your sister know you." She went up on her tiptoes and pressed her lips to his cheek. He caught her and pulled her to him, holding her tightly as though he might never let go. She wrapped her arms around his back and rested her head against his chest.

From the hallway the sound of hurrying feet and raised voices filtered into the room.

Elise lifted her head. "Welcome home, Your Grace," she whispered, before stepping away from him completely.

In the next second, the door of the drawing room was pushed all the way open, Roddy darting out of the way of Lady Abigail as she came to an abrupt stop just inside the door. Her hair was coming loose from its braid, she had a smear of flour across one reddened cheek, and a soiled apron was draped over her plain dress. Elise heard her gasp as she caught sight of Noah.

"The lad said the Duke of Ashland was here," she said, her voice breaking. "I thought he was telling tales."

"No." The duke crossed the room to stand in front of his sister. "He was telling the truth."

"Noah." It wasn't quite a question.

"Yes." His hands were clenched at his sides. "It's still me. Though I imagine I look and sound a little different than you remember."

Abigail put a hand to her mouth, a single tear escaping and making a sharp track through the flour on her cheek. A sob caught in her throat.

"This belongs to you." He held out the steel rose. "And it's long past time I returned it."

Abigail reached for the brooch, her hand stopping just shy of Noah's. "I'm afraid, if I touch you, I'll wake," she whispered. "And discover that this is a dream and you're not real and you'll vanish again."

"I'm real, Abby. And I'm not going anywhere."

Abigail's hand closed over the rose, and another tear slid down her cheek. "I've missed you, Noah."

In a heartbeat Noah had enfolded his sister in his arms, Abigail clinging to him as she cried in earnest now. "I've missed you too, Abby," he said fiercely.

Elise watched them, a lump in her own throat. She caught Roderick's eye and jerked her head in the direction of the door, and the boy nodded before ducking out the way he had come. Elise followed silently, slipping past Noah and Abigail and making her way to the door.

Abigail was trying to talk through her tears now, a rapid string of questions and exclamations that were barely coherent. Elise couldn't make out Noah's murmured responses, but she didn't need to.

The Duke of Ashland was finally home.

Chapter 16

"I might suggest jumping off a bridge was somewhat foolish." Ivory Moore, owner of Chegarre & Associates, poured more whiskey into a crystal tumbler and put it on the desk in front of Elise. Outside, the sun had given up its hold on the day, and the room was cast in a soft glow from the hearth and the lanterns that had been lit.

"It was a controlled leap," Elise said irritably, and took a healthy swallow, embracing the fire that burned its way down her throat into her belly. She shouldn't be feeling quite so contrary. She had defied ridiculous odds. She had succeeded in her mission. The Duke of Ashland was safely in London, tucked away in their drawing room with his sister until such time as they could plot his return to his rightful place. She should be celebrating.

Except Elise had spent the better part of the hour detailing the events that had led to the discovery and return to London of one Noah Ellery, Duke of Ashland, and none of it had given her any pleasure. It had been a heavily edited version that she had carefully recited, a monotone list of facts and events as they had happened, starting with Lady Abigail's frantic plea and ending with Noah Ellery's reunion with his sister in the drawing room down the hall. And it had left her with an empty coldness that had settled in her gut.

Because, deep down, she knew that in finding the Duke of Ashland, she had lost Noah. She had lost the man who had claimed her heart.

Ivory resumed her seat behind her desk and sat back, and Elise could feel her shrewd brown eyes assessing her. She took another swallow, hoping that Ivory would attribute the color in her face to the liquor. "How was Chelmsford?" Elise mumbled, in an effort to redirect the conversation.

"Successful. Profitable." Ivory waved her hand dismissively, not biting. "Tell me about Ashland."

Elise looked up warily. "I just did."

"No, you told me where he was. How he was living. The details of his past. The names of those closest to him. How long it took you to travel. You told me nothing about the man. His strengths. His weaknesses."

Elise stared into her whiskey, the amber liquid offering no clever inspiration for answering that question without betraying the depths of her feelings. She took a steadying breath and adopted a mask of neutrality.

"He's kind. Intelligent. Loyal." God help her, but it sounded as if she were describing a three-legged dog named Square. "Extremely protective of those he cares about," she tried. Bloody hell, that wasn't any better. "Socially aware."

Ivory had leaned forward and was watching her carefully, a brow raised.

"He endured Bedlam for five years and the streets of London for another three," Elise continued. "And he believed that what he was forced to do to survive made him...lesser, somehow."

"Believed? But not anymore?" Ivory missed nothing.

"No. He's made at least some sort of peace with it."

"How do you know that?"

Elise fought to keep her expression blank. She wasn't sure she succeeded. "He mentioned as much."

"To you?"

"Yes."

"He trusts you then." It wasn't a question, though it needed to be answered.

Elise had a sudden, vivid memory of moments spent in a moonlit river and the storm that had followed. "Yes."

"Mmmm."

"I'm not so sure he's made peace with the choices his mother made." Elise took a careful sip of her drink, if only to give her hands something to do and prevent her having to look at Ivory. "An abandoned child has a long memory."

"Indeed. I would imagine that would be more difficult. He's only a man. Not a saint."

Elise snorted, unable to help herself. "No, he is not a saint."

"Mmmm."

Elise hated when Ivory did that. That single sound told her that Ivory understood far more than required explanation. "Don't *mmmm* me," she grumbled. "Just ask me what you want to know."

"Are you in love with him?"

Elise looked up at her then. There was nowhere to go but the truth. "Yes."

Ivory sighed and sat back again. Her eyes softened in sympathy, and she picked an opened letter off the desk, a piece of blood-red wax crumbling from the broken seal. "There is a situation that will need attention in Bath shortly," she said. "If you like, you can leave immediately—"

"No." Elise placed her glass on the surface of the desk with utmost care. She knew Ivory was offering her a painless exit. Well, not painless, because it was far too late for that, but an easier exit nonetheless. "He is not mine to keep, I know. But I will see this through. I will see him rise to the station he was born to because he was destined to be a leader among men. He has a wonderful heart and a brilliant mind."

Ivory appraised her. "You're sure?"

"Yes."

"Mmmm." She turned the letter over in her fingers, a faint line between her brow. More wax crumbled to the desk.

Elise scowled. "You don't think it's a good idea that I stay. Being that he's a client. And a duke."

Ivory dropped the letter, a rueful expression on her face. "I didn't say that. God knows I cannot cast stones on that account. It would be...neater if you removed yourself from the situation, for both your sakes. But I cannot discount the fact that he will need you and your skills."

Elise stood, unable to remain seated any longer. "Good. Because I won't leave him." She realized that wasn't quite right. She would leave him. When he didn't need her anymore. But that wasn't yet. "I will see this through."

Ivory picked up a heavy ledger that rested next to the

letter and opened it to a marked page. The ledgers, which chronicled the secrets and scandals of some of the most prominent English families, had been started by Ivory's late husband, the wily and elderly Duke of Knightley, and had been continued by his widow and her associates.

"I assume you've already looked at this," Ivory said.

Elise stopped by the hearth, the heat drying whatever dampness still lingered in the fabric of her trousers. "Of course. Immediately after Lady Abigail arrived. But there was nothing of note, other than the scandal of Lady Abigail marrying beneath her station."

"Agreed." Ivory scanned the brief entries. "The late duke and his father before him were exceedingly ordinary. Managed the ducal estates with a reasonable degree of competency, or at least hired those who could. Participated in Parliament. Invested carefully with better-than-average results. If they kept mistresses, they did so discreetly and predictably. Likewise, if their wives involved themselves in anything beyond what was expected of a duchess, I have no record of it. No duels, no extortions, no scandalous affairs, no illegitimate children. The late duke was a shining example of a perfect English aristocrat."

"Until that perfect, shining example decided his ten-year-old heir was flawed and had him committed to Bedlam."

Ivory closed the ledger. "Yet there is nothing here that suggests that. Which means that however the late duke had his son secreted away, he did it well. If there had been rumors, Knightley would have heard them. Would have confirmed them and recorded them."

"Then it is safe to assume that we may construct a past for the new duke as we see fit."

"Perhaps." Ivory reached across the desk and retrieved Elise's glass, downing the last of the whiskey.

"Perhaps? No one knows where Noah Ellery has spent the last twenty years of his life."

"Except, possibly, the man who paid you to find him. You told me King knew Ashland had been in London twelve years ago."

Elise braced her hands on the mantel, leaning closer to the fire. That still bothered her because of its lack of transparency. "'I owe him a great debt.'"

"I beg your pardon?"

"'I owe him a great debt.' That's what King said to me when I asked why he cared."

Ivory was silent for a moment. "Noah Ellery lived on the streets for a good while. I think it's likely that your duke might have had the opportunity to save his life, or perhaps that of another who was important to King."

"Then how did King know who he was? His true identity?"

Ivory shrugged. "Perhaps Ashland told him?"

Elise frowned.

"Even if he didn't, there is very little that King cannot discover for himself should he take the notion," Ivory reminded her. "King is a businessman first and foremost."

Elise gave Ivory a long look over her shoulder, thinking about the last time her employer had done business with the man.

"Don't start," Ivory said, catching Elise's eye.

"Don't start on what, Duchess?" The voice came from the doorway.

"Alex," Ivory said warmly as she rose, coming around her desk, "you made good time. Thank you for coming."

"Of course. Roddy had quite a bit to say when he showed up at my door."

Elise pushed herself from the mantel and turned, watching her brother greet Ivory before stepping toward Elise and regarding her intensely, as if searching for damage.

"Little sister," he said, drawing her to him briefly before holding her out at arm's length. "You look…"

"Like a boy?" Elise supplied.

"Different."

Elise laughed, though it sounded forced. "I look different every day, Alex. It's my job."

Alex considered her, and Elise was afraid she hadn't fooled anyone. "Roddy tells me you found our long-lost duke."

"I did," she said carefully, metering her words to sound nothing less than professional.

"That was quick, even for you."

Elise shrugged carelessly. "I had some good luck on the way there. And the service of a mail coach on the way back."

Alex winced. "Barbarous way to travel."

"But fast."

"And what about the small issue with the assassins?" he inquired.

"They are no longer an issue."

"Ah." Alex considered her. "You dispatched them?"

"Ashland did. Well, one of them. The other he left for me."

Her brother looked reluctantly impressed. "I think I might like this duke." He paused. "Though I must confess I find myself less than pleased that Francis Ellery's actions might have put you in more danger than I would have liked." His voice was cold. "I wish I'd known this earlier."

"What are you talking about?"

"Francis Ellery will shortly be on his way to a delightful weeklong country retreat, courtesy of the Marquess of Heatherton's rather…unexpected yet generous invitation. I went to his lordship's home immediately after Roddy's arrival and caught the marquess just as he was preparing to leave. I suggested that Heatherton might wish to travel with a guest. I thought it might be helpful if Ellery was absent from London in the immediate future."

"Well done," Ivory murmured.

"Wasn't it?" Alex looked rather pleased with himself.

"And the marquess just agreed to this?" Elise asked.

"Heatherton took with him three cases of my finest French brandy as a…parting gift. His lordship was well compensated." Alex's eyes narrowed. "But now I wonder if I shouldn't have just left Ellery for King to toy with."

Ivory frowned at him.

Alex held up a hand. "Just because I don't like King doesn't mean he's not useful, Duchess."

"The last thing we need is for Francis Ellery to show up dead somewhere right now. Coinciding with Ashland's sudden appearance, it would be too suspicious," Ivory said.

"She's right. Francis Ellery's absence buys us time," Elise interjected. "Which is important because His Grace has been missing for twenty years. A seamless reintroduction into London society is going to require some skill."

Alex steepled his fingers in front of his chest. "How much skill, exactly?"

Elise glanced at Ivory. "I'm not entirely sure."

"Why?" He looked pained. "Please tell me the new duke is not a half-wit."

"He is not a half-wit," the Duke of Ashland said from the doorway.

~

Noah took in the study, and the people gathered in it.

There was Elise, standing close to the hearth, watching him with eyes he couldn't read. Next to her stood a man with the same dark hair, the same rich complexion. His eyes were a shade more golden than Elise's, and a narrow scar traveled from his ear to catch the side of his upper lip. Her brother, Noah surmised, noting the instinctive way the man positioned himself in front of her. His respect for the man grew.

The other occupant of the room was a simply dressed woman, her chestnut hair caught up elegantly. She wasn't vibrant like Elise, but she was beautiful nonetheless in a way that he couldn't quite describe. Dark-brown eyes assessed him as she leaned against the front of a massive desk.

"Your Grace." It was this woman who spoke first. "Welcome to London." She straightened, and her eyes slid past him and she smiled warmly. "Lady Abigail. I trust you are most pleased to be reunited with your brother."

Behind Noah his sister sniffed. "You have no idea," she said.

It had been an emotionally wrought hour, an impossible time in which to share two lifetimes' worth of regrets and happiness, but they had made a start. And if the gods were willing, they would have years ahead to make up for those already lost.

"Your Grace, may I introduce Miss Ivory Moore." Elise

pushed by her brother to come and stand closer to Noah. "Miss Moore is the proprietor of Chegarre and Associates and will be assisting you in your return to London society."

"A pleasure, Miss Moore." Noah inclined his head.

"It is a pleasure indeed," she said sincerely, and pushed a loose piece of hair behind her ear with her hand. A golden band glinted from her ring finger, exotically fashioned and set with a polished ruby. Noah might have thought it a wedding ring, had she not been introduced as Miss Moore.

"And this is my brother," Elise said, shifting slightly, "Alexander Lavoie. He too will be working with us."

"Lavoie?" he asked, confused.

"DeVries was our mother's name. I made it mine when I started acting."

"Ah." Noah eyed the hard-looking man whose attempt at a pleasant expression was not quite enough to mask his underlying suspicion. "Mr. Lavoie. Miss DeVries has spoken of you quite highly."

Lavoie's gaze slid to Elise briefly, and a faint wash of color rose into her face.

"Indeed?" The word held a speculative note. "How... nice." His eyes returned to Noah. "Then, Your Grace, since my sister has proven to be so very conversational, I must assume that she has made you aware of the current circumstances surrounding the duchy of Ashland? And further impressed on you the need for swift action, given your long absence?"

There was a challenge in his words, Noah knew. A test of sorts.

"Miss DeVries has indeed made me aware of the current situation, Mr. Lavoie," Noah said evenly, not looking at

Elise. "And whatever you may think of my absence to date, please rest assured that I do not care about your opinion. At all."

Lavoie raised a brow, though there was a gleam of grudging approval. "He sounds like a bloody duke at least," he muttered in his sister's direction. "I can see why you're—"

"Perhaps, since everyone is here, we might turn to the matters at hand," Elise suggested a little louder than was necessary.

"Agreed," Miss Moore said just as loudly. "Please, be seated." She took the chair behind the massive desk, and Noah waited until the ladies had been seated in the chairs facing it. He pulled over the small bench from a beautifully carved pianoforte that graced the far wall of the study. A sheet of music, disturbed by his movements, fluttered to the floor from the top of the pianoforte. He bent to retrieve it.

"'S'ei non mi vuol amar,'" he read. It had been a long time since he'd spoken the language, and it made the words all the more pleasing.

Four heads swiveled in his direction.

"Yes," Miss Moore said. "It's an aria from Handel's *Tamerlano*. One of my favorite composers. Are you familiar with it?"

"No." Noah looked down at the music. "I've never heard it. But the title is beautiful." With a sudden start, he realized Miss Moore had addressed him in Italian, and he had replied in the same language.

"How fluent are you?" Miss Moore demanded, her eyes narrowing.

"Enough to be having this conversation," Noah replied, still speaking in Italian. "I might ask the same."

"I sing," she said simply.

Noah glanced at the sheet music in his hand. "You're an opera singer."

"I was an opera singer. Now I do...other things."

"How did you learn to speak Italian?" Elise interrupted, looking at Noah, a furrow in her forehead. Abigail was watching him with wide eyes.

He switched back to English. "Joshua taught me."

"And just who is Joshua?" Alex inquired from near the fireplace.

"An old acquaintance," Noah responded, without taking his eyes off Elise. "Said it was the only civilized language worth knowing."

Elise was gaping at him. "But—"

"I had found my voice by then. Joshua took great pleasure in adding to it. We had some hours to fill."

"Do you speak French?"

"Enough to get by. He thought the language vulgar."

Elise suddenly grinned. "It depends how you use it."

Lavoie cleared his throat loudly. "This is all very fascinating, but might we turn our attention to business?" he said irritably. "How we might best resurrect a duke who's been presumed dead for two decades? With all due respect, Your Grace, it's not like you will simply be able to stroll into the House of Lords and say, 'Sorry I'm late, gentlemen. What did I miss?'"

Noah dragged his gaze from Elise. "I am aware."

Miss Moore placed her hands on her desk. "Alex is right. When your cousin learns of your return, he will do everything within his power to discredit you. Claim you are an imposter. Unless we can reinvent the truth and establish beyond any sort of doubt that you are the duke, it will be his word against yours."

Noah lowered himself to the bench, suddenly feeling exhausted, the long hours of travel, and everything that had come before and after that journey, taking their toll. "How do you hope to accomplish that?" Noah asked.

"We don't get paid to hope things will happen the way we wish, Your Grace," Alex said smoothly from his post near the hearth. "We get paid to make it so."

"There is the advantage that Parliament has ended." Elise was on her feet now, prowling the room. "A good percentage of the ton has likely departed for their country estates to immerse themselves in house parties and hunts. By the time these individuals hear of you, your existence will simply be fact, and not speculation. We will be able to leave no room for gossip except for that which we control." She turned to Miss Moore. "This needs to be done subtly."

"Agreed." Miss Moore ran her hands over the leather cover of a thick ledger that lay in front of her. "There are enough individuals in London at the moment who, with enough finesse, will have the opportunity to remember that they are, indeed, acquainted with the new Duke of Ashland."

"Finesse?" It was Abigail who spoke, and she sounded apprehensive. "What does that mean?"

Noah knew very well what that meant. "It means with enough resources, there are any number of individuals who might be..." *Blackmailed? Coerced? Bribed?* He trailed off, uncertain just how far the reach of Chegarre & Associates went.

"Convinced," Elise suggested.

"Encouraged," Miss Moore added politely.

"Yes. That." Noah rubbed his face. The word mattered not.

"I see," Abigail said, and Noah was quite sure she did.

"I'll make the necessary arrangements," Miss Moore

said, and her voice was all cool business. She turned to Noah. "You'll need to move back into the house in Mayfair tomorrow," Miss Moore told him. "Both you and your sister. You staying anywhere else would be strange and will not help us convince anyone you are the Duke of Ashland."

Noah shook his head. "I don't want Abigail there. If Francis knows we're there—"

"Francis is out of town at the moment. He will be for the better part of this week."

"How coincidental."

Miss Moore glanced in Lavoie's direction. "Not coincidental. Smart." She turned back to Noah. "Regardless, I will assign a number of men to guard the house."

"And that won't be considered strange?" Noah asked cynically.

"You won't know they're there."

Noah made a noise of disbelief.

"I give you my word." Miss Moore leaned across her desk. "The men I employ are good enough to be invisible. You will not see them. You will not hear them. The only person who will discover their presence will be Francis Ellery if he returns and tries something stupid." She paused. "In that case it will be unlikely that anyone will find his body."

Noah stared at her.

"You'll need to get His Grace out in public as soon as possible, Duchess." Lavoie came to sit on the edge of Miss Moore's desk. "Time is ticking."

"Agreed," Miss Moore said again, considering the man. "The solicitors first, of that there is no question. We should be able to deal with the situation at Bedlam then as well. I think we can all agree those are our two most pressing needs, and they will be attended to before Francis Ellery is even aware that it has happened." She paused. "We'll need Alderidge. His Grace is going to need someone with visible power whose word will not be questioned. And when they get to Bedlam, we'll likely need a physician."

"I know a good one," Elise murmured.

"Good."

"Consider using my club to stage one of the social introductions." Lavoie crossed his arms and glanced at his sister and then Miss Moore.

The woman was drumming her fingers on her desk. "Absolutely. But we'll need something to draw a crowd. A tournament, perhaps? Something novel. Something different than what any other club offers."

Lavoie nodded. "I like the idea. It will bring in a good number of the ton who are still stewing in London and looking for something to alleviate their boredom."

"Set it up." Miss Moore turned to Elise and paused. "Do you still wish to assist in this context, Miss DeVries?"

The last question lacked the brisk efficiency that her prior ones had had, and it made Noah sit up. The query had been posed softly, almost gently, as if Miss Moore somehow regretted the necessity of asking.

"Yes," Elise answered, avoiding his gaze.

Miss Moore nodded. "Very well," she said, and the efficiency was back in her tone.

"Titled?" Elise asked. "French? Austrian? Or something else?"

"French, I think, because you speak it better than most. Let's not add risk we don't need."

"Understood."

Well, at least Elise did. Because for the life of him,

Noah couldn't begin to make sense of the conversation that had just blown by him. It might as well have been in Russian, for all he understood.

"Who the hell is Alderidge?" Noah demanded, trying to start in order.

"The Duke of Alderidge is a friend," Miss Moore told him.

Lavoie rolled his eyes. "Bloody hell, Duchess. God save me from a lifetime of friends then."

Noah paused suddenly at the use of Lavoie's address. He'd thought Duchess a strange nickname for Miss Moore when he'd heard it the first time, but now...his eyes fell on the gold band on her finger. "He's your husband."

"He is."

"You're a duchess."

"I'm a lot of things." She shrugged.

"But your name—"

"Is just a name." Her rich brown eyes penetrated his, concealing the secrets that he knew lay within. "And perhaps, Mr. Lawson, one day I'll tell you the story of mine."

Noah held her gaze.

Lavoie pushed himself from the desk. "End of the week then? I imagine you want to chum the waters a bit before you unleash the sharks in my club." He strode to the door.

"Of course. I will arrange an array of social appearances over the next days," Miss Moore replied.

"We will also need to turn our attention to the situation that is Francis Ellery by then as well." It was Elise who said it.

"Leave him to me," Lavoie said, and Noah looked up, startled by the cold ruthlessness of his words. Lavoie caught his gaze and shrugged unapologetically. "I take exception to the fact that his minions might have put my sister in danger."

"No." Noah braced his hands on his knees and rose. "You will leave Francis Ellery to me."

Lavoie considered him for a long moment. "Very well, Your Grace." He looked between Elise and Noah and opened his mouth to say something, but then seemed to change his mind. "I'm glad you're back safe, little sister," was all he said before disappearing from view.

"What can I do?" Abigail asked suddenly into the silence. "I want to help."

Noah turned to where his sister sat. "I want you to go back to Derby. Back to your husband and your children, where you'll be safe."

Lady Abigail lurched to her feet and stomped over to Noah. "My husband and my children are not dependent on me for their survival, Noah Ellery," she snapped. "Granted, the quality of their meals might be suffering as of late, but they'll be fine. I'm not leaving you. Not now."

"But it might be dangerous—"

Abigail planted her fists on her hips. "It might. Especially if you suggest again that I should tuck my tail and run from our cockroach of a cousin. I never backed down from him when I was ten. Do you honestly believe I'd do it now?"

It was so reminiscent of the girl in braids and pinafores he remembered that he felt his throat thicken. "No."

"Good. That's the smartest thing you've said in this entire conversation."

Noah raised his eyes to find Elise watching him, a soft, gentle smile on her face.

"Whatever you need me to do, whatever needs to be done to make this right, I'll do it," Abigail declared.

And so would he.

Chapter 17

She should be sleeping.

Elise knew she should be exhausted, knew she should seek her bed and find the rest she would need to keep her wits sharp and her mind clear. Except the house had been silent around her for hours and still Elise tossed and turned, her mind unable to quiet.

Her rooms seemed cavernous suddenly. Empty. A little like the way she was feeling inside. The last days of travel had been a gift, each minute with the man who had stolen her heart something to be treasured. But she was out of those minutes now. This night, she knew, marked the beginning of the end. Elise would do what she did best over the coming week, and with the help of Ivory and Alex, she would see Noah restored to his rightful place.

Elise fingered the brooch the Barrs had given her, the steel gleaming softly in the light from the single candle she'd left lit on her washstand. She traced the strands of the branches with her index finger, the metal warm beneath her touch. Courage and strength were what the twisted oak represented. Two things that she was going to need in order to walk away from Noah Ellery. She only hoped she had enough of each to survive it.

Elise shoved her twisted sheets back and rolled out of bed. Lying here in her bed was pointless. Sleep was as elusive as it had been an hour ago. She lit a small lantern and wandered into her massive dressing room, setting the light and the brooch on the long counter in the center of the room. Around her were shelves and shelves of costumes. Most were folded, sorted by function and style, but some of the more extravagant gowns had been settled over dressmaker's dummies in order to keep their silks and satins from being crushed or creased.

She went to the shelves first, selecting the items she would need tomorrow. The clothes she laid out on the counter by the lantern, along with the appropriate wig and accessories. Then she turned her attention to the gowns on the dummies. There were a dozen of them, obscenely expensive, elaborate creations that belonged in the dressing rooms of royalty. She ran a hand over one, a masterpiece of ice-blue silk and blonde lace, pearls sewn along the edges of the bodice. It was stunning, and one of her favorites, but it was inherently English in appearance. She needed something far different, she mused as she examined each gown and dismissed it in order. The cream one was too virginal, the saffron too proper—

She stopped abruptly at the last. She hadn't worn it in a long time. And it was perfect.

"Do you actually wear all of this?"

The voice came from behind her, and Elise nearly came out of her skin. She whirled, her heart in her throat.

"*Merde.*" She put a hand out on a shelf to steady herself.

Noah was leaning back against the counter, dressed only in his breeches and a shirt he hadn't bothered to fasten at the neck, staring at the array of clothing surrounding them. "I couldn't sleep."

She forced herself to take slow, deep breaths. "So you thought you might sleep better in my room?"

He looked at her then. His eyes followed the smooth arch of her neck and dropped to the deep V of her chemise where it was tied loosely at the tops of her breasts. His gaze continued down, and he stripped her with his eyes where she stood. "No. I hadn't thought to sleep at all."

Fire tore through her, stealing her breath and making her feel as if she might come apart right there. She should be making an effort to distance herself from him, she knew. Prepare them both for the time when they would be nothing to each other but a memory. She should not be standing in a dressing room in her chemise wondering if there was enough room on that counter for him to take her there. It would only make things more difficult. Elise forced herself to think through the fog of desire that had risen.

She stepped back, as if inches of space would make this easier. "Noah—"

"I want you, Elise." The soft light carved austere shadows across his features. "I need you. And not just now. But for always."

She shook her head, his words twisting her heart. "You don't need me, Noah."

Noah picked up the brooch that still lay on the counter beside him. "You're wrong. You've made me better."

"I only showed you what you could be. You were always better."

"Will you stay?" he asked, staring down at the polished steel.

She knew what he was asking. She knew what he wanted her to say. But she couldn't promise him more than she could offer. "I'll be here to see this through," she whispered, knowing that reality needed to find purchase in this conversation. Anything less would only hurt them more in the end. "But you must know that my role here is not the one it was in Nottingham. The upper realms of London society are where Miss Moore excels. Trust her guidance. She will not lead you wrong."

Noah nodded.

"After tonight, when you see me, I won't be me. Once this starts, Elise DeVries will no longer exist. I'll be whatever person the Duke of Ashland needs me to be at any given moment. Do you understand?"

He straightened and closed the distance between them. They were separated by a breath, their bodies nearly touching.

"Yes. It means I won't be able to do this." He bent his head and kissed her softly.

"You won't be able to do that," she agreed with quiet regret, her heart breaking into small, jagged pieces.

"Or this." He ran his hands over her face, tracing her brows, her cheekbones, the outline of her lips, with gentle, tender touches.

"No." The backs of her eyes were burning.

He pressed a kiss to her forehead before resting his own against it. "I should have believed you at the very beginning."

Elise shook her head. "It doesn't matter. You believe now."

"Yes. Whatever you say, I promise to believe—"

"No," she interrupted. "You believe in you now. No matter what happens." She put a hand on his arm, feeling the solidity of him beneath his shirt. "I'm proud of you, Noah Ellery."

He went completely still.

She lifted her head and looked at him.

"No one has ever told me that." It came out as a strangled whisper.

She touched his face. "They should have."

He released a shaky breath.

"You'll stumble in your speech at one point in time," she said quietly.

"Yes." He covered her hand with his. "I can only imagine the rumors that my cousin has fostered over the years. I know that at some point someone will suggest that I am a simpleton. And when they do—"

"You will not challenge them to a duel," Elise intoned.

"Agreed. I'll hire you to shoot them instead."

"Very funny."

"If I find myself caring about opinions that do not matter, I will think of you. Of your faith in me. I will think about what truly matters." He pressed the steel brooch he still held into her hand.

Elise felt her breath catch in her throat.

"I will think about what Francis Ellery might have taken from me that has nothing to do with the duchy of Ashland. And I will see him pay for his actions."

"There might be a line," Elise murmured, thinking of King and whatever stake he had in this.

"Do you know what the most ironic thing about this entire thing is?" Noah asked.

"The fact that the socially ambitious Miss Silver called a duke a nothing?"

"Well, there is that," he said, a shadow of a smile touching his mouth.

"Then what?"

Noah gazed at her. "Bedlam cured me. Not the institution, not the mad-doctors, not the purges or starvation, but the company they chained me to."

"Joshua?"

"Yes. As I child I couldn't form the words I wanted to say fast enough. I missed words or used the wrong one. And the more my tutors or my father tried to beat my errors out of me, the worse my mistakes became. And the less I spoke. Until I just didn't."

Elise rested her head against his shoulder.

"Bedlam was always so loud. People crying. Talking. Screaming. Joshua and I would be locked in a room sometimes, where there were no windows. No light, just darkness. But there was no sound either, so it wasn't so much a punishment as a reprieve from the constant din. And there Joshua would talk about paintings."

"Paintings? Like art?"

"Yes. The knowledge he possessed about artists, especially those of the Renaissance, was staggering. The painters, the sculptors, the men who created worlds out of nothing but a bit of canvas and oil, marble and bronze. He'd traveled the Continent as a boy, had seen many of their works himself, or plates of those he couldn't."

Elise frowned and raised her head, a strange sensation creeping up her spine.

"I think it was his way of keeping himself sane," Noah continued, oblivious to her disquiet. "After a year I worked up the courage to ask him a question. After two years he would listen as I recited the names and their works back to him. It was easier for me to repeat things I heard. He never once criticized my speech, only corrected. I think he cared more about my ability to remember that it took one hundred and twenty years for St. Peter's Basilica to be completed and to be able to describe the *Navicella* mosaic that might be found inside. Or that I might recall that Sansovino's statues of Mars and Neptune that guard the Giants' Staircase at the Doge's Palace were meant to represent Venice's power by land and by sea."

Holy, holy hell. The loose ends that had bothered Elise were suddenly tying themselves up into knots at a blinding speed.

"What happened to him?" Elise asked, striving for a neutral tone.

"For three years after we escaped, we stayed together. Survived in the streets." Noah was tracing patterns along her arm with his fingers. "He was a born leader there. Where I only survived, he flourished."

"And after three years?"

"Abigail eloped. Not that I was part of her life, but my sister was the only reason I had stayed in the city as long as I had. I could still watch out for her, even if it was from a distance. So when she left London, so did I." He paused. "Joshua chose to stay. That was the last time I saw him. I'd like to think he survived. I'd like to think he found his own measure of happiness."

Elise swallowed with difficulty. The boy Noah had known as Joshua had certainly survived, though she wasn't sure she could comment on his happiness.

I owe him a great debt.

Joshua was King. King was Joshua. And what he owed Noah was his life. The man who now rested at the pinnacle of London's underworld had once been chained to a boy who had been quick with a knife. The ruthless dealer who specialized in stolen art had once taught a young duke to speak.

"Elise?" Noah was staring down at her strangely. "Are you all right?"

"Yes." Her mind was racing. She had given King her word that his involvement would remain confidential. Not only did the repercussions of breaking her word to such a man give her pause, it went against her honor. The violent and unspeakable acts that these two men had endured and the bond that had resulted were things that were theirs. Whatever existed between Noah and Joshua, and whatever might yet one day lie between them, were not for her to meddle in.

"I think he would have survived," she said simply.

"I talked with Abigail tonight," Noah said suddenly. "After we went upstairs. She's agreed to stay at the dower house near Kilburn."

"How did you manage to convince her of that?" Elise asked with some surprise.

"My mother will need somewhere to recover. Abby will see to it."

It made sense on many different levels. "I think that's a good idea," she told him.

Noah gathered her against him again, wrapping his arms around her. They stood in silence for a long minute.

"What if I can't forgive my mother?" Noah asked, and his voice was bleak. "What if I'm not a good-enough person to forgive my own mother for what she did?"

Elise pulled back and looked up at him. "Then forgive yourself, Noah."

Noah closed his eyes briefly, before opening them to gaze at her. After a heartbeat he moved away from her and stopped near the doorway of the dressing room, holding out his hand.

Elise placed the steel brooch on the counter with careful deliberation. Courage and strength could wait until tomorrow. Tonight would be theirs, and though it would make everything hurt so much worse, Elise couldn't bring herself to care.

Silently she padded toward him, taking his hand and allowing him to lead her to the side of her bed. His hands went to the ties of her chemise, and one by one the laces loosened until the garment simply slipped over her shoulders and fell to the ground soundlessly. Elise shivered as the cool air touched her skin.

"I don't wish to speak of the past anymore tonight," he said. "I don't wish to speak of the person I was or the person I might be tomorrow." He lifted his shirt over his head, letting it fall on top of her chemise, and his breeches followed. He bent his head and kissed her, a long, sensuous kiss that left her gasping. His mouth moved from her lips to her neck, over her collarbone, and then to her breasts. Elise closed her eyes as he toyed with each nipple, his tongue and his teeth making everything in her body ache with need.

He pulled away suddenly and got onto the bed, lying back against the pillows at her headboard. "Come here."

Elise stood for a moment, admiring the magnificent man now sprawled out in the center of her bed, his eyes simmering with desire. The light caught the scattered blond hair across his chest, the whorls darkening slightly as they descended over the ridges of his abdomen and between his hips to end where his cock jutted, hard and ready for her. With each of his rapid breaths, with each of his movements, muscle rippled beneath taut skin, demanding to be touched. And he was, for this moment, infinitely touchable. He was, for this moment, still Noah. Still hers.

This would be goodbye, even if he didn't know it yet. She would keep this memory and put it away carefully with the others. When she was strong enough, she would retrieve them. She would remember every moment of what it had felt like to fall in love with this man. This duke.

Elise lowered herself to the bed and crawled over him, coming to straddle his thighs. She ran her hands over his chest, her fingers playing with the hard pebbles of his nipples. She bent and replaced her hands with her lips, sucking each one. Her own nipples brushed his abdomen, and his erection pressed against the soft skin of her belly. She moved her body forward, then back, a gentle friction along the length of his cock that had him arching beneath her.

Elise lifted herself off his body, pushing forward on her knees and bracing her hands at the sides of his head. His own hands went to her shoulders before sliding down and cupping her breasts. He pinched her nipples just hard enough to send bolts of sensation straight to the juncture of her thighs, stirring the acute ache that throbbed there into a relentless pressure.

She could feel his length pressing up against the folds of her sex, and she reached down between them to position him, her fingers brushing against her own wetness. She rocked forward just a little farther, and now she could feel the blunt head of his cock poised at the entrance to her sex.

Beneath her his hips bucked, and the movement forced the tip of him into her. She kept them there, unmoving, letting anticipation amplify the pleasure that was building, a vortex of craving and yearning and need that was escalating in every cell of her body.

Noah's hands were on her hips now, his skin bathed in perspiration. Wanting. Waiting.

Elise lowered herself back to her elbows, careful to keep their bodies connected, and kissed him, a hot, openmouthed kiss that he returned. She licked his lower lip, ran her tongue along the edge of his jaw and down his neck. She sucked gently on the tendon that was straining there, licking the salt from his skin.

He made an inarticulate noise but didn't move.

Ever so deliberately Elise rolled her hips back, seating him halfway within her, reveling in the feel of his completing her the way no man would ever do again.

"Who do you want to be right now, Noah?" she whispered against his ear, feeling her body reach deep within itself. She was close. So very close. She moved again, felt his cock slide deeper, and she gasped as the first spasms of her climax took hold deep within her.

His hands tightened on her hips, his fingers biting into her flesh. "Yours," he rasped, as he pushed her down, impaling himself fully within her. "Yours," he repeated, thrusting hard and sending Elise hurtling into an abyss of ecstasy. "I want to be yours."

Chapter 18

Ned Miller was an excellent solicitor.

Or at least that was what Ivory Moore had told Noah. Mr. Miller had been the first one in his family to lever himself to such a lofty station, and he took great pride in that, she'd said. How else might the son of a shopkeeper find himself rubbing shoulders with the upper echelons of the peerage? And not only rubbing shoulders with them, but *advising* them?

Noah strode through the door of the solicitor's office, letting it bang shut behind him, his polished boots rapping loudly on the wooden floor. He'd dressed this morning with a care he had never taken before and in clothes that were finer than anything he could ever remember wearing. Appearances were critical, but Noah knew that even the damn prince would not be able to find fault. He knew he looked every inch a duke. Now he just needed to convince everyone here.

Noah registered a pause in the hum of industry as heads

snapped up to examine the new arrival. All around him were men bent over desks, with stacks of paper and ledgers and pots of ink piled in front of them. On his left a narrow staircase led up to a second story, a series of doors visible along the hallway. On his right a row of chairs lined the wall, currently occupied by a well-dressed woman and what looked to be her maid, as well as two young gentlemen. All waiting for the services of Mr. Ned Miller, it appeared. And all eyeing him curiously.

Perfect.

Noah stopped, looking around with ill-concealed impatience, all the while making sure every soul in the room got a good look. He was quite sure most of the clerks and assistants were familiar with his family's legal affairs. At least those affairs that concerned a missing heir. And those who weren't soon would be.

As if on cue, a young clerk approached him nervously. "May I help you?"

"Yes. You can take me to see Mr. Miller," Noah replied briskly.

"Ah yes, well, Mr. Miller is unavailable at the moment." The clerk's eyes darted to the top of the stairs.

Noah let his brows inch up his forehead. "He'll see me."

The clerk looked back at Noah, uncertainty flitting over his face. "Would you care to leave a name?" he asked.

"Yes." He allowed impatience to bleed into his words. "Tell him that the Duke of Ashland wishes an audience. He will be expecting me. My sister wrote earlier on my behalf to advise Mr. Miller of my arrival."

The bustle around him, which had slowed, now came to an abrupt halt. The clerk in front of him was blinking rapidly. "The Duke of Ashland? But—"

"Would you like me to write it down for you?"

"N-no." The clerk was backing up toward the stairs. "I'll tell him, of course, Your Grace. If you would just wait but a moment."

"Thank you." Noah watched him hurry up the wooden stairs and knock on the first door.

"Mr. Miller?" The clerk's voice floated down as he pushed the office door open, hovering in the hall.

Noah was pleased at how easily the sound carried to where he stood.

"Not now, Donnelly." The response from within was laced with disapproval. "I'm currently busy."

"Begging your pardon, but there is a man downstairs—"

"I'm busy, Donnelly." Now the voice sounded angry.

Noah headed to the stairs and started climbing, aware that his audience wasn't even trying to pretend to work any longer.

The clerk was shifting back and forth on his toes. "He claims he's the Duke of Ashland, sir."

"*What?*" Noah had reached the top of the stairs and he heard the scrape of a chair being shoved back.

"He said that you should have been advised of his arrival by his sister . . ." The clerk's voice trailed off.

Noah ignored the clerk and pushed the office door the rest of the way open. "Mr. Miller?" he asked, addressing a middle-aged man with a pair of spectacles perched on the end of his nose. He was standing behind a desk, his hands on his hips. In his peripheral vision, Noah saw another person seated in the room, but for now he kept his attention on the solicitor.

"Can I help you?" Mr. Miller was examining Noah's appearance and frowning slightly.

"Your clerk wasn't sure if you were available." Noah made it sounded like an accusation. Behind him the clerk slunk away.

The solicitor bristled. "I have appointments with other clients, sir. Important clients. So if you care to wait downstairs, I will be there in due time." He turned to the other occupant of the room. "I'm so sorry, Your Grace. This is most irregular—" He stopped in alarm as the man drew himself to his feet.

Noah looked over. The man Miller had addressed as "Your Grace" was clad completely in black, a day's worth of stubble on his face and his sun-bleached hair tied back in a careless queue. He was tall and imposing and met Noah's eyes with his own ice-grey ones, giving Noah an almost imperceptible nod.

"Alderidge?" Noah forced himself to grin widely. "Bloody hell, Alderidge, you look like a damn pirate. Don't they have valets in India? Or at the very least, scissors?"

The Duke of Alderidge met his broad smile with one of his own. "And if it isn't Ashland crawling out from the Tuscan vineyards or wherever the hell you've been hiding."

From the corner of his eye, he saw the solicitor's mouth fall open.

"I've been hiding in the English countryside as of late, if you must know. The weather is not nearly as agreeable as Italy. However, if one is to become a duke, one must understand the people who form the very foundation of this country, do you not agree?" He waved his hand in the direction of Mr. Miller. "One does not become a successful solicitor without studying the law first, aye?"

"Indeed. Though I can't imagine your father was overly enthusiastic at the idea."

"My father wasn't overly enthusiastic about any of my social...explorations. They mortified him," Noah admitted with a wry shake of his head.

Alderidge sobered abruptly. "My condolences on his death."

"Thank you." Noah let the joviality slide from his face. "We certainly had our differences, but I will miss him. I came as soon as Abigail's letter finally caught up with me notifying me of Father's passing."

Alderidge nodded. "Please let me know if there is anything I can do."

"Thank you. I came directly here as soon as I arrived in London. Haven't even been to the house in Mayfair yet. Perhaps, if it's not too much of a hassle, you might stop by and let my mother know I've arrived back in town? I wrote, of course, advising her and Abigail of my intention to return, but it was impossible to give them more than a vague idea. Travel is notoriously unreliable."

"Of course. I've only been back in London a day myself. Happy to do so."

"Drinks later? Cards?"

"Aye. I'd like that. You still owe me a good bottle of brandy from the last time we played in Bombay."

"I'm still not convinced you weren't cheating."

"All good pirates cheat, Ashland."

"Your Grace?" Mr. Miller finally spoke up, though Noah wasn't sure whom he was addressing. Judging from the look of horror on the solicitor's face as the man looked between them, Noah wasn't sure he did either.

"Are we done, Mr. Miller?" Alderidge asked. "If I'm to stop by Mayfair to see the duchess, I'll need to get moving. I'm sure there is a pile of paperwork waiting for you here, Ashland. But you're in good hands with Mr. Miller."

The solicitor swallowed audibly. "Er, about that."

The Duke of Alderidge looked at the solicitor and then at Noah. "Are Mr. Miller and his associates not handling your estate anymore, Ashland?"

Noah shrugged. "He was listed in my father's papers, and my father always spoke highly of this firm. But I fully admit I have been absent for far too long to be sure. A failing on my part, I know."

"You are the Duke of Ashland?" Mr. Miller blurted.

"I am." Noah frowned.

"What a bizarre question," Alderidge commented, sounding displeased.

"In Mr. Miller's defense, we've never met," Noah pointed out.

"Ah, of course." Alderidge shrugged. "Well, you can take it from me, Mr. Miller. The man who stands before you is indeed the Duke of Ashland. If you do a good job on the paperwork, maybe he can find you a good bottle of brandy too."

The solicitor sat down hard in his chair. "But you were presumed dead."

"What?" Noah laughed, though there wasn't any humor in it. "That's absurd."

"Your father never spoke of you."

"My father had a seizure two years ago and couldn't speak," Noah snapped.

"B-but before then. You didn't exist. You were nowhere to be found in England."

"This may come as a surprise to you, Mr. Miller, but there are other places on the globe where one might receive an education befitting a duke. An absence on the roll at Eton does not negate my existence."

"I never attended Eton either," Alderidge interjected.

The solicitor cleared his throat. "But there was nothing that—"

"I know I've been away from London for a very long time, but I was in contact with my family. Ask my sister or my mother. Either one will certainly vouch for my continued existence, if not for my exact location at any given time." Noah found himself speaking slowly, concentrating on each word.

Behind his desk the solicitor was sweating.

"Is there a problem, Mr. Miller?" Alderidge asked.

Mr. Miller pulled at his collar, as if he found the air in the room suddenly a little thin. "Your sister ... er ..."

"Lady Abigail?" Noah supplied.

"Was difficult to reach."

Noah scoffed, but it wasn't a pleasant sound. "What do you mean, difficult? She lives in Derby, not in Damascus."

"Um, yes. Of course, but—"

"What about my mother? She lives a half mile from here in Mayfair." Noah spoke carefully. This was the critical part.

"Um." The solicitor's eyes were shifting about the room, as if he were searching for escape. "It would seem that your mother has had some difficulties as of late."

"Difficulties?" Noah placed his hands on the edge of Miller's desk. "What sort of difficulties?"

"What the hell is going on, Mr. Miller?" Alderidge demanded from behind him.

The solicitor looked up at Noah. "Perhaps this should be a private conversation, Your Grace—"

"Alderidge stays."

"Right. Very good then." Mr. Miller took a deep breath. "It would seem your mother has been committed to Bedlam."

A deafening silence fell in the office, and Noah let it stretch. Mr. Miller's fingers were white on the arms of his chair.

"By whom?" Noah kept his tone even.

"Er, by your cousin. Mr. Ellery. I have been told that he makes a monthly payment to the hospital on her behalf. Out of his own funds, of course, not the duchy's," he added hastily, as if this detail might lessen the awfulness.

"Why was my mother committed to Bedlam?"

"Well. Um. It would seem that she was suffering from some, ah, delusions."

"What sort of delusions, Mr. Miller?"

"Um. She, er, insisted that you were . . . alive."

Noah stared down stonily at the solicitor. "She was committed to Bedlam for insisting that I was alive," he repeated.

"Y-yes."

"Are you delusional, Mr. Miller?" Noah asked.

"N-no."

"So you will attest that I am standing before you, very much alive—"

"Showing a remarkable amount of restraint, I might add," Alderidge growled from behind him.

"Yes, yes." Ned Miller nodded.

"Is my sister aware of my mother's current predicament, Mr. Miller?" Noah asked grimly.

"She is." Mr. Miller was trying not to squeak.

"Did she not petition you for assistance?"

"She did."

"And is there a reason that you chose...not...to provide that assistance?" Anger on Abigail's behalf had arisen, making each word a chore.

Mr. Miller flinched. "Your cousin, Mr. Ellery, was handling it, Your Grace. And being that it was a family matter, I thought it best to respect the privacy of yours."

"Ah yes. Francis." Noah took his hands from the edge of his desk and straightened. He smiled, but it wasn't a pleasant one. "I should have known."

Mr. Miller frowned and watched warily as Noah flexed his hands into fists before relaxing them again. "Would you like me to—"

"I would like you to listen very carefully, Mr. Miller. You will see to the paperwork that is required for me to assume control of the duchy. I will be back tomorrow at this time, and I expect everything to be in order. Can you do that, Mr. Miller?"

"Y-yes."

"Good. Because right now I need to leave to extract my mother from Bedlam, where, as I understand it, she languishes for the crime of telling the truth."

"I will come with you," the Duke of Alderidge said.

"But Mr. Ellery said you were dead," Miller wheezed. "Insisted on it."

"My cousin is up past his eyeballs in debt, Mr. Miller. Something that you might have determined for yourself should you have taken the time to investigate. Where else would he get the funds he so desperately needs if not from my family's coffers?"

The solicitor reddened, and he started to splutter. "He's not had a penny from me," he managed.

"And for that I am thankful. Francis Ellery tried to make a fool of the both of us, Mr. Miller," Noah said quietly. "And as such, you will not mention this conversation to my cousin should you have the unfortunate opportunity to see him."

Miller nodded fervently.

"I will handle Mr. Ellery."

Noah retreated back down the staircase to the main floor, his footsteps preceded by the sounds of frantic scuffling as the legion of clerks who had been listening at the bottom of the stairs fled back to their desks and feigned work. The expensively dressed people waiting in the chairs along the wall simply gawked. Noah kept his eyes straight ahead, his posture stiff, and his expression grim. There was little need for acting now.

He stepped out into the brilliant sunshine of the street. He took a deep breath, letting some of the tension of the morning drain from him.

It had taken an extraordinary amount of concentration to keep his words in order. But he had done it, and any slip would likely be attributed to his fury. A fury that hadn't required much fabrication as that little drama had played out. He would have given anything to have had Elise at his side with her calm determination. But he knew that that was impossible. Instead he owed a great debt to the man who had now stepped out into the sunshine behind him.

He turned to address a duke he had never met. "Thank you for that," Noah said, making sure he couldn't be overheard. "And it is a true pleasure to meet you."

"The pleasure is all mine," Alderidge replied. "I'm sorry about the circumstances."

Noah inclined his head. "As am I."

"You were splendid, by the way," Alderidge added. "I think Mr. Miller was suitably convinced."

"Mr. Miller looked like he was going to cast up his accounts."

"A good start then." Alderidge watched him. "You'll get used to it, you know," he said suddenly.

"Used to what?"

"Being a duke."

Noah stared at him.

"I'm discovering it has far more advantages than disadvantages." Alderidge paused. "Certainly more advantages than being a pirate."

Noah wasn't sure if he was joking or not.

"Your Grace?" The raspy address came from behind Alderidge. "I hope I am not late."

Both men turned to find a stooped, plainly dressed man holding a leather doctor's bag. Spectacles sat under a mop of shaggy brown hair, and an unfashionable beard covered most of his face, giving him a slightly studious and somewhat antiquated appearance.

"Not at all. You are right on time, Dr. Rowley."

"This is good to hear." The doctor shifted his bag. "I trust your meeting was successful," the man said, and met Noah's gaze for the first time. The spectacles that the man wore could not completely conceal the worry in his hazel eyes.

Noah froze in stunned recognition.

It was eerie how completely she had transformed herself. The way she held herself, her mannerisms, the way she spoke and moved, there was nothing left of Elise DeVries in this slightly stoop-shouldered physician. Except, of course, for the eyes he knew so well.

"It was," Alderidge confirmed for them, since Noah couldn't yet speak.

Elise transferred her gaze to Alderidge. "Ah. Then this too I am happy to hear."

"Yes." The duke turned to Noah. "I've been remiss, Ashland, in not introducing my personal physician, Dr. Rowley. Dr. Rowley has agreed to accompany us today to give us his professional opinion on the health of the aging Duchess of Ashland, in the event that it is required."

"Of course." Noah finally found his voice. He wanted to touch her. Wanted to reach out to draw her to his side and keep her there all day. All night.

Forever.

But he didn't, because dukes did not kiss stoop-shouldered physicians senseless on a London street. This was what she had meant when she had said that she wouldn't be herself. That she would be present, but inaccessible to him. It was harder than he had thought it would be.

"Then we should go, yes?" Elise pulled a timepiece from her pocket and consulted it pointedly before glancing back in the direction of the solicitor's office.

A half-dozen faces that had been watching through the window ducked from view.

"We should," Alderidge agreed. "The first domino has fallen and set the rest in motion. My carriage is just up the street."

Elise tucked her watch away and put a hand on Noah's sleeve, a familiar, fleeting gesture that meant everything. "Let's go fetch your mother, Your Grace."

Chapter 19

Bedlam had been as awful as she had remembered it.

The only advantage this time was that she got to watch as the Duchess of Ashland was unchained and carried through the hospital corridors under the chilling direction of not one, but two, dukes. Her expert opinion and services had not even been needed, at least when it came to Miriam. When it came to Noah, however, she'd stayed as close to his side as she dared.

He'd gone white as a sheet as he'd entered the building. And though it might have been a new building with halls that were less crowded and walls that were unmarred by cracks and rotting masonry, the sounds and the smells would have been the same. The constant din he had described, the lingering stench of urine and too many bodies.

Yet he'd stridden through the institution without hesitation, tight-lipped and stone-faced, issuing orders with precision and control. It was only when they were unchaining the limp, unconscious duchess that Noah had pressed himself against her for support. The heavy clanking of the chains as the keepers frantically worked the key at the duchess's ankle had his fist curling unseen into the back of her coat where they stood, as if he needed to anchor himself to something.

And then they'd released the duchess and Noah had released Elise, and within a half hour they were back in the Duke of Alderidge's carriage. They'd let Elise out a quarter mile from Covent Square before the driver had urged the horses on, heading out past the edges of London, to Ashland's closest estate, near Kilburn. Lady Abigail had already left that morning, not happy about leaving her brother but unable to argue with the fact that the duchess was going to need a great deal of care if she was to recover. Noah would return to the house in Mayfair by early evening, but as Alderidge had said, the first domino had been tipped and now the others behind were falling faster and faster.

The Duke of Ashland would entertain tonight, a small, informal soiree arranged by Ivory. This was Ivory's specialty, this subtle and skillful manipulation of society, and she did it better and with more cunning than anyone. Elise's role in the instating of Noah Ellery to the Ashland title was drawing to a close.

Tonight two earls and a viscount, along with their wives, would offer their condolences but profess their delight and pleasure that Noah was back safely to take over where his father had left off. There would be a carefully staged ride along Rotten Row tomorrow afternoon, where a marquess and the wealthy widow of a baron would create a very public, joyful scene as they welcomed the new Duke of

Ashland back to London. And there were more arranged events just like those, each time and location chosen with deliberation, each person selected with meticulousness and made to understand exactly what might be at stake for him or her. And all were encouraged to share with others the news of their happy meeting with the new duke.

As Elise watched Alderidge's carriage disappear from sight down the road, she now fully understood just how far out of her reach Noah Ellery had already slipped. By the end of the week, Elise would witness the final act in the production that would see the Duke of Ashland assert his full dominion and power and take control of the life that had always been his.

A life where she would not fit. She had known that all along. But it didn't keep a black, yawning chasm of emptiness from making her feel like a hollowed shell of who she had once been.

Her eyes blurring, Elise turned from the spot where the carriage had been and started walking. She'd reached Covent Square and had almost made it to the stone steps of Chegarre & Associates when a man stepped into her path.

"Good afternoon, Doctor."

Elise stopped, her hand tightening around the handle of her doctor's bag as pale eyes inspected her disguise with interest. "King."

The man flicked a nonexistent piece of dust from the front of his coat. "I wonder, for the number of times I see you in the guise of some sort of physician, if you've actually picked up any doctor-type knowledge."

Elise cleared her throat and selected her words carefully. "I know when a man's throat is slit, the blood pumps bright red and in copious amounts. I know that when a rifle bullet lodges itself in the muscle of a second man's leg, that blood is darker, the bleeding slower, and it will take him longer to die."

King tipped his head, his red-gold hair glinting in the sunlight. "Indeed?"

"Noah Ellery knows this too."

His pale eyes shifted. "I see."

"I thought you might."

"The Duke of Ashland is back in London." It wasn't a question.

She was not surprised. "He is."

"I'm impressed, Miss DeVries. It would seem that your services are worth every penny. And then some."

"What do you want from him, King?" Elise asked, tired of the game.

The man looked thoughtful. "You care for him."

Elise ignored the way her heart thumped erratically and painfully. "He is a client, King. I care about all my clients," she said, aiming for bored impatience.

"Of course you do." He ground the tip of his walking stick into the dust at their feet. "Tell me, Miss DeVries, did you disclose my involvement in this…affair to your duke?"

"Of course not." She left it at that, knowing that anything else might betray the conclusions that she had only so recently drawn regarding the past that these two men shared.

His cold eyes impaled hers. "Strangely enough, I believe you."

"Good. Now what do you want, King?" she asked again.

"Only to settle my account in full."

"I beg your pardon?"

King extracted a small velvet bag from the inside of his coat and pulled at the string. From the depths of the bag, diamonds sparkled, a thousand rainbows trapped in brilliant stones. "I regret that I don't have coin on hand. But in truth it's bulky and difficult to transport with any discretion. I trust that these will cover the outstanding balance I owe to the duchess and yourself." He closed the bag and held it out to her.

She accepted it, her hand closing around the velvet. "Your debt has been settled then."

King straightened his shoulders. "Not quite yet."

"What does that mean?"

"It means not quite yet." He turned then, disappearing back into the crowded market, and Elise was left standing on the steps of Chegarre & Associates, clutching a bag of diamonds and understanding nothing.

Chapter 20

Francis Ellery had been surprised by the Marquess of Heatherton's sudden invitation to join him at one of his vast country estates.

But at the time it had pleased him immensely. Not only would he be living, eating, and drinking like a bloody king at Heatherton's expense for a week, he was looking forward to the distraction. Surely there would be pretty women, maybe a good shoot or two for birds, and certainly evenings filled with games and other...attractive entertainments. If Francis played his cards right, perhaps the influential marquess might even be able to put in a good word with the solicitors and courts on his behalf.

Except there hadn't been a party. There hadn't been women or card games or shoots. Instead there had been sheep. Hundreds and hundreds of sheep that the marquess had dragged Francis out to view each day.

Heatherton, it seemed, was under the impression that

Francis would be interested in agriculture, in the sense that it applied to large estates not unlike the ones that the Ashland duchy boasted. Unwilling to alienate the powerful man, Francis had endured lectures on enclosures, wool prices, and breeding stock. He'd suffered through conversations that the marquess had had with mere peasants, discussing things like forage crops and hoof rot, for God's sake. And after five days Francis had been ready to shoot every one of those damn sheep, or possibly Heatherton himself, if only to stop the agony of boredom.

So when the marquess had been called away to one of his other estates, Francis had inwardly rejoiced. He'd waved off Heatherton's apologies for their visit's being cut short with what he hoped was a suitable show of disappointment, and packed immediately. He'd never been so relieved to see the city of London rise up on the horizon.

In truth he was also anxious to return for another reason.

He'd received only one brief message from the men he'd hired to find Noah—a barely legible letter that had revealed they'd discovered information that had set them on Noah Ellery's trail. The two men were confident that it wouldn't be long until they tracked his idiot cousin down and dispatched him, should he still live. Francis had been delighted. Really, how hard could it be to find a half-wit?

Except that had been the last message he'd received. There hadn't been anything since, and there had been nothing waiting for him when he'd finally returned home. No confirmation his cousin had been found, no affirmation that he was dead. Nothing but silence.

Which was vexing.

Francis recognized that unfortunately, there was very little he could do about it at the moment. He reminded himself that he needed to be patient and told himself that, however dull his country sojourn had been, it was a step in the right direction. Important men like the Marquess of Heatherton were already doing the smart thing and aligning themselves with the next Duke of Ashland. That knowledge buoyed his spirits. And, coupled with the excruciating boredom of the past week, it was enough to drive Francis out to find the types of diversions that he had sorely missed.

Perhaps he'd start with a mutton steak.

~

Noah had seen a leopard once.

It had been part of a traveling fair, the exotic cat trapped in a large, ornate cage. Noah had stood back and observed the creature that paced back and forth, back and forth, hemmed in by beautifully painted bars and subjected to a long line of gawking onlookers. The leopard had snarled when someone had gotten too close to the cage, before resuming its incessant pacing.

Noah had never felt more like that cat than he did now. Though he was careful not to snarl.

The week had been endless, a steady stream of the same gawking onlookers come to examine the new creature in their midst. Many of them had been planted by Miss Moore, he knew, and however she'd managed to...encourage them to embrace the new Duke of Ashland with nary a whispered doubt had been effective. With each new face that came and went, word spread, and more followed in their wake, not wanting to be the only ones ill-mannered enough not to welcome a duke back into the bosom of society.

And to satisfy their curiosity, of course.

Under the tutelage of Miss Moore, he took care to control the conversations. Any error in his speech was followed with a self-depreciating muttering in Italian and a rueful explanation that he still found himself slipping into a language that had become more familiar than English over the years. Though errors happened far less than he had feared.

He also took care to supply believable generalities. Yes, he had spent most of his childhood abroad. And yes, he had spent time in England. If one was to be an effective duke, one must understand how the people of this nation really lived, wouldn't they agree? No one had yet disagreed.

And there were indeed benefits to being a duke, Noah was discovering, and one was his ability to ignore any questions he didn't care to answer. A cold gaze or an annoyed frown was enough to stop even the most impertinent. It was strange, though, being surrounded by an army of people all the time. In Nottingham he'd gotten used to the quiet, used to the unobtrusive presence of Mrs. Pritchard, and used to the seclusion of his farm. But here there was a constant stream of humanity, in and out of his house, be they visitors or the host of servants employed to make a duke's household run smoothly.

And for all the people around him, Noah had never felt as lonely as he did now. He missed Elise. Terribly. He understood that she had taken a step back, letting her colleagues do what they did best to make this work. Elise had told him what would happen. She had told him that she wouldn't be at his side. And he had told her he'd understood.

Yet he hadn't been prepared for the reality of it.

He'd finally sent a message to Chegarre & Associates, asking after Elise, but it had been Roddy who had shown up at his door a few hours later, informing him that Miss Elise was unavailable, that she was helping another client whose son had gone missing. Missing into the bottom of a bottle of blue ruin, Roddy had opined with a disgusted shake of his head, but still. Miss Elise didn't get to pick who she went and found.

He felt as if he was losing her. She had been his once, for a glorious window of time, but now, here, in this place, he felt as if she was slipping through his fingers as surely as water. He had last seen Elise in Bedlam, her presence the only thing that had managed to stay the memories that had threatened to crush him with their potency. It had taken every ounce of his self-control to remind himself of his responsibilities. To remind himself that he needed to see his mother safely deposited with Abigail and not simply step from the carriage with Elise when she disembarked and slipped into the crowds.

He stood by the window in his bedroom, watching as the streets of London darkened, wondering where Elise was now and desperately hoping she was safe. And wondering if she might be thinking of him.

There was a sharp rap on his door and it swung open. "Are you ready to dress, Your Grace?" His father's—well, now his—valet stood in the doorway. Noah glanced over to where the man had already set out his evening clothes, the severe black of the garments suiting his mood perfectly.

After a week of performances, this evening at Lavoie's club would be the last. Miss Moore had assured him that, in the dearth of social events in the city at this time of year, the tournament Lavoie had arranged was eagerly anticipated and would be well attended. It would be a decisive finish to the week's worth of work on his behalf. All he had to do was follow the script that had been given him.

And after that he would go and find Elise.

~

Francis Ellery had settled into his club. Well, he called it that, but it wasn't really. Not like White's or Brooks's or Boodle's. He wasn't sure which one he would patronize when he became the Duke of Ashland. Maybe White's. Or maybe all three just for the hell of it.

The establishment he was sitting in now was nowhere close to St James's, but at least the alcohol wasn't watered much and the gaming tables weren't always rigged. And there were women. Willing women who didn't much care that you were a mere mister, even though you were related to a goddamn duke.

"Another?" A serving wench was bent over the table, holding a bottle of...well, something alcoholic in her hand. Gin, perhaps? Francis didn't much care what it was, only that he was enjoying the spectacular display of cleavage.

"Yes." He held out his glass to have it refilled. God knew there had been a dearth of gin and women this last week.

The girl finished filling his cup, and Francis patted his lap. The girl complied with that too, tucking the coin he gave her into her bosom.

"Where is everyone?" Francis asked. The card table at which he sat was still empty, though the night was far from young. Unusual.

"At Lavoie's. He's having a card tournament." The girl shrugged. "Everyone knows that."

Ellery seethed. Now there was a man who was the very epitome of insufferable arrogance. Lavoie had had the gall to evict him from his club for a simple misunderstanding and then forbid him any further access to his establishment.

When Francis was a duke, he would see the man destroyed. Ruined and run out of town.

Just for the hell of it.

"I guess that's why ye didn't bring yer cousin along with ye tonight, Mr. Ellery," the girl said as she wiggled against him.

Francis almost sloshed his drink down the front of her dress. "What?" he said rudely. Hell, but he must be drunker than he thought. He'd thought the girl had said—

"Your cousin. The duke." The girl gave him a wink, and her fingers wandered over his chest. "I would have liked to have...served a duke."

"My cousin," Francis managed, "is dead."

The girl on his lap had set the bottle aside, and her hands were wandering lower now. She had her fingers in the front of his trousers, but Francis was too disturbed by her outlandish comment to even notice.

"Well, there is certainly one thing that's dead, and it's not the Duke of Ashland," she muttered, her fingers becoming bolder.

Ellery surged to his feet, sending her tumbling off his lap and careening into the side of the table.

"Who...how...why are you asking me about my cousin?"

The girl righted herself, rubbing a rapidly swelling lump on her forehead, and gave him a scathing look.

"Is there a problem here?" A man built like a bull had materialized next to the girl. His eyes slid down the length of Francis, and his lip curled.

Belatedly Francis realized he had spilled the contents of his drink down the front of his trousers. He ground his teeth. "No."

"I asked him about his cousin. The duke. And then he got mean," the girl pouted. "I think he's jealous."

"I think it's time you leave, Mr. Ellery."

"My cousin—"

"Has money and more manners than you," the man sneered. "Now get out."

"My cousin is dead," Francis shouted.

The bull of a man lunged toward Francis and picked him up by the collar, dragging him toward the door. "Your cousin is at Lavoie's along with all the rest of the titled sots still left in London." He kicked open the door and tossed Francis into an ignoble heap on the pavement. "Let me give you some advice, Ellery, though it is certain you don't deserve it. Lay off the gin," he said, wiping his hands on the front of his coat. "It's making you sound like a lunatic."

Chapter 21

The crowd at Lavoie's was impressive.

More people than Elise had anticipated had not yet abandoned the malodorous summer heat of London for the clean air and cool breezes of the English countryside. The men, resplendent in formal evening attire, created a perfect dark foil for the women who swirled through the room in brilliantly colored gowns.

Like her, each woman wore an elaborate mask, an artful creation of filigree and feathers and all manner of decorations. Absurd, really, because the identities of many were obvious, but the charade of anonymity allowed indulgence in things that etiquette otherwise made impossible for females. It was one of the things that made Lavoie's so popular.

Her gaze skipped over each of the tables, where the games of chance were in full swing, the press of players surrounded by even greater throngs of people laughing and drinking and flirting and competing to be heard. Suddenly Elise froze, her surroundings dropping away and her eyes riveted on the man in the center of the room.

Noah was standing near a faro table, surrounded by a bevy of masked women, some fluttering fans in practiced, rapid movements, and others simply gazing up at him. There were a number of men in his circle as well, and Elise could hear a great deal of easy laughter along with the requisite giggles.

Noah was turned out to perfection, his valet quite obviously a man worth his salt, and the effect was stunning. But beyond that, it was the way he held himself that made her fingers curl and her pulse skip. He looked utterly at ease, perfectly at home against the backdrop of wealth and power and titled privilege. He looked every inch a duke. He looked as if he belonged.

"Did your draper run out of fabric, little sister? Or did your dressmaker only get paid for half a gown?"

Elise turned from the heavy curtain that concealed them from the gaming floor. Her brother stood beside her, pretending to study the contents of the glass he was holding casually in his hand.

"Good heavens, Alex, but you certainly know how to compliment a woman. It's a wonder you aren't mobbed every night."

"I'd find more compliments if you had managed to find more clothes," he said testily.

Elise smoothed her hand over the cool silk of her gown. "There is nothing wrong with my gown."

"That's not a gown, that's a felony waiting to happen."

"I am dressed no differently than any number of women out there."

"And any number of those women are not my sister."

"It's just another role for me to play tonight, Alex."

Alex's eyes met hers. "A role," he repeated, before taking a sip from his glass. "This night is only the icing on the proverbial cake, as it were. From what I hear, your duke has taken London by storm. In the space of a week, he's got the ton falling all over themselves in an effort to outdo each other in welcoming Ashland's heir. It's become a competition, and the only winner is Noah Ellery."

Elise felt her chest compress, a reaction that had gotten worse, and not better, with each day that went by without Noah. While she was overjoyed by his success, the hole he had left in her life when he had spread his wings was suffocating.

"Ivory has been brilliant," Elise said, using cool professionalism to hide the turmoil she felt deep within.

"The duchess only laid out the framework. It's your duke who has been brilliant."

"He's not my duke."

A dark brow rose slowly. "He might beg to differ. He's asked after you, you know."

"I know. Roddy told me." But it didn't change anything. She was no longer part of Noah's world. "I'm leaving for Bath tonight," Elise said suddenly. She hadn't made up her mind until this moment.

Her brother crossed his arms and gave her a long look. "The Rumsford affair."

"Yes."

"Did the duchess ask you to handle that?"

"Yes," Elise told him. The exit Ivory had offered to her was still on the table. And now would be a good time to take it, if only for her own sanity.

"Does your duke know that? That you're leaving?"

Elise frowned. "Why would that matter?"

"He might take exception to your absence."

"You just said yourself that he is doing just fine without me. *Brilliant*, I think was the word you used. I can't imagine anything will change or that I can offer him anything further to benefit him in his new role." Each word that she spoke was like a tiny shard of glass, penetrating what pieces of her heart remained.

Alex ran his hands over his face. "I see the way you look at him. He looks at you the same way. As your brother, I don't have to like it, but—"

"There is no room for me in his life," Elise said, and she knew Alex could hear her heartbreak.

"Because he's a duke?"

Elise looked away.

"Alderidge is a damned duke. And that didn't stop—"

"Alderidge and Ashland are very different men. There was never any uncertainty as to who Alderidge was. But Ashland is different. We need people to continue to believe in him as a duke. To take him seriously. Which means he's going to have to marry seriously. A woman with the weight of a title behind her name. Otherwise everything I've done, everything we've done, has been for nothing. You know this as well as I do, Alex."

"Perhaps," he said reluctantly, though he didn't appear convinced. "I just want you to be happy, Elise."

"I am happy."

Alex gave her a look of disbelief.

She held up a hand in defeat. "Or I will be. Honestly, I'll be fine. I just need to get back to work."

"Maybe you should—"

"It's best if I go, Alex." She couldn't stand here and try to justify herself anymore. "I'll play my part here tonight, and then I'll go."

"What about Francis Ellery?" Alex demanded.

Elise blew out her breath, feeling suddenly weary. "What about him, Alex?"

"You hate loose ends."

"Francis Ellery is a loose end that will be snipped very shortly, once he returns to London. Either by the firm's employees, or more likely by the Duke of Ashland himself. If there is one thing that I've learned, it's that Noah Ellery can take care of himself." She smiled a little sadly. "He doesn't need me hovering."

Alex's mouth was set, making the scar above his upper lip stand out in stark contrast to the richness of his complexion. But he didn't offer any further comment.

"Shall we get this over with then?" she asked.

Alex gazed at her before he jerked his head. "If it allows you to put some damn clothes on sooner, then by all means."

⁓

Noah's face felt as if it might fall off from the strain of the smile he'd kept plastered on it the entire night.

Be likable, Miss Moore had told him. Approachable and polite. Because, she had lectured more than once, people are far more likely to support those whose company they enjoy than those whom they view as insufferable bastards.

Noah was done with being likable. And approachable. And polite.

He forced himself to relax his fingers around the

brandy he'd been nursing all night, afraid that he might break the glass if he kept his current grip. There was still one more act to go, he knew. A coincidental meeting with a member of the French aristocracy who would publicly identify him and remind him of a chance meeting in Venice before moving on. But all he wanted to do was excuse himself from this crush of people and head directly to Covent Square. And Elise. He would not, could not, let another day slip by without seeing her. Touching her. She was as necessary as air.

And it didn't matter if she wasn't there when he arrived. Roddy would know where she was. And he'd happily gift the boy the entire Ashland fortune in exchange for her whereabouts. It was likely Elise was—

Walking toward him.

Noah felt the floor shift under his feet, felt the world around him blur, every sound in the room strangely muffled. He put a hand out, finding a chair back on which to steady himself.

Her hair was pulled off her face and left to cascade down her back in a curtain of dark, shining curls. Thin ropes of tiny crystals had been woven through her coiffure, and with each movement they sparkled and danced. From behind her mask of gold, her beautiful eyes were expertly rimmed with kohl. And her gown, what there was of it, was a vision of sin. Deep-emerald silk covered in more tiny crystals that dove daringly low, skimming the swell of her breasts just above her nipples. The silk clung to her waist and her hips before sweeping down and swirling at her feet.

He had fantasized about this dress once. And he had fantasized about the woman wearing it more times than he could count since then. She looked exotic and untouchable, and Noah knew very well that there wasn't a man in this room who wasn't imagining just how good all those curves would feel. Or taste.

And the fact that Noah already knew made his breathing shallow and sent heat searing through his veins.

Elise was on Lavoie's arm, the man looking mildly bored in a calculated, casual way, and Noah gave him credit for not baring his teeth at all the males who sent his sister covetous looks, every debauched thought stamped all over their faces. Lavoie had his head tipped, as if listening to something Elise was saying as they strolled past, and Elise suddenly looked up, meeting his eyes.

It was as if he'd been struck by lightning, with the force with which her gaze sizzled through his body. He tried to think, tried to remember how to breathe. Tried to remember why he shouldn't pick her up and run out of here as fast as his legs could carry him.

Because, dammit, he had a carriage now. With a door. And a lock.

"Oh," Elise breathed in startled recognition, stopping before Noah, looking up at him and putting her hand to her magnificent cleavage. "*C'est formidable.*"

Lavoie raised a dark brow. "*Comtesse*, are you acquainted with His Grace?"

The extensive knot of people he had been standing with parted to make way for Elise and Lavoie. Elise removed her hand from her brother's arm and extended it toward Noah. "But of course we are acquainted."

Noah took Elise's hand in his, feeling the heat of her fingers. He brought her hand to his lips and pressed a kiss to the backs of her knuckles. He watched as her eyes went hot and her breath hitched. "Indeed. We had the good fortune...meeting..." He stopped, his mind blanking, his concentration and train of thought disrupted by the almost uncontrollable need to possess her.

"Of meeting in Venice," she said easily. "His Grace showed me the gods."

"Neptune and Mars."

"In the Doge's Palace."

"Yes." With an effort Noah released her hand. It was easier to think when he wasn't touching her. "I am very sorry to hear of the death of your husband."

"And I of your father."

Noah nodded in acknowledgment. "You are visiting then?" he asked.

"*Oui*. I very much like your country, Your Grace."

"Perhaps I might be able to show you more of it sometime."

"*Oui*, I would like that very much. Mr. Lavoie can give you my direction. But please, do not let me keep you from your friends and your fun." She gave him another slow smile, but this one seemed bittersweet. "*Bonne chance*, Your Grace," she whispered.

She placed her hand back on Lavoie's arm. That was all that was supposed to happen, Noah knew. A quick but necessary public affirmation from a wealthy widow that Noah had indeed existed beyond the borders of England.

But as he watched her walk away, there was a growing sense of disquiet, his initial exhilaration at seeing her giving way to something that approached dread.

Bonne chance, *Your Grace.*

She had wished him well, but now, as Elise disappeared from view with her brother, it sounded like a goodbye.

Elise wasted no time pulling a shawl tightly over her shoulders and slipping through the private door from Alex's office that led into the narrow dead-end alley that ran between the buildings. She headed in the direction of the street. She would hire a hackney to take her back to Covent Square so that she might pack for her departure for Bath. The Rumsford file was in Ivory's top desk drawer, Elise knew, and she would review it once she had made her travel arrangements.

Tonight had been a mistake. She should never have insisted on playing this part. Because being so close to Noah, yet being impossibly far away, had been almost more than she could bear. She willed herself not to cry. It had been everything she could do not to simply throw herself into his arms in front of—

The door behind her crashed open, and Elise jerked and spun, only to find Noah standing at the end of the alley. They remained motionless for a long minute, staring at each other.

"Where are you going?" he demanded.

"Go back inside. Please." She turned and kept walking toward the street.

"Where are you going, Elise?" Noah repeated, and she could hear the sounds of his boots behind her.

Elise stopped at the top of the alley, her back to the street. "I'm going home, Your Grace." She wished she'd asked Alex for the use of his carriage. She wished she were already rolling away from this club. She wished she were anywhere but here. Because she didn't know if she would be strong enough to say goodbye to Noah a second time.

He closed the distance between them, stopping in front of her. "Stay with me."

The backs of her eyes burned. "I can't, Noah. I will not risk everything that you have accomplished and the future that lies before you. You will do so much good. I can't be visible in this world."

"Then I don't want this world if I can't have you in it." He reached toward her but she stepped back.

"I will not let you sacrifice everything." Elise glanced up the street, looking for a hackney, but the stretch was devoid of equipages, with only a handful of drunken revelers laughing as they stumbled along the pavement. "Your Grace—"

"Stop calling me Your Grace," he growled. "I want you to say my name. The way you did when we first met. The way you did when you refused to let me hide." He took another step closer. "And the way you did when I was deep inside you and you were stealing my very soul."

She squeezed her eyes shut, and the heart she'd thought was already broken shattered further. Her hands tightened involuntarily around her shawl, the edges of a steel brooch she had pinned at the front cutting into her palm. Courage and strength. She had never needed them more than she did now.

"I—" she started, but never got a chance to finish because a heavy arm snaked around her neck and yanked her backward, the cold blade of a knife biting into the skin at her throat.

"Yes, do stop calling him Your Grace." It came from behind her, and with every syllable the blade at her throat bit a little deeper.

She froze, forcing herself to remain calm. Forcing herself to acclimate before she reacted mindlessly. Her assailant was strong, far stronger than she. He reeked of gin, and his accent was not that of the street. In fact it was a cultured voice that was familiar.

Francis Ellery.

"Don't struggle, my little ladybird," Ellery said in her ear. Something cold and hard was dragged across the tops of her breasts, and with horror Elise realized he held a dueling pistol in his other hand.

Noah had also frozen, his hands clenched at his sides, but now they relaxed as his entire body uncoiled. She'd seen that look once before. Except this time he did not have a knife. In his elegant evening clothes, he had no weapon. No knife, no sword, not even a rag with a piece of broken glass.

"Let her go," Noah said, and his voice was flat. "For I must warn you, the lady has far more resources at her disposal than the creatures you tormented in your childhood."

"Christ on a pony, it really is you," Ellery said. "A talking version of the little idiot boy who hid behind his sister's skirts. I honestly didn't believe it when I heard."

"I can imagine your disappointment, Mr. Ellery."

"*Mister.* I should be called Your Grace. Not *mister.*"

"Yes, the men you sent to kill me mentioned as much."

Elise felt Francis tighten his hand on his knife.

"They won't be coming to collect the rest of their payment, if you were wondering." Noah looked as if he was trying to gauge where his best angle was going to be. "Let the woman go. Your quarrel is with me."

"It is. But I'd as soon kill you both." He extended his pistol and aimed it at Noah. "Perhaps they'll think it was a lover's quarrel." He laughed at this. "Kind of sounded like one."

Elise felt an icy-cold sweat prick her skin. Noah was circling, looking for his opening. She knew he was going to get one chance at this, but there was a voice in her head telling her that he wouldn't be fast enough. It would be hard for Francis to miss with his pistol at such close range.

"My father was an idiot," Francis said. "But he always maintained that, if one wanted a job done properly, one should do it oneself. He was right in that, at least."

Elise's fingers brushed the brooch at the front of her shawl. She wriggled slightly, enough to hide her movements as she slid the steel from the fabric, grasping the sharpened end between her fingers. Noah's eyes dropped briefly, an instant acknowledgment, before they flickered back to Ellery.

"I can't let a half-wit become a duke," Francis sneered. He adjusted his grip on Elise. "You'll breed nothing but more half-wits." The pistol left her chest and wavered in front of her. "But at least you won't be breeding with this one—"

Elise brought her hand down and slammed the pointed end of the brooch into Ellery's thigh, as close to his groin as she could manage.

He grunted in pain, his hold slackening enough for Elise to twist and wrench herself from his grip. At the same time, Noah charged forward, putting himself between Francis and Elise, his shoulder driving into his cousin's waist.

The report of the pistol was deafening.

Noah staggered back onto Elise, her heavy skirts tangling around her legs, and she found herself trapped under Noah's weight as they both fell to the ground. Francis had been knocked onto his back, but he was stirring, pushing himself to his feet. Elise struggled under Noah, her heart in her throat.

Noah was breathing still, she could feel it, but the side of his head was covered in blood that looked almost black in the dim light. He groaned and tried to rise, but his movements were sluggish and unsteady, and he collapsed back on top of her almost instantly.

Francis had gained his feet now, and he approached them, tossing the pistol to the side. He brought his knife up in front of him.

Elise tried to free her skirts and her legs from underneath Noah's bulk, but they were hopelessly tangled. She was trapped. Rage such as she had never known coursed through her, obliterating the fear.

"You'll never survive this," she told Francis. "If you kill either of us, you will be hunted down like an animal and destroyed. And you will never see it coming."

"No, I'll be a duke," he said as he met her eyes. "As soon as this one dies—"

The man stopped abruptly midsentence, the knife sliding out of his hands. He had a faintly surprised expression on his face as he dropped to his knees, before sinking into an ignoble heap.

In the spot where Ellery had once stood, there was another figure. Against the gaslights of the street beyond, it was difficult to make out his face. The man bent slightly, pulling the long rapier-like blade that was buried in Francis's side out from the corpse, wiping the blood on Francis's coat before sheathing it in what looked like a walking stick. He turned a little into the light, and now Elise saw the red-gold hair and aquiline features.

With smooth movements he stepped over Ellery's body and crouched beside Noah. He pushed him gently onto his back, away from Elise. She scrambled out from underneath Noah and came to kneel beside him, her fingers pushing his hair aside, looking for the wound. Whatever rage she'd felt had drained away, replaced with a numbing terror.

"Take a deep breath, Miss DeVries," King said from beside her. "He's survived much worse and lived to tell the tale."

Elise exhaled, trying to steady herself.

King peered closer. "The bullet only grazed his skull. He'll need stitches, and he'll have a ghastly headache, but he won't die."

Noah stirred, his eyes opening. They found Elise, and he smiled faintly. "You did say dueling...pistols... unreliable."

This time Elise didn't fight the burn behind her eyes or the tightness in her throat. Relief poured through her, making her wobbly. "I did," she said, as a tear leaked down her cheek.

Noah's eyes went to the man crouched beside her, and this time he frowned, as if trying to reconcile the face he saw with the present.

"I do believe my debt has been settled," King said.

The sound of raised voices intruded. King stood and peered around the corner of the alley and up the street toward the entrance to Lavoie's. "We're about to have company in a few minutes," he said. "There is a small crowd gathering, no doubt to investigate the sound of that shot, though it will be somewhat difficult for them to determine exactly where it came from in this warren of buildings." He stepped out onto the pavement and raised his walking stick, and within seconds a carriage rolled to a stop in front of the alley. A giant of a man stepped from the interior and waited, presumably for orders.

"Fetch the body," King instructed. "Wrap it and put it in the carriage. It has a hole in it, so have a care with the upholstery."

Beside Elise, Noah was struggling to his feet. Elise stood, her shawl slipping from her shoulders. She wrapped her arms around Noah's waist and braced him, though he swayed like a sapling in a windstorm and his eyes weren't quite focused.

"Joshua?" Noah sounded dazed.

King went to Noah's other side and drew the duke's arm over his shoulder. "I'm going to need a minute to get His Grace safely away from here," he said to Elise. "I don't think any of us want anyone wondering at the coincidence of the Duke of Ashland suffering a wound from a dueling pistol on the same night Francis Ellery vanished." His eyes evaluated Elise's bare shoulders and cleavage in cool detachment. "Distract and delay these would-be heroes, Miss DeVries. Redirect them. Ideally, keep them from ever making it to this alley. I will put my trust in your clever tongue and the fact that you currently look like a courtesan only a king could afford."

"The body can't be found," Elise said, finally finding her voice.

King gave her a look of sharp disapproval. "Please desist from insulting my intelligence, Miss DeVries. Or I may start questioning yours."

Elise slid out from Noah's side. She bent and retrieved an object from the ground where it lay. She straightened, and with fingers that were no longer shaking, pinned the steel brooch to the inside of Noah's evening coat. "Courage and strength, Noah," she said. "You have both."

A shout came from somewhere on the street.

"Miss DeVries, you need to go," King warned. "Or this is going to become a situation that not even Chegarre will be able to explain away."

Noah's brow had wrinkled. "Don't leave me, Elise," he said, his words slow and slightly slurred.

The sound of voices was drawing closer.

"Hurry, Miss DeVries—"

"I'm not leaving you, Noah," she whispered, brushing her lips against his one last time. "I'm setting you free."

Chapter 22

The Viscountess Rumsford was as cold a woman as Elise had ever had the unfortunate opportunity to come across.

She sat in the corner of the room, perched on an over-stuffed chair, glaring at her daughter. Every once in a while she would sniff, her discontent dripping from every contrived nuance.

"How long since your last courses?" Elise asked gently of the sixteen-year-old, red-eyed girl who sat wretchedly on the edge of a bed draped in a pretty floral fabric.

"Fourteen weeks," her mother snapped.

Elise suppressed the irritation that rose. Lady Rumsford had effectively prevented her daughter from answering any of the questions Elise had put to her.

"It was only once," the girl sniveled. "It was a mistake."

"Fourteen weeks," Lady Rumsford repeated. "And she waited until a fortnight ago to tell me. And only because

I asked her after I overheard her lady's maid telling the scullery maid that her mistress ought to lay off the scones if she ever intended to entice Lord Durlop into more than the occasional poke once they were wed."

Lady Rumsford's daughter looked down, her hands twisting her skirts in her lap.

"I let both those impertinent tarts go without a reference," Lady Rumsford continued, "though it doesn't change the fact that Edith here has already let someone have an occasional poke."

"There is no need to be crude," Elise said evenly.

"It's not your daughter who is supposed to wed an earl when she turns eighteen, is it? Do you know how hard we worked to secure such an advantageous marriage? Do you know how much of her father's money it took? The title of countess does not come cheap. And this is how she chooses to repay us." Lady Rumsford had worked herself into a high dudgeon.

"Is this what you want?" Elise suddenly asked the girl.

Edith looked up at her. "I want to be a countess," she cried miserably, bursting into a new round of tears.

"Can you make this go away?" Lady Rumsford demanded.

Elise suddenly felt tired. "We have a place in which your daughter may spend her confinement," she told her, thinking of the isolated property Chegarre & Associates owned north of York for exactly this purpose. "Not only will your daughter receive excellent care from our staff, which includes two midwives, she will have the opportunity to take a number of classes."

"Classes?" The viscountess's lip curled.

"Of course, my lady. Your daughter will be departing

shortly for an exclusive girls' school to continue her stud-
ies in all the things required for the day when she should
become a countess."

"I see."

"I'm glad you do. Now, I must warn you that such
a...school is expensive—"

Lady Rumsford waved her hand, indicating that this was
of no consequence.

"Does your husband know?" Elise asked.

"God, no." Lady Rumsford shuddered. "Nor will he
ever. Is that understood?"

"Of course."

"How soon can she leave?"

"It will take me two days to make the necessary arrangements."

"Do it."

"When the child is born, we will find it a good family—"

"I don't care about the child," Lady Rumsford interrupted. "So long as you can guarantee me that no one
will find out about this unfortunate circumstance and my
daughter will not suffer any lasting consequences."

Elise stared at the viscountess, suddenly needing to get
away. Away from the ambitious deceit and the callous ruthlessness and the heartless greed. "I'll be in touch," she said
abruptly.

And she fled.

⁓

The River Avon flowed lazily beneath her, the clouds that
drifted in the sky reflected and framed between the edges
of the banks. A family of ducks disturbed the portrait, rip-

ples blurring the images as they swam across the surface. Elise leaned on the edge of the bridge, the stone wall warm beneath her touch from the late-afternoon sun. She stared down at the water beneath her, watching it slip away.

The unhappiness that had plagued her since she'd left London returned with renewed vigor. She glanced around her at the pretty town, beautiful architecture rising majestically into the air, trees swaying softly along the riverbank, the sun drenching everything in gold. Once upon a time, Elise had lived for this. The adventure, the possibility, the novelty of each new place.

But now she just felt like an imposter. Now she just felt lost, each new place and each new role she stepped into foreign and unwelcoming.

She could try to blame it on Lady Rumsford and her ilk. The constant exposure to the rot that dwelt beneath the perfectly polished surface was certainly starting to wear on her. But that wasn't quite it. If Elise was being honest with herself, it was the fact that, for a brief window in time, she had been given the gift of belonging.

The moment she had taken Noah Ellery's hand on a muddy riverbank, she had become his. And in the process she had found herself again. She had been reminded of the things that mattered. The simple things that made her happy. And she had found true love.

Her thoughts drifted to Noah. She'd stopped keeping track of the number of times that happened during each day and each night, because it was an exercise in futility. And it wasn't getting better. She'd hoped that distance would ease the empty ache that all but consumed her on most days, but that too had been an exercise in futility. Even if she returned to Canada, it wouldn't be far enough to change a thing. One did not walk away from the only man one had ever loved without scars.

It was hard to sleep most nights, difficult to eat most days, and impossible to think—

"Please tell me you're not thinking of jumping."

Elise's head snapped up, and her elbows slipped on the stone, scraping her skin. Very slowly she turned to find the Duke of Ashland standing a dozen paces from her, watching her intently with those smoky green eyes of his. He was dressed casually, his coat and breeches simple, his boots dusty, his blond hair mussed by the wind. In his hand he held a pink rose.

She stared at him, her mouth dry, her heart pounding. "How did you find me?" she blurted.

"Your brother suggested I start here."

"I see." She wasn't sure if she would kiss Alex or just shoot him for his meddling ways the next time she saw him.

"This is for you, milady," Noah said, closing the distance between them and extending his hand.

Wordlessly Elise accepted the rose. She curled her fingers around the stem, realizing they were shaking. "Is your head all right?"

Noah glanced at her. "Are you asking about my injury, or questioning my motivations in giving a beautiful woman a rose?"

Both. "Your injury."

"Ah. You're referring to the gash I sustained in the rather embarrassing tumble I took from my horse."

"Of course."

"I'm quite recovered. Nothing that a handful of stitches and two days of sleep didn't fix." He gazed at her, his eyes becoming serious. "He's different. The boy I once knew as Joshua."

"I imagine he might say the same of you."

"You know who he is. Who he once was."

"Yes."

"You never said anything."

"No," she replied simply. "Those secrets were not mine to share."

Noah leaned against the wall beside her, gazing down at the river. He was silent for a long time. "If you jump, I can't save you, you know," he said suddenly. "Because my swimming instructor up and left before we could finish my lessons. Which, for the record, grieved me greatly."

Elise turned back to the river as well, not looking at him. She swallowed with difficulty. "There are many people who could teach you to swim, Your Grace, if you took the notion."

"I don't want many people, Elise. I want you."

Elise remained silent, unable to answer.

Noah slid a shilling onto the stone wall between them. "Turnips," he said.

"I beg your pardon?"

"You once wagered a shilling on whether Miss Silver would slide off her pony like a sack of turnips or if she would go ass over teakettle. I say turnips."

Elise stared at him.

"I need to return to my farm to settle some details, such as the piece of land a smith is currently trying to purchase from a recalcitrant baron. I thought I'd introduce myself properly and speed things along. I had hoped you might accompany me. If only for the entertainment value."

Elise felt her lips quirk. "Be kind, Your Grace."

"I'll try." There was a shadow of a smile on his lips as well. "Someone once told me that I could do good things as a duke. I'd like to start there."

She nodded, afraid to speak.

"My cousin has offered no contest to my return, which has silenced whatever doubters may have remained. It would seem that he has taken the notion to travel the Continent, having been released from the responsibility of the duchy."

"You don't say?"

Noah looked up at the sky, watching the clouds drift across the sea of blue. "And Abigail tells me my mother is making a good recovery." His smile faded.

"I'm glad to hear that." She paused. "Have you seen her?"

"No," he said, and transferred his gaze to the family of ducks that were now swimming along the near bank. "I'm not ready to see her yet."

"I understand."

"I know you do." He turned to her. "You are the only person who truly does. Or who will ever do so."

She put a hand on his arm, unable to help herself. "Give yourself time."

"I will."

She made to take her hand from his arm but he caught it and held it fast.

"Your Grace—"

"Noah," he said. "No matter what name I had, I've always been only Noah with you."

Elise tried desperately to remember why this couldn't happen. "Why are you here?"

"I came to fetch you."

"Why?"

"Because when you left, you took my heart with you." Not waiting for her to respond, he caught her face in his hands and kissed her softly. "You took my soul, you took my very life with you. And I can't live without you."

Her fingers tightened around the stem of the rose, a thorn pricking her flesh. "I can't—we can't—"

"Can't what?"

"You're a duke," she whispered. "You need a woman with a title. Someone else—"

"You're wrong. I don't need anyone else. But you're also right. I am a duke. And that, I have recently discovered, gives me the power to do just about anything I damn well please." He kissed her again and then pulled back, watching her face.

She stood immobile, afraid to hope. Afraid to let herself believe.

Noah sighed and took his coat off, placing it neatly over the low stone wall. He swung himself up onto the wall beside it, sitting on the edge facing the river and letting his feet dangle over the side.

"I love you, Elise," he said, beginning to work his left boot off.

Elise gaped, even as she was swept into a tide of emotion made up of joy and exhilaration so intense she thought she might suffocate from the force of it.

He tossed his boot to the side and began working on his right one.

"What are you doing?" she croaked.

His second boot thumped to the ground, and he peered over the edge. "Do you think it's as cold as the Leen?" he asked.

"Noah. What the hell are you doing? You can't swim."

"Well, I told you that I loved you."

A laugh escaped her, bordering on hysterical. "And you're going to prove it by jumping off a bridge?"

"I'm counting on you jumping in after me. Because I'm not leaving here without you." He wriggled his backside closer to the edge. "You will accompany me back to London or Nottingham or wherever life may take me, and whether you do so as Elise DeVries or the Duchess of Ashland, it matters not. I, of course, have a preference for the latter, but I am prepared to wait."

She was laughing in earnest now, tears starting to run down her face.

Noah glanced back at her. "You might want to take your boots off too. It will take a team of oxen to pry them off later if they get wet."

Elise scrubbed at her eyes, her vision a blurry mess.

"Your boots?" he prompted, gesturing at her sturdy half boots. "I'll wait."

"I'm not taking my boots off," she whispered, all the love she had for this man swelling within her heart. "And you don't have to wait."

He swung one leg back over the wall toward her. "I don't have to wait for what?"

Elise searched his eyes. "I love you too, Noah Ellery."

He swung his other leg back over. She closed the distance between them, her hands resting on his chest. Beneath her palms she could feel the steady beat of his heart. He reached up to the collar of his shirt and unpinned something that had been fastened to the inside.

"This belongs to you," he said, opening his hand. Against his palm a steel brooch gleamed in the afternoon sun. "Courage and strength. It was what you gave to me.

And now I wish to return the favor. Forever." Noah pinned it at the top of her bodice with infinite care. "Say yes, Elise," he rasped. "Say you'll marry me."

"Yes." She thought that she might simply burst from the happiness and the love that filled her.

He caught the back of her head and pulled her toward him, kissing her deeply. "Thank God," he whispered against her lips. "I thought I was going to have to dare you to become my duchess."

To save his family's reputation, Maximus Harcourt must turn to a company known throughout London for managing the most dire of crises. But when he meets the firm's beautiful owner, Max discovers his desire for her may cause its own scandal…

Please see the next page
for an excerpt from

DUKE OF MY HEART.

Chapter One

London, February 1819

T he silk was the color of sin.

It shimmered where the candlelight danced across its surface, its rich crimson and sumptuous garnet hues swirling in the cascading lengths. The silken ribbon was wide, its superior quality was evident, and it must have been expensive, a luxury only the very wealthy could afford. On the brim of a bonnet, it would have been impressive. On the bodice of a ball gown, it would have been spectacular.

Wrapped around the limbs of a dead earl, however, it was a problem.

Ivory Moore pressed her fingers over the pulse point at the man's neck, knowing she would find none, but needing to confirm. Beneath her touch the soft flesh was already cooling, and she let her fingers move to the bindings covering his wrists, tracing the silk to where it was knotted deftly around the bedpost.

"He's dead." It was a statement, not a question, from her pretty associate standing just behind her.

"He is indeed, Miss DeVries," Ivory murmured.

"That is the Earl of Debarry," Elise DeVries hissed urgently in her ear.

"I am aware." Ivory stepped back slightly to consider the tableau in front of her. The naked earl was spread out across the mattress like a marooned sea star, his wrists and ankles tied to the four corners of the bed. His barrel chest rose like an island amid a scattering of rose petals and decorative ostrich feathers and rumpled bedclothes. He was instantly recognizable, even stripped of the wildly expensive clothes he favored, whose absence exposed a body that was just beginning to lose its battle with fine wine and idle living.

The earl was still handsome despite the fifty-plus years of vice he'd enjoyed before this last unfortunate encounter. He was powerful, wealthy, and widowed—and everywhere he went in polite society, he was treated with the deference befitting his title. But privately, behind closed doors, he was known to all as the Earl of Debauchery, more famous for his love of women and his outrageous sexual exploits than anything else. Finding him tied to a bed wasn't a surprise.

Finding him tied to the bed of the demure Lady Beatrice Harcourt, the Duke of Alderidge's eighteen-year-old sister? Now that was more of a shock.

Ivory took another step back, pushing the hood of her cloak off her head, and placed her bag gently on the floor. There was little time to waste, but before she could analyze the potential damage and formulate a solution, there were preliminary matters to consider.

"The door is locked, Miss DeVries?" she asked briskly. Containment was critical.

"Of course."

"Good." Ivory turned to address the woman standing stiffly near the hearth. "Was it you, my lady, who summoned us?"

Lady Helen Harcourt was worrying an enameled pendant at her throat, but at Ivory's question she dropped it, clasping her hands in front of her hard enough to make her knuckles as white as her face. "Yes."

"A wise decision on your part, my lady." Ivory eyed the woman's greying hair, which had been pulled into a severe knot, softened only by a jeweled clip that matched her green ball gown. Deep grooves of distress were cut into Lady Helen's unyielding face, but despite her pallor, there were no signs of impending hysterics.

Ivory felt a small measure of relief. "May I ask who found the body?"

"Mary. Lady Beatrice's maid." Lady Helen unclasped her hands long enough to make a gesture in the direction of a red-eyed maid sitting in the corner, who, at the mention of the word *body*, had started to sob.

Ivory exchanged a look with Elise. The maid would need to go.

"And where is Lady Beatrice at the moment?" Ivory inquired.

"I can't find her. She's just...*gone*." It came out in a rush, the news delivered in a tone barely above a whisper.

Well, that wasn't surprising. Beatrice had very likely fled, and while the girl would need to be found, it wasn't the immediate priority.

Ivory eyed the crumpled bedclothes beneath the body,

and the lavender counterpane that lay in a forgotten heap on the floor. She took in the size of the room, and the pretty dressing table with its collection of bottles and pots. A pale-pink ball gown, embroidered with tiny roses, had been tossed over the back of the chair, layers of costly fabric and lace abandoned with little care. Stockings and slippers, along with Debarry's evening clothes, had been discarded and had fallen in disarray on the floor. Two empty wine bottles rested on their sides at the edge of the rug.

Ivory frowned. If it had been Lady Helen's rooms, she would have had more options. An affair between an aging spinster aunt and a peer of the realm—no matter how unlikely—if properly presented, would cause gossip, but not ruination. A dead earl tied to the bed of a debutante in her first season posed a much greater challenge.

There was very little time to waste. Who knew how long they had before someone—

A sharp banging on the bedroom door snapped Ivory's head around and caused Lady Helen to emit a squeak of shock.

"Helen?" came a disembodied voice through the thick wood. "Are you in there?"

"Who is that?" hissed Ivory, her mind racing through the possible excuses Helen might offer for locking herself in her niece's room.

The older woman was staring at the door, her hand pressed to her mouth.

Another rap sounded, the urgent impatience of the blow making the wood shake. "What the hell is going on, Helen? Is Bea in there with you?"

"My lady!" Ivory snapped in low tones. Whoever was standing on the other side of that door was not going away.

Worse, he would soon draw attention to this room with all his banging. Every servant in the house would descend on this scene, and even Ivory wouldn't be able to contain that.

"It's Alderidge," Lady Helen whispered faintly, as though she didn't quite believe it.

Ivory started. "The duke? I was given to understand he was currently in India."

"He was. Apparently he's decided to grace us with his presence." Lady Helen's words were tight with bitterness. "Too little, too late, as always."

Ivory fought the urge to groan aloud. It was clear there was no love lost between the duke and his aunt. Ivory only hoped the man held his sister in higher regard. She did not need family turmoil to complicate what was already a terribly complicated situation.

"Aunt Helen!" The knob rattled loudly. "I demand you let me into this room at once!"

"Can he be trusted?" Ivory asked, though she feared she had little choice in the matter. Someone was going to have to let him in or risk having the door knocked clean off its hinges.

Lady Helen's lips compressed into a thin line, but she gave a quick, jerky nod. That was all Ivory needed. She flew to the door, twisted the key in the lock, and wrenched the door open. She had the vague impression of a worn greatcoat, battered boots, and a hulking bearing.

"What the hell is going on?" the stranger bellowed. "And who the hell are you?"

"Welcome home, Your Grace," said Ivory, and grabbed the sleeve of his coat. She yanked him into the room. "Please do come in and cease making so much noise, if you would be so kind."

The man stumbled past her a couple of steps before coming to an abrupt halt, but not before Ivory had closed the door behind him and once again turned the key in the lock.

"Jesus Christ," Alderidge swore, getting his first look at the scene in front of him.

Ivory was standing just behind the duke, and she could feel the chill of the night still clinging to his coat. The only things she knew about Maximus Harcourt, Duke of Alderidge, were that he had inherited his title a decade ago and that he spent much of his time overseas captaining an impressive fleet of trade ships. But she knew nothing about his personality, his family relationships, or the motivations that had brought him home to London tonight.

She desperately hoped Alderidge was not going to be a problem. "Did anyone see you come up here?" Ivory asked.

"I beg your pardon?" The duke swung around to face her, and Ivory felt the impact of his icy grey eyes clear through to her toes.

"Is anyone else looking for your aunt? Or your sister, for that matter?" She refused to look away, dismayed to realize an involuntary flutter had started deep in her belly, radiating out to weaken the joints at her knees and send heat flooding through her body.

Good heavens. She hadn't had this sort of visceral reaction to a man in a very, very long time, and she wasn't pleased. Desire was a distraction, and distractions were perilous. Maybe it was because Alderidge was such a radical departure from the long line of polished, simpering aristocrats she'd been dealing with for years. Dressed completely in black, he looked a little like a pirate who had just stepped off the deck of a ship, what with his long, sun-bleached hair, his wind-roughened skin, and at least a week's worth of dark-blond stubble covering his strong jaw. A scar ran along the left side of his forehead, disappearing into his hairline. His clothes were plain, his salt-stained coat meant to be serviceable and warm. He looked dangerous and, at the moment, furious.

"No, no one saw me. I left my ship and crew at the damn docks after a long journey across uncooperative seas and came here, thinking to find some peace and quiet. Instead I find a swarm of gilded strangers packed into my ballroom, and more strangers locked in my sister's room with my aunt and a dead body. Someone damn well needs to tell me very quickly and very clearly just what the hell is going on here." The duke was making a visible effort to remain calm.

Lady Harcourt made little disapproving sounds with her tongue for every curse that erupted from the duke's mouth—and Alderidge flinched, as if on cue, after each of his aunt's tiny clicks and sighs. Ivory might have found this exchange funny in other circumstances. Right now, however, she needed to take control and make sure the duke and his aunt were aligned. Otherwise she hadn't a prayer of extracting the family from this mess unscathed.

"You may call me Miss Moore," Ivory said pleasantly, "and I am from Chegarre and Associates. This is my colleague, Miss DeVries." Out of the corner of her eye she saw Elise make a brief curtsy.

"And Chegarre and Associates is what?" Alderidge demanded. "A solicitor's firm?" He paused, a shadow of uncertainty flickering in his eyes as he regarded her. "I've been away from England for quite a long time, but I feel certain I would have heard the news if a group of women had set up shop at the Inns of Court."

"We are not lawyers exactly, Your Grace."

"Then what—"

"Your sister seems to have gotten herself in a spot of trouble," Ivory continued, nodding at the naked form sprawled across the sheets. "We've been summoned to get her out of it."

"That is not possible. My sister is the Lady Beatrice Harcourt."

"We're aware," Ivory agreed grimly, turning and marching over to the bed. "And the dead man currently tied to her bed is the Earl of Debarry."

The duke's jaw was clenched so hard that Ivory imagined his teeth were in danger of shattering. He turned to his aunt. "Where is Bea?"

"I don't know."

"What do you mean, you don't know?"

Angry color had flooded Helen's face. "I came looking for her when I couldn't find her downstairs in the ballroom, thinking maybe she was feeling poorly. The ball is in her honor. It took *months* to plan. Everyone who is *anyone* is downstairs." She stopped abruptly, as if suddenly realizing the awful import of that fact.

"She's missing?" Horror colored his words.

"The precise location of your sister is not known at this point, Your Grace," Ivory confirmed. "Though I have every confidence that we will locate her shortly."

The duke swung around to face her again, those ice-grey eyes impaling her as if she were somehow responsible for this debacle.

"We have a much more immediate problem that needs

to be addressed, Your Grace, before we can focus our efforts on locating Lady Beatrice. And that is the body currently tied to her bed." Ivory jerked her chin in the direction of the maid still sniffling into her apron. "Your sister's maid, Mary, discovered this unfortunate scene, and most fortuitously, it was your aunt who intercepted her before anyone else could. It was also your aunt who did the sensible thing and hired us."

"Hired you? What the hell for?"

"We manage situations such as the one your sister has currently found herself in."

"And what sort of situation is that, exactly?" His tone was threatening, but Ivory didn't have time for niceties.

"You are a man of the world, Your Grace. I feel certain you are able to guess."

The duke's eyes darkened to the color of an approaching storm, and another unwanted thrill shot through Ivory. She curled her fingers into her palms, letting her nails bite into the skin.

"Have a care, Miss Moore," he snarled. "I assure you, you do not wish to insult my sister's—"

"I deal in facts, not in fairy tales." Ivory cut him off and was absurdly gratified to see shock wash across his face. "There are no signs of a violent struggle, nor are there any obvious wounds or marks on the body. It is likely that the earl died from natural causes induced from the exertions that usually follow being tied with red silk to the bed of a healthy young woman."

Helen Harcourt wheezed. "You can't possibly be suggesting that Lady Beatrice—"

"Further," Ivory continued, "it is also likely that Lady Beatrice panicked and fled the scene once she realized her companion had drawn his last debauched breath. It is a very common reaction, and in my experience, the young woman in question will return when she has had a moment to collect her wits and invent a suitable explanation for her absence. And if Lady Beatrice lacks the requisite powers of invention, Chegarre and Associates shall be happy to supply her with a credible lie that she may repeat to the ton." She paused. "Your loyalty is admirable, but I suggest you save the moral outrage for someone else. I care more about rescuing your sister's reputation than the truth of what happened here tonight. And frankly, so should you. We've got a great deal of work to do if your sister's future is to remain as bright as it was this morning."

The duke's expression was positively glacial. "I give the orders here, Miss Moore, not you. Don't presume that I will ever follow your lead."

Irritation surged. "Take a look around you, Your Grace. Do you see a crew of sailors anxiously awaiting your direction?" She put emphasis on the last two words. "This is not your world. This is mine."

"Get out of my house," the duke said, his voice as sharp as cut glass. "Now."

His aunt made a strangled sound of distress.

"If that is your wish, Your Grace, we will be happy to comply, of course. But I ask that you consider carefully. Our firm has been brought here by your aunt to preserve your good name and honor. Our objective is the same as yours: we want only to protect Lady Beatrice and the rest of your family. And what you must understand is that there is a window of opportunity here that is rapidly closing. Downstairs there is a ballroom filled with some of the most important and influential people in London. Soon those people will begin to wonder where the Earl of Debarry has gotten to. Soon people will start wondering where the comely Lady Beatrice—the guest of honor—is hiding. Soon people will come looking. And should they find a dead earl tied to Lady Beatrice's bed, I will no longer be able to help you. But it is your choice, of course, if I stay or if I go."

"I don't need you to fix my problems," the duke growled.

Ivory resisted the urge to roll her eyes. The duke was in so far over his head that he couldn't even begin to see the surface. Instead she adopted her most neutral tone. "I'm not here to fix your problems, Your Grace, I'm here to fix those of Lady Beatrice."

Lady Helen swayed slightly before straightening her shoulders with resolve. "Don't be a fool. We need help. Neither you nor I can make this all disappear."

The duke was shaking his head. "I can handle this."

"Can you really?" his aunt asked. "How?"

Alderidge blinked, and Ivory suspected the duke was finally getting over his initial shock and was now considering the magnitude of the problem before him.

Helen continued on, relentless. "How will you make certain the honor of the Alderidge family is preserved? How will you prevent this, this…scene from becoming known to everyone? Do you intend to let malicious gossip and baseless slander ruin poor Beatrice's life?"

Ivory rather suspected Lady Beatrice was doing a fine job of ruining things all on her own. But it was not for her to judge. Especially since a little ruin was always good for business.

"You're supposed to be her guardian," Lady Helen said

bitterly. "A lady should have the protection of her brother. If you had ever once thought of anyone but yourself, we would not now find ourselves here, in this sordid and disgusting position."

"My lady," Ivory snapped, sensing that this conversation was in danger of veering badly off track. "Now is not the time to point fingers. If you must lay blame, I would suggest you conduct that useless exercise tomorrow over tea, when your guests are gone and there is no longer a body tied to your niece's bed."

Whatever color had been left in Lady Helen's stoic face fled, and her mouth gaped slightly. Ivory noticed Alderidge's was similarly hanging open.

She put her hands on her hips. "Now, what is it going to be? Do you require our services on behalf of Lady Beatrice or not? Make a decision. Time is running out."

The duke swore again, his expression black. "Very well. Consider yourself hired. My sister can't . . ." He trailed off, as if searching for words.

Ivory pounced. "You must agree to defer to my instruction and trust in my expertise, Your Grace."

Icy grey eyes snapped back to her. "I will agree to no such thing. I don't even know you."

"And I don't know you, which is irrelevant. But I will not be able to do my job if you get in my way. Dissent will cost your sister everything."

The duke muttered something vile under his breath. "Do what you must." It sounded strained.

"Do I have your word?"

"You heard me the first time, Miss Moore. I do not need to repeat myself."

"A wise choice then, Your Grace." She produced a small

card from a pocket sewn into her cloak and handed it to the duke. "In the event you need to find me in the future."

Alderidge shoved the card in the pocket of his coat without even looking at it. "After tonight, Miss Moore, I hope to never see you again."

That stung a little, though Ivory had no idea why it should. No one in their right mind *wanted* to see her. Her presence in someone's home meant the parallel presence of some sort of acute social or family disaster.

She sniffed. "The feeling is quite mutual, Your Grace. The sooner we conclude this unfortunate bit of business, the better it will be for all involved. But I must warn you before I begin, if I may be so gauche, that the services provided by Chegarre and Associates are expensive."

"Are they worth it?" Alderidge asked in a harsh voice.

Ivory held his gaze. "Always."

～

Maximus Harcourt, tenth Duke of Alderidge, couldn't remember ever having felt so helpless—or so furious. He had stepped into a nightmare that defied comprehension, and making it worse was the knowledge that he was not the person most qualified to handle it.

Unruly crews could be reformed. He could deal with tropical storms and raging seas. Pirates and smugglers could be summarily dispatched. Max had rarely met a problem he couldn't best. He'd rarely met a problem with the power to confuse him. But this? Well, this was an altogether different sort of beast.

Which meant he was now at the mercy of Miss Moore. A woman who treated the discovery of a dead, naked earl tied to a missing virgin's bed as though it were no more serious than a cup of spilled tea on an expensive rug. As though this sort of thing happened every day.

He'd never in all his life met a woman with such nerve. Or maybe it wasn't nerve at all but simply arrogance. It was difficult to tell how old she was, though certainly she wasn't any older than he. Even beneath her plain clothing and mundane cap, she was striking, in a most extraordinarily unconventional way. Her skin glowed like unblemished satin, framed by tendrils of hair the color of rich chestnut, shot through with mahogany. Her dark eyes were too wide, her mouth was too full, her cheekbones too sharp. Yet all of that together was somehow... flawless.

"Was that the ball gown your niece was wearing tonight?" Miss Moore was asking his aunt, pointing at a pile of abandoned lace and rose silk draped over a chair.

Max wrenched his gaze away from her face and, with a jolt, recognized the embroidered silk that he'd shipped to Bea the last time he'd been in China. He'd been sure his sister would love the detail.

"Yes." Lady Helen pressed a hand to her lips, her face a peculiar ashen color.

"Then she'll not be downstairs," the dark-haired woman who had been introduced as Miss DeVries murmured. "Nor does she have any intention of returning to the ball." She plucked the gown from the chair and held it up to her body with consideration.

Miss Moore nodded. "Let's hope she has the good sense to stay away until we have a chance to speak with her." She paused, eyeing the gown critically. "Can you make it work?"

"Most certainly," said Miss DeVries, replacing the

gown and then inexplicably loosening the ties on her own shapeless woolen dress. Max frowned, perplexed, then horrified, as the top half of her chemise was revealed. It slipped over a shoulder, revealing smooth skin puckered by scar tissue from what looked like an old bullet wound. He gaped before hastily averting his eyes. What kind of woman stripped in the middle of a room full of people? What kind of woman had cause to have been *shot*?

"Excellent." Miss Moore turned to his aunt. "If you wish to preserve your niece's reputation, and your own, you need to return downstairs. Your absence may have been noted by now, so I need you to circulate, smile pleasantly, and ensure everyone is having a marvelous time. If anyone comments on your absence, cite your nephew's unexpected, yet welcome, return. I can't stress enough the value of a good distraction, and the duke's arrival will be splendid."

"My sister is missing and you're telling my aunt she should go and dance a quadrille?" Max could feel a vein throbbing at his temple.

Miss Moore glared at him and then turned her attention back to his aunt. She didn't even give him the courtesy of a response. Bloody, bloody hell.

"Can you do that?" she was asking Helen.

Lady Helen nodded stiffly.

"If anyone asks about the whereabouts of Lady Beatrice, mention you just saw her at the refreshment table. Or near the ballroom doors. Somewhere that cannot be immediately verified." Miss Moore put a hand on the older woman's arm. "Your behavior is critical right now. No one must suspect you are anything but pleased with how successful the ball is. Do you understand?"

"Yes."

"In thirty minutes you will visibly exit the ballroom and make your way to the bottom of the main staircase."

"Why—"

"Thirty minutes. Can you do that?"

"Yes."

He'd never heard Helen so tractable in his life.

Despite himself, Max was grudgingly impressed that Miss Moore had managed to handle his battle-ax of an aunt with a deft touch. That was something he hadn't mastered, nor did he suspect he ever would. She was a good woman, but also a mighty annoyance. She delighted in repeating to him just how much she had sacrificed for *his* family, and it wore sorely on his nerves.

Miss Moore led her over to the door and cracked it open, peering out into the empty hallway. She turned back and softened her voice. "This will turn out all right, my lady. I suspect your niece is rather terrified right now. She'll need you, and your forgiveness, when she comes home."

Helen nodded and met Max's eyes, her expression stony. "Your parents would be turning in their graves," she said coldly. "If you have any regard for your sister, you will help Miss Moore do whatever it takes to find her and fix this."

Max fought the acerbic response that jumped into his throat. As if he were incapable of recognizing that Bea's future was hanging by a perilous thread. He became aware that Miss Moore was glaring at him again with those impenetrable dark eyes, and he swallowed his retort, nodding instead. Arguing with his aunt would get them nowhere.

"Arguing will get us nowhere." Miss Moore stole his thought as soon as his aunt had departed and she'd locked the door behind her. "She's upset, and I need everyone to keep a clear head."

Resentment rose hard and fast. How dare this chit lecture him on maintaining composure in difficult circumstances? He was a sea captain, for God's sake. Every day of his life brought difficult circumstances. The only difference being that he knew what to do with those.

Miss Moore had returned to the bed and was diligently working on the knots that bound the dead man's wrists. Max strode to the footboard and began working on the bindings at his ankles.

"I refuse to believe my sister had anything to do with this," Max said. He wondered for whose benefit he'd made that statement.

Miss Moore straightened slightly, brushing an errant strand of hair out of her eyes. "Your Grace, there is one thing you must understand. I do not get paid to form opinions or pass judgments." She bent to retrieve a cloth bag by her feet and began stuffing the silk ribbons into it. "Frankly, I don't really care if Debarry was your sister's lover or not. What I do care about is ensuring she is not ruined, or worse, because of it."

"Worse?"

"The earl is dead." She was now collecting feathers and rose petals, and they too disappeared into the bag. The wine bottles followed with a loud clink.

Max felt his skin prickle with unease. "You can't be serious. You think she *killed* him?"

"If she did, he went out a happy man," Miss Moore remarked.

Max recoiled. "Bea is barely eighteen. She is beautiful and innocent and—"

Miss Moore had stopped and now turned to meet his eyes. He hated the sympathy that was in them, yet somehow he couldn't bring himself to look away.

"My apologies. My comment was insensitive." She approached him, searching his face. "How long have you been away, Your Grace?"

"What?"

Miss Moore remained silent, simply waiting for his answer.

Despite himself, he couldn't think of a reason not to answer. "I own and captain Indiamen, Miss Moore. I am rarely in England. The last time was two years ago."

"Ah." She nodded, as if this bit of information somehow explained the situation in which they currently found themselves.

"I may not know my sister as well as you think I should, but I know she wouldn't have an earl tied to her bed," Maximus said, ignoring the tiny voice in the back of his head that was telling him he knew no such thing. "And I resent any implication otherwise."

Miss Moore was still studying him carefully, and for the life of him, he couldn't tell what she was thinking. Though he had the inexplicable feeling she was somehow seeing more than he cared for her to see.

"Is there a guest room on this floor?" she asked abruptly.

Max frowned, caught off guard. "There are two of them. At the end of the hall."

"I'll need your help to move his lordship." She left him at the bed, discarding her own cloak, and bent to collect the abandoned clothing strewn about the room. A pair of trousers, then a shirt and a waistcoat. "We'll need to redress him first to stage this properly."

Maximus stared at her. Bloody hell, but this woman was unnerving.

She returned, the clothes draped over an arm, a faint look of annoyance across her face. "Quickly. Time is of the essence, Your Grace." She plucked the ribbons from his unfeeling hands.

Max scowled. "If we're going to dress a corpse together, then at least give me Debarry's trousers."

Miss Moore gazed at him with shrewd speculation.

"I have my limits, Miss Moore."

"A gentleman," she murmured, and he wasn't sure at all that she wasn't laughing at him.

"A poor assumption on your part," Max muttered, but the woman's only response was to toss the trousers in his direction.

"Good" was all she said.

~

Ivory yanked the shirt over the corpse's head, careful not to touch the duke where he had the dead man braced. Alderidge had shed his greatcoat, and beneath the bulky winter garment lay a pair of broad shoulders and an impressive collection of muscles in all the right places. His own shirt and waistcoat hid some of them, but not enough to slow the pulse she could feel pounding at her throat.

It was ridiculous, but it was an effort not to simply stare at him.

He looked a bit untamed, Ivory thought, as she jammed a lifeless arm through the opening of Debarry's striped waistcoat. Like a lion that had suddenly appeared amid a clutter of domesticated house cats. She diligently attacked the row of waistcoat buttons, wrestling them into their buttonholes, considering further. It was obvious Alderidge was a man used to power and control, yet it would seem his sister's welfare trumped his disinclination to surrender either. That was certainly a relief—

"Miss Moore?"

Ivory blinked and looked up. "I'm sorry?"

"I asked you if you think I should retie his cravat."

Good God. This was no time for flights of fancy about untamed pirates. They were dealing with the Earl of Debarry here, and she could not afford any missteps. The man had too many powerful friends. The situation at hand required her undivided attention.

"No," she said, gathering her wits. "Leave off his cravat. And his evening coat and his shoes. But bring them with us." She pushed herself off the bed, where she had been kneeling. "Elise, stay here with Mary. Get her to stop sniveling and pick out the appropriate wig from the kit. She'll know what hairstyle Lady Beatrice was wearing tonight. I also need to know if there is anything missing of Lady Beatrice's. Clothing, shoes, jewelry."

Elise, now in nothing but her chemise, nodded, busy examining the rose ball gown. "Of course."

"There's water in the basin," Ivory said, pointing toward the washstand. "I'll need that. Please leave it just outside the door."

"Done. Anything else?" Elise asked.

"No, I think that will get us started. His Grace and I will take Debarry to a guest room." She gestured at the duke to get under one of the corpse's arms.

Alderidge frowned. "Why are we taking him to a guest room?"

"Because he's too big to stuff up a chimney." Ivory pulled a lifeless arm over her shoulder and together they hauled the man off the bed.

The duke's jaw clenched again. "I don't appreciate your humor."

Ivory sighed. "No, I don't suppose you do."

They made their way to the door, Ivory puffing under the dead weight. Thank God the duke and his muscles had shown up when they did. She and Elise would have managed it, but it would have been a struggle. She unlocked the door and cracked it open, peering into the hall. It was still deserted.

"Quickly now."

They made their way down the hall, the duke doing most of the work to support the body. Mercifully, the hallway remained empty, and they shoved their way into a guest room, Ivory pushing the door shut behind them with her foot. The room was dark, the only faint light coming through the window from streetlamps burning below.

She ducked out from under their lifeless load and pulled back the sheets. "Put him into bed," she whispered.

Alderidge dropped the bundle of clothing he had under his other arm and heaved the corpse onto the mattress. Together they arranged his limbs into a pose of peaceful slumber.

"Now what?" he asked in a clipped voice.

"Debarry was feeling poorly when you ran into him," Ivory said, pulling up the sheets and tucking them around the earl. "Though you had just returned home and hadn't even had a chance to change for the ball, you offered to have his carriage brought around. He refused, declaring that he was certain he would feel better with a brief rest.

Being a gracious host, you offered him your guest room. You saw to his needs yourself, as the servants were all busy downstairs."

"Why don't we just take him back to his own house?" the duke hissed. "I don't particularly want him found dead in any of my rooms. People will talk."

"Probably. But Debarry shows no obvious symptoms of anything save a lifetime of overindulgence. His untimely death will be unfortunate but not shocking." She retrieved the earl's pumps and set them neatly by the bed. The forgotten evening coat and cravat she laid out over the end of the footboard, as if Debarry had been planning on redressing. "And the risk of taking him back to his own house is too great. Downstairs there's an army of guests and footmen and coachmen and grooms to get past, and then assuming we arrive safely at our destination, we'd have to navigate Debarry's own servants. It would be almost impossible."

"Almost?"

"I've done it once or twice when there has simply been no other option."

"What the hell does that mean?"

"It means I've helped others out of worse situations than this."

"Worse? How could it be worse? This man is dead, and my sister is missing!"

Ivory winced slightly. There was absolutely nothing she could say at this moment that the duke wanted to hear about Lady Beatrice. "I need you to dress for the ball now," she told him instead. "And you need to hurry."

"Have you lost your mind? I should be out looking for Bea, not prancing around a ballroom." His voice was absolute, and Ivory suspected that he was very good at commanding his crew.

Too bad for him she wasn't one of them.

"And you will look for her. But not right now." She was careful to keep her tone steady but firm.

"You think this is partly my fault, don't you?"

"As I said earlier, I am not here to form opinions, Your Grace. I'm here to make sure your sister returns safely to your protection. And to do that, I need you to trust me."

The duke raked his hands through his hair, creating an impenetrable shadow across his face. Ivory didn't need to see his features to know that furious indecision would be stamped there.

She took a step forward and placed her hand gently on his shoulder. The man might be a controlling ass, but he was clearly worried about his sister. And she needed his full cooperation if she was going to pull this off. "This is what will happen next. You will dress. Go downstairs. Welcome your guests, regale them with tales of your last voyage. Be visible. You are the perfect distraction, and your presence here will doubtless aid your sister tonight. Somewhere over a card game, mention to at least two people, but no more than four, your regret that Debarry is missing the hand because he was feeling poorly. In one hour you will instruct your butler to check on his lordship. Not a footman, but the butler. Butlers are far more discreet." Beneath her fingers his muscles were tight.

"What about Bea?"

"Leave her to me. Just for right now. Now let's get you dressed. Which one is your room?"

Alderidge opened his mouth twice before he managed a response. "You've done quite enough, Miss Moore."

"I will tell you when I've done enough," Ivory said. "You can either tell me which one is your room or I will simply find it myself. But I will remind you again that time is not our friend."

"I don't need—"

Ivory blew out a breath of exasperation and tiptoed to the door. She checked the hallway, but it remained empty, the only sound the muted noise of the music and the crowd below their feet. Silently she slipped from the room and started down the hall. She bent to retrieve the basin that Elise had left outside Beatrice's door, careful not to slop the water on the rug. "Which room, Your Grace? I will open every one of these doors, or you can just tell me."

"Jesus." Alderidge was on her heels, and not happy about it. "This one." He pushed by her and stalked to the end of the hall, opening the last door on the right.

The room was dark, yet the faint musty smell she had expected from a room left unused too long was absent. Though the room was chilled, it would seem the town house enjoyed the attentions of an exceedingly diligent staff. Ivory closed the door behind her and waited for her eyes to adjust, light suddenly flaring as the duke lit two lanterns.

The room was sparsely decorated with the basics, and there was not a personal touch in evidence anywhere. A bed with a Spartan headboard and footboard was covered in a plain white coverlet. A cumbersome wardrobe loomed against one of the walls, and there was a washstand with a porcelain bowl resting empty and cold in the center. A small cheval mirror stood near the washstand, and at the foot of the bed rested a battered trunk, the only indication that this space might belong to somebody.

"No dressing room, Your Grace?" Ivory asked, heading for the washstand. She dumped the water into the bowl and put Lady Beatrice's basin on the floor. Then she moved to the wardrobe.

"A waste of space." He was still standing near the cold hearth and the lanterns.

"Spoken like a man who chooses to live on a ship, I suppose," Ivory replied mildly. "I must assume you have a shaving kit in here somewhere?"

"Of course I do."

"Then I would advise you to get started."

"Are you ordering me to shave? Now?"

"Anything that deviates from an expected appearance will be remembered. Remarked upon. Speculated on. You cannot appear like a barbarous, disheveled pirate on the same night that your ball ends because there is a dead man in your guest room."

"What did you just call me?"

"I didn't call you anything. I simply commented upon your current appearance." Ivory had reached the wardrobe and stopped. "Do you need me to shave you?"

Alderidge's jaw dropped open. "*What?*"

Given his expression, she might as well have suggested she take him on a flying carpet to the moon. "Time, Your Grace, is ticking. I don't know how many more times I need to stress this to you before you understand that we simply must find a way to get done what needs to be done. Either you shave, and make yourself look presentable to society, or I will do it for you."

"No, I don't need you holding a razor to my throat," Alderidge muttered, but at least he was moving now. He knelt before the battered trunk and released the buckles. He opened the lid and rummaged in its interior, then pulled out a leather case. He stalked over to the washstand and started extracting items.

Satisfied, Ivory turned back to the massive wardrobe, just as a terrible thought struck her. "Do you even have evening clothes?"

"Of course I have evening clothes." He stopped. "Somewhere. In there, maybe?"

Dear God. Ivory yanked open the two center doors and nearly swooned with relief when she wasn't met with a swarm of moths. The clothes, like the room, were neat and orderly, folded on shelves, as though the duke had just stepped out for two hours as opposed to two years. When it came to the domestic details, Lady Helen, it would seem, ran a tight ship.

Ivory ran her fingers over a collection of crisply folded linen shirts, waistcoats, breeches, and more formal pantaloons. The drawers below revealed an array of stockings, braces, and pressed cravats, each one separated from the next by a thin piece of tissue. Opening the long door at the side of the wardrobe, she discovered a collection of jackets sorted by function. It had been a very long time since she had had the pleasure of choosing evening wear. Of any sort.

The sharp scent of shaving soap had filled the room, and Ivory could hear the faint swirl of water in the basin, followed by the scrape of a straight blade against stubble. A faint twinge of melancholy struck her, old memories surfacing of the pleasure she had derived from simply watching a man shave. In those memories she sat on the edge of the bed while her husband went about his ablutions, most often preferring to do it himself, as this duke did. In those memories those stolen moments of privacy were always filled with banter and conversation and laughter.

But they were just that. Memories. And they had no place in the present.

Pushing the melancholy and memories aside, Ivory carefully selected a shirt, waistcoat, and tailcoat, draping each over her arm. She stood on her tiptoes and pulled a pair of pantaloons from a shelf. The clothes were all of fine quality and understated in their color, making it easy to coordinate.

"I'll lay your clothes out on the bed," she started, turning around. She had the tailcoat and his shirt spread neatly on the coverlet when she made the mistake of looking up. And found herself staring.

The duke had stripped off his worn waistcoat and shirt, and had his back to her, peering into the cheval mirror as he ran the blade over his skin. He'd moved one of the lanterns to the washstand so that he might see better, and the light created an impressive silhouette, putting his torso in stark relief. The muscles in his arms and shoulders flexed each time he lifted the razor to his face—raw, male, physical power sculpted into beautiful lines. His spine created a valley of shadow that started beneath the ends of his long hair and traveled down through the ridges and planes of his back to dip into the waistband of his breeches.

She couldn't draw enough air into her lungs, and a peculiar light-headedness seemed to have impaired her ability to remember what she was supposed to be doing. He was stunning, and she couldn't even begin to imagine what that power and strength might feel like beneath her hands or between her—

"Am I not doing this fast enough for your liking?" the duke said irritably, and with some horror, Ivory realized he was watching her in the mirror.

"Are you almost done?" she said, and it was a monumental effort to keep her voice even.

"Yes." He picked up his discarded shirt and dried his face.

"Good." She placed the last items of clothing on the bed and turned back to the wardrobe, under the guise of fetching stockings. And while she was fetching him silk stockings, she would try to remember how to breathe normally.

Bloody hell. She needed to pull herself together.

"Get undressed," she ordered, not turning around. "I need you downstairs in ten minutes."

"And I don't need you in here at all."

Ivory jumped, not having heard the duke come up behind her. She turned and was presented with a view of his broad chest.

His broad, shirtless, beautiful chest.

She stumbled backward, only to be caught by a pair of strong hands. She could feel the warmth from his palms on her upper arms.

"I've been dressing myself since I was two, Miss Moore. I do not need further assistance."

"Congratulations, Your Grace." She was pleased that she seemed to have regained her sanity.

His icy eyes bored into her. "And the last woman who ordered me to undress was rather naked herself."

It was meant to shock her, she knew. He wasn't the first man to try to do so.

Ivory snorted. "Congratulations again, Your Grace."

The duke's jaw clenched again. Clearly not the response he'd been expecting.

"If I thought it would get you downstairs faster, you'd already have my gown at your feet," she said, silently cursing her traitorous body and the twist of lust that pooled deep within her at the very thought of her clothes on the floor at his feet. "But I trust that it won't come to that." She had to tip her head up to look at him.

It was he who now looked a little shocked.

Ivory ducked her head. Playing the flirt was entirely counterproductive and unwise, no matter that it felt deliciously wicked. She would leave him to his own devices. "Ten minutes, Your Grace." She turned, slipping from his touch. She had barely a second to miss it before one of his hands caught her own and forced her to turn back.

"I'm trusting you, Miss Moore." He dropped her hand. "Don't make me regret it."

Fall in Love with Forever Romance

NACHO FIGUERAS PRESENTS: RIDE FREE

World-renowned polo player and global face of Ralph Lauren, Nacho Figueras dives into the world of scandal and seduction with this third book in The Polo Season. Antonia Black has always known her place in the Del Campo family—a bastard daughter. And it will take a lot more than her skill with horses to truly belong within the wealthy polo dynasty. She's been shuttled around so much in her life, she doesn't even know what "home" means. Until one man shows her exactly how it feels to be safe, to be free, to be loved.

Fall in Love with Forever Romance

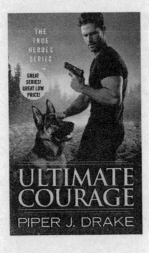

ULTIMATE COURAGE
By Piper J. Drake

Retired Navy SEAL Alex Rojas is putting his life back together, one piece at a time. Being a single dad to his young daughter and working at Hope's Crossing Kennels to help rehab a former guard dog, he struggles every day to control his PTSD. But when Elisa Hall shows up, on the run and way too cautious, she unleashes his every protective instinct.

WAKING UP
WITH A BILLIONAIRE
By Katie Lane

Famed artist Grayson is the most elusive of the billionaire Beaumont brothers. He has a reputation of being able to seduce any woman with only a look, word, or sensual stroke of his brush. But now Grayson has lost all his desire to paint... unless he can find a muse to unlock his creative—and erotic—imagination...Fans of Jennifer Probst will love the newest novel from *USA Today* bestselling author Katie Lane.

Fall in Love with Forever Romance

LOVE BLOOMS ON MAIN STREET
by Olivia Miles

Brett Hastings has one plan for Briar Creek—to get out as quickly as possible. But when he's asked to oversee the hospital fundraiser with Ivy Birch, a beautiful woman from his past, will he find a reason to stay? Fans of Jill Shalvis, Susan Mallery, and RaeAnne Thayne will love the next in Olivia Miles's Briar Creek series!

A DUKE TO REMEMBER
By Kelly Bowen

Elise deVries is not what she seems. By night, the actress captivates London theatergoers with her chameleon-like ability to slip inside her characters. By day, she uses her mastery of disguise to work undercover for Chegarre & Associates, an elite agency known for its discreet handling of indelicate scandals. But when Elise is tasked to find the missing Duke of Ashbury, she finds herself center stage in a real-life romance as tumultuous as any drama.